Megan,
Thank you doesn't seem like enough words. Your friendship is more precious than gold and I will always cherish it.
Jae H

Someday, Too

Jae Henderson

Someday, Too

Imprint: *RiverHouse Publishing, LLC*

ISBN: 978-0-9839819-4-7

Printed in the United States

RiverHouse Publishing, LLC
80 Broad Street, 5th Floor
New York City, NY 10004
www.riverhousepublishingllc.com

This book is printed on acid-free paper.

This book is dedicated to my nieces: Victoria, Javani, Raquel, Regina, and Vania. May the words found within these pages encourage you to live a life of integrity and righteousness as you grow into the amazing women that God has predestined you to become. Auntie loves you more than life!

Acknowledgments

Becoming a published author has been an enjoyable, educational and enriching journey. I am thankful for my amazing and supportive family and friends. Your love gives me wings! Thank you to my publisher and friend Latrivia S. Nelson and RiverHouse Publishing. Your guidance has been immeasurable. I couldn't have done this without you.

To my editors, Megan Mottley, Kiara Rainey and Joyce Oscar, thank you. I am also grateful to my friends Dr. Dorsha James, Dr. Valencia Walker and Tracy Robinson for your support and editorial advice. I want to be just like you when I grow up!

Olivet Fellowship Baptist Church, there aren't enough words to describe why I love being a part of the Place of the Outpouring. We're not just a church, we are a family. Thank you for embracing me and my book.

I appreciate all of you who took the time to read *Someday* and offer your words of praise, encouragement, suggestions and constructive criticism. You have no idea how much joy you have placed into my life by doing so. I hope to continue to give you quality literature that you can apply to your daily life for many years to come.

To every bookstore, corner store, church, etc. that saw fit to feature my book, thank you. Your assistance in helping me present my book to the world is greatly appreciated. To the book clubs around the nation who read and discussed my book, you are invaluable.

Thank you to everyone, no matter what role you have played in making my dream of being a published author come to fruition. Whether it was purchasing a book, telling a friend about the book or saying a prayer, you are appreciated. None of us are perfect but we're blessed to have the opportunity to serve a perfect God. Don't waste your time or your talents.

To My Heavenly Father, thank you for delivering your message through me. May my humble offerings to the world encourage women across the globe to follow you and live a life of righteousness. You've placed a calling on my life that I don't take lightly. My God is truly amazing!

I wish peace, love and prosperity to all of you!

Chapter 1

Mr. & Mrs. Michael Stokes

Today is the last day of Mr. and Mrs. Michael Stokes' honeymoon. For the past week, the newlyweds have been living in marital bliss on the beautiful island of Anguilla. Although, neither Michael nor Tee could tell you much about the island. They were celibate for a combination of four years and waited until their wedding night to fully explore one another. They spent most of the week in their cottage repeatedly consummating their marriage.

Michael loved waking up each morning to the love of his life. He believed you saw the true essence of a woman in the morning. How a woman started her day said a lot about her. He didn't believe in subjecting himself to the essence of just any woman. You had to be special to wake up next to him, and this woman was more special than any other. She was his wife.

It was the dawn of a new day for both of them. While Tee quietly slumbered, he pulled back the covers to admire her beauty. She stirred slightly in response to his act. The morning light that streamed through the blinds of their cottage cast a soft glow on her naked body. Michael delighted in every inch of her--from her shoulder-length extensions to her French manicured toes. As he visually feasted on her beauty, his eyes drifted to the unsightly scars that served as physical reminders of the multiple stitches that were once on the left side of her right breast and the right side of her abdomen. Sadness briefly interrupted his joy as he remembered the day that his ex-girlfriend, Becca, escaped from a mental institution and attacked the two of them with a knife during a charity event. The scars from the cuts he received on his right arm during the altercation seemed miniscule next to Tee's deep puncture wounds. That was almost two months ago. He still blamed himself for her misfortune but thanked God every day that it had not been any worse. The attack made him realize that he didn't want to live without her. Michael was determined to make sure that all of Tee's days from that day forward were good ones.

October was a busy month for both of them. After his hospital bedside proposal, Michael and Tee decided that they wanted to get married as soon as possible and get all of the ugliness out of the way before the ceremony. Tee harbored no ill will toward Becca or her daughter, Michelle. Her gratitude and newfound zeal for life dwarfed any anger she might have had. She went out of her way to make Becca's death as painless as possible for her soon-to-be niece.

After she recovered, Tee, an event planner by trade, took it upon herself to plan Becca's memorial service. It was also Tee who insisted that Michael hire private investigator Ida Foster, the woman who killed their attacker, to try and locate Becca's family to invite them to mourn, too. Unfortunately, none were found because Rebecca DeFoy was not her birth name, and whoever she used to be was very well hidden and long forgotten.

The only attendees at the service were Tee and the Stokes family: Michael and his parents Michael, Sr. and Vanessa; his brother Maxwell; his sister Tomeka; and Michelle. Tee's family could not bring themselves to attend the funeral of the woman who almost robbed them of her. It was a brief but beautiful graveside service that was dedicated to giving a four-year-old girl the opportunity to say goodbye to the only family she had known, until six months ago when her mother revealed to Michael her existence.

Two weeks later during a breathtaking ceremony, orchestrated by Tee as well, she and Michael became man and wife. Michael, a retired NFL player turned motivational speaker told Tee to spare no expense. After everything Tee had been through, she deserved to have her dream wedding. But her true heart's desire was to move on and start their lives together. She loved Michael like no other. Having a fairytale, princess wedding was an added bonus to her. She was also quite fond of her large 24-karat diamond and white gold wedding ring; they affectionately referred to it as Godzilla.

Michael enjoyed having Tee all to himself the past seven days. He used his index finger to gently trace her scars and then softly kissed each one. He was startled when Tee let out a hearty laugh and said, "Good Morning, Mr. Stokes. I guess you are to blame for the cold air that has invaded my space. You do know I'm naked, right?"

"I'm sorry, pretty lady. I didn't mean to wake you. I was just admiring one of God's greatest creations. You look so adorable when you are asleep."

"Oh really? Is that all you're going to do is admire?"

"I was but if you have something else in mind I may be able to accommodate you," teased Michael.

"I most certainly do. Come here and I'll show you."

Chapter 2

Guess Who?

While Tee took a shower, Michael ordered room service so they could dine out on the patio one last time. Their cottage held a magnificent view of the Caribbean and the coolness of the morning was the perfect time to enjoy it.

He ordered assorted fruit, bagels with cream cheese and bacon. As he set the trays on their small patio table, he heard the familiar chime of his cell phone. Michael had been avoiding phone calls all week, and he usually let them roll over to voice mail. Since his honeymoon was almost over, he figured he might as well take the call. What could it hurt? Tee was busy at the moment. The number was restricted, but he decided to answer it anyway. He immediately wished he hadn't.

"Hello, Binky. Are you enjoying your honeymoon?"

The voice sent a chilling panic throughout his entire body. This had to be a mistake. The madness was over, and he was beginning a wonderful new life. Someone must be playing a sick joke.

"Becca?"

"What's wrong? You don't sound happy to hear from me. You sound as if you heard a ghost."

"But you're dead. I buried you," said Michael.

"Are you sure? If I'm dead how am I on the phone talking to you?"

"Whoever this is, this is not funny. I'm going to find out who you are, and I'm going to beat you until you can no longer utter a single word," he threatened.

"Michael, calm down. There's no need for violence. I'm only calling to congratulate you on your wedding. I have no intentions of bothering you or your bride for now. I want the two of you to be happy and take really good care of Michelle for me. But be aware that I am watching and when the time is right you'll see me again, whether it's in this life or the next."

"Look, whoever you are, don't call this number or try to contact me again!" Michael shouted.

"Oh, you'll be hearing from me again. You can bet your life on that. But no worries, I plan to give you plenty of time to enjoy your family. Keep doing your speaking engagements, write another book, make some babies and then I'm going to come take it all away because the life you share with that woman is supposed to be mine."

The phone clicked, indicating that the caller hung up.

What Tee saw when she emerged from the shower sent the beat of her heart into overdrive. Her new husband was lying motionless on the floor.

Chapter 3

Home Sweet Home

Tee and Michael wheeled their carry-on luggage through Memphis International Airport and outside to the driver who stood waiting for them next to a black limousine. They then went back inside to retrieve the rest of their things. It felt good to be home. Tee had a wonderful time in Anguilla with Michael but she missed her friends and family dearly and could not wait to catch up on whatever good news and activities took place without her. She also couldn't wait to get back to work. She was an event planner to her very core and the tropical peaceful atmosphere of the island gave her several ideas she planned to incorporate into her upcoming events. As they waited to retrieve their larger pieces of luggage from the carousel, Tee thought about the morning's events.

When she saw Michael stretched out on the floor, her heart started racing and her breaths began to come in short spurts. She was relieved and grateful to her Heavenly Father when she realized Michael had only fainted. Tee was able to revive him and assisted him with moving from the floor to the bed. Michael refused to allow her to call the paramedics or take him to the hospital to be checked out. He told her he merely fainted from lack of food and would be fine after eating something. Tee didn't believe him but decided not to push the issue at that moment. She would try to persuade him to see a doctor later. It was obvious during the flight something was bothering him, but she was learning that Michael only told what was on his mind when he was ready. He generally did not enjoy being coerced, manipulated or begged to reveal his private thoughts.

Michael tried to push the disturbing phone call from his thoughts. He must be hallucinating. He told himself that the combination of lack of sleep and lack of food caused him to imagine receiving a call from Becca. He saw the body for himself. He knew the woman who tried to kill him and his wife was dead. He resolved within himself that he wouldn't speak of it for fear someone would think he was losing his mind. That phone call never happened.

Once Tee and Michael reached the limo with all of their luggage, the driver put their bags in the trunk and took his position behind the wheel. The limo traveled swiftly taking Tee and Michael to their home in an area known as Hickory Hill. Once there, Michael helped unload their luggage and placed it outside the door. He then effortlessly picked up Tee's small body and carried her over the threshold. This would be their first night in this house as husband and wife. Tee enjoyed being cradled in her husband's strong arms, but her enjoyment was interrupted by a phone call from her sister, Sandy. Tee knew she needed to answer it or she would never hear the end of it. Michael sat her down.

"Are you home?" asked Sandy.

"Hello to you, too. Yes, Michael and I just made it to the house."

"Good. I'm going to f-ing kill her. That witch spelled with the letter b is still calling my husband. I see I'm going to have to stomp a mud hole in her behind for her to understand I'm not playing with her assets."

Tee could hardly contain her laughter. Her sister was such a square. Even though they were both from the hood of North Memphis and heard profanity regularly outside their home, neither she nor Sandy used profane language. As children, they were forbidden to use bad words and they carried that behavior into adulthood. For some reason, over the past few months whenever she got upset, Sandy would say some variation of the profane word she seemed to want to say. Tee figured it had something to do with the pregnancy. She was extremely upset about something though, and the fact that her sister was almost six months pregnant and wanted to fight someone was cause for concern.

"Stomp a mud hole in who?" asked Tee.

"That heifer Sheniqua. My husband has no contact with her, but she is still calling him."

"How? I thought Patrick got his number changed?"

"We decided that too many important contacts had his number. So, we got him a new number and kept the old. I take the calls on the old one and give him the important messages," explained Sandy.

"Don't answer and eventually she'll stop," said Tee.

"I don't, but she's also texting and leaving sexual messages on the voice mail. Evidently, she's been following him because sometimes she mentions where she saw him and what he was wearing. Last week, she sent a picture of herself naked. It's only a matter of time before she approaches him. My marriage has suffered a lot of damage because of this woman. Tee, I will kill her before I let her rip us apart. I'm about to have three kids. I'm not raising them alone."

Sandy sounded like she was at her wits' end. Patrick's former lover and receptionist was at it again. Their affair was over a year ago. What would it take for her to get a clue? He fired her and stopped seeing her. He and Sandy went to counseling and were working hard to move on with their lives, but Sheniqua found a way to weasel herself back in. A few months ago, Sandy discovered that Patrick was giving Sheniqua money to help with her kids until she found another job. Patrick is a good man, and when he found out Sheniqua's boyfriend left her alone with three kids after finding out about the affair, he felt bad and started paying some of her bills and hiding it from Sandy. After Sandy found out she kicked him out of the house because she believed they were still sleeping together. Fortunately for him, there was overwhelming evidence that they weren't. Sandy forgave him, Patrick moved back home and it appeared everything was getting back to normal, or so they thought.

"Sandy, that's the hormones talking," said Tee. "You are not going to kill anyone. Calm down. It's my first night home, and I am exhausted. Tomorrow we will figure out what to do about this. I'm sure there's a way to get this woman out of your marriage for good without ending her life."

"I hope you have an idea because I have already got my nine millimeter ready to go. You know how much I love my husband, and I'm not about to lose Patrick to another woman!" yelled Sandy.

"Sandy, quit lying. You don't own a gun. Calm down before you end up with an ugly angry baby. I'll help you, I promise. Don't forget we're meeting the girls tomorrow at Mae Lillie's for lunch. We can talk more about it afterward."

"I'll try but this isn't easy. I'll see you tomorrow, and tell Michael I said hello. Bye," said Sandy.

"Bye."

Before Tee could put down the phone, she had another call. It was her brother-in-law.

"Hey, Sis!"

"Hey, Patrick. How are you?"

"I'm good. I need to talk. Do you have a few minutes?"

"Sure. What's up?"

"It's your sister. She doesn't seem happy about this pregnancy," he said.

"What do you mean?"

"When Sandy she was pregnant with Donovin and Nicole she was all smiles and laughter. She was truly glowing. With this pregnancy, all she does is cry and complain and I seem to be the trigger. As soon as I walk into the room, she starts crying and talking about what's wrong with her life. I try to console her, but she cries even harder. All I can get her to say is I'm friggin', freakin' or f-ing sorry."

"She seems to dread her doctor's visits and anything that has to do with planning for this baby. With the other two pregnancies, you couldn't keep her out of maternity and baby stores. She was buying up everything she could before we even knew whether we were having a boy or a girl. With this one, she hasn't done any shopping for herself or the baby. All Sandy's clothes are too small now, and she doesn't seem to care. It's almost embarrassing some of the stuff she wears. You know how fashion-conscious she usually is. This isn't like my wife at all," said Patrick.

Tee realized her brother-in-law was right. The entire pregnancy her sister hadn't said much about the baby. In the past, you couldn't shut her up about swelling breasts, cravings and feeling the baby move. She also went on and on about the cute baby outfits she found and how she was going to decorate the nursery. Maybe she wasn't talking because this baby was their third child. It could be a *been there, done that* kind of attitude.

"I'll admit that does seem odd," said Tee. "She and I will be getting together soon. I'll see if I can get to the bottom of this."

"Thanks, Tee. Let me know what you find out. If I never told you, you are an amazing sister to my wife and to me. I love you as if we were born from the same mother. You have never turned your back on me no matter how bad I messed up. Michael is a lucky man, and I know I'm probably not one to talk, but if he ever hurts you I'll make sure he knows the meaning of pain."

"My man knows what a good woman he's got. The last thing I'm worried about is him hurting me. Besides, what I'll do to him is far worse than anything you could do," she joked. "You make sure you do right by my sister, my adorable niece and nephew and the one on the way. You two belong together."

"I couldn't agree with you more. I have to go now. A dentist's work is never done."

"Okay, Patrick. We'll talk soon."

Michael stood listening to Tee as she held her conversations with his new in-laws. He gave his spouse of one week and a day a hug.

"Sounds like trouble in the Pierce home. Welcome home, Superwoman."

Tee stood on her tiptoes and gave her man a kiss on the cheek.

"Welcome home indeed. Neither one of them even bothered to ask how our honeymoon was, but Sandy did say to tell you hello. I'll deal with them tomorrow. This is our first night in our home. I think we have a bed to christen, Mr. Stokes."

"We sure do, Tina Desiree Long-Stokes but not just the bed. We can take care of the floor, the table, the couch, the desk, the kitchen counter………"

Tee laughed while her husband continued to name all the various places they could make love. He was an excellent and spontaneous lover, and she welcomed whatever he had in mind.

Chapter 4

B-A-B-Y Spells Baby

Sandy tried to take Tee's advice and calm down. Sheniqua managed to infiltrate her marriage twice already and she was not about to let there be a third. What made this woman think she could waltz in and take another woman's husband?

She took the day off from her successful soul food restaurant, Mae Lillie's, because she wasn't feeling well. Lately, she could hardly keep anything down. She was in her 20's with her first two pregnancies. She was now 35 and figured that the age difference was probably why this one seemed to be tiring her. She was always exhausted. She decided to do something more productive than worry and checked emails to take her mind off things.

Sandy went to the computer in her home office and logged into her email account. She had five emails from Armondo. Her mind drifted back to their forbidden afternoon. She was still beating herself up for cheating on her husband, but she was feeling so unloved and vulnerable at the time. She thought Patrick was seeing Sheniqua again, and some attention from Armondo seemed to be exactly what she needed to feel better. Boy was she wrong. She made a terrible mistake. She was so afraid that the little girl she was carrying was Armondo's instead of her husband's.

God please let this be Patrick's baby, she prayed silently.

Sandy didn't tell anyone about the affair, not even Tee. The possibility that soon there could be evidence of her indiscretion and the guilt of what she did was weighing heavily on her and troubled her day and night. Armondo was Italian with brown curly hair, so if she gave birth to a biracial baby she knew there was no way she could hide the affair. She was part Creole and light-skinned and her husband was a deep dark chocolate. There was no telling what hue their new baby would be. Their son, Donovin, was light-skinned and Nicole was a beautiful brown like her mother, Pearl. They both inherited her wavy hair. Nicole's was so long her ponytails hung to her shoulders.

Initially, Sandy thought about secretly having an abortion, but she couldn't bring herself to terminate the pregnancy. After all, it was still her child. Sandy spent many days and nights crying and praying that God would hear her pleas and have mercy on her and her family.

Sandy read the emails, and in each one Armondo asked her to reconsider staying with her husband because he loved her and wanted to be with her. She couldn't believe that after one afternoon together this 22-year-old thought he was in love. She laughed at his youthful folly. Sandy read each email and deleted it afterward. There were several others like them already in her trash. She never responded. However, in the fifth one Armondo threatened to start sending mail to the house if she didn't answer. The last thing she needed was for Patrick to intercept one of those letters. Before she logged out of her account, she sent him one in return.

I'm sorry but my decision has been made. I am dedicated to my marriage and my family. Patrick is the only man for me. You're young, nice, intelligent and handsome. You'll have no problem finding someone else. Thank you for being there when I needed a friend. Please don't contact me again. Goodbye, Armondo and God bless.

Mrs. Cassandra Pierce

Sandy hoped he would leave her alone now because Patrick was the only man she wanted or needed in her life. There was no way she and Armondo could be together. Armondo was scheduled to be deployed in Iraq for seven more months, and he had no idea she was pregnant. If he knew, he would probably question the paternity as well. She had to keep that news from him until she was sure whose baby she was carrying.

Chapter 5

Food, Friends & Fellowship

Tee spent her first night back in Memphis in the arms of her husband. She enjoyed their honeymoon immensely. She was definitely enjoying married life, thus far. Now that they were back in the real world, she didn't know how much longer the two of them could keep up their marathon love making sessions. They each led busy lives. During her recovery, Michael took some time off from promoting his children's book, *Victory Is Mine*, and cut back on his speaking engagements to help nurse her back to heath. Now that she was better, they would both be resuming their hectic work schedules soon.

She was amazed at how skillful Michael was in bed. He caught on quickly to what she liked and used his newfound knowledge to release her love each night. He was a kind and patient lover. He told her repeatedly how much it meant to him to be able to please her, but she was also eager to please him. Before their marriage, she bought several instructional books and videos to show her how to blow his mind. She knew her husband used to be a player. Although he never discussed his sexual past with her, she was sure he enjoyed more than his fair share of uninhibited lovers. Tee wanted to make sure she ranked in at least the top three, if not number one. Michael often told Tee how much he loved her body and in return, she shared it with him freely. She did things with her new husband that she never felt comfortable enough to do with anyone else because she felt bad about fornicating. She saw no shame in pleasing her husband. She discovered his most sensitive areas and made it her business to make Michael smile, moan and at times even scream in response to her efforts.

Tee emerged the next day looking like she hadn't slept a wink. She tried to apply her makeup to hide the tell-tale bags under her eyes before meeting the girls at 11:30 a.m. Teresa, Lenora, Lenice, Tiffany and Cassie were as much a part of her life as Sandy. Even though, she didn't see or talk to them nearly as much. Their routine get-togethers were a priority for her and gave Tee a chance to see what was going on with them. She also wanted to discuss her women's motivational website, www.Imagoodwoman.com. This online business venture specialized in novelty items like t-shirts, mugs, bags and stationery with the I'm A Good Woman logo on them. She also posted inspiring messages to help keep women motivated to live a life of integrity. Sales on the site were steady and plans were going well for the first I'm A Good Woman Empowerment Conference. Her friends all agreed to assist with the event, and she wanted to update them on the latest developments.

It was fall and Tee admired the lovely foliage as she drove the streets of her hometown. The once green leaves were now yellow, auburn and brown. Many had fallen from their branches and littered the ground beneath the trees that bore them. She saw several of her neighbors outside raking and bagging leaves for trash pick-up. She needed to call her lawn service and ask them to come do the same. Tee arrived at Mae Lillie's looking stunning in skinny jeans, brown suede boots, a brown cashmere wrap and a cream blouse. She was running behind and was the last person to arrive.

Everyone was already seated in the private dining area of the restaurant.

"Look at the newlywed Diva!" quipped Lenora. "I remember when I was a newlywed and looked like I wasn't getting any sleep."

Tee was busted. She laughed and made her way around the table distributing hugs and air kisses. No amount of make-up could hide lover's fatigue. Although, she gave it a gallant effort.

"Yeah girl, you look happy and crappy at the same time. I could use those bags under your eyes for a hammock. I don't have to ask what you did during your honeymoon because it's written all over your face," chimed in Lenora's twin sister Lenice.

"Leave Tee alone. I'm happy for her," said Tiffany. "Since I left Quincy, I haven't had any in almost two months, and I feel like I'm about to die. I feel sorry for Michael. Tee unleashed years of pent-up sexual energy on that poor man." She was sure to give the word *years* added emphasis in her southern drawl. "It's a wonder he can still walk."

"Well, I'm going to ask the question the rest of these high and mighty princesses won't ask. How was it? Is he packing like a meat truck or a hot dog stand? A man with a body that fine and feet that big rarely disappoints," said Cassie.

You never knew what was going to come out of that woman's mouth.

"Cassie! Good girls don't tell." Tee pushed her lips tightly together and made the zip and lock motion with her right hand. She was never one to discuss her bedroom business with anyone other than her big sister. Her mother told her when she was young that a lady exercised discretion and kept that information behind closed doors where it belonged. Doing so helped to guard your reputation and your relationship. When you have something good other women always seem to want it, and some are bold enough to try and take it. Cassie would have to use her imagination to answer that one, but she thought to herself, *my man's got enough meat to fill the refrigerator in the house and the deep freezer in the garage!*

"You're no fun," said Cassie.

Teresa could tell Tee was feeling uncomfortable and jumped in to run a little interference. "Why did you ask a stupid question like that? The girl looks so tired I almost made her a pallet on the floor. It's obvious her husband is turning her every which way but loose. The size of her husband's pecker is none of your business."

Tee changed the subject.

"I missed you guys, and I really would like to begin our lunch by talking about the positive changes in our lives. Each of you has agreed to be brand ambassadors for I'm A Good Woman so we need to keep ourselves on point. Let's start with you Tiffany. How have you been?"

Tiffany Tate looked beautiful as usual. The orange sweater dress she was wearing fit right in with the fall foliage. Her wooden earrings, necklace and bangles were the perfect accessories. Her shoulder length tresses were perfectly curled to frame her face and, as usual, those big doe-like eyes of hers were adorned with thick faux eyelashes.

"I guess I'm okay. As I stated, I left Quincy and he has been almost unbearable since. He started showing up at my house all times of the day and night unannounced. I almost had to change the locks because he would use his key to walk in and scare the bee gees out of me. More than once, I awoke to find him in my kitchen trying to cook a meal for his family, as he likes to say. That may sound nice, but Quincy can't cook. He even set my fire alarm off. I ran into the kitchen thinking my home was in flames, but it was him burning up breakfast. Did he really think he was going to get me back with runny eggs, under cooked grits, and burned bacon and toast?" The girls laughed.

"He finally got it through his head we were really over when I threatened to go to the police and file a harassment report. Of course, with him being on the city council Quincy didn't want that bad press. He left me alone but to punish me, he stopped giving me money for Quincy 2. I had to go to juvenile court and file for child support. I'm now waiting for my time before the judge. It's been hard, but I am determined to make it without continuing to participate in a relationship with a married man.

"On a brighter side, I am almost done with massage therapy school, and I love my new career. I've always been good at giving massages and now I'm using them to make people feel good and earn a living. I would like to open my own massage parlor. Instead of the traditional spas around here, I want to create a bathhouse like the ones they have in Hot Springs, Arkansas."

"Tiffany, I think that's a great idea," said Tee. "I know you would be great at that. You are so hospitable to everyone you meet. Start working on your business plan now so when you think you've got enough experience under your belt you will be ready to roll."

Tee then reached in her bag and pulled out an I'm A Good Woman baby doll t-shirt and a gold necklace with an I'm A Good Woman charm dangling from it and handed it to her friend. "These are some of the promotional items I'm thinking about selling and a small gift to let you know how proud I am of you. Stay strong. God will provide and give you the victory in court."

Several women at the table said, "Amen."

"Now, who's next?" asked Tee.

"I'll go," said Lenice. "First, I want to say thank you to all of you for being sisterly enough to tell me how much of a bitter woman I had become. I have been going to therapy to help me resolve my man-hating issues, and my therapist said I am making good progress. She even suggested I start going on a few dates. No relationships, but an occasional lunch or dinner with someone who seems nice. I'll admit that I'm scared I'll meet another man who wants to use my heart for kickball practice, but I won't let it stop me. I want to get back to the old me. I used to love everything about love. Now, I'm skeptical about anything that starts with the letter l and for a while, I only thought the worst. Tiffany, please forgive me for being so mean to you about your relationship with Quincy. Yes, he's married, but I know you love him. He is the father of your child, and I can understand that you wanted to try to make it work. You had to realize for yourself how detrimental he was to you and how he was telling you lies to keep you in his life. I couldn't do it for you no matter how bad I wanted to and being mean to you wasn't the right way to go about it, anyway. I'm glad you finally realized you were better off without him. I'm proud of you, too."

"But it was those harsh things you said to me that made me begin to re-examine my priorities," said Tiffany. "I was setting a bad example for my son and after he saw Quincy in the paper with his wife and kids, he kept asking me when he could go over to his Daddy's house and play with his sisters. I didn't know how to answer that because I knew Quincy's wife would never allow it. She hates me and the fact that I gave Quincy the son he always wanted and she didn't. Lately he hasn't acted like it, though. Quincy hasn't tried to see Quincy 2 once since I ended it. Apology accepted, Lenice. We're cool. Don't give it another thought. I am also proud of you. There's a man out there looking for a woman like you. Keep smiling girl, it looks much better than that scowl you used to wear all the time."

The two stood up and embraced to comfort and encourage each other. This was a momentous occasion. Tiffany and Lenice used to argue like enemies whenever they were within five feet of each other. It seems that with healing came some maturity and the realization that they really didn't have a valid reason to hate one another. They both had a lot more work to do on themselves to completely heal their emotional and mental wounds, but each was ready to do it. Support from one another would help as well.

"Enough of this mushy stuff," said Teresa. She pushed her chair back from the table and stood up as if she were about to make an important announcement. "My name is Teresa Atkins, and I'm an alcoholic. I have been sober two months and five days." Everyone in the room burst into applause.

Teresa waited for them to stop before she resumed speaking, "Thank you. Ladies, I am determined to keep my drinking under control. It's not healthy for my body, my career or my marriage. My job as a cop is hectic, but drinking is not a good way to deal with the stress. It got so bad, I was getting drunk every night after work and barely remembered how I got home, and I would be in no shape to interact with my husband when I did arrive. Half the time, I had no idea whether he was home or not when I got there. I was so ashamed of myself. Zachary deserves better.

I want to be the kind of wife he can be proud of. Now, instead of drinking I go swing on a pole."

"WHAT!" said Tiffany.

"You're stripping now?" asked Sandy.

"Don't be silly. I'm a police officer, but I do take a pole dancing exercise class. I thought I was too old to be participating in such foolishness at 40, but it makes me feel sexy, flirty and alive. I even put a pole in the house so I could exercise at home. Zachary loves to watch!"

All of the girls hooted and hollered as Teresa gyrated her hips to an invisible beat all the way down to the floor. "We're going on a cruise in a couple of days to celebrate his birthday. I have some dance moves I've perfected for the occasion," she said before settling back in her seat.

"Oh my goodness. You have got to tell me where this class is so I can go, too," said Lenora. "Well, I guess I'll go next. My life isn't as exciting as you guys' because I am a stay at home mom, but I have decided to lose some weight. I started last week so I don't have a report yet but next time we meet, I will tell you how much I've lost. I used to admire my body, and now I don't want to look at it. I went to the doctor and he said I am in danger of becoming a diabetic, and my cholesterol and blood pressure need to be put in check. He told me if I didn't lose weight, he was going to have to put me on medication. I don't want to take any type of medication, if I don't have to. So, I am taking control of my life for better health. I've been eating better, watching my portions and exercising. You guys wish me luck because I know I can do this. Twin, pretty soon you're gonna have to keep your dates away from me because I'll be thin again, and they won't be able to tell us apart.

Lenice reached over and grabbed her sister's hand. She supported her decision to lose weight wholeheartedly but only she knew that the number one motivating factor behind her sudden urge to shed the pounds. Lenora's husband, Herman, was constantly nagging her to lose weight. He called her mean names like fatty, Jell-O booty and Ms. Piggy regularly. On more than one occasion, after Lenora called her upset, Lenice wanted to go over there and tell him to be nice to her sister or she would kick his behind. Lenora begged her to stay out of it because she would only make things worse. As far as Lenice was concerned, NOBODY had the right to abuse her sister in any kind of way. NOBODY! She was overjoyed her twin decided to lose weight, even if it was for a man. She had never been over 140 pounds, but Lenora was more than twice that. It was obvious that it affected her self-esteem. Lenora rarely wore make-up or anything other than some hideous shapeless jeans and large dresses that resembled a housecoat or a mumu. Today, she had on a particularly hideous one with purple and yellow flowers all over it.

"We are so happy for you," said Sandy. "I've got some great low-fat recipes I'm going to give you. Healthy food can taste delicious if you season it right."

"Thank you, Sandy. I would appreciate that," said Lenora.

The only two people left to give an update were Cassie and Sandy. Cassie began to speak but stopped. She began again then stopped. She was obviously choked up about whatever she had to say. Tee was sitting next to her and began rubbing her back while she composed herself. A single tear rolled from Cassie's right eye. She brushed it away and began to speak.

"I came to tell all of you goodbye. I'm moving back to Sunflower, Mississippi to help my parents with the farm. As you know, my Dad's been ill, and he can't get out in the fields like he used to. I finally persuaded him to sell the farm. I'm moving home to help get it in top condition and to make sure some vulture doesn't try to take advantage of my parents and offer them less than what it's worth. I was a stranger to this city, and Tee, meeting you was one of the best moments in my life. You brought me into your world and introduced me to your wonderful friends who later became my friends, too. Some of you I haven't known long, but it's not the quantity of time you've known someone but the quality of the time you've spent with them. I'm leaving tomorrow to get things ready for my move, but I'll move officially in a week or so. If all goes well with the sale, I'll be back in Memphis with my parents sometime next year. I hope they can adjust to city life. Tee, I can sell your I'm A Good Woman products in Sunflower and maybe we could even do a mini conference there. We are a small town, with little for young people to do, and it's important we keep them busy. That way, we don't have a bunch of teen parents. I want to do something with young girls to keep them from being somewhere they're not supposed to be with their legs all up in the air with some boy in between them."

"That sounds like a good idea, Cassie," said Tee. "When you get home and settled, tell me what you need me to do. I'm really going to miss you. You've been my girl since we pledged Phi Beta Pi at The University of Memphis. We had some really good times, didn't we?"

"Yes we did!" The two gave each other a high five and threw up their sorority hand sign. Sandy threw hers up too. She was also a member of Phi Beta Pi and pledged both of them. Even though she thought Cassie's mouth could use a good cleaning out with soap from time to time, she hated to see her go, too. She handed her a napkin in case she started to cry again.

"I guess I'm last," said Sandy. "As you can see, I am pregnant. Initially, Patrick and I decided not to find out the sex of our child, but we changed our minds. Tee, while you were on your honeymoon we found out we're having another girl."

"That's wonderful," said Tee. "Have you come up with a name yet?"

"No, we haven't really discussed it, but we have a little time before the baby gets here." Sandy wore a smile as she spoke, but there was no excitement in her voice. She acted as if she announced she planned to go watch paint dry instead of the gender of her baby. Tee wondered what was stealing her sister's joy but decided not to bring it up until everyone was gone.

Sandy then addressed the rest of the group. "Cassie, we will miss you. Your parents are blessed to have a daughter like you who realizes that family comes first. Sunflower's only a few hours away. I'm sure we can plan a trip there, and you can show us around your hometown. You are never alone.

"In this life, we owe it to ourselves to get stronger, wiser and better as we move along. I would like to commend all of you and the progress and positive decisions you've made. Kudos to each of you. Give yourselves a hand."

The ladies applauded one another and Tee finished handing out t-shirts and necklaces to everyone in the room along with the first draft of the I'm A Good Woman Empowerment Conference itinerary she completed earlier that morning. This was the inaugural year for this event, and she was eager to get everyone's feedback. She really wanted it to be a vehicle to inspire and motivate woman of all ages to love God and live a life that was not only pleasing to Him but prosperous. She believed that life is too short not to accomplish your dreams. She wanted to let women know that being a Christian wasn't boring. She loved her life, and it was exciting. Her career as an elite event planner gave her the opportunity to interact with the rich and famous and earn a nice salary doing it. Other women could do the same thing if they found something they were passionate about and worked hard at it.

The meeting proved to be very productive, and each woman was given an assignment to help move the event along. Tee also talked a little about her honeymoon and how happy she and Michael were. Before they dismissed, the ladies joined hands for a word of prayer. Then, parting embraces and well wishes were passed around the room.

Tee asked Lenice to stay for a moment so they could discuss Sandy's problem with Sheniqua. She had an idea that might help get that woman out of her sister's marriage, but she would need Lenice's help to make it work.

After their strategy session, Sandy said she was tired and wanted to check on her staff one last time before heading home. Tee decided to wait a little while longer before she asked her sister why she seemed so glum during a time she should be elated about the life growing inside her.

Chapter 6

Friend vs. Foe

Lenice Langston had always been a small woman with a big attitude. She refused to let her size or her beauty give anyone an excuse to believe for one second she did not possess brains and brawn to go along with her model thin frame. She was bold, almost fearless, and sassy. Lenice was not accustomed to biting her tongue, especially when she thought someone was wrong. It was killing her inside not to call her brother-in-law and tell him to mind his mouth when it came to her sister, but she promised Lenora she wouldn't.

Her brassiness allowed Lenice to move up the ranks and become a director at the Memphis Division of Wellness and Welfare. It was her job to make sure thousands of parents and their children were adequately provided food assistance, health care and subsidized housing. She loved her job because she loved helping people.

She was as protective of her friends as she was of her family. So, when Tee asked her to help get Sheniqua Alexander out of Sandy's marriage she was more than happy to assist. Tee and Sandy gave Lenice plenty of information that allowed her to devise a plan she hoped would send her on her way. She was now ready to put her plan into action. She couldn't go over to Sheniqua's house looking like herself, so she invested in non-prescription glasses and a long black wig to cover her chic pixy cut. She also wore a horrible pea green, short-sleeved, two-piece suit she found at the thrift store. The skirt came all the way to her black Mary Jane shoes. The real Lenice would never go out looking so geeky, but this look was perfect for what she was about to do. Earlier in the day, she borrowed Lenora's car so no one would recognize her Volkswagen Rabbit. Tee didn't tell her to get rid of Sheniqua this way, but Lenice felt this was the only way to get that home wrecker's attention without jeopardizing her job in the process.

Lenice arrived outside Sheniqua's place a little after 7 p.m., when she was almost certain the single mother would be home fixing dinner for her children. She walked up to the apartment her office helped Sheniqua secure through the Section 8 subsidized housing program and rang the doorbell. An adorable little boy who appeared to be about eight years old answered.

"Hello, son. Is your momma home?" asked Lenice.

"Yes," he said sweetly.

"May I see her?"

"Momma, it's a lady at the door for you!" he yelled and waited for his mother to appear. You heard her before you saw her.

"Boy, what did I tell you about opening my door for any ole body? I told you not to answer that door unless I told you to." Sheniqua immediately stopped in her tracks when she saw Lenice standing in her doorway holding up the doctored up Wealth and Wellness badge she wore around her neck. The name on it read Priscilla Price. Although she was perfectly within the policies of her division to pay Sheniqua a visit, she had not gone through the proper channels to do so. One of her subordinate's should be making a home visit such as this, but it may have taken as much as two weeks to get the paperwork processed to get it done. Lenice thought it was best to bypass protocol and do it herself. This woman had to be stopped.

Sheniqua was wearing nothing but her undergarments--a bra, panties, half-slip and flip-flops. She was in shape but the stretch marks on her exposed stomach provided evidence of her motherhood, as did the sleeping toddler she carried on her right hip. He seemed unaware to the world as he lay with his head resting on his mother's shoulder sucking his thumb.

"Oh, hello. I wasn't expecting anyone today. I usually get a phone call or something before you guys come. How can I help you?" she asked.

"Sorry to disturb you this evening, but are you Sheniqua Alexander?" asked Lenice

"Yes, I am."

"I came to discuss your benefits with you. May I come in and talk with you for a minute?"

"Yes, of course. Please excuse the mess. Let me go throw something on."

She led Lenice to the living room, asked her to have a seat and instructed the children sitting in front of a 50-inch flat screen TV to go to their rooms. She and the baby then headed to the back of the apartment. This wasn't the first time Lenice had entered the home of someone on public assistance to discover that their house looked almost as good as hers. The TV sat on a large oak and glass entertainment center. It also housed a Nintendo Wii, a Play Station, a Blu-ray player, a full surround sound system as well as a stereo. The furniture was navy blue leather and consisted of a couch, love seat and chaise lounger.

Lenice knew for a fact the furniture set was about $2,500 because she had once priced it for purchase herself. A Mac laptop and a large Coach purse lay on the coffee table and underneath it, was a pair of Jimmy Choo pumps. Sheniqua should not have been able to afford half of this with the amount of government assistance she received. Although, Lenice was quite aware that a pretty girl like her would have no problem securing male sponsors. She may have had some gullible man buying everything in the house.

Sheniqua reappeared in a red terrycloth robe without the baby. She nervously asked Lenice if she would like a beverage. Lenice declined.

"Ms. Alexander, please have a seat. I'll get straight to the point. It has been brought to our attention that you have a full-time job as a receptionist at a local dental practice. If this is true, I am almost positive you would not qualify for any of the public assistance programs in which you are currently enrolled. Is this true?" asked Lenice.

Sheniqua tugged on the long strands of her auburn lace front wig while avoiding making eye contact with Lenice.

"No, it's not. Who would tell you such a bold face lie?" she stammered.

"I cannot reveal our sources, but are you sure you are not being paid in cash by your current employer to avoid having your benefits terminated? Let me warn you, I am a thorough researcher and I already know the answers to the questions before I ask. Please choose your words carefully, Ms. Alexander. Lying on your benefits application is considered fraud. If you are found guilty of fraud, you will be required to pay us back every dime, including the cost of the medical benefits you received from the government while employed. Failure to pay it back is punishable with jail time and a hefty fine. My file indicates that you now receive $500 a month in food stamps and only pay $50 a month for this fine apartment here. Section 8 pays the balance. You and your children are also covered by a government healthcare plan." Lenice flipped through the portfolio in her hands looking for some notes she wrote down.

"You reported to us you were only working part-time at Kmart. If this is true, you should have no problem producing check stubs."

Sheniqua tugged harder at her wig. She hadn't worked at Kmart in years. She realized she was caught and continuing to lie would not be beneficial.

"Jail time? Who would take care of my children if I went to jail? I meant no harm. I was just trying to do right by my babies. It's hard being a single parent. What you give me isn't enough to take care of all of us!"

"I'm not finished, Ms. Alexander," interrupted Lenice. "My initial investigation revealed you make at least $2,500 a month on your job. Ms. Alexander, this is absolutely unacceptable. I estimate that your repayment of the government funds and health care benefits you have received over the past two years would be at least $80,000. If you are unable to repay it, you would be required to serve jail time."

Sheniqua's mouth dropped. She tried to hold back the tears that were now forming behind her violet contacts. She pushed strands from the wig out of her face and began fanning herself furiously.

"My, it's hot in here. Please ma'am, I'm sorry. Tell me what I can do. I don't have that kind of money and I can't go to jail. I'll do anything you want. I'll even quit my job if I have to, but I can't go to jail. My children have no one. Their daddy left us over a year ago. They're the only joy I have right now."

Lenice stared at her blankly. She was not moved one ounce by this woman's words. Her plan was working perfectly. She had this wanna be home wrecker exactly where she wanted her.

"Perhaps, we can strike a deal. It has also been brought to my attention you are still attempting to make contact with your former employer…." Lenice flipped to another page in her portfolio as if she was looking for something.

"Here we go, a Mr. Patrick Pierce. It is true you had an affair with him last year and are currently attempting to re-enter his life? Your doing so would cause great harm to his marriage. He and his wife would like you to stop trying to contact him immediately."

Lenice showed no emotion as she spoke. Her only expression was a serious stern stare.

Sheniqua stood up. "What? Ms. Price, what does any of that have to do with my benefits?"

"Everything, Ms. Alexander because I am offering you the opportunity to avoid embarrassment, a huge fine, an arrest and jail time if you forget about Patrick. That man is happily married. You should be ashamed of yourself."

"Who sent you? His wife?" shouted Sheniqua. "Is she afraid I'm going to steal him from her? I could you know. I had him once. I know I could have him again. She don't deserve him no way. She don't even appreciate him."

Lenice continued her serious unconcerned demeanor and added a bit of edge to her voice. She was the one holding all the cards. Sheniqua was in no position to argue about anything. "Who sent me is no concern of yours nor am I here to discuss the conditions of their marriage. However, your main concern should be preserving you and your children's way of life. If you go to jail they will probably be placed in foster care while you serve your sentence. Unless, you have a family member who is willing to care for them."

"This sounds like blackmail to me!" screamed Sheniqua.

Lenice released a sarcastic laugh. "Call it what you like, but if you want this issue to go away you are to have no contact with Patrick from this day forth. No phone calls, no letters, no text messages, no emails, no naked pictures and absolutely no face-to-face conversation. Don't even send him so much as a Facebook friend request or a poke. If you happen to be in the same place as him or his family, I suggest you treat them like total strangers. Don't even think about approaching to say hello. If I hear that you have done any of the above, not only will I report your fraudulent behavior, but I will also have words with your employer. After I tell him I am planning to launch a probe into his business practices, he will probably fire you to save himself."

Lenice stood up and looked up into Sheniqua's face. She was at least six inches shorter than Sheniqua, but she could be quite intimidating when she wished to be and this was one of those times.

"Have I made myself clear, Ms. Alexander?"

It didn't take Sheniqua long to decide she needed to agree to everything Lenice was offering or risk getting into a lot of trouble. Although she really did like Patrick, he was not worth $80,000, jail time or losing her children. She still looked good and would have no problem catching the eye of another rich man.

"Ms. Price, you got yourself a deal. You said Patrick, right? Patrick who? I don't know no Patrick."

"Wonderful. I was hoping you would see it that way. As long as you keep up your end of the bargain, I will not reveal you are working and filing fraudulent information in order to obtain government assistance. Let me give you some advice, young lady. Stay away from married men before you meet one whose wife believes in taking vengeance. You may find yourself dead in a ditch stanking. Then, who would take care of your children?"

"Is that a threat?" asked Sheniqua with a cold stare.

"Not at all. Patrick is Sandy's husband, and she wouldn't hurt a fly. Be glad it's not my husband because this conversation would include my taser. You're a pretty girl, and there is a single man out there who is fully capable of loving you and your children. Pray and ask God to send him your way. Patrick is taken. Good day, Ms. Alexander."

Lenice walked to the door and let herself out. She was sure that Sandy and Patrick would no longer hear from that gold-digger. She was not the one to play with. If someone she loved was hurting, be it friend of family, Lenice took it very personal.

She was all smiles as she drove to her sister's house to retrieve her car so she could get ready for her date with Deacon James. It was her first date in two years. After her boyfriend of five years left her for a man, she found it hard to trust any man. At the urging of her therapist, she was now slowly reentering the dating scene. She was a little apprehensive when a sweet shy deacon, at the church she and her sister attended, asked her out. She was a strong woman and in her opinion, it would take a strong, somewhat abrasive, man to handle her. She didn't think Deacon James was the man for the job. Yet, it was only a date, and maybe she needed a change. As she drove, Lenice tried to calm the nervous butterflies fluttering in her stomach. She truly wanted to believe there were still some good men out there, but her faith and her heart were severely damaged by someone who claimed to be something he wasn't. She was hoping Deacon James was a good man. She didn't think her heart could take much more abuse.

Chapter 7

Lenora Langston James

Lenora paced the floor anxiously waiting for Herman, her husband of eight years, to come home. It was their anniversary, and she prepared a special romantic dinner for two to celebrate. Everything had to be perfect. Her husband hadn't touched her in months and her body was yearning for his familiarity and some attention.

Their marriage wasn't ideal, but she and Herman proved all those who said they wouldn't last wrong. Most people didn't think they would last eight months let alone eight years. Her family was shocked when she came home from college one Christmas break and introduced them to her new Caucasian boyfriend. Race never mattered to either of them. At the time, Herman was one of only three white men attending the historically black Morehouse College. She was attending the Atlanta location of Savannah College of Art and Design. During their first meeting in the line at Wendy's, he made her feel more beautiful than any of the black men she dated before him. He was full of compliments. Herman was also smart, funny and handsome. She loved the way his shiny black locks curled up on his forehead like Clark Kent, and his blue eyes always seemed to see right through her. Yet, something was different between them. Herman was no longer kind, attentive or complimentary.

Lenora wasn't like her twin sister. She was quiet, docile and sometimes a tad too nice. She often bit her tongue when she should speak up for herself or some cause she was passionate about. She was a giver, not a fighter. She volunteered at church, a shelter and local daycare that catered specifically to children who were HIV positive. She was skilled in the art of crochet and often made blankets for the children to make them feel special.

On the inside, Lenora was the same good natured gentle spirit she had always been but her outside appearance had changed drastically over the years. The once skinny woman was now undeniably obese and she had her three children to thank for it. Lenora was able to lose the weight she gained while pregnant with their first child, Herman, Jr., relatively easy. He was now five. However, with the twins, Heather and Heston, things were entirely different. During her pregnancy, her petite physique ballooned from 125 pounds to 180 pounds. After giving birth, she developed post partum depression and ate constantly to make herself feel better. Eventually, the depression passed, but the weight remained and she continued to eat constantly. She was now tipping the scales at 300 pounds.

Although, Lenora no longer looked like her model thin sister she had many other noteworthy attributes Herman seemed to have forgotten. She was still loving and attentive. She was a homemaker and a darn good one. Their two-story brick and vinyl siding house was always spotless. She did the landscaping herself, and the yard was always well maintained. Her peach hybrid roses were the envy of her neighbors. More than once, she caught someone trying to snip a few blossoms for themselves. She kept her man looking good, too. Herman's clothes were heavily starched the way he liked them. She cut his hair for him, carefully trimming his nose and ear hair. She even shined his shoes.

Lenora could cook with the best of them. She made almost everything from scratch. Her vegetables came from fresh produce instead of a can or the frozen food section. She would probably kill the pigs, chickens and cows herself if she could. She was also a good mother--attending to her children's every need and making sure they were properly educated was very important to her. Their oldest was in kindergarten and always received an "E" for excellent in conduct and his academics. The twins were now three years old and two of the happiest children you ever saw. They spoke quite well for their age and could even read some. As far as Lenora was concerned, she was still doing all the things that really mattered so a little weight gain was no reason not to get some lovin' from her hubby every now and then.

Lenora knew her weight bothered Herman. In an effort to do something about it, she began eating healthier and walking daily around the track at the high school near their home. She was also taking some diet pills, called Melt the Fat, she saw one day while in the grocery store. She was certain that it was only a matter of time before the pounds started falling off.

The dining room table was set with their best china and several tall lit candles. She prepared Herman's favorite dinner. Baked chicken, Caesar salad, extra cheesy macaroni and cheese and baked russet potatoes with a red velvet cake for dessert were all ready to be consumed. The real feast would take place in the bedroom.

Their bed contained fresh linen sprinkled with the alluring scent of jasmine. She tried to make herself look more appetizing with some lingerie she purchased at Plush, a plus size lingerie store she heard about. Lenora tried not to worry that Herman was almost an hour later than he said he would be. Instead, she remained optimistic he would arrive any minute. What could be keeping him?

When she heard someone at the front door, Lenora almost tripped over her own feet as she ran to see who it was. Herman usually entered through the kitchen door but maybe he was trying something different today. Disappointment showed all over her face when she opened the door and saw Lenice standing there with the keys to her car.

"I was dropping off the car and noticed Herman hadn't made it home yet. So, I decided to hand you your keys rather than stick them under the seat like we discussed," she explained.

Lenice was pleased to see Lenora had enough sense not to wear a mumu for her anniversary. What she did have on resembled a pleated curtain. The black and white monstrosity was void of any shape or definition. It swallowed Lenora whole. She looked like an eight ball on a pool table.

"That's fine. Now, get out of here before he gets here," said Lenora ungratefully.

"I'm leaving, but you don't have to be so mean. Happy anniversary! Why do you always want me to leave before Herman comes home?"

"If you must know, it's because I used to look like you. He is always making mention of how good you look, and how I used to look that good and with a little exercise I could look as sexy as you again someday."

"You mean your husband has been checking me out? How gross. Don't listen to him, girl. I know for a fact you are beautiful no matter what size you are," comforted Lenice.

"I'm glad you think so, but your opinion doesn't count because you aren't the one whose bones I want to jump tonight. Now get out," Lenora said as she pushed Lenice toward the front steps of her porch.

"I'm going. Here," said Lenice. She reached inside her oversized leather purse, pulled out a bottle of Atalon Cabernet Sauvignon from Napa Valley and handed it to Lenora.

Lenora gushed with gratitude at the gift. "It's his favorite. You didn't have to do that. This bottle is 100 bucks."

"I want you to have a great time tonight because you deserve it. I figured this might help. Call me tomorrow."

"I will. Drive safely and have fun on your date." Lenora gave her sister a hug and walked back into the house, securely locking the door behind her. She then went to the kitchen to put the wine in the kitchen and make sure their dinner was still warm.

If she hadn't been in such a hurry for her to leave, she would have asked Lenice why she was dressed like she was auditioning for a remake of the movie, *Revenge of the Nerds.*

Lenice was the only company Lenora had that evening. Herman didn't come home until 11 p.m., making for one unhappy anniversary. The dinner was cold, the candles were nothing but a puddle of melted wax and Lenora was miserable. Herman's reason for being late didn't make things any better. According to him, he was working late and fell asleep at the office. He was so busy, he completely forgot it was their anniversary. Lenora may have believed him if he hadn't smelled like peanuts and beer.

Chapter 8

Can You Keep A Secret?

Today Tee and Michael were making room for his belongings throughout their home. Before they left for the honeymoon, he instructed his housekeeper in Miami, Ms. Sophia, to box up his fall and winter clothes and a few other treasured items and ship them to Memphis. They arrived that morning. She had lived here alone for five years and decorated the three bedroom/two bath home to suit her tastes. She wondered how having a man in the house would change things.

There was a his and hers walk-in closet in the master bedroom, but Tee's abundant wardrobe, shoes and hand bags took up both sides. She planned to spend the majority of the day deciding which items she wanted to donate to charity and which ones she wanted to distribute to closets in other areas of the house. She laid them out in piles on the floor. Her honey-colored cocker spaniel, Chesnutt, playfully jumped over and rolled through them making it impossible to keep them neat.

Michael wasn't exactly thrilled about the size of the house. He commented more than once that they should start looking for something larger in the near future. Tee didn't object, but she did take issue with his scrutiny of her home. This was the first house she purchased, and she was proud of it. It was a foreclosure and she got it for half of what it was worth. She painted it in rich colors and added furniture to suit her classic taste. The only place Tee instituted fads was in her event planning and her wardrobe. Everything else she liked to be able to stand the test of time. Fifty years from now her home and the majority of everything in it would still be in style. Maybe it wasn't as spacious as the sprawling 8,200 square foot mansion Michael lived in before downsizing to his Miami condo, but it was hers. She knew he didn't mean any harm, but his words were somewhat irritating. Peter Parker, Michael's manager, agent and best friend, called while she tried to find drawer space for Michael's t-shirts, underwear and socks. Tee preferred to talk to him in private, but she didn't want to make Michael suspicious. So, she answered it in his presence.

"Hello, Peter."

"Hello, Mrs. Stokes. I was calling to make sure everything is set," said Peter.

"Yeah, we're good. Everything is arranged the way you wanted it."

"Great. You're the best."

"No problem. It's been a blast preparing for this rendezvous."

"Michael doesn't suspect anything does he?"

"Not a thing," said Tee.

"Even better. Eight o'clock, right?"

"Eight o'clock."

"I'll be there waiting, and I even have a couple of surprises."

"I'm sure it will be a night to remember."

"Tee, there's no one I would rather keep a secret with," said Peter.

Tee laughed. "Me neither, Peter."

"Tell Michael I'm going to call him next to talk business."

"Will do. Bye."

"Bye, Tee."

Michael tried to act as if he wasn't listening, but Tee knew he was. She prepared herself for his questions.

"Was that Peter? What did he want?"

"Yeah. I've been helping him with the arrangements for his sister's surprise birthday party. I set up a meeting for him with an event planner in Miami tomorrow," she lied. "He said he's going to call you in a few minutes to discuss some business."

Michael and Tee hadn't been together long, less than a year, but he knew his wife well enough to know when she was lying. She and Peter became friends while they were dating, but now that they were married, for some reason, he was a little uneasy about their friendship. It was not beneath Peter to inappropriately flirt or bed another man's wife. Although, he was positive he wouldn't be ignorant enough to try to sleep with Tee. He trusted his wife, but she and Peter obviously had a secret they weren't willing to share with him. He decided to play it cool for now, but he would keep his eyes and ears open.

"That was nice of you," he responded. His phone rang with the distinctive "Pick up the phone boss, pick up the phone boss," ring tone he used especially for Peter.

"What's up, man?" he answered.

"Hey, newlywed. I wanted to call and talk to you for a minute about an opportunity at The Centrillium.

The Centrillium was the most popular gentleman's club in Miami. It used to be one of his and Peter's favorite spots to unwind and look at some flesh. Michael hadn't been in over a year. Since he rededicated his life to Christ, he tried to stay away from any kind of club. They didn't hold the same excitement for him like in the past. He'd rather stay at home and watch his wife take off her clothes instead of women he barely knew.

"Before you say no hear me out," continued Peter. "They want you to host twice a month and they're willing to pay you $20,000 to do it. Having you there was always good for business, and with a new club opening up down the street management has decided to play offense rather than defense. It's a win-win for them because the ladies loved having you in the place and the men think you're a cool dude. They even told me each night you're there, they'll reserve your favorite girl, Porsche, especially for you."

Michael felt warm at the mention of Porsche's name. She had to be one of the baddest women to walk the earth, and she was every bit as fast as the car. Images of DD breasts, thick hips and thighs and a big backside flooded his thoughts. She was so bad she had her own stage upstairs and only the club's high dollar clients were allowed to enter. Her show was more like a nude concert instead of your normal strip tease. She liked to lip sync to popular songs while she danced seductively. She believed in putting on a performance her audience wouldn't forget. It included costume changes and sometimes even back up dancers. It was like she was doing an exotic musical or something.

Back in the day, when Michael felt the pang of loneliness, he would invite Porsche over to the house for a private show. She became somewhat of a friend. The two chatted from time to time about their personal and professional lives. He stopped taking her phone calls after he became injured and was forced to retire. Those were dark days for him. He became depressed and shut almost everyone out of his life. He knew Porsche would have no problem finding another baller to replace him. After all, she was super fine. There wasn't a day he didn't thank the Lord for allowing him to survive that ordeal and become a better man.

"No deals, Pete. I'm through with that life," said Michael.

"Come on, Mike. Did you hear me? He's going to pay you $10,000 a night to stand on stage, crack a few jokes, introduce the dancers and say hello to a few people. Look, I'll sweeten the deal for you. He's giving me a personal VIP room for my clients and distinguished guests. I'll cut you a piece of the money that's made there as well. Mike you owe me this. I'm not making nearly the amount of money I used to make managing you since you don't play ball anymore and you adopted all these rules about what you can and can't do since you're saved now." Peter's voice dripped with sarcasm.

"Six months. That's all I'm asking, six months. By then my room should be one of the most popular in the club and you can quit," rationalized Peter.

"No. God would not be pleased with me hosting in a strip club. My mind is made up and that's my final answer. Don't mention that place or Porsche to me again. That's my past."

"Alright, man. No disrespect. All of us aren't like you. Some of us believe if God really intended for us to be with one woman, he wouldn't have given us all this sperm. I'll see if Ray Lewis or somebody wants the gig," joked Peter.

"Do what you like. You know I'll be in Miami tonight. I have a gig tomorrow morning but maybe we can hang out before I leave. I'm sure we can come up with other ways to make some money that don't involve naked women. Okay man?"

"Alright, man. See you then." Peter sounded like a kid whose balloon was popped by the neighborhood bully.

Tee could tell their conversation hadn't gone well. They were having a pretty good day, and she didn't want anything to ruin it.

"Baby, are you ready to take a break? We can get something to eat before I drop you off at the airport," she suggested. A good meal usually made him smile.

"That sounds like a great idea."

Michael walked over to Tee. She was kneeling over a pile of clothes she was packing into a box. He reached down to give her a hand up. She eagerly accepted his assistance. As she rose, he looked deep into her eyes and said, "Have I told you how beautiful you are?"

"Not today, but I never get tired of hearing it," replied Tee.

"Well, Mrs. Michael Stokes you are absolutely stunning, and I am so glad I married you. I love you."

"I love you too, baby." Michael kissed her the way she liked—as if she were the only woman in the world who mattered.

As they drove to Mae Lillie's, Michael continued to wonder about Tee's phone call with Peter. He had a speaking engagement in Miami the next day, and he planned to spend the night at his condo so he would be well rested for the event. He hadn't been to the condo in over a month, but he was sure Ms. Sophia was keeping everything in top condition. He didn't have much use for his bachelor pad these days, but Tee persuaded him to keep it for a sunny getaway. Memphis could get pretty cold during the winter.

He really wanted to know why those two felt the need to be so secretive. He hoped he could get some kind of explanation in Miami. He also wanted to help Peter understand why he couldn't do the things he used to do anymore. He prayed often for his friend and asked God for wisdom to bring him to Christ, but Peter had other ideas. He said he had no use for church and that he and God had an understanding. Although, he didn't elaborate on what that understanding was. For now, all Michael could do was try to be a good example for his buddy in hopes that living right might rub off on him one day.

Chapter 9

D-A-N-G

Sandy was tired of Patrick's frequent questions about why she was taking her time preparing for the baby. When he found out she asked Tee to push her baby shower back until two weeks before the baby was due, he hit the roof. He said that was too late. What if she went into labor earlier? Patrick insisted she and Tee have the baby shower no less than a month before the due date and start decorating the nursery now. He did not want to have to scramble around at the last minute to get things done. If there was one thing Patrick hated, it was procrastination. He was also scared she was suffering from some type of pregnancy related depression and thought that keeping her busy might help. But, it wasn't like she didn't have enough to do with two children, a husband and a restaurant.

In an effort to quiet Patrick, Sandy agreed to his demands. Tee was supposed to drop Michael off at the airport and then meet her at Booties, her favorite baby boutique, to help her select items for the room and to talk about the baby shower. Sandy decided to check her email before she left. There was another message from Armondo. Didn't he know how to follow directions?

Hello Cassandra,

My sister said you came in my grandfather's store and you're pregnant. Is this true? Is it mine? If I'm going to be a father I have the right to know. I still love you.

Armondo

She deleted the email and walked out the door. Armondo's sister had a big mouth. She definitely wouldn't be going to Sebastian's Grocery Store anymore. Sandy was tired, and her conscience was starting to get the better of her. She wasn't eating the way she should to provide proper nourishment for the baby, and she was barely getting any sleep. She needed to confess but couldn't. She was too afraid of how Patrick would react.

Tee was running late as usual, and rather than wait in the parking lot for her, Sandy went inside Booties and headed straight for the section that housed the nursery furniture. The most popular colors for girls seemed to be pink and brown. She admired the skillfully crafted furniture that was specifically designed to welcome new life into the world. She looked at cribs, bassinets, dressers, hampers and cute little throw rugs in the shapes of animals. She wished Tee would hurry up. She didn't want to be there, and she didn't want to make these decisions. She was too distracted to decide much of anything lately.

A saleswoman approached her to see if she needed any assistance. Sandy quickly declined and told her she was waiting on someone to give her a second opinion.

"I understand. This is a big decision," said the saleswoman. "If you don't mind me asking, who are you waiting for, the baby's father?" Although a seemingly innocent question, it caused Armondo's face to flash before her eyes, followed by the face of a very angry Patrick. Sandy's mouth went dry, and her face felt flushed. She became hot and found it hard to breathe. She rushed past the saleswoman, without providing an answer, and headed for the door to get some fresh air. What was happening to her?

As she exited the store, she bumped into Tee and almost knocked her over. Tee saw she was upset and guided her to one of the colorful rocking chairs outside. Tee was drinking a bottle of water and offered it to Sandy. She snatched it from her hands and took several large gulps.

"Sandy, what's wrong with you? And don't tell me nothing," said Tee.

The water helped to calm her nerves and her temperature. Sandy's breathing returned to normal. She began rocking back in forth in the chair and rubbed her stomach. The baby kicked.

"I'll tell you, but you have to promise not to tell a soul," Sandy whispered while looking around to make sure no one was in earshot of their conversation.

"Done, now spill it."

"I did something horrible, and I'm afraid this dang baby might not be Patrick's."

Tee wasn't sure she heard her correctly. "What? You mean you slept with someone else. Who? When?"

"Armondo, and it was the day of my surprise birthday party."

"Armondo? You mean old man Sebastian's grandson? The cute kid who used to sack our groceries?"

"Yes, but he's not a kid anymore. He's a full-grown man in every sense of the word. I mean, he's gorgeous. Absolutely gorgeous."

"It doesn't matter how fine he is, Sandy. I knew you were upset with Patrick, but I didn't think you would commit adultery. What in the world were you thinking?" asked Tee.

"I wasn't. It happened the day after I found out Patrick was paying Sheniqua's bills. I thought he was cheating on me, again. I ordered some food from Sebastian's, and Armondo brought it over. He started flirting with me, one thing led to another and before I knew it we were—you know. Little sister, I feel horrible."

"But Patrick wasn't cheating on you, Sandy."

"Shucks! I didn't find that out until after the affair and of course, with it being my birthday, I had sex with Patrick after the party that night."

"You had sex with two men in the same day? What did you do?" Tee couldn't believe her sister's behavior.

"The question is, what am I freakin' gonna do, Tee? I can't tell Patrick, he'll leave me. Thanks to Lenice, Sheniqua is out of our lives for good. She hasn't called or texted since we met at the restaurant. I can't give him a reason to go back to her. By the way, did Lenice ever tell you how she did it?"

"No," said Tee. "She said if she told me she'd have to kill me, and I like living so I left it alone. Do you think Patrick suspects anything?"

"No. He thinks its hormones or something and wants me to snap out of it. But it's not that easy. I feel so guilty, and I'm so scared. I want to wait until I give birth and see who the baby looks like. If it looks like Armondo, I'll confess. But I may not be about to wait because Armondo's nosy sister told him I was pregnant. He sent me an email today asking if it was his."

"Well, what did you say?"

"Gat dang it, nothing. I deleted the email without responding. He's in Iraq right now working for Uncle Sam so he's easy to ignore," Sandy explained.

"Wow. Honestly Sandy, right now I don't know what to tell you. Waiting does sound like a good idea because there's no need to upset Patrick if you don't have to, but you kind of owe it to him to confess. He confessed about his affair, and it might be a good idea to tell him before Armondo takes it upon himself to do so. But he can tell something is wrong because of your attitude about this pregnancy. He even asked me to see if I can find out what it is."

"He did? What attitude? I don't have an attitude."

"Sandy, it is obvious you are not happy about having this baby. I've never seen you this stressed, tired, irritable and unfashionable. Look at you, you're a mess. What are you wearing? Keeping this secret is not good for you."

Sandy had on a pair of stonewashed jeans that were too small. She couldn't zip or button them. Instead, they were held together in the front with a large safety pin and a white scarf that was supposed to be a belt. The pink shirt she wore wasn't long enough to cover the safety pin or her protruding stomach. Her baby bump was exposed for the world to see. She was a prime candidate for the maternity version of, "What Not to Wear." Tee was embarrassed for her.

"What do my clothes have to do with anything? I can't tell him. He'll be so angry. I treated him badly after he told me he cheated. What if he decides to treat me the same way? He might even leave me. You better not tell him either. I don't want to talk about this anymore, and don't you say a word to anyone. Now, help me go in this store and decorate my nursery."

"But…"

"Fudge that! No buts, little sister. If I confess anything today, it will be that I spent an obscene amount of money on things for this baby. I'll worry about the rest later. Now get your arse in this friggin' store."

Tee giggled at her sisters feebly attempts at profanity. If she only knew how ridiculous she sounded. She was glad she only did it when she was upset.

Tee helped Sandy temporarily relieve some stress with one of her favorite past times---shopping. They selected furniture along with artwork for the walls and a few toys. She also picked out a few outfits to carry the baby home in following her arrival. Sandy arranged for everything to be delivered to her home the next day.

Tee insisted they visit the maternity boutique next door and buy some new clothes for Sandy. She forbade her sister to go out in public looking like that ever again.

Afterward, they went to Sandy's house and ate dinner with Patrick and the children. He almost choked on his smothered pork chop after Sandy told him she spent $12,000 on the nursery for their new bundle of joy. She also spent another $2,000 on herself.

Tee avoided being alone with Patrick so he couldn't ask if she found out what was bothering her sister. He would have to figure it out without her help.

Chapter 10

Surprise

Michael arrived at the condo safely. He was tired and couldn't wait to get into his bed and rest. He had only been gone from home a few hours, but he was missing his wife already. Michael opened the door and reached for the light switch to illuminate the room. What he saw caused him to rub his eyes because they must be deceiving him. He was much more tired than he thought. Maybe he was losing his mind. There were three women in short naughty nurse's uniforms standing in the middle of his living room. Each woman was wearing a mask to hide her face, but their short, cleavage-baring outfits weren't hiding much of anything. Two of the women were petite but the one in the middle was thick and curvaceous. Something about her was vaguely familiar.

"Good evening, Mr. Stokes. Are you ready for your evening massage?" asked the woman on the right in a seductive tone.

"Excuse me ladies, but I think you have the wrong man. I'm married, and I didn't order a massage. How did you get in here?"

"No, we have the right man. You didn't order a massage but someone very close to you did," said the woman on the left.

"Well. I appreciate the sentiment Miss but I'm going to have to ask all of you to leave," said Michael sternly. This had to be a trap. He wasn't going to be a sucker.

Michael felt his cell phone vibrate and pulled it out of his pocket. There was a text message from Tee. He was thankful for the distraction. His wife was beautiful, but he was still a man and it wasn't easy to divert his eyes from the three chocolate beauties standing in front of him. It read, I love you baby! Surprise! Enjoy your post-bachelor party.

"Bachelor party?" Michael said to no one in particular.

Peter, Maxwell, several of his buddies from the NFL and others appeared from the doorways of various rooms around the condo. They were all laughing.

"What's up, man? You should have seen your face!" yelled Peter. "Congrats on the wedding. Now, let's celebrate the way we should have. Tee felt bad she had a bridal shower but you didn't get a chance to have a bachelor party, so we got together and decided to throw you one tonight. I knew you wouldn't want exotic dancers. So, I arranged for these ladies here to give us a different type of entertainment in the form of massages."

Michael was pleasantly surprised and began laughing. "You guys are crazy. You know you were about to get these ladies booted out. And you're right, I wouldn't have wanted strippers, but I can deal with a massage."

He went around the room greeting his friends and family. So, that was the big secret. The ladies removed their masks. Michael didn't recognize the two shorter women, who were obviously twins, but the curvy sister in the middle was one of Tee's closest friends, Tiffany Tate.

"Tiffany, what are you doing here?" he asked.

"Well, as you know I'm in massage therapy school, and Peter asked me to arrange tonight's G-rated entertainment.

I am going to administer your massage personally because I know your wife wouldn't want strange women putting their hands on you. Right this way, Cowboy," she said.

Michael was smart enough to know this was Tee's way of keeping an eye on things without being there, but he didn't mind. He hung out with Tee and her girlfriends a couple of times, and he thought Tiffany was pretty cool. A massage would probably do him some good. He followed Tiffany to his bedroom where her portable massage table was set up. She instructed him to strip down to his boxer shorts and lay face down on the table. She then went into his bathroom to wait for him to take his clothes off. He wasn't too sure about this because she was his wife's friend, but he did as he was told.

Tiffany returned wearing something that resembled a cloth utility belt, but instead of tools it contained massage oils and lotions.

"I know you're probably a little nervous about me touching you but Michael, please relax. I'm a professional, and this massage will not help you if you don't relax," said Tiffany.

"Sorry, but you are one of my wife's best friends," said Michael.

Tiffany began rubbing his shoulders.

"That's exactly why I'm giving you this massage myself. I'm sure the twins would take this opportunity to try to feel you up or something," laughed Tiffany. "You're in excellent hands. Besides, I owe Tee and Peter big time for this. The amount of money Peter is paying the three of us along with the tips we'll make tonight is a big help right about now. It's been hard for me. I'm enjoying school, but I'm so used to being able to go to the bank and withdraw money whenever I need it. When I left Quincy he cut off my funds and right now I'm fighting him for child support. Until the judge makes a decision, I'm on my own. I really need this money."

"I can understand that. I commend you for your decision to leave. That was brave. Not many women would be willing to do what you did. Oooh that feels nice."

"Thank you. I really think I have a calling for this. I'll be happy when I finish school and can increase my clientele. I was thinking of trying to do parties like this all the time. Peter said if the twins and I do a good job he would help me."

"That's good," said Michael. "I'm going to help you tonight. I'm going to give you a list of who, in that room, is most likely to give a big tip. You make sure you go out there and get them."

"Oh thank you, Michael! Tee always says you're the sweetest man on Earth."

"I'll be sure to thank my wife for that when I get home. That's enough work on me. Let's get you some more money." Michael sat up and swung his legs over the side of the table. "Go get some pencil and paper off my night stand so I can write down those names."

Instead, Tiffany pulled a notepad and a pen out of her cloth belt. Michael then told her the names of the most generous athletes and businessmen in the room. He even gave her a fifty dollar tip.

Chapter 11

First Date Fun

Lenice hadn't had this much fun in the company of a man in years. James was smart, funny and considerate. Like Lenice, he had never been married, and he didn't have any children. James told her he had been watching her for the past couple of years and finally built up the courage to ask her out. He wanted to make sure she enjoyed herself and arranged for a horse and carriage ride downtown. It was a little cool so they huddled beneath a blanket while admiring the bright lights of downtown Memphis and listening to the steady clopping sound of the horse's feet. They exited on historic Beale Street in front of one of the clubs there that featured karaoke. They went inside, and the two of them playfully belted out their favorite tunes. They even did a duo to Ashford and Simpson's "Solid." For dinner, they walked to a nearby restaurant and dined on crawfish, shrimp and crab legs. Lenice adored seafood.

They were having so much fun that neither of them wanted the night to end. James suggested they go see a double feature at the drive-in. Lenice hadn't been to the drive-in since she was a teenager and thought it was a nice way to end the evening. However, it was late, and they fell asleep before the first movie ended. James awoke to find they were the only car left. The second movie ended almost an hour earlier. James woke Lenice up and drove her home.

He escorted her to her door and stood patiently while she located her keys inside her purse.

"I had a good time, Lenice," he said.

"I did too, James. I enjoyed listening to you sing. You have a nice voice."

"Thanks. You're not too bad yourself."

"Boy, please. I can't carry a tune in a bucket and you know it. Well, it's late and here we are acting like we don't have to go to work tomorrow."

"I know, don't remind me," said James.

They were now at the awkward part of the evening where both individuals want to kiss, and each one is contemplating if he or she should make the first move. James was nervous, but he decided to go for it. He pulled Lenice toward him and gave her a sweet kiss on her cherry lips.

Lenice blushed. James made her feel like a giddy school girl. In an effort to hide it, she gave him a tight hug and buried her face in his shoulder. He smelled good. She breathed him in deeply. James enjoyed having her close to him. Her small body fit snugly within his embrace. Lenice let him go when she thought she could look at him without grinning from ear to ear.

"Goodnight, Deacon James."

"You mean good morning. It's 1 a.m. You go inside now, and I hope you have sweet dreams."

Lenice disappeared into the house and was greeted by her Chihuahua, Webster. She treated him as if he was her child and dressed him regularly. Today he was wearing a blue, white and pink argyle sweater. She stooped down to pick him up and kissed the top of his brown head.

"Mommy got a kiss tonight, too," she said. "I hope it's not the last."

He licked her face. She smiled. That made two kisses.

Chapter 12

Memories

The bachelor party wound down around 2 a.m. Beer bottles and used paper plates with remnants of barbecue, coleslaw and fries, littered the rooms of Michael's condo. He would tell Ms. Sophia to come in later and clean it up. He enjoyed seeing his buddies for a change. Other than Patrick, he hadn't made any friends in Memphis. The only people left at the party were Peter, Maxwell, his college roommate Dexter, and a couple of other retired NFL players. One was Deuce Edwards, who used to play tight end for San Francisco and Roscoe Floyd, an old buddy from his days with the Dallas Cowboys. He told Tiffany and the twins they could spend the night in one of his guest rooms. He had plenty of room.

The six men sat around talking about sports. Eventually, the conversation shifted towards women. All of them were married, except Maxwell and Dexter, but the guys always got a kick out of reliving their sexual conquests from their single days in the form of a good tale. They often swapped stories just for fun. Although, they had all been told many times. There was one story they never got tired of hearing. It was the one that persuaded Michael to change his womanizing ways; the story of Daneisha Crawford. Patrick and Maxwell were the only ones who hadn't heard it, and the fellas asked Michael to tell it again for their entertainment. At first, Michael was a little apprehensive because he tried hard to shield his little brother from his philandering ways in hopes he would be a better man. Since he was a changed man, and more importantly married, he figured it couldn't do any harm. Besides, his little brother was now grown and after finding out that Maxwell slept with Becca and fathered Michelle, it was safe to say his innocence was out the window. The brothers were trying to get past the rift it caused between them, but it was happening slowly. They hardly talked anymore and when they did, conversation was often awkward between them. Michael was still glad he came to Miami. It showed Maxwell cared. Everyone gave Michael their attention.

"One thing you have to understand about me is I have never believed in spending the night with every woman you sleep with," began Michael. "When I was really out there my bedroom was a revolving door, but no one was allowed to spend the night. There's something about waking up with someone special. It's almost like you can feel her essence. So, if a woman wasn't special to me I saw no need to experience that great- start-to-a-new-day feeling with her. If she was a gold digger, insincere or a liar, I knew it in the morning because her essence was funky. If I took a woman home she had to trail me in her car and when I got through banging her back out, I put her out. This wasn't very bright or considerate, but I didn't care. I was Michael Stokes, and in my arrogance, I believed there was nothing they could do to me. I got called every name in the book and had my car keyed up three times by women I told to get out. One chick even tried to kill me by turning all the eyes of my gas stove to full blast before she left. That should've been a sign that what I was doing could end in disaster but nothing changed. Except after that, I walked them to the door instead of telling them to let themselves out. I didn't feel anything for any of those women. What made me change my ways was a life-altering experience I had one night after an away game in Chicago.

"After the game, I went to the restaurant in the hotel for a drink and met a 20-year-old college student working there as a waitress. From the moment she brought me my drink, I could tell she wanted me. Her name was Daneisha. She was cute, about 5'6," bowlegged, with hazel eyes and long brown hair pulled into a neat bun. She wore a white tuxedo shirt and a black skirt, that were both too big, and fishnet stockings. Even in too large clothing I could tell she had a nice body underneath. After making small talk and acting like I cared about what she thought, I told her to come to my room after work, and I would teach her a few things that weren't in her textbooks. The entire time I was talking to her I had this feeling of familiarity. I knew I'd seen her somewhere before, but I couldn't put my finger on it. I asked her if we'd met before, and she said we hadn't. So, I just assumed I was buggin."

"She arrived at my room about midnight and still had on her work uniform. She was so young and naïve. I guess she didn't know you were supposed to go home and get all prettied up first if you wanted to entice a man. Maybe she was just really eager to be in my presence. I told her to take off her uniform and go take a shower because she smelled like fried food. I stood in the door of the bathroom and watched her get out with water dripping down her cinnamon body and realized her uniform was hiding an almost perfect physique. Her hips could have stood to be a little wider but give her about two to three more years or maybe a kid and she was going to look like Beyoncé. I grabbed a towel and dried her off. Then, I picked her up, carried her to the bed and rubbed lotion all over her tender, young and extremely soft skin. If it's one thing I can't stand it's an ashy woman. Once she was thoroughly moisturized, I pounced on her like a monk who recently left the monastery. After about two hours of nude gymnastics, I was finished with her and told Ms. May I Take Your Order it was time for her to leave. That girl started to cry and screamed at me, 'What did I do? I thought this would make you happy? I wanted to wake up next to you. Why are you treating me like this? I've adored you since I was a little kid. I used to dream of marrying you!'

"I had become such a cold-hearted, insufferable bastard that I wasn't moved by Daneisha's tears or her words. I told her I was flattered and handed her clothes and shoes to her. She continued to cry. As she put on each article of clothing, she cried a little louder. I was still unmoved. She had to go! By the time she finished putting on her shoes, tears and mucus were streaming down her face. She looked like a child who got beat with a switch from the back yard. Her performance was wasted on me because I didn't care about her tears. I just wanted her to shut up and leave so I could get some sleep. I escorted her to the door. Her eyes were red and she hadn't even bothered to comb her hair, which as a result of our prior activities, was all over her head. Before she stepped into the hallway, she turn toward me and wiped her nose and face with her sleeve. It was so gross.

"I watched snot string from her nose to her shirt before she opened her mouth wide and screamed, 'I'mma tell your momma Michael Stokes! She's gonna be so ashamed of how her big, strong son the NFL player turned out to be a bigheaded selfish turd! I hate you! I'm gonna tell my daddy too and he's gonna beat you senseless!'

"Her threats meant nothing to me. I was Michael Stokes. I just looked at her little nasty, snot-nosed behind like she was crazy and hoped none of the other people on the floor called security. I shut my door and called room service for a new set of sheets. The next morning, the team and I boarded a plane and headed back to Miami. I forgot about her before the plane landed.

"That night, I was relaxing on the couch playing Madden and the phone rang. I didn't even get a chance to say hello before my momma started talking. She was very upset about something."

Michael increased the pitch of his voice to imitate his mother. 'Michael Alexander Deontae Stokes, Jr. what have you become?'

'Calm down, Ma,' I said. 'What are you talking about?'

'I'm talking about you sleeping with young girls and then putting them out of your hotel room in the middle of the night. Not only is that rude but unsafe. What if she had been mugged or raped while riding the subway home? I raised you to be a respectable young man not a gigolo.'

"The whole time she was talking I was wondering, *how in the world did that girl find my momma?* My momma was so mad she was now yelling at me and she hardly ever raises her voice.

'That young girl you used for your sinful fornicative pleasures last night is a member of our church. She's up there in Chicago going to school. That poor baby called me all in tears. You may not remember her because she's older now, but she's the little girl who used to follow you all around the sanctuary when you came home to visit from college. She used to worship the ground you walked on, and you treated her like some streetwalker. I'm disappointed in you Michael. Are you trying to go to hell on purpose?'

"I was dumbfounded. I knew she looked familiar. Why did she say she didn't know me? She said her name was Daneisha, but she was little Dee Dee from First Baptist Progressive in Akron, Ohio. I was like *dang, what did I do*? Unfortunately, Momma wasn't finished.

'That's somebody's daughter you're treating like that. Deacon Crawford's to be exact. You remember him don't you? Your old tee ball coach. Would you want someone to treat me like that? What about your little sister, Tomeka? I admit she was wrong for coming to your hotel room like some Jezebel, but she's still a human being and you don't treat human beings like that. If I was up there, I would take the strap off my purse and wear your behind out! Lord, help me! I try to raise my boys to be respectable men and look what the devil does. The flesh sho' is weak. Senior, come get this phone and talk to your son before he catches AIDS or gets somebody pregnant! Senior, I said get this phone!'

"Before I could ask her not to put Pop on the phone, she handed it to him. I wished she hadn't told him. My father is the head deacon at our church. He and my mother were each other's first. He never played the field and couldn't understand me. Can you believe he's only had sex with one woman his entire life? Also, they are both saved, sanctified and Holy Ghost filled Christians and if you do wrong, they will hurl the word at you like a grenade.

"Pop said, 'Son, I raised you to treat women with the same respect I treat your mother. You know right from wrong. You went to church three days a week so there's really nothing I can say that you don't already know, but I'm disappointed in you, boy. You keep treating women this way it's going to come back on you. Stop this foolishness. Why would you want to engage in such unhealthy behavior? I know Dee Dee wasn't the first woman you've done this to. Every time you sleep with someone, you give them a piece of yourself. Briefly, for one moment, you become one spirit and one flesh and when you separate, that person takes a piece of you with them. You keep giving yourself away like that, there's not going to be anything left to give the woman God has chosen for you. I know you're grown, and I can't make decisions for you, but you've got to do better. Get on your knees, repent and ask the Lord to forgive you. You also need to ask that young lady for forgiveness. She's devastated. She sat on the phone with your momma and cried for a full 30 minutes. You also need to apologize to her parents. Deacon Crawford called here and asked for your address so he could come to Miami and kill you. I talked him out of that by pointing out his daughter willingly came to your room and hid who she was. He's still pretty mad and if he sees you, he might try to beat you up. I don't blame him. You wiped your feet on his child. His only child at that.'

"I told my Pop I was sorry, and I would try to make things right. I asked him to give me the girl's number. He handed the phone back to my mother. She gave it to me but not before she made me join her in prayer. I was half-listening, but I know I heard her use the words HIV, Satan's pawn and hell-bound in there somewhere. I felt really bad. I had to come up with a creative way to make this up to Daneisha but first, I needed to call and apologize.

"I dialed Daneisha's number. She answered the phone on the second ring. When I told her it was me, she launched into another wailing session. I told her to please stop crying. I told her that I was sorry, I never meant to hurt her and my actions had nothing to do with her. I was going through some things and taking it out on women at random.

'Really? I thought you put me out because I wasn't very good. I haven't been with very many guys, only one to be exact,' she said.

"I said, 'Baby girl, you were one of the best I ever had.' I was lying, but I wanted to make her feel better. After all, she was the unsuspecting fly in my expertly crafted web. When I turn on the charm very few women can resist.

"I told her, 'It can't happen again because I'm not good for you. Now, no more tears. I'm going to make this up to you.

"She said, 'Okay, but it had better be good because you made me feel like a total whore.'

"I apologized again and gave her a piece of advice. I told Daneisha, 'Never sleep with a man who hasn't taken the time to get to know you. He won't treat you like the princess you are because he hasn't developed any feelings for you. Most men are dogs on the prowl for their next bone. Do you know what a dog does when he's finished gnawing on a bone? He discards it. Don't put yourself in a position to be discarded that easily by any man. There are some good men out there. You just have to take your time and learn to separate the good from the bad. If a man really likes you, sex won't be the only thing on his mind. If you want to be positive that he's really into you make him wait until you're married.'

"She said, 'But Michael, I thought I did know you. I've had a crush on you since I was a five. I didn't want to pass up an opportunity to spend time with you. I got way more than I bargained for. I understand. I had an image in my head of what you were like. It's not your fault I worshipped you, and you turned out to be a jerk.'

"I could tell she was trying to keep from crying again. When she said that, I felt like the mold that develops at the bottom of a refrigerator after it hasn't been cleaned for a while. I apologized once more, and I told her it would never happen again.

'It wasn't a total disappointment,' she responded and then started to giggle hysterically. 'Your body is bangin! You should walk around naked because clothes don't do you justice! I'll probably never be with a man as fine as you again in my life. I never did all those things we did before. I didn't know there were so many different positions. I was hoping that was the beginning of something. You sure you don't wanna do it again?'

"I had turned this girl out in one night! Sometimes being handsome, athletic, rich and well endowed can be a curse. I had to do some damage control before she became the campus freak.

'Sweetheart, I'm too old for you and in the future, don't have sex with anyone unless he's your man. If a relationship is what you're really looking for, then hold out for that. Men rarely keep the woman who gives it up on the first night. If you don't remember anything I've said, remember that,' I advised.

"She told me she'd remember, and she sounded real disappointed that we wouldn't be having sex again. I had to say something to make her smile so I said, 'Daneisha, you don't look too bad naked either.'

'Really?' she asked cheering up.

'Really,' I said. 'Now get some sleep.'

"A few weeks later she went home for fall break, and I surprised Daneisha by going to her house and giving her a $500 gift certificate to go shopping. I even took her and two of her friends out for a night on the town in a stretch Hummer. You should have seen them with all the windows down and hanging out the sunroof so everybody in Akron could see them. I took them to a club and got them in VIP. They were underage, so I made sure they only served them soft drinks and juice. I had to be careful, though. They were all half-naked, young breasts and booty everywhere. I could tell Daneisha was trying to get me to do her again, but it wasn't going to happen. Especially, after the conversation I had with her father when I went to pick them up.

"It was ugly. He stared me down like a rabid dog ready to attack. He always was a big man. As a boy, he used to tower over me as he showed me and the other tee ball players how to hold a bat properly. Even though I'm a grown man now, he's still a little intimidating. I could see nothing but anger in his eyes. I'll never forget what he said.

'I wanted to kill you for what you did to my little girl. No father wants to imagine his baby having sex, and I sure don't want to know that someone has used sex to take advantage of her. But she's so excited about going out with you and her friends tonight I decided to let you live a little while longer. I can forgive, but I won't forget. If you ever touch my child again, I'm going to split your head to the white meat, cut off your genitals and watch you writhe in excruciating pain. I have an aluminum bat and a hunting knife. I know how to hit a home run and gut a deer. You catch my drift, son?'

"I knew I was deserving of every word he said, so I sat there and took my tongue lashing like a man. Under normal circumstances, if a dude threatened me like that he'd be picking up his teeth.

"I told him, 'My behavior was inexcusable. I assure you it will never happen again, so you can keep using your bat for tee ball games. You won't need to use it on me.'

"We shook hands and that was the end of it. Daneisha had a great time that night but when I dropped her off at home, what she said threw me for a loop.

'Michael Stokes, you were my first crush, and this is a dream come true. Please go back to the man you used to be; the one I admired when I was a little girl. He was so much better than the man you've become. I don't know who broke your heart, but you gotta let go of the pain she caused you before you either run Mrs. Right away or meet some psycho female who'll shoot you. She then gave me a kiss on the cheek and went in the house. I realized the kid was right. I had to let the hurt other women caused me go. I was better off without them."

***

Halfway through the story, Peter tiptoed out while Michael continued to entertain everyone else. He had heard it several times and didn't want to hear it again. Michael may have been a changed man but he wasn't. He believed in enjoying life, and although he still loved his wife, Ce Ce, he craved variety. Michael may have sworn off misbehaving but he hadn't. He wanted to call several of the exotic dancers he knew and throw his best friend a real bachelor party. He wasn't as much fun since he got saved. They used to go to bars and strip clubs together all the time. They'd buy the bar and all the babes. Now, the only thing Michael wanted to do was go home to his wife in Memphis or his parent's house in Akron.

Peter knew Michael told the girls they could stay in one of the guest rooms for the night. The twins were in their early 20's and wanted to take full advantage of their free trip to Miami and went out to have a little fun. They each made a little over $500 in tips and felt like they had money to blow. Thanks to Michael's advice, Tiffany made $800 in tips.

Tiffany was older than they were, 31 years old to be exact, and had no desire to go party. As far as she was concerned, those days were over. She had a son to take care of and needed to spend her tip money on more important things like tuition and tutors. After her last massage, she retired to the guest room alone and settled into the soft queen-sized bed to watch TV. She knew the guys were out there having guy talk and didn't plan to come out until the next morning when she left for the airport.

She heard a light tap at the door. When she opened it, Peter told her he was so busy coordinating everything he didn't have a chance to get his massage and wanted to know if he could get it now.

Chapter 13

Busted

"Haaaa! I never get tired of that story!" yelled Deuce. "Your mama sounds like mine. She don't play that sleeping around mess, either. She's the reason I married my wife. She made me feel so bad about having two kids by a woman I wasn't married to that I went ahead and popped the question." He leaned forward and held his sides as the laughter escaped his body.

"Big bro, you hit that!" said Maxwell. "Daneisha is fiiiine. It was foul how you did it, but if I had the chance I would have gone for it, too! I was wondering how ya'll became so cool all of a sudden. She was bragging for weeks about how you spent your ends on her!"

Dexter wiped his eyes as if he were crying and said, "That's so sweet. You took the time to make sure she didn't become the campus slut."

"Shut up, man. That wasn't one of my proudest moments," said Michael. "I had to do something. The last thing you want to do is scar a young girl for life. One man really can make a woman hate all men. Does anyone know where Peter went? His cell phone has been vibrating for the last ten minutes."

"Naw," said Roscoe. "Check the bathroom. He might be taking a dump."

Peter's phone was on the coffee table near Michael's favorite chair. It began to vibrate again, and Michael checked to see who it was. It was Peter's sister-in-law, Audrey. She must really need to talk to him because the calls were coming back to back. He decided to answer it. What he was told made it imperative he find Peter right away.

Michael checked the bathroom in his bedroom and the one in the hallway, but no one was there. Where did he go? He had a total of four guest rooms in the condo. He checked the rooms the guys would probably sleep in and left the one where the girls were sleeping for last. He assumed Tiffany was in there asleep because he hadn't seen her since the twins left and that was hours ago. Peter couldn't be in there, could he?

He knocked on the door several times, no one answered but he distinctly heard Peter's voice. He knew his boy and if he was in that room, he was up to no good.

"Peter, I know you're in there, come to the door," said Michael. The door opened. Peter was shirtless and mad. "Ce Ce's mother had a stroke. Your wife needs you to get to the hospital. I'll go get your car to save time. Meet me in front of the building."

"I'll be out in a minute," he hissed.

"Now, Peter. Tell Tiffany I said get dressed, too. I'm taking her to the airport. You and Miss Magic Hands have to leave my home NOW!"

Peter was sick of Michael's blessed and highly favored mess. He was a grown man. What right did he have to interrupt him while he was enjoying the company of a woman? Peter's blood began to boil. He felt like a man who was bitten by his own dog. He used money, influence, blackmail and street savvy to make Michael one of the highest paid athletes in the history of the NFL. Michael had no idea how many under the table, back door deals he orchestrated on his behalf. Evidently, he didn't realize what his retiring was costing them both, but Peter was the one left holding the shorter end of the stick. Michael could still command millions using his name and likeness. Very few people outside the sports world even knew who Peter Parker was. Peter felt Michael could have at least tried to soften the financial blow by helping him bring in some money other ways. Hosting at the Centrillium was easy money. Michael Stokes needed to be taught a lesson. But first, he needed to go to the hospital and check on his wife and her mother.

Chapter 14

I'm Sorry

Herman apologized profusely for missing their anniversary and promised to make it up to Lenora. She didn't understand how he could have done that nor was she trying to. When she got fed up, she preferred to display her anger quietly like a lethal injection. To punish Herman, she did not get up the following morning to fix him breakfast as she normally did. Instead, she pretended to be asleep the entire time he got ready for work.

Herman knew he messed up big time. He didn't enjoy the bowl of cold cereal and toast he made himself for breakfast. He preferred hot food. Although his physical attraction to Lenora had decreased, he recognized the valuable role she played in his life and their children's lives. It was quiet in the house without them. It was even quieter without the sound of Lenora swishing around doing her wifely duties. She didn't fix his lunch or kiss him on the cheek and tell him to have a good day. He needed that. Herman was having problems at work and these days, home was the only place he felt valued. Lenora's willingness to please him was a major contributing factor.

Herman loved the allure of African American women. The moment he met Lenora, he wanted to cup her cocoa-skinned face in his hands and kiss her luscious full lips. She was little, cute and sexy. He wished she still looked like Lenice. He understood weight gain came with childbearing, but she barely resembled the woman he married. Fat, stretch marks and cellulite seemed to be everywhere. She had a double chin and a chubby Cabbage Patch doll face. She was so wide he now had to use both arms to wrap them around her when he used to be able to take one arm and wrap it around her entire waist. He still loved her, but he wasn't sure if he was still in love with her. He realized he was changing, too. His hair was thinning and he had a small bald spot in the top of his head. Each day he tried to arrange the remaining hair so it wasn't easily visible. He also had a small potbelly but for the most part, he thought he looked the way he did when they met. He refused to let himself go like Lenora. Fat or not, he had to make Lenora feel better or his house would cease to feel like home.

Herman worked a half-day, came home early and surprised Lenora with a bouquet of flowers and a small box containing a diamond tennis bracelet. She was delighted when he informed her he arranged for the children to stay a second night with his parents so they could spend the rest of the day together. They went to one of her favorite restaurants, The Olive Garden, for a late lunch. Lenora was particularly proud of herself because she did not take this opportunity to cheat on her diet. She ordered a grill chicken salad with a light vinaigrette dressing and a diet Coke. She also selected a low-calorie key lime pie for dessert. Afterward, they went downtown to Tom Lee Park and took a romantic stroll along the river walk. It was a little cool outside, but Lenora didn't mind. She moved her body closer to Herman's for warmth. This was the Herman she remembered; the kind attentive one who doted on her.

They also went to the South Main arts district and perused its many art galleries. Lenora studied to become an art teacher in college but only taught two years before marrying

Herman and becoming a homemaker. He was adamant about his wife being at home until all three of their children were of school age. She was looking forward to returning to work in two years when the twins began kindergarten. She loved art galleries but rarely found time to visit them. This was certainly a treat. She admired the work of new and established painters, photographers and sculptors. She once dreamed of having her own art featured in a gallery.

Herman wasn't exactly a fan of art galleries, but he did a great job of behaving as if he were interested. They ended their evening with a viewing of *Porgy and Bess* at the Orpheum Theatre. It was one of Lenora's favorite operas. It broke her heart at the end when Bess left Porgy to resume her riotous lifestyle. She wondered if this were a true to life story would Porgy have ever gotten past the pain. She didn't think she would recover if Herman ever left her and the children.

After the play, Herman and Lenora drove home for what she hoped would be the cherry on top of their incredibly wonderful day. Beneath her dress, she was wearing the lingerie she purchased the day before and couldn't wait to show it off.

They arrived home and made their way to the bedroom. Herman seemed different. They had done it hundreds of times. Why was he acting funny? He took off her clothes and didn't make a single comment about her lingerie. He fumbled like a teenage boy while taking them off. He barely kissed her. His motions were almost robotic and lacked any kind of passion. When Herman completed his poor, romanceless display of affection, he slapped her on the behind, rolled over and went to sleep. Lenora laid there in disbelief. This was the big climactic finale to her anniversary celebration? Lenora punched her pillow wishing it was Herman's face.

Herman saw no problem with his actions and drowsily reached a heavy arm over and pulled her toward him. *Maybe he needs a little rest before round two. It will be better*, Lenora thought. She would try again in an hour or so. As she nuzzled her backside against her husband, he whispered, "Good night, Tia and Tamara. You two were great."

She couldn't have heard him right. Was her husband thinking about those little Mowry twins while in the bed with her? She wanted to slap him out of his slumber, but she didn't. This was her fault. She let her weight get out of control, and now her man was thinking about other women. She rose from the bed and walked to the kitchen. She was hungry. They ate over six hours ago, but she refused to open the refrigerator door in search of food. Instead, she opened the cabinet and retrieved her Melt the Fat weight loss pills. There was no way she was going to lose her battle with the bulge. Her marriage depended on her slimming down. She popped twice the recommended dosage in her mouth and swallowed hard. She chased the four pills with a glass of water and slowly went back to bed. Tomorrow she was going to cut her meals to once a day and exercise twice a day. She was going to show that fat who was boss.

Chapter 15

Welcome Back

Tee walked into Innovations Marketing & Events feeling refreshed. She didn't communicate with anyone at the office while on her honeymoon and left strict orders not to be disturbed unless it was an emergency. She delegated anything that needed to be done in her absence to the other event planners within the company. She told her assistant to take a vacation while she was gone because she had no assignments for her. Tee looked forward to seeing everyone. Especially, her best guy friend Edgar.

Tee entered her office and noticed a foul odor. It smelled like rotten eggs. She checked the bottom drawer of her desk and sure enough, there was the egg salad sandwich she forgot to consume before she left. The smell was almost unbearable. She opened the windows and went to the ladies restroom to find some disinfectant. She was happy when she spotted a small can of Lysol. She showered her room in a heavy haze of germ-fighters and odor eliminators and waited for them to take effect. She found it odd that her assistant hadn't been in her office to ready things for her arrival. Evelyn usually had the room in top condition and a cup of coffee on her desk when she arrived. She needed her morning cup of coffee, especially on chilly November mornings. She located her I'm A Good Woman mug and headed toward the break room. She rounded the corner and met Edgar at the elevators.

"Mamacita, I am so happy to see you. You look lovely, and I see you have those newlywed bags under your eyes. Did you bring your compact? If you like, I can help you get rid of those. I learned a new application technique," he said.

Edgar was one of the best-dressed men Tee knew. Today, he was wearing a grey Brooks Brothers suit with a custom-made canary yellow shirt and a grey tie with yellow, blue, black and grey polka dots on it. His black shoes were shined to perfection, and his yellow men's hosiery peaked from beneath his perfectly creased slacks.

He recently began doing makeup. Edgar said it was something he always wanted to do but put it off for years because he didn't want anyone to think he was gay. Now that he was older, he no longer cared what people thought. His wife, Marva, knew he wasn't gay and that's all that mattered to him.

"I have some good news and some bad news and under the circumstances, I think I should tell you the bad news first."

"Okay, shoot," said Tee.

"Evelyn was fired while you were gone."

"What! I loved Evelyn. Why didn't anyone tell me? I have to get her back. I've never had anyone as efficient or in tune to what I need."

"I know, but I don't think Jesus could help you save her after what she did," said Edgar in a most serious tone.

"What did she do? It couldn't be that bad. She wasn't even supposed to be here. I told her to go on vacation."

"Obviously, she didn't follow your advice. You know she started hanging out with Katty Kathy and picking up her bad habits. I knew no good would come of that. I tried to warn her, but she went on and on about how Kathy wasn't as bad as everyone thought she was. Just like Kathy,

Evelyn began talking about people behind their backs only she wasn't as careful as Kathy. She made ugly comments to anyone and everyone who would listen. The boss' baby girl, Celesteina, came to visit last week. You know that girl is as ugly as sin, but her being Mr. Anderson's youngest, he is crazy about her and spoils that wilder beast rotten."

"The day she came to visit, Evelyn was in the break room talking about how she looked like a cross between a gorilla and a llama. Unfortunately for her, Mr. Anderson and his daughter happened to be walking past the door on their way to lunch. Celesteina heard her and started crying and Mr. Anderson fired Evelyn right there on the spot. He told everybody in the office if they called and told you we would all forfeit our Christmas bonuses because he was the boss and what he says goes. He told Evelyn if she called you, he wouldn't pay her for the two days she worked that week."

Tee shook her head. "Oh my. That explains why no one told me. I know how much our boss loves his daughter, and I think you're right. My stellar persuasion skills aren't enough to help her on this one. That was mean, but how can he get mad at someone for telling the truth? He looks at that girl every day; he has to see how unattractive she is," said Tee.

"Probably not. One day I heard him say she looks like his mother, so she's probably the most beautiful girl in the world to him. Who doesn't think their mother is radiant?"

Edgar followed Tee to the break room and fixed himself a cup of hot honey lemon tea. Tee poured herself a cup of coffee.

"Darn, I hate this!" Tee stomped her foot. "That is terrible news. I could trust Evelyn with my life. What's your good news? I need it," inquired Tee, poking out her bottom lip.

"To make you feel a little better I had Papa make you some of his world famous Suspiros de Monja. I know how much you like them. I put it in the refrigerator for you. Consider it comfort food. Also, Evelyn's replacement has already been found. Her name is Sheba, and she should be here tomorrow. Be nice to her, Tee. She was handpicked by Mr. Anderson. I'm almost positive she was hired to spy on you. He heard about your I'm A Good Woman project. He asked me the other day if you were working on it on company time. I told him I didn't know what he was talking about. Watch your back, girl," advised Edgar.

"What? As much money as I bring this company. How dare he spy on me!"

"He dares, and he is. Proceed with caution. I've already taken control of the situation. I told Ebae, in graphic design, to delete any files on his office computer for artwork he did for you because I'm sure if Mr. Anderson knew he would try to say the company owned some rights to it. I also got rid of all the IGW info you had in your office. It's at my house. You don't have to thank me because I know you would do it for me."

"I paid Ebae for the work he did for me out of my own pocket and thank you just the same. Good looking out, homie," said Tee.

"You're welcome. And yeah, I know but Ebae works for this company, and he did your artwork during office hours. Trust me. I know how men like Mr. Anderson think. He's an opportunist. By the way, your office stinks, girl. I didn't have time to look around to see where that stench was coming from. I had to get in and out before anyone saw me. You need to do something about that. Smells like somebody boo booed on themselves then died. I have to go. I've got a 9 a.m. meeting, and I can't be late. I'm glad you're back. I missed you."

He gave Tee a hug and was gone. That wasn't the welcome back Tee was expecting at all. She knew Mr. Anderson was a little jealous that she often received credit for the success of the events division instead of him. He was quick to point out Tee worked for Innovations Marketing & Events, but she never thought he would go so far as to plant a spy on her team. She brought in almost $500,000 last year. She opened the refrigerator and saw a container with her name on it. She pulled off the lid and stuck her finger into the authentic Mexican dessert for a taste. Yum! She made a mental note to thank Edgar's father for her comfort food and to dig up some information about this Sheba woman.

Tee was on pins and needles all day and couldn't wait until she left the office. She decided to spend some time with Lenice after work and get the scoop about her date. She really hoped it went well. Lenice almost lost her mind when her ex-boyfriend, Scott, left her for the lawn man. No one even suspected that Scott was on the down low. Maybe she should call Lenora, too. Lenice told her Herman was a no-show on their anniversary. She could probably use some cheering up.

Chapter 16

So Ashamed

Tiffany knew she should have flown back to Memphis like Michael suggested, but Peter arranged for her and the twins to stay in Miami a couple more days and give massages to some of the celebrities he knew. She really needed the money. She was also afraid to face Tee. She figured Michael must have told her everything by now. He seemed really disgusted with her, and she knew Tee would be disappointed. He hardly said two words to her as he escorted her out of his condo and put her in a cab. He thought she was headed to the airport, but she was really headed to the Mandarin Oriental Hotel. Peter sent her the information via text message while she was packing her things.

The twins were sent to take care of some artist, but Peter refused to reveal his name beforehand. She was sent to take care of a politician living in Fort Lauderdale. He even sent a limo to pick her up from her hotel. As the car pulled up to her destination, she received a text that read, OMG IT'S USHER! We r giving Usher n his friends massages!!! – Twin, 2 is better than 1.

She always laughed after reading the signature Sierra and Siendy attached to their text messages. She couldn't help but be a little jealous that she hadn't been sent to help them. A job was a job and whoever she was servicing was going to get the massage of his life. She prided herself on exceeding her client's expectations. Tiffany checked her makeup and exited the limo. She was summoned to an exquisite peach colored house near the beach. The driver unloaded her supplies from the car. She rang the doorbell and waited to see who was waiting on the other side. Once again, she was surprised to find Peter on the other side.

"Welcome, Sexy," he said.

"Peter, I thought you would be at the hospital with your wife," said Tiffany.

"I was, but there is nothing she or I can do. My mother-in-law had a massive stroke and she is in a coma. The doctors don't expect her to last past a few days. My wife is there with her now."

"I'm so sorry. Shouldn't you be with her?"

"My wife is fine. Her sisters are there. We've been having issues for quite some time, and she didn't seem comforted by my presence. I'm exactly where I should be, here with you. Have a seat, Tiffany. I have a business proposition for you."

Tiffany felt uneasy. Thanks to Michael, she avoided having sex with him once. She didn't want to be placed in that situation, again. She was trying so hard to be a good Christian woman but poverty didn't agree with her at all. Tiffany wasn't used to struggling to make ends meet. She was behind on several of her bills. Without Quincy's help, she could no longer afford the tuition at the elite Christian school their son attended. She couldn't really work because she was in school. What little money she had, she spent on the necessities: groceries, gas and utilities. Tee was always talking about how the Lord would make a way. She needed Him to move now. It couldn't hurt to hear what Peter had to say. Maybe it would be a blessing. Tiffany sat down on a plush emerald green couch accented by red decorative pillows. Peter sat next to her, leaned back and opened his legs wide. He toyed with her long tresses before speaking.

"Tiffany, I see a lot of potential in you and with your beauty, talent and my connections I'm sure we could actually make a traveling massage service work. I got rave reviews on the work you and the twins did last night. Those men really enjoyed the way you ladies rubbed them down. This is Miami, and there are hundreds, if not thousands, of men who would pay top dollar to have a beautiful woman put her hands all over them."

"I'm glad you enjoyed my work, Peter, and I would welcome the opportunity to make some extra money. Things have been mighty tight for me lately," said Tiffany.

Peter found Tiffany very attractive but that country hick accent of hers drove him insane. He hated to hear her talk. To him, she sounded like she was from some part of Mississippi where they didn't have running water and still used an outhouse. He cringed every time she spoke. He preferred for her to sit there looking pretty and being silent.

"I'm glad you feel that way, but I want you to work with me, not for me. I'm not as young as I used to be, and I'm tired of chasing tail. Beautiful women come a dime a dozen here, but I've come to the realization that I can get by with one or two extra. I'll be honest with you. I've got too much invested with my wife to leave her. I don't have a prenup. I'm pretty much stuck in my marriage. Unfortunately, our flame went out years ago. I'm a passionate man, and I need a passionate woman. Looking at you ignites my fire, Tiffany. You are an incredibly beautiful woman." He moved closer to her.

"Thanks, but I'm not sure I follow you," said Tiffany.

"I want you to be my lover and my business partner. In return, I will give you everything you want. This house you're in is mine. It's fully furnished, and you and your son can live in it rent-free if you like. As long as you understand I will never leave my wife for you and I will not have an open affair with you and embarrass her. I owe her that much. However, I will make sure that you and your son are very well taken care of."

Being able to resume the expensive life style she used to have sounded like a dream come true to Tiffany. She didn't have to be Peter's mistress forever. Only until she could build up her massage clientele. Then, she would leave him alone and strike out on her own. She looked at him thoughtfully. Peter appeared to be about 45 years old. He was vertically challenged with crooked teeth, but he wasn't horrible on the eyes. He worked out regularly and had a decent body, although his neck was a little thick. He wasn't really her type, but she could persuade herself to sleep with him for the sake of herself and her son. She'd been the kept woman of a married man before, what harm would doing it again temporarily make? Only this time, she would go into it with a plan to make it work in her favor instead of his. She would also make sure she didn't fall in love with Peter, like she did with Quincy. Miami seemed like a good place to live. The weather was nice.

Tiffany tried to mentally convince herself that this time it would be different. At least Peter was honest about what he wanted from the beginning. Maybe she could convince him to get some braces. His teeth really looked bad. They were bunched together like someone was trying to bundle them for easier transport.

She turned to Peter and answered, "Sure, Sugah."

"Wonderful. Now, come show me everything you would have done if we hadn't been rudely interrupted last night."

Tiffany took off her clothes and stood in the middle of the room completely naked so her new lover could admire the view.

Her honey colored skin, large breasts, thighs and buttocks caused an inferno to rise up within Peter. Tiffany ran her hands all over her body drawing attention to her curves. *It's amazing what a big booty and breasts can get you*, she thought. As he examined her lustfully, she had another thought. Her mind drifted back to the words the very wise Teresa, once said to her. *Never let a man's money be the noose around your neck* played over and over again in her head like a bad ballad.

Chapter 17

There's No Place Like Home

Michael was happy to find out there really was no speaking engagement in Miami. His booking agent only told him that to make sure he would be in town for his bachelor party. He enjoyed kicking it with the fellas and was grateful his wife was secure enough to help organize it for him. When he called her to say thank you, Tee shared with him how bad she felt that he didn't have a bachelor party. They planned their wedding quickly, and Michael decided not to have one because he wasn't able to give his friends adequate notice. Several of them didn't make it in town for the wedding, either. It was mostly attended by Tee's friends and family. Michael didn't mind; he wanted Tee as his wife as soon as possible. As long as she and his family were there, that was all that really mattered to him.

The bachelor party went well except for Peter trying to get with Tiffany. Before she left for the airport, Tiffany asked Michael to let her tell Tee what happened herself. He didn't say yes, but he didn't said no either. He decided not to say anything to Tee. Michael was actually more disappointed in Peter. He was the one who was married, and he knew how Michael felt about cheating. It angered him Peter was bold enough to do it in his home. When he came downstairs to get his car, Peter cussed Michael out and called him a cock-blocker for interrupting him like he was some teenager having sex in his parent's house. Michael tried to explain it was only because Audrey told him Peter needed to get to the hospital right away, but Peter didn't believe him. He even accused Michael of being jealous because he wanted to "tap that" himself.

Michael's new Christian life and Peter's worldly one didn't seem to be gelling very well. Peter was a great manager, and Michael had to admit he owed him quite a bit. Peter negotiated all of his endorsement deals and helped him land his multi-million dollar football contracts. Yet, if he couldn't respect his beliefs and his home, Michael didn't know how much longer they could do business together.

Everyone at the bachelor party left the next morning, including Michael. Instead of heading to Memphis, he decided to fly home to Akron, Ohio to spend the day with his parents, Tomeka and Michelle. He still wished Michelle had turned out to be his child instead of Maxwell's. He was sure he would be a wonderful father, but for now he was determined to be a wonderful uncle. She seemed to be adjusting to the death of her mother and her new family well. He knew one day he would have to explain exactly what happened to Becca, but he was glad that it wouldn't be anytime soon.

He offered to let Michelle come to Memphis and live with him and Tee, but Maxwell decided it would be best for her to stay with their parents. His plan was to graduate from UCLA and then move back to the Ohio area to attend medical school, so he could see her more often. Even though their relationship was strained, Michael continued to be a good big brother and paid his college living expenses. He was actually doing it for Michelle. As a doctor, Maxwell would be able to provide a good life for her, without his help. Perhaps in time, their relationship could get back where it used to be.

Michael's parent's lived in a neighborhood called Sky View. The gated community was home to some of the most affluent citizens of Akron. He entered the house and announced his arrival. Michelle screamed and ran and jumped into his arms.

"Uncle Mike, I missed you so much," she said planting a juicy kiss on his cheek. The four-year old appeared to have grown taller since he last saw her and picked up a little weight, too.

"I missed you," he said and swung her around until she was dizzy. She giggled with glee.

He sat her down and held her until she gained her balance. She then took her little index finger and pointed down. "Look," she said. Michelle's small butterscotch knee had a Mickey Mouse band-aid on it. It wasn't large enough to cover the entire span of the sore it was supposed to be protecting from infection. The scab could be seen clearly.

"Granddaddy took the training wheels off my bike, and I fell off," she explained.

After hearing his new title mentioned, Michael Stokes, Sr. entered the room.

"Hey, son. What a surprise! You should have told us you were coming. Now Michelle, don't go trying to get Granddaddy in trouble with Uncle Mike. It's a scratch."

"Hey, Pops," Mike said and embraced him in a manly hug.

Michael, Sr. and Jr. were about the same size. They were both tall with a muscular build and broad shoulders. They even shared the same dark complexion. In his hay day, Michael, Sr. had been a pretty good football player himself. Although, he never made it to the NFL. After college, he married his girlfriend, Michael's mother Vanessa, and enlisted in the army. He was ecstatic when Vanessa wrote him while he was away at boot camp to tell him she was pregnant. He always knew he was going to have a son, and the minute he laid eyes on him, he knew Michael, Jr. was going to be someone special. Michael, Sr. only served three years in the army and now worked as a supervisor for the United States Postal Service. He lived a very comfortable life because of his oldest son's generosity. He didn't work because he needed the money. He worked because he liked to stay busy. He was actually thinking about retiring and running for public office next year.

"I'm not, Granddaddy. I wanted Uncle Mike to see I have a hurt knee, too. I'm just like him," said Michelle.

Michael was amazed at her intelligence.

"You sure are, Princess. You know what would make my knee feel better and I'm sure it would make yours feel better, too?"

"What?" asked the brown-eyed angel.

"Ice cream!"

"Ice cream would make me feel muuuch better!" squeaked Michelle jumping up and down.

Michael hoisted his niece up on his shoulders, and the three of them made their way to the kitchen. He decided a couple of days at home with Michelle would do them both some good. He'd be back home with Tee before the week was out.

Chapter 18

Here's Sheba

Lenice informed Tee that Lenora would not be able to join them tonight because her husband was still trying to get out of the doghouse. Teresa left for her cruise that morning, and Tiffany was still out of town. They decided to go out anyway, just the two of them.

The Max contained the perfect atmosphere for a night of adult socialization. The classy establishment specialized in a 30 and up professional crowd. Their happy hour was a weekday favorite for many, and the place was packed. The music was always the right volume so as not to impede conversation, and the food was delicious. They stood near the bar hoping seats there or a table would open up soon. While they were waiting, a woman with naturally curly hair approached them and stopped near Tee.

"Excuse me, Mrs. Stokes. I probably should wait until tomorrow to meet you, but since we're both here, I thought I would come over and introduce myself. I'm your new assistant, Sheba."

Sheba was at least 5'9"and extremely thin. She wore a tight leopard print dress with a plunging neckline that dipped to show her small breasts and hugged her barely there hips. Sheba had a very pretty face that reminded you of a Jennifer Aniston. Her makeup was extremely well done. Her eyebrows were perfectly arched, and she had beautiful blue eyes. Sheba's skin was the same shade as Werther's coffee candy. Her curly hair was brown with blonde high-lights. It was hard to tell what ethnicity she was, but it was obvious that she was a mixture of something. Tee guessed she was probably between the ages of 22 and 25.

What has Mr. Anderson gotten me into? She's a baby, Tee thought. The two ladies shook hands.

"It's a pleasure to meet you, Sheba. I'm glad you came over to introduce yourself. I look forward to working with you. You come highly recommended," said Tee.

"Thank you," Sheba said putting her hand on her chest and batting her eyelashes to signify she was flattered. "I am a fan of your work. I've watched you from afar for quite some time. Your event planning and eye for décor is truly a work of art. I know I'll learn a lot from you."

"Oh, that's so sweet. By the way, this is my friend Lenice."

"Hello, Lenice," said Sheba.

Lenice smiled and waved.

"You should probably know that I'm going to come in a little late tomorrow. So, you can get to the office around noon, if you'd like," instructed Tee.

"Great! I can sleep in tomorrow. Thanks, Boss Lady. I like you already. I won't continue to disturb you and your friend. Nice to meet you, Lenice. Enjoy yourselves."

Sheba shook her little booty to the beat as she walked away. Lenice didn't know whether to laugh or give Tee a hug. Her new assistant was a sight to behold.

"Don't you say a word," said Tee.

"What? I was only going to say she seems nice," smirked Lenice.

Tee rolled her eyes and turned her attention to the house DJ who was playing a great mix of music from the

70's, 80's and 90's. He transitioned from "Two Occasions" by The Deele to Michael Jackson's "Off the Wall."

"I know better. You have some snide remark in the making," said Tee and snapped her fingers to the beat.

She was in no hurry to go home. Last night was the first night Michael wasn't lying in bed next to her since they said "I do." She missed him terribly, but she knew how close he was to his family and was accustomed to spending time with them regularly. For the longest time, they were all he had.

"Tell me about this Deacon James," said Tee.

"Tee, I didn't think I would like him but I do. You know how much I love athletic men, and he's a little smaller than what I'm used to but he's so nice. He put a lot of effort into our date, and I had a really good time. I'm looking forward to the next one. We're supposed to go out again soon," gushed Lenice.

"I'm glad you had a nice time but try not to get too attached too soon. I don't want to be a pessimist, but in my experience that almost always ends in disaster," said Tee.

"How can you say that? You were going to Jamaica with Michael less than a week after you met him."

"I said almost," said Tee. Her whirlwind life-threatening romance wasn't the norm, and she wished people would stop comparing their situations to hers.

"I adore my husband, but did you forget I got thrown off the side of a boat and stabbed all in the name of love? Is that what you want? You want a relationship that will land you in the hospital? That probably wouldn't have happened if we took things slow. I don't regret a thing, but I'm telling you from experience, take it slow. He may have some skeletons in the closet that need to come out before you decide he's the one."

Lenice never really stopped to think about everything Tee endured to be with Michael. She was happy Becca was no longer in their lives to cause the two of them any more pain.

"I hope we get a table soon. These shoes weren't made for standing," said Tee.

"I feel you, girl. These stilettos are about to make me hit a falsetto. I'll buy you a soda," said Lenice and summoned the bartender in their direction.

***

The next morning, Tee arrived at Innovations at 9 a.m. and requested a copy of Sheba's resume and cover letter from human resources. She was qualified. She had an associate's degree in Office Administration and worked previously for two other corporate companies in town. Bethany, in the human resource department, assured Tee she called each one of Sheba's references, and they all gave her glowing reviews. *Okay, you're qualified, but can I trust you?*, wondered Tee.

Chapter 19

Redeemed

Tiffany felt horrible. Her head was throbbing like she was hit with a hammer in her sleep. She looked around at what was supposed to be her new house. The walls were a bright orange---way too bright for her. She preferred softer colors like white and pastels. The furniture was contemporary with hard straight edges. She preferred furniture with curves and was partial to pieces with shapes other than square.

She was glad she was alone. Peter left earlier to check on his wife. He gave Tiffany the keys to the house and a $10,000 check to help pay off some bills and move to Miami after graduation.

This was a mistake. Everything about it was wrong. She couldn't settle for less than she deserved, again. She deserved to have a man who was willing to date her openly for the world to see. Peter was a good lover, but she wanted more than regular sex and a full bank account. She wanted love.

Tiffany wanted to believe so badly God could fix all her problems, but it was difficult for her to trust in someone she could not see. Yet, she was willing to try. She didn't pray much, but she decided that now was as good a time as any. She kneeled on the side of the bed and said:

Dear God. It's me Tiffany. I know I haven't been perfect, but could you find it in your heart to help me? I'm not doing too well financially, and I'm not doing too well in the love department, either. The thing is, I want to do better, and I'm going to do better. I need a little strength and a little money would help, too. I know I don't deserve it, but Tee tells me you're merciful. Please have a little on me. I could really use it. Amen.

Her prayer was short but sincere. She actually felt better, and she knew what she had to do. Tiffany picked up the phone and called Tee. She told her everything and asked if she and Michael could loan her some money until she got on her feet.

"You know we would be happy to loan you some money. Why didn't you tell me you were in need?" said Tee sympathetically.

"You know how I am, Tee. Being raised in a family of politicians, you learn how to smile and hold your head high even if the rain is beating you in the face."

"You don't have to fake anything with me. Call yourself a cab and get to the airport. Use the money you made at the bachelor party to buy yourself a ticket home, and I'll give you the money back when you get here. You have no idea how proud I am of you. Peter did have a good idea, though. A traveling masseuse enterprise would be perfect for you. Let's talk about it later. Maybe I can help," offered Tee.

Tiffany was surprised she believed in her that much. "You would do that for me, Tee?"

"I sure would. I know doing right isn't always easy, but I promise you that the Lord is going to bless you for making the right decision. God is more than capable of providing for you and your son. Hurry up and leave that house before Peter gets back. I love you."

"I love you too, Tee. I'll call you to come pick me up as soon as the plane lands."

Tiffany called a cab and packed up her portable massage table and everything else she brought before heading to the hotel to pick up the rest of her things. She placed the keys Peter gave her and the check in the middle of the island in the kitchen with a note.

Peter,

After careful reconsideration I have decided to decline your offer. God would not be pleased with my having an ongoing affair with you. You really shouldn't be cheating on your wife. I'll be praying for you. Thanks for the masseuse idea. I plan to put it to good use.

Tiffany

Peter returned to the house about an hour after Tiffany left. He was looking forward to ravaging her voluptuous body again before he went to his office for a couple of hours.

He read Tiffany's note. Then, he tore it and the check into pieces, placed them in the fireplace and set them on fire. He picked up the poker by the fireplace and swung it into walls, vases and lamps to blow off some steam. Shards of glass and porcelain flew in every direction, dirtying the house and cutting Peter on his bare arms. He was so angry he didn't feel a thing. He was tired of everyone trying to push their religious views on him. First Michael and then some woman he regarded as one step above a whore. He needed that business venture to help generate some additional income. Living in Miami was expensive. He had thousands of dollars worth of bills to pay each month. It was a sure fire moneymaker. He had already lined up appointments with some of the guys from the bachelor party who specifically requested Tiffany. Did she actually think he was going to let her take his idea and do it without him?

He was sure this was Michael's fault. He probably talked her into leaving.

Chapter 20

That's What Friends Are For

Tee picked Tiffany up from the airport late that afternoon and treated her to lunch at ISIS, one of their favorite downtown eateries. As usual, Tiffany Tate looked flawless. Her hair was in a classy up do with soft tendrils outlining her square face. She was wearing a black Donna Karen dress that hugged every curve, and she expertly accessorized it with black boots, a black clutch and expressive gold jewelry. The big bangles on her wrists clanged loudly as she walked. She loved wearing dresses and showing off her legs. In the past, Tiffany would have worn such a head-turning ensemble to greet her lover. Quincy's approval meant so much to her, but today she was looking her best for herself. He strung her along with promises of marriage for over a decade. He even gave Tiffany her most treasured accomplishment—her son, but that event was bittersweet. When he was born, Quincy wouldn't give his own son his last name or sign the birth certificate. He said he didn't want to shame his family. She called him Quincy 2 because he wasn't a junior, but he did share his father's first and middle name. She was still upset with Quincy, but it felt unnatural for him to be absent from their lives.

ISIS had an eclectic dining atmosphere and a diverse group of patrons. Everyone from popular politicians to hippie wanna be's ate there. They specialized in spicy dishes with a Caribbean influence. Tee and Tiffany arrived after the lunch rush and were easily seated. Their server took their drink and appetizer order and brought them out quickly. Tiffany slowly sipped her raspberry lemonade. She had a lot on her mind.

"Tee, do you think God is mad at me because I backslid?" she asked. Even though she left Peter and did not intend to see him again, guilt and shame were still nibbling away at her.

Tee ate a large peppered gulf shrimp with cocktail sauce before she answered her friend's question.

"Mad, no. Disappointed, yes. You asked God for forgiveness, and I assure you, He has given it to you. I'm sure He's very proud you now that you've decided not to take another married man up on his offer to make you his mistress. The key now is to take steps to make sure you don't find yourself in bed with another one."

"This celibacy thing is hard. I don't know if I can do it. Aren't we humans supposed to want to experience one another? Sexual desires are natural, aren't they? Why does God hate sex so much?" asked Tiffany and then bit into a seasoned jerk chicken wing.

Tee coughed and wiped her hand.

"Sweetheart, you've got it all wrong. God doesn't hate sex. He created it. He made that incredible attraction men and women have toward one another. He made sex pleasurable for a reason. He wants a man and his wife to be able to enjoy each other on a level that only the two of them should share. There's actually a whole book in the Bible dedicated to it. It's called Song of Songs, and it talks vividly about a man's attraction to a woman and how beautiful she is. It does so in intricate detail. King Solomon describes the beauty of his woman's smile, her breasts, her smell and everything. It's deep reading. Some think it's a metaphor for how Christ loves the church. Ephesians 5:35 tells husbands to love their wives as Christ loves the church. So, it still applies to couples, if you ask me.

"What God hates is sin and the things that lead to sin such as lust. Sex is a natural desire but what separates us from the animals, which are also sexual beings, is that we have the gift of intellectual thought. Animals do it instinctively when they're in heat. We have the option to decide when, where and with whom we do "the do" with. We're not supposed to give ourselves to any man simply because we're horny."

"So, God hates lust?" asked Tiffany

"That's right. For example, there is nothing sinful or lustful about noticing that someone of the opposite sex is attractive. Lust comes into play when you begin to imagine that person naked and fantasize about what they would be like in bed. Your lust has allowed sin to plant a seed that can grow into a tree if you decide to act upon it and invite that attractive man into your home later to find out if he has skills," explained Tee.

"I don't see how you did this, Tee. Quincy and I had sex regularly and not being able to get any at all has me all in a tizzy. I mean I didn't even find Peter all that attractive, but I was so lonely and horny when he came in my room that I didn't care. I wanted some affection."

"You see what satisfying your sexual desires outside of wedlock has gotten you, don't you? A child who can't visit his father's home or meet his sisters, a broken heart, broke, busted and disgusted and another indecent proposal from a man who wanted to make you his chick on the side. I know Peter made it sound nice, but his intent was to buy you so he could continuously fulfill his fantasies with you while keeping his marriage intact. Don't you deserve your own family?

"I've known you for years, Tiffany. I love you, and I want something better for you. God wants something better for you. You deserve your own husband and your son deserves a father figure who doesn't have to go home to his other family at night. Giving up sex wasn't easy for me either, but it was worth it. It also let any man who came into my life know that if he wasn't coming correct don't come at all. He wasn't going to part my legs and then leave me alone. I'd had more than my fill of that mess. I encourage you to wait until you're married to have sex again, but if you can't wait at least promise yourself that you will wait for a committed relationship with a SINGLE man who loves and appreciates you. You owe yourself that much. However, you must recognize that fornication is still a sin whether it's with a married man or a single man. There are consequences to sin. I can't tell you how to live your life. I can only tell you how God says we should live in His word," Tee said and then motioned for the server to refill her water. Her mouth was on fire from the shrimp.

"You're right Tee, but you have to remember my entire adult life I've been the other woman. I was fed lies the entire time that I would one day be number one. Not having someone and refraining from sex is all so new to me." Tiffany licked two fingers and picked up another wing. They were really good.

"That's why I'm so proud of you. You are willing to do what you have never done in order to have what you've never had. Not only did you leave your lover, but you also left your security blanket and your lucrative spending account. You're in school learning a trade that will help you to be self-sufficient. That's why I want to help you until you get there. In the meantime, I want you to stop playing the role of the victim. Yes, Quincy was wrong and you were young, but he never twisted your arm. You willingly participated in his affair, and over the course of the years, you have willingly stayed."

Tiffany was not exactly pleased with that statement, but she held her tongue. Right now she needed her friend, emotionally and financially. Besides, in her heart she knew Tee was right. The words sounded so harsh, though. Hadn't she been beat up enough?

"I hope God sends me a baller like He sent you. I want to get married someday, too. Being Ms. Independent is overrated. I will gladly let my rich Christian husband take care of me," she said.

"Stop looking for a man to take care of you and wait for a man to love you. God will send you what you need, and he may not come in a high tax bracket. Don't overlook a good man because his bank account isn't as lucrative as you're used to. There are plenty of lonely rich women in the world. I encounter them all the time at the charity events I plan. Standing by their husbands' sides with fake smiles plastered on their faces pretending they're happy. They reveal the other side when we're in planning sessions. They pour their hearts out about how their husbands are never home, how he doesn't talk to her or how he's hooked up with yet another mistress. God gives each of us unconditional love, and you have never had that from a man. A husband is called to love his wife with that same type of love, a love that sees your flaws but loves you in spite of them."

Tiffany chewed thoughtfully on her chicken. She couldn't imagine dating an average man. Nothing about her life had ever been average. She came from a privileged political family. She attended private school and charm school. She shopped at high-end boutiques and had a hair and nail appointment every week. At least, she used to. She looked down at her nails. She was trying to learn to do them herself but still had a lot to learn. Her cuticles looked rough.

She looked over at Tee and Godzilla wistfully. That ring was massive, and it sparkled like spring water. Some days she caught herself staring at it as if she were hypnotized. Quincy could never afford a ring like that. She always thought the ring looked out of place on Tee. She never really saw what Michael saw in her physically. Tee was cute, but she believed the wife of a NFL great should be glamorous. Tee hardly wore any makeup. Her hairstyles were functional when they should be fierce, but Tiffany had to admit she had an eye for fashion. Tee was always in the latest and greatest. She was almost positive the outfit she had on was Michael Kors along with her purse. She was happy for her friend, but she couldn't help occasionally wishing that the life she lived belonged to her.

"I understand what you're saying, but I want what you and Michael have. Your husband adores you. I see the way he looks at you, like you're the only woman in the room. It doesn't hurt he's beyond fine and rich," said Tiffany.

"I'm a blessed woman, but you know my story. How many frogs did I kiss before I found my prince? My advice to you is not to worry about a man right now. You should worry about you and Quincy 2. God still has you under construction but when the time is right, He will send Mr. Righteous your way. That I know for sure," said Tee.

"I hope you're right," said Tiffany. "But you're wrong about one thing. I do have unconditional love. I get if from my son. I also get it from you, Sandy, Teresa and Lenora. None of you ever approved of my relationship with Quincy, but you never made me feel terrible because of it like so many others tried to do."

Tee was genuinely moved after hearing her friend's words. "I'm not perfect and because I know that, I never felt I had the right to judge you too harshly. I hated what you were doing but like I said before, I know what a good person you are. You made a bad decision. We all make them from time to time. The Tiffany that I know you're capable of being is only beginning to shine. I can't wait until you pull the rest of that veil you've been hiding under off. You're going to blind the world."

Tiffany smiled. "Darn right I am! So you had better make sure you always have a pair of shades in your purse."

"I got them right here!" Tiffany reached in her bag and pulled out a pair of Moss Lipow sunglasses trimmed in alligator, leather and ostrich."

"Girl, are those what I think they are? Let me see!" Tiffany wiped her greasy fingers and snatched the expensive lenses from Tee's hand.

"What? Michael bought me these a couple of months ago. No big deal."

Tiffany was flabbergasted. "Do you know how much these cost?"

"No. Fifty bucks, maybe?"

"Honey please, try about $3,500 or more!"

Tee was about to put another shrimp in her mouth and dropped it in her lap. It landed on the black cloth napkin she placed there when she sat down.

"No way! That's a mortgage."

"Yes way! Don't believe me, Google it when you get home. See, that's what I mean. I want a man who thinks money is no object when it comes to me," said Tiffany.

"I admit that is an ample amount to spend on accessories, and I would never spend that much for eyewear. Tiffany, when it's all said and done, these are just sunglasses. I could accidently step on them and break them tomorrow. It's the unbreakable things Michael gives me that makes him such a wonderful man. As long as you're more interested in what's in a man's wallet than you are in what's in his soul, you will never find true love."

She lifted the shrimp from her lap and popped it in her mouth. "I have something for you." She took out her checkbook and a pen and wrote Tiffany a check for $12,000. She then gave her the numbers to the offices of two corporate CEO's she talked to that morning concerning a complimentary massage from her personal massage therapist. She told them it was her way of saying thank you for their sponsorship of some of Tee's past charity fundraising events.

"Call their assistants and set something up," she instructed. "They are expecting you."

Tiffany thanked her for her generosity and agreed to call as soon as she got home. They finished their meal, and Tee drove her home. Before Tiffany exited her truck, the two of them prayed together. Tee prayed for her strength, patience and prosperity. She genuinely wanted God to bless her college buddy. Tee then handed her a piece of paper with a list of scriptures she thought she should read for encouragement. They agreed to try to meet again soon. Tee knew if Tiffany was going to stay on the straight and narrow she was going to need someone to not only hold her accountable, but also, hold her hand until she was ready to walk on her own.

Tee was on her way back to work when she received an urgent call from Lenice. Something was wrong with Lenora, and she needed her to come to the hospital right away.

Chapter 21

Lord Help

Lenice swerved dangerously through traffic as she raced to the hospital in her vintage Volkswagen Rabbit. She yelled at red lights, stop signs and other drivers---anything and anyone that prohibited her from getting to her destination faster. She didn't know what to expect when she arrived because the nurse who called wouldn't give her any information over the phone. All she would tell her was her sister was at the hospital, and she needed to get there soon. On the way, she called Tee and James and asked them to meet her there. They both said they would. She tried to call Herman, but he didn't answer.

Lenice parked her car and rushed up to the information counter and demanded someone tell her something. She was directed to another information counter located outside the emergency room. Once she arrived, the nurse there informed her that Lenora overdosed on diet pills and had to have her stomach pumped. The pills she took contained ephedrine, which speeds up your heart rate and could have caused serious damage. However, she was lucky and everything appeared to be fine, but they planned to keep her overnight for observation. Lenora was now in stable condition and resting comfortably, but she made a request not to be disturbed by anyone. She said she wanted to be alone. Therefore, the nurse could not tell her what room she was in. Lenice was relieved to hear Lenora was alright, but she wouldn't be fine until she saw her sister.

"What? My sister has never done that before. We're twins. We shared a womb. She always wants to see me even if she doesn't want to see anybody else. You have to tell me where she is," protested Lenice.

"Ma'am, the patient has the right to refuse visitors, and we have to respect her privacy," said the nurse.

"So, what am I supposed to do?"

"You can go have a seat in the waiting area, and I can let you know when she wants to see you or you can give me your phone number and I can call you," she said calmly.

Neither of those is acceptable!" yelled Lenice and stomped away.

She knew this wasn't the nurse's fault but she needed to take it out on someone. Lenice turned around, apologized and asked her to please tell Lenora she was there. She would hang around the hospital for an hour or so in case she changed her mind. She gave the exact location where she could be found within the hospital. Lenice didn't want to sit in the waiting area with other jittery family members waiting for positive news. Instead, she headed toward the chapel. She figured it would be quiet there.

Lenice hated hospitals. For her, hospitals represented sickness and death. Her grandmother and both her parents died while in a hospital. Her father died of congestive heart failure when she and Lenora were only seven. Afterward, the twins and their mother moved in with their grandmother and stayed with her until she died. Madea passed away at that exact hospital after the doctors discovered she had a severe case of pneumonia. Her grandmother was old and frail and couldn't seem to fight the illness off. She died after spending two weeks in intensive care. She and Lenora were

15 then. When they were 25, their mother lost her battle with breast cancer. She fought so hard to live. The endless doctor visits, chemotherapy and medication didn't seem to improve her situation. Eventually, their mother got tired of it all and decided to let nature take its course. Lenice was thankful that as her health diminished their mother's spirit didn't. Lenora and Lenice were by her side the day she passed. She had a smile on her face until she took her last breath. She was 50 years old. That's too young to die, and she was greatly missed. Each year, she and Webster ran during the *Susan G. Komen Race for the Cure* in her memory. She had a special pink jersey she wore with the words "In Memory of the World's Best Mom" on the front. She even bought Webster a special pink stroller just for the occasion. His little legs couldn't run an entire half-marathon but he was right there with her just the same. Lenice had nothing but bad memories associated with hospitals. They were definitely on her list of places to avoid.

She made her way to the hospital chapel and quietly opened the door in case there was anyone else in there seeking solitude or answers to a prayer. It was the only place in the hospital she didn't mind being. It was so peaceful. The room was decorated in a rich shade of purple. There were five or six long wooden pews lined one in front of the other before the altar. Above the altar, was a painting of a brown haired, blue-eyed Jesus with his arms stretched wide open as if he wanted to welcome you or hug you. It was illuminated at the bottom with soft light that gave him an ethereal glow. Lenice spent many nights in this room asking God to spare her mother. Later, her mother was in so much pain, Lenice asked Him to end her suffering. It was the merciful thing to do.

The room was quiet and still. There was one other person there. He sat on the front pew with his head bowed toward the altar. Herman turned around and greeted her with a smile. Lenora also refused to see him and having Lenice's familiar face there warmed his aching heart a little. He was sure she shared in his pain. He didn't understand why Lenora took so many pills at one time. Was she trying to hurt herself?

Lenice could no longer hold her anger within. Why was Herman sitting there smiling? He was the reason her sister was in the hospital. She took those diet pills to lose weight for him. She yelled, "You!" and propelled her body quickly toward him. Before Herman could react, Lenice had both her hands wrapped solidly around his neck. As she cut off his air supply, she said, "She is God's gift to me. How dare you abuse her like that? I'll kill you before I let you kill my sister!"

Herman gasped for air. He tried to pry her hands off him but it was no use. Her small, yet strong fingers were solidly locked in place. He could feel her nails digging into his skin. His face turned red and then purple. He looked up at the painting of Jesus with his arms outstretched. That's exactly what he needed at that very moment, a Savior. His body began to weaken and he sank to his knees.

Lenice was so engrossed in her murderous task that she did not hear Tee and James enter the chapel. She appeared to be possessed. Her eyes were narrowed. Her face was contorted into a sinister grin as if she were finding great satisfaction in choking the life out of Herman. Normally, quite coherent and articulate when speaking, she spoke one-syllable words loudly.

"Hate! Kill! Die! You!" she screamed.

Tee ran to Herman's aid. She shouted Lenice's name repeatedly and shook her several times before she came to her senses and let Herman go. Lenice looked at her hands in disbelief. She then brought them to her face and collapsed on a pew. Herman crawled away as fast as his legs could carry him, gasping for air.

"He tried to take her from me. She's all I got, Tee. He tried to take her from me. She took those pills because of all those mean things he said to her. It's his fault," she sobbed.

Tee sat down next to her and rocked her gently in her arms. "It's okay, Lenice. The nurse said Lenora will be fine. She's not going anywhere. You still have your twin. She's not going anywhere."

James helped Herman to his feet and escorted him from the room. As he left, Herman rubbed his neck and looked at Lenice as if she were Satan with breasts.

"Keep her away from me!" he said as loudly as he could. "I'll be filing an assault report tomorrow!"

"Go to hell!" Lenice screamed in between sobs. She didn't understand why James helped Herman instead of her, but that wasn't her primary concern at the moment. She had to get her sister away from that man.

Chapter 22

The Legend

It felt good being on a field again. Michael hadn't stepped on the grass since he retired from football a little over a year ago. This time, instead of suiting up he was the guest assistant coach at his old high school. Coach Marion Nickelberry was used to having a winning season. He had been coaching for the last 40 years and refused to retire even though he was eligible to do so. So far this season, his team's record was 15 – 0, and he aimed to keep his opponent's wins at 0. He ran a tight ship and hated to lose. He blew his whistle and told the boys practicing on the field and the rest of the coaching staff to gather around. Michael stood next to Coach Nickelberry as he spoke.

"I'm sure you all know who this is. He's an alumnus of this great institution of secondary schooling we call Marshall High School. If you're lucky, you'll achieve half the success he has. He's my special assistant coach for the day. I thought maybe he could pass you girls some wisdom. Once upon a time, he stood right where you're standing and did those same exercises you do. You got a NFL great among you and I--"

A snicker was heard from the group. "He ain't great no more with that busted knee," someone said.

A couple of students laughed, and the coach Michael remembered emerged.

"Who said that?" yelled Coach Nickelberry. "Somebody better spill their guts or all of you will be running the bleachers until I get tired, and I took a nap right before practice! I swear they put sedatives in that cafeteria food!"

It was as if Moses were parting the Red Sea. All the players stepped to the left or to the right leaving one lone boy standing on the middle.

"Steinbeck, I should have known it was you. If you were as smart as those comments you attempt to make, you might be doing more than riding my bench this season. Come here, boy."

A cocky young man who looked to be about 16 stepped forward. He was tall and lean with a 10-inch high-top fade. Michael wondered how he got his helmet on over all that hair. Coach grabbed him by the front of his practice jersey, looked him in the eyes and said, "This man is like a son to me and by disrespectin' him, you disrespectin' me and you know how I feel about disrespectful chill'un. He was making touch downs when you were still a useless little sperm waiting to escape from yo' daddy's scrotum. You owe Mr. Stokes an apology. Then, to make sure you learned yo' lesson, I think I'll sentence you to a long day of running the bleachers and after that I'll think about letting you dress out for tomorrow's game."

Michael didn't appreciate Steinbeck's comment, but he didn't think it warranted suicide runs.

"C'mon Coach, don't be so hard on him. I'd be satisfied with the apology," said Michael.

"You questioning my authority to run my team?" snarled Coach Nickelberry.

He always did need to be in control at all times. Some things never change. Coach Nickelberry wasn't as young as he used to be. He had lost most of his hair except for a small patch of grey on each side of his head and was still as ornery as he was the day Michael met him as a scrawny high school freshmen. He owed this man more than respect. He owed him the majority of his football skill set. The fundamentals he taught Michael allowed him to become one of the greatest players to ever grace the field. His high school letters, his scholarship, his Heisman, his MVP trophies all were a result of Coach Nickelberry's dedication to his players. He worked them hard, teaching them the value of hard work, dedication and excellence, in hopes they would emerge as one of the best. Not only on the field, but also in life.

"No, sir. I know from experience you run a fine team. It's just that—"

"Shut your face then before I make you run," he said cutting Michael off. "I ain't heard an apology, Steinbeck."

The kid who looked so cocky a minute ago now seemed terrified. Michael wondered if it was from the possibility of having to run the bleachers until he puked or not being able to wear his uniform the next day. They were playing their biggest rival, Oaktown High School.

"I'm sorry, Mr. Stokes. I didn't mean any harm. I've been watching you my whole life. My cousin Terrance played with you when you were here. I'm sorry you hurt yourself. It is truly an honor to have you at our practice today. I look forward to hearing what knowledge you have to bestow upon us," said the youth.

"I said apologize, Steinbeck not kiss his behind. Your feet should be moving by now," growled Coach.

"Yes, sir!" said Steinbeck and took off in the direction of the bleachers.

"The rest of you girls get to work!" he barked at the other players.

Michael watched 30 or so young men take off down the field and begin running drills.

It always amazed Michael how people thought they could talk down to him because he didn't play on a NFL team anymore. Even little kids. They all seemed to have forgotten all the things he accomplished and records he'd broken over the years. He was about to be a NFL Hall of Famer. People seem to only care about what you've done lately. He busted his knee giving others the opportunity to see an excellent performance during a game they loved to watch. Michael was thankful for people like Coach Nickelberry who never forgot. It felt good to be home.

"Mike!" yelled Coach Nickelberry.

"Yes, sir."

"I'm real proud of you, son. Real proud of you. Do you remember those drills I taught you?"

Michael thought about the endless hours he spent on the field learning the game under the watchful eye of a much younger version of the man who stood before him.

"I sure do."

"Go put those girls to work!"

"It would be my pleasure, sir." Michael walked down the field to show those boys what practice with a pro felt like.

Chapter 23

He Loves Me, He Loves Me Not

Lenora laid in her hospital bed wondering how she got to this point. How she could have put her life in danger for the love of a man? No man was worth that. What would happen to her children if she died? When she woke up from her nap, one of the nurses told her about the incident in the chapel. Word circulated quickly throughout the hospital that two adults where fighting in front of the picture of Jesus like some sacrilegious heathens. Hospital security ordered Lenice to leave the premises and not to come back until someone called her. Lenora was upset that Lenice choked her husband, but she understood why she did it. She couldn't imagine living without her sister, either. She had hoped to go home, but the doctors decided to keep her overnight and run some additional tests to make sure the pills hadn't done any serious damage. If everything checked out, she could go home tomorrow. She finally agreed to have visitors.

There was a soft knock on the door, and Herman appeared holding a teddy bear and a single rose.

"Hello, my beautiful wife," he said before handing her the gifts.

"Oh, now I'm beautiful. Not too long ago I was Ms. Piggy, wide load and buffalo butt," said Lenora.

"I'm sorry I ever called you such horrible names. You are beautiful. I had no right to be mean to you. I'll admit I would like for you to lose weight, but the healthy way with diet and exercise. Or maybe we can look at gastric bypass," he said.

"I haven't been in the hospital 24 hours, and you're bringing up how I should be losing weight, again! You are so insensitive."

She took the teddy bear and knocked it on the floor. It fell face down on the hard linoleum squares. She eyed the purple bruises and nail marks on Herman's neck indicating where her sister wrapped her hands around it. She laughed inwardly. What a sight that must have been! Lenice really needed to get control of her temper.

"I almost died trying to please you. Since the day I married you, I have been living for someone else. I quit the job I loved because you didn't want your wife working. I moved into that ugly house far away from my friends and family because that's where you wanted to live. I drive the car you like. I keep my hair long even though I want to cut it because that's what you like. I spend my days attending to the needs of you and our children. I hardly have a moment to myself. Somewhere along the way I lost myself. I used to have a life. I had hobbies and interests that didn't involve you or our children. I've made a decision. When the doctors release me I'm going home with my sister to recuperate. While I'm there, I'll decide if I want to stay in this marriage. It's not worth dying for."

Herman knew he messed up royally, but he didn't think it was bad enough to leave him. He couldn't believe she said that.

Rather than fight with her, he simply said, "Okay." He was sure after a couple of days with Lenice's crazy behind, she would come running back home. "I'm glad you're alright, Lenora. I love you, and I am grateful for you."

"I'll see if my parents will keep the kids a little longer." He kissed his wife on the cheek again and walked out.

A sea of salty tears rolled down Lenora's pudgy face. Had she really told her husband she was considering a divorce and all he had to say was, "Okay"? There was no "Baby, I need you, please don't go," no "I'm sorry, we can work this out." Nothing! There must be another woman. She decided she had better start looking for jobs and get ready to be a single mother because if all her husband had to say was "Okay," that was a good indication her marriage was coming to an end.

Chapter 24

Lesson Learned

Tiffany completed one of the appointments Tee arranged for her the next morning, but the other gentleman asked her to go visit his mother instead. She agreed and scheduled it for later that afternoon. The man she did see was Mr. Luther, the president of a local electronics company named Precision, Inc. After his 30-minute massage, Mr. Luther raved about how good he felt, handed her a $40 tip and asked her to come again next week for a paid appointment. Tee was right! Giving free massages was a great way to build her clientele. All those years in the marketing industry had taught her a thing or two about how to reel in the big fish. Tiffany was also finding the list of scriptures Tee gave her useful. She read a few of them that morning and then followed them up with prayer. She always considered herself a Christian. She attended church as a child and was baptized at the age of 10. Now, she had to take the time to understand what being a Christian truly meant and if her behavior had ever been Christ-like. She was a good person. She was nice to others. She gave to the needy. She even volunteered from time to time, but she knew she needed to make some changes in her life. She no longer felt good about herself. Tiffany had some time to kill before her next appointment and decided to read a few more scriptures. She turned to Ephesians 5:3.

"But among you there must not be even a hint of sexual immorality, or of any kind of impurity, or of greed, because these are improper for God's holy people."

She then turned to 1 Thessalonians 4:7-8.

"For God did not call us to be impure but to live a holy life. Therefore, he who rejects this instruction does not reject man but God, who gives you his Holy Spirit."

Lastly, she read Galatians 5:22-25.

"But when the Holy Spirit controls our lives, he will produce this kind of fruit in us: love, joy, peace, patience, kindness, goodness, faithfulness, gentleness and self-control. Here there is no conflict with the law. Those who belong to Christ Jesus have nailed the passion and desires of their sinful nature to His cross and crucified them there. If we are living by the Holy Spirit, let us follow the Holy Spirit's leading in every part of our lives."

"Holy Spirit, I really need you. I need you to take control because I really like me. I'm used to doing things my way, but I'm going to try yours," Tiffany said aloud.

She then fixed herself a chicken breast sandwich on rye bread with mayo, lettuce and tomato. She ate it and headed to her next appointment. She was going to visit Mrs. Loretta Tolliver. Mrs. Tolliver was the granddaughter of Edward Tolliver, the founder of Southwest Railroad. Back in the early 1900's before planes became a popular way of travel, he dominated the industry. His trains carried freight, humans and livestock, making him one of the richest men in the South. His family never had to worry about money again. The company was now headed by Mrs. Tolliver's two sons. She, like her mother, was an avid philanthropist and gave money frequently to worthy causes. She and her son often sponsored whatever charitable event Tee asked them to support. She was particularly fond of organizations that assisted women and children.

Tiffany arrived at her beautiful antebellum-inspired home, located in one of the historic parts of Memphis that was known for attracting those with "old money." These were families who possessed wealth for generations and didn't really care to live among the younger generations who were now coming into their own. Tiffany rang the doorbell, and a young African American woman opened the door and escorted her to the room where Mrs. Tolliver was waiting. Tiffany had never been in a house so elaborate. It was spacious with large bay windows that allowed the sun's rays to bathe the antique furniture found throughout. One of a kind paintings lined the walls and above the fireplace, in the parlor, was a portrait of Mrs. Tolliver and three young children, two boys and a girl.

Mrs. Tolliver was very fond of hydrotherapy and often spent hours in her Jacuzzi but rarely did she indulge in massages. She only agreed to see Tiffany because her son insisted she do so. He wanted to do something nice for her. The 60-year-old wasn't in the mood today. She recently received word from a very good friend that her husband was seeing a younger much prettier woman. He had even been so bold as to take his new play thing to a social function the night before while she was out playing bridge. Mrs. Tolliver actually forgot Tiffany was coming. Rather than send her away, she figured a massage might make her feel a little better before she called her lawyer and asked him to start divorce proceedings. She would not tolerate a wayward husband. She wasn't like her friends who turned a blind eye so as not to upset their privileged way of life. She would leave him before she gave him permission to have a mistress.

Mrs. Tolliver looked like she was getting dressed and then changed her mind. She wore a navy blue dress that reminded you of Audrey Hepburn in the movie *Breakfast at Tiffany's*. She wasn't wearing pantyhose or shoes, and her hair was still in rollers. A small locket nestled in the hollow of her throat served as her only jewelry.

Tiffany set up her portable station and sprinkled the sheets with lavender to give them a calming fragrance. Mrs. Tolliver told Tiffany her temples and lower back were bothering her and instructed her to do something about it, if she could. After turning on some soothing music, Tiffany asked the millionairess to lie face down on her table in her underwear underneath the sheet. Once she was comfortable, Tiffany applied her oil and began massaging Mrs. Tolliver's milky white shoulders, slowly working her way down. She noticed every few minutes Mrs. Tolliver would make a sound that sounded like laughter. This was nothing new to Tiffany because several people found themselves a little ticklish during massages. The sounds became more frequent, and Mrs. Tolliver's body began to shake. She realized the woman was crying, not laughing. Tiffany stopped the music and inquired if something was wrong.

Mrs. Tolliver wrapped herself in the sheet and sat up. It took a few minutes for the woman to compose herself in order to tell Tiffany what she was going through.

"My husband is having an affair. The woman is younger and prettier, and I don't think I can compete," cried Mrs. Tolliver. "I love my husband. I have loved him since I was a young girl. We were playmates as children. His mother cleaned our house. We've been married almost 40 years. How could he do this?"

"How do you know he's having an affair?" Tiffany moistened a towel with warm water and handed it to Mrs. Tolliver to wipe her face.

"I asked him this morning, and he confessed. He apologized and said he didn't mean for it to happen. I asked him if he planned to continue to see her. He said he didn't know because she made him feel alive when he was with her, and he likes feeling that way. He claims he's never cheated on me before. Evidently, I don't make my husband feel like he has a pulse anymore. What is it she's doing that I can't do? I used to be enough." Her body shook again as a new set of tears spilled from her eyes.

"Mrs. Tolliver, you've got to pull yourself together. The fact that he told you is a good sign. She may make him feel good, but he doesn't feel good about what he's doing. That means there's hope. Do you still want your husband?" asked Tiffany.

"Yes, but I can't allow him to have a mistress. I'll divorce him first."

"That might not be necessary. If there's one thing I know about, it's married men. Allow me to offer you some advice. Men like your husband usually cheat when they become bored or unhappy with what they have at home. Instead of worrying about what she is doing, worry about what you could do better," said Tiffany.

Mrs. Tolliver sat up straight and looked at Tiffany with a stare that fully showed her disapproval.

"I beg your pardon, Ms. Tiffany. I am good to my husband. I have been a dedicated wife. We share three wonderful children and two grandchildren. I loved that man when he didn't have a dime in his pocket. My daddy didn't want me to marry him because he was poor. He believed Larry wanted me because my family was rich. I looked my father in the eye, told him he was wrong and I was going to marry Larry with or without his blessing. It was the best decision I ever made," declared Mrs. Tolliver.

"You sure have a lot of spunk Mrs. Tolliver, and I like that. I'm sure you are a good wife and I know for a fact you're a fine upstanding member of the community as well. But let me ask you a few questions: when was the last time you cooked for your husband, ran him a hot bath or massaged his shoulders after a long day's work?"

"I don't have to. We have servants, and we pay people like you for massages and such," she said with a pompous air.

"And as much as we appreciate your business, it would mean more to your husband if the woman he loved was doing it. I bet he has a favorite dish you haven't prepared in years. When was the last time you told him he looked hot or sexy? And please forgive me for being so invasive, but when was the last time you made love to your husband?"

Mrs. Tolliver didn't like her line of questioning, but she realized she was only trying to help. To her, Tiffany looked like she had been around the block a time or two, and maybe she could use whatever wisdom she possessed to help. She had never really been single or dated. She got married when she was 20 years old. Mrs. Tolliver softened a bit. What did she have to lose in confiding in her? Her husband was already taking that hussy out in public.

"My husband knows I find him attractive. I married him didn't I? I was quite a looker in my day. I could have had any man I wanted, but I chose him. My husband and I last had intercourse on his birthday."

"When was that?" asked Tiffany.

"About six months ago."

"Mrs. Tolliver! Do you really expect a married man to go six months without sex and be fine with that? He doesn't have any problems in that area does he?"

"No. He's as spry as a chicken in the springtime. He and I are both in pretty good shape for our age. I'm just not in the mood like I used to be. As you get older, sex becomes less and less important."

"Maybe it has for you, but it sounds like it's plenty important for him. Now, listen to me Mrs. Tolliver. Yes, your husband was wrong for stepping out on you, but the good thing is he's not gone. If you want to keep him you've got to get past his indiscretion, get in the mood and make him feel desirable so he doesn't need or want to go to that other woman. Let me ask you some more questions. How's your communication? Do you have good conversations? Do you argue a lot?"

"This past year or so, yes. We used to have wonderful conversations. Larry and I could talk for hours about everything and nothing. We had a lot in common. We laughed at one another's jokes. We were affectionate. We never seemed to tire of one another's company," said Mrs. Tolliver with a wide smile.

"And now?"

Her smile disappeared. "All we seem to say is good morning and good night. He's never home. He's always working. He rarely takes me anywhere. When he does have free time, it seems he prefers to spend it with his friends."

"I'm not taking sides here, Mrs. Tolliver but try to see his side. If you were hard at work all day and all you had to come home to was an unhappy woman complaining about how you don't spend enough time with her AND she won't have sex with you, would you want to come home and spend time with her? He probably doesn't say much or come home because if you're not talking you can't argue. His friends don't pick fights with him."

"That's the only way he seems to pay me some attention! So, this is my fault?" said Mrs. Tolliver.

"No, not entirely. You do seem to be the key to making it better. It sounds to me like he's yearning for some attention. You know your husband better than anyone. Cater to him for a while, and I bet you get the attention you desire. There's nothing better to a man than a woman's touch and some kind words and compliments to boost his ego. If you're not giving them to him you best to be darn tootin' sure he's going to get it from someone else. Because he's rich, there are plenty of women who would love to take your spot. You lay back down on this table, and while I finish working the kinks out of this body I'm going to tell you how to work the kinks out of your marriage," said Tiffany.

Mrs. Tolliver decided she liked Tiffany. She had spunk as well. She did as she was told and listened attentively to a woman who was well versed in the whims of a married man. She gave a wonderful massage, too.

Some of the things Tiffany told Mrs. Tolliver actually made the old woman blush, but she promised she would try them if they would keep her husband home. After Tiffany finished her massage, she went to Mrs. Tolliver's wardrobe room. It was actually a large bedroom that was converted into a closet. There was a department store in there! The long racks of clothes, shoes, purses and accessories were neatly organized by color. The two of them selected several outfits that were sure to make her husband smile. She then took Mrs. Tolliver to her favorite intimate apparel boutique and helped her select a few age appropriate negligees for bedtime.

Chapter 25

Media Mayhem

On his way home from practice, Michael received a call from his father.

"Son, you haven't heard the news yet have you?"

"No Pop. Why? Did Tiger get caught with another woman?" he joked.

"This time it's about you, son. You're all over the TV. It seems you are under investigation by the NCAA for violations that have suddenly come to their attention."

"Are you serious? I haven't been in college for over a decade."

"I know but apparently, there seems to be no statute of limitation for this kind of thing."

"What kind of thing? I haven't done anything."

"It's about the Corvette you drove your senior year. They are claiming it was bought with money from one of the college's boosters. If they find that to be true and personnel at the college had knowledge of the money, it could be a bad situation for everyone involved. They are threatening to take back your Heisman, your All American designations, and wipe your name from The University of Miami annuals. All your record-breaking performances would cease to exist. They could even go as far as to make the team forfeit every season you played."

"That was over ten years ago! This makes me no sense. You bought me the car with money you received from Pop Warner's insurance, right?"

The elder Stokes hesitated a little too long for Michael's liking before saying, "Of course I did. I've already taken the liberty of calling Elbert, and he's trying to set up a meeting with the NCAA to get to the bottom of this. I'm sure this will all work out fine. Come on home, son. Your momma's already got dinner on the table."

"I'm on my way, Pop."

Elbert was an old friend of his father's and one of Michael's lawyers. He hoped he could help him make some sense out of this. He hung up the phone, and it rang again. He thought it was his father calling back and answered without looking. What he heard made all of the hairs on the back of his neck stand up.

"It seems you've got yourself in a pickle," said the familiar voice.

"I don't know who you are, but you've got a sick sense of humor. Why are you impersonating a dead woman? Don't you have anything better to do?" Michael refused to believe it was Becca.

"Binky, is that any way to talk to the woman who bore your favorite niece? I called to offer my sympathy for your current situation. While I find it somewhat amusing, I wouldn't have wished such a misfortune on anyone. I need your picture perfect life to stay that way before I take it all away."

Michael had no desire to continue this conversation. "Kick rocks," he said and hung up. He needed to call his wife. He had several missed calls from her.

Tee and James left the hospital with Lenice. He agreed to take her home. While driving home to get ready for Bible study, Edgar called and told Tee Michael was all over the news. She pulled over and searched for updates on her smart phone. Tee didn't pay much attention to football before marrying Michael, and she didn't quite understand everything she read but she knew it wasn't good. She tried to call him several times, but he didn't answer. She called his parent's house, and Tomeka said they were all watching the news but Michael wasn't there. She drove home, watched some of the newscasts and wondered why anyone would go dig up such old news. She received several calls from unknown numbers and there were messages on the answering machine from reporters wanting an interview. She decided not to speak to anyone until she spoke to her husband. Tee changed clothes and headed to the church. As she parked in front of Faith Persists Christian Church, Michael's name appeared in her caller ID.

"Michael baby, I have been trying to reach you for the past hour. Have you seen the news?" she asked.

"I left my phone in the car. I sat in on football practice at my old high school today. No, I haven't seen any of the news broadcasts, but my dad called and told me what they're saying. Is it that bad?"

"It's everywhere. CNN, MSNBC, Sports Center, FOX Sports, Ultimate Sports, Yahoo and the local newscasts. Reporters have been calling the house and my cell phone non-stop trying to get a statement. I've been pretending like I'm the housekeeper, and I don't uh speak uh no Inglés," Tee said with a bad Hispanic accent.

Michael chuckled. She was so funny, and it was times like this he appreciated her humor. "Baby, I don't have all the details myself but my lawyer is trying to get them now.

As soon as I know more I'll give you a call. Don't answer the phone and whatever you do, do not issue a statement on my behalf. I'm sure I will make one myself at some point. Just so you know, I didn't do it. I would never do anything to jeopardize my chances of going pro."

"I know you didn't. That's why I didn't ask. Don't worry; I won't say anything to the media. Are you still coming home tomorrow?"

"No, under the circumstances I think I need to stay here."

"Why? Your attorney lives in New York? Why does it matter where you are? Do you want me to come there?"

"No. That's not necessary. You just returned to work. This is not that serious. I know you have a couple of events coming up, and you need to work on the details for the I'm A Good Woman conference."

"I have staff and committees for that and this is serious. I can be there tomorrow," said Tee.

"Tee, no. I need to do this alone. Stay put!"

Michael had never spoken to her like that before. Why was he pushing her away?

He realized his tone was too forceful and lowered his voice before continuing. "Baby, there is nothing you or I can do at this point. Stay in Memphis and handle your business. I'll call you soon. Please, Beautiful."

"I'll stay put for now, but I expect to hear all the details as soon as you have them. Bye, Handsome. I love you."

"Ditto. I promise you'll hear from me soon.

During Bible study Tee tried to focus on the words of the ministry leader, but she couldn't. She closed her eyes and prayed for her family and friends. "God fix it," she said. "Fix it like only you can."

Chapter 26

Rage

Lenice and James sat in Starbucks across from each other. There was only a small table between them, but at that moment the distance seemed much greater. Neither one knew what to say. James was at a loss for words after witnessing the wrath of Lenice at the hospital. Lenice was too angry to speak.

Ever since she was a little girl, Lenice possessed a bit of a temper. In elementary and middle school, it was common for her to come home with bruises and scratches after pummeling some poor boy or girl who made the mistake of teasing her about her skinny legs, buckteeth or flat chest. She and Lenora were late bloomers. They were extremely thin until they reached their mid-teens. They were told on more than one occasion that they resembled the stick-figured Olive Oyl from the cartoon "Popeye." Lenora, the quiet one, either laughed or cried during the taunting, depending on the taunter and what mood she was in. Lenice often flew into a rage, enacted her own brand of punishment and dared the person to say it again.

One never knew when it was going to occur, and it turned on and off like a switch. One minute she was slapping some little girl for calling her a name and the next she was in the office cracking jokes with the principal. Lenice was charming with an entertaining way with words when she chose to exercise it, which she did to avoid several suspensions as a youth. She was feared by boys and girls alike. The word around the school was don't mess with the Langston Twins because one of them was crazy. However, around age 15, the twins hit puberty and pockets of fat began to develop in all the right places. All of a sudden, people were commenting that they looked like models instead of cartoon stick figures. Still thin but curvaceous and braces helped to transform their buckteeth into perfectly straight pearly whites.

Luckily, Lenice discovered a passion for sports and found an outlet for her aggression. Her anger was channeled into softball, basketball and tennis. She was fiercely competitive and excelled in all three sports. Although, she enjoyed tennis the most. In her senior year of high school, she was recognized for her stellar sportsmanship statewide.

Lenora preferred art and all things domestic. She could paint a picture and decorate a delicious cake. She was an excellent seamstress as well and enjoyed difficult patterns. She made both of their dresses for junior and senior prom. They both received full scholarships to their respective schools. Lenice got one for tennis and Lenora for art. They were the topic of several newspaper articles from publications that wanted to laud praises over such talented twins. Lenice kept them in a scrapbook and read them again from time to time.

Lenice often wondered what happened to them. She was supposed to be playing Venus and Serena at Wimbledon, and her sister should be featuring her art in her own art gallery or her culinary skills as the young, hip, African American Paula Deen. Instead, she was sitting in a coffee shop wondering if the man she was interested in was still interested in her, and her sister was in the hospital recuperating after taking too many weight loss pills.

She and James continued to sit there sipping lattes in silence. It felt good having him there. Lenice's therapist told her to take things slow, but the head and the heart are known for doing two very different things. She was smitten with this man after their first date. James was the first person she had taken an interest in since her last relationship. Before him, she blew any man who approached her off.

James was unsure of what to think of Lenice after seeing her bring a grown man to his knees. She seemed so sweet and docile when they were together. Evidently, there was a side to her he wasn't aware of. He was sure if Tee hadn't intervened, she would have killed Herman right there in the hospital. He wondered if she generally handled intense situations with unbridled anger and violence. Yet, her actions also heightened his intrigue for her. She possessed great passion, and she loved hard. That could mean she would love him like no other, but it could also mean she could turn psychotic at the drop of a hat. He decided he wouldn't label her, yet. He would continue to spend time with her and get to know her and then draw a conclusion. They said they would take things slow, and that's what they would do. People are multi-faceted and all of us behave differently when faced with a tragic situation. Having a temper didn't make her a bad person. She seemed perfectly calm now.

He knew he looked foolish sitting there staring into her eyes without speaking, but he thought Lenice Langston was gorgeous. To him, the woman sitting in front of him was classy, chic and funny. She scared him somewhat, but he wasn't ready to let her go.

James was a hard working accountant. He loved numbers and everything about them. He never thought a woman like her would even be interested in a man like him. One could say he was a little bit of a nerd. He wasn't unattractive but not strikingly handsome, either. He was conservative and often wore polo shirts, khakis and Birkenstock shoes. He also wore thin wire framed glasses. He loved music. His collection included Barry Manilow, Bette Midler, Alicia Keys, Beethoven, Herbie Hancock, Lil Wayne, Mos Def and NWA. He was generally quiet and soft-spoken and avoided emotional outbursts. His reserve allowed him to perform well in high-pressure situations. Although, when engaged in a conversation he found particularly interesting, he could become talkative and spirited.

Lenice blushed under his stare. James noticed and smiled. Her hands were wrapped around the hot chocolate he purchased for her. He stretched out his arm and gently touched her hand with his. She loosened her grip on the cup and eagerly enclosed hers within his. His touch felt nice, and the smile across his face was even nicer.

"Are you alright?" asked James softly.

"I'm better now. I'm so angry at Herman for what he's been putting my sister through. Lenora is sensitive and to have the man she loves tell her she is unattractive repeatedly was breaking her inside. She took those pills to please him. She was trying to lose the weight rapidly so he'd look at her the way he used to."

"I can understand your anger, but you tried to kill him," said James.

"I wasn't trying to kill him. At least, I don't think I was. I don't even remember choking him. What I do remember is Tee shaking me and yelling at me to stop. When I came to myself, I realized my hands were around his neck. I guess

I was overcome with emotion. I hope I didn't scare you away."

"Not at all," he lied. "I like a woman with passion and a strong dedication to the ones she loves. You did scare Herman, though. I spoke with him before we left. He seems to be doing fine except for a couple of bruises on his neck. I also think he's embarrassed such a small woman got the best of him. He initially intended to press charges against you, but I think I talked him out of it. I'm sure he'll let it go. At some point, the two of you are going to need to talk about what happened. But for now, I suggest you avoid each other."

"I'm inclined to agree with you," said Lenice. "Thank you for talking to him. I think he deserves what he got, but I don't want to go to jail over it."

"No problem. I like you, Lenice." He stroked her hand with his thumb.

Lenice felt a tingle move through her body. She wondered if he could tell the effect he had on her. Maybe if she kept talking, he wouldn't notice.

"I like you as well, Deacon James."

"Please always call me James. Such a formal title has no place among two informal people."

"James, thanks for staying with me."

"No problem. Herman seems to be very sorry. He never meant for Lenora to hurt herself. He merely wanted her to look like the woman he fell in love with. You have to understand something about men; we are visual creatures. When we marry a woman we consider to be beautiful we don't want her to change. It's the outer beauty that initially attracts us to her. Once we get to know a woman, it's her inner beauty that keeps us. Yet, we still need the outer beauty to be there. We need to be able to look at our significant other and still say *wow!*"

Lenice didn't like James trying to defend any part of Herman's actions. There was no excuse for what he did.

"What happens if it doesn't? Do men forget about the inner beauty and abandon the chick. Outer beauty fades, you know. We all get old and develop wrinkles. We might lose our hair and some of our teeth. Gravity may pull our breasts to our no longer flat stomachs but what we can do is keep the same mannerisms and personality he fell in love with. The inner beauty is still there," Lenice pounded her fist on the table. "Why are men so stupid?"

James laughed nervously. "Don't go putting us all in the same category. There are men who have been with their wives for 25 or more years and wouldn't dream of leaving her. Then, there are those selfish individuals who will abandon their woman while she's ill if he feels he has a better offer. We cannot control other people. We can only control ourselves, but more importantly, how we react to the things others do."

"I suppose you're right. Which one are you?" asked Lenice.

"I'm like that dog Old Faithful. I'll stay right by your side and love you with everything I've got once I decide that's what I want to do. Lenice, I want you to know I would never say harsh words to you. I respect you too much."

Lenice blushed again. She thought to herself, *James may be quiet but he sure knows how to make a woman feel special.*

They continued to sip their beverages in silence, smiling at one another and holding hands.

Chapter 27

Turn It Off

Michael's parents had every television on in the house. There were five in all, and each was set to a different channel. The newscasters were pretty much saying what his dad told him, and they were all running footage of him driving off in his Corvette after a big game against the University of Florida his senior year. It was after that game he was informed that he would be receiving the Heisman trophy.

Michael, Sr. hated to see any of his children in distress. He instructed Tomeka to turn off all the TV's, and he gathered his family together for dinner. Before eating the delicious fried catfish, spaghetti, greens and cornbread his wife prepared, they all joined hands and thanked God for the meal. He asked Him to take control of the situation that was unfolding right before their very eyes and work it out in Michael's favor. His father suggested they try to change the subject. He liked pleasant conversation during dinner. They tried to talk about anything but the shocking news but realized ignoring it was not going to help and the outside world wasn't going to let them ignore it. The doorbell rang.

"I'll get it," said Michael, Sr.

He looked out the window and saw two news reporters, from different television stations, filming on his front lawn. Another reporter was on his porch waiting for him to answer. He opened the door and shouted for them to all leave, but they didn't budge.

"Mr. Stokes, we've received reports that Michael is in town. Is he here? I'd like to talk to him if he is," said the female newspaper reporter standing in front of him.

"This is private property, and you have no right to be here. You want news. I'll give you some news!" he shouted before closing the door and heading to the hall closet.

He returned to the door, opened it wide and stepped out onto his front porch. He cocked his Remington shot gun and fired three shots in the air. They rang loudly into the evening sky. The reporter on the porch screamed and ran, almost tumbling down the front steps. In less than three minutes, not a single solitary soul was left standing in front of his house. They all left as fast as their wheels could roll.

Michael, Sr. slammed the door shut, put his gun back in the closet, returned to the dinner table, poured himself a glass of sweet tea and said, "Nobody interrupts my time with my family. Makes no sense that a man can't even enjoy a meal with the people he loves. Finish eating everybody." He took a couple of bites of his food. "Vanessa, I think you make the best fried catfish on the planet."

"Why, thank you, Senior," Vanessa responded as if it was perfectly normal for her husband to scare the living daylights out of three reporters. "The devil sho' is busy."

"He sure is," agreed Michael, Sr. "Junior, I know you're worried, but put it to the back of your mind and try to enjoy dinner with your family. You don't see us every day, and you going hungry won't fix anything. You looked tired too, boy. When you finish, why don't you try to get you some sleep while you're here."

"Pop, you're something else!" He chuckled at his father's actions as he cut a piece of the crispy fish on his plate. He was always looking out for his children. He planned to be that kind of father one day. He looked at Michelle. She had spaghetti sauce and fish crumbs all around her mouth.

"Is it good?" He asked her.

"Yes, sir. Reaaaaal goooood. Can I go play fire crackers with Granddaddy when I finish?"

Everyone laughed except Tomeka. She sat in silence wondering if her father would make the news tonight, too. The kids at school would never let her live it down.

"Grandaddy's done playing for tonight, Pumpkin. Maybe some other time," said Michael, Sr.

After dinner, Michael went to his childhood bedroom and checked his cell phone messages. There were several from Tee, various friends and family members, and one from Peter. He decided to call Peter back first.

"Hey, Superstar. Are you enjoying the news coverage?" asked Peter.

"I'm not watching it. I cut it off for now. It was getting to be a bit much."

"This is only the beginning. Wait until I tell them about all the other under the table gifts you received while in college," said Peter.

"What? You did this?"

"Who else knows all the deep dark secrets to your success?"

"Why are you spreading lies? I thought I was your brother." Michael was confused. He knew Peter was mad, but what would make him turn into a liar?

"It's nothing personal, Bro. It's just business. I needed to show you who's really in control. This incredible life you lead, you owe it all to me. I was guiding your career before you had a career. How do you think a boy in Akron, Ohio came to the attention of a school like the University of Miami? You and I both know they rarely look as far as Akron for talent.

"You may have gotten them to look at me, but it was my talent that made them accept me," defended Michael.

"You're talented for sure, Mike, or at least you were before you hurt yourself. But talent without recognition becomes little more than a hobby. When you put that talent in front of an audience is when it truly becomes something special. That's when the world loves you, people are willing to pay you ridiculous amounts of money and women become willing to do anything to please you. You owe me more than you know. I did all the dirty work while you remained ignorant and squeaky clean."

"All these years I've been your pet project, Peter?"

"Don't think of it like that. You are a talented man with a beast for an agent. Now that I'm older, I have no desire to work as hard as I used to, which is why I need you to recognize what a valuable asset I am and stop slapping away the hand that fed you all these years. I brought you to Miami because this is my home base. I needed you closer to me so I could keep tabs on you. The good thing was you were genuinely a good kid, so I didn't have to worry about the nonsense that most superstar athletes get into. You weren't trying to be hard and constantly testing the laws. You didn't do drugs or alcohol and you didn't allow women to manipulate you---not a whole lot anyway. I watched you your entire high school career and got my scout friends to steer Miami your way. Then, I sat back and waited for the right opportunity to become your agent. When I heard of your father's financial problems, it was the perfect opportunity to get him in my corner."

Michael couldn't believe what he was hearing. He struggled to make sense of it all and to determine if it was true or if Peter was pulling his leg.

I alerted the NCAA to your father's behavior to show you this thing is bigger than you. You thought your Daddy bought you that car. Your daddy was barely making ends meet when I approached him. He had been laid off from his job, and your momma was pregnant with your little sister. I talked to a few of my associates, and they agreed to float him some cash, but your father was greedy. He didn't want enough to get by. He wanted enough to buy you the Corvette he knew you wanted. He was so proud of his boy and thought you deserved to ride in style like your fellow teammates who came from rich families."

"My Pop wouldn't do that. He knew how that could jeopardize my career if word got out," Michael said.

"Man, please. Ask him. I can get you out of this but you've got to do whatever I tell you to do. You seem to be under the impression this Christian life you lead only affects you. Well, it doesn't. It affects me, too, and you need to stop expecting everyone to get with your program. I am the only deity you need. I've been calling the shots in your life for your benefit for years."

"Peter, I admit I owe you a lot, but you act as if you weren't paid handsomely for your services. You received more than fair compensation for your hard manipulative work. You've been able to live a good life because of my talent. If I wasn't a great athlete, I wouldn't have lasted 10 years in the game. I wouldn't have been offered multi-million dollar endorsement deals for you to broker. As far as I'm concerned, my debt to you is more than paid. I see now, more clearly than ever, it's time for us to part ways. I no longer want you as my agent, manager or friend."

"If that's what you want, Mike. Let's see you get out of this mess without me," mocked Peter.

"I am more than certain that the God you scoff at will make a way. Now, get off my phone!"

"Stay tuned. The second act of this show is much better than the first," said Peter.

Michael didn't respond. Instead, he clicked the end call button. He'd had enough of evil people for one day. Michael didn't know what was going on, but he knew who to call to help him figure it out. He put in a call to Private Detective Ida Foster.

Chapter 28

Mac III

"Good morning," said the voice.

"Morning," said Mac.

Mackenzie Elbert Patton III hated he became involved with a woman he had never seen. He received a call on his cell phone one day while sitting outside of Tee's office waiting for her to arrive. He watched Tee whenever his schedule allowed. He liked looking at her, even if she was married to someone else. The mystery woman told him that if he helped her get revenge on Michael, she would deliver Tee into his hands. He figured she was a woman scorned, but he really didn't care. Her offer to get rid of Michael for him was too good to pass up. He was sure if Michael hadn't come into her life, Tee would have taken him back. The voice initially asked him for $5,000 to help her enact her vengeance. It seemed like a small price to have the woman he loved back.

His only method of contacting her was through email. Although, she would call him periodically from a restricted number. Today was one of those times.

"I have some news for you. I'm sure you've seen the news about Michael. He was in Ohio when the news reports started. Tee asked him to come there to be with him, and he told her no," shared the voice.

"I know how much of a nurturer she is. I'm sure that is tearing her up inside," said Mac.

"Exactly. I suggest you become her shoulder to lean on before someone else does. She's working from home today. Goodbye."

Mac knew exactly what to do with that information. Within the hour he was at Tee's door.

Chapter 29

Good Morning

Tee was beside herself with worry over Michael. She wanted to hop on a flight to go comfort her man, stand by his side or bring him a cup of coffee, if he needed it. Marriage was new to her, and she was unsure of how to handle this. She called him earlier that morning and all he would tell her was he was fine and he and his father were going to figure out how to keep his name from being dragged through the mud. The bad publicity was already costing him money. Michael had upcoming speaking engagements at two colleges, and both of them called to cancel that morning and requested their deposit back. He was sure more would follow if he didn't clear this mess up fast.

There were no new developments, but the media was repeatedly running that same speculative story and footage of him driving off campus in his Corvette over a decade ago. What happened to responsible journalism?

Tee decided she would honor her husband's request for now and stay home, but she didn't know for how long. Doing a little work might keep her mind off things. She called Sheba to discuss a few projects and confirmed her schedule for the rest of the week. Sheba was doing well as her assistant. She was intelligent, efficient and eager to help. Tee still wasn't sure she could trust her, but she couldn't deny the girl had fantastic clerical skills and was extremely organized. She was even mechanically inclined. The icemaker in the break room hadn't worked in months. Sheba went to her car and got her toolbox and fixed it in less than 10 minutes. You don't find women who carry a toolbox very often.

Tee got up that morning and worked out to an exercise video. She was still wearing her black spandex bottoms and a pink top that showed off her flat stomach. She heard someone at the door. She was surprised to see Mac but didn't mind him being there. Especially, after he announced he brought her breakfast from Cracker Barrel. The workout left her hungry, and the thought of consuming some of her favorite breakfast foods without having to prepare them was enticing. She was hesitant about letting him inside the home she now shared with her husband, but she didn't want to be alone. It hurt that she was told to stay away when she only wanted to comfort Michael. She gave Mac a heartfelt hug and invited him in.

Mac didn't expect to be greeted in that manner. It felt good to hold her again. He held Tee as long as she allowed, breathing in her scent, rubbing on her back and feeling her heartbeat against his chest. His mind shifted back to the close moments they shared less than a year ago. Tee stepped away from him and he reluctantly let go. The shiny spandex she wore hugged her body perfectly. Her abs looked great. Tee noticed him staring, but she also noticed he was wearing the black shirt and red tie she bought for him when they were dating. He always did look good in black. She announced she was going upstairs to freshen up, and told Mac to head to the kitchen and make himself at home. She would be back shortly.

Chapter 30

Lies, Lies, Lies

Sandy dropped her children off at school and went home to work on the nursery. She wasn't feeling the best and preferred to stay close to her bed and her bathroom in case she needed them. She walked to her office, sat at her desk and removed her shoes. After receiving Armondo's last email, she was more determined than ever to get him out of their lives for good. She decided to lie and tell him she was only three months pregnant. That should get him to stop because their affair happened almost six months ago.

She and Patrick shared an office. Her desk was near the window and his near the door. His desk was made of wood and hers of glass. They were different in so many ways but similar in the ones that really mattered. They both possessed a no nonsense approach to life and an entrepreneurial spirit. They were dedicated to being good parents and making their marriage work. They were lovers, business partners and friends.

She hated Patrick was so messy. Papers were all over his desk as well as empty cups and dishes he was too lazy to take back to the kitchen. She started to clean up, but she remembered the last email Armondo sent and decided that it might be a good idea to respond to him now. She logged into her account, and there was another email from Armondo waiting in her inbox. What did he have to say now? She was going to put a stop to this once and for all. After she sent her email to him, she was going to block him from sending her anymore. The email read:

> I have tried to be patient and civil with you but since you refuse to answer my email regarding the paternity of your baby I have put in a request to come home to ask you face to face. I fully expect it to be granted. I can't wait to see you.
>
> Armondo

"Oh pooh! No, this can't be! He can't come here! Not now. If he sees me, he'll know I'm more than three months pregnant. Fiddlesticks!" She said out loud to herself.

She tried to call Tee. She didn't answer. Sandy spoke with her last night about what was going on with Michael and Tee informed her that she planned to work from home today. She said she was alright, but Sandy wasn't thoroughly convinced she was. Tee liked going to the office. She decided to pay her a visit. She needed to talk, and it couldn't wait.

Sandy arrived at Tee's house and saw a truck she didn't recognize sitting in the driveway. She parked on the street so she wouldn't block whoever was there. She always disliked the steep incline of Tee's driveway, and she disliked it even more now that she had to waddle up it while pregnant. She rang the doorbell twice and didn't get an answer. She really didn't expect anyone to hear it because of the loud music playing inside the house. Sandy had a key but normally didn't use it unless Tee took too long to answer the door. She found it on her key ring and let herself in. She followed the music to the kitchen and was quite surprised to see Mac in an apron squeezing oranges. He was singing along to "You're My Lady" by D'Angelo at the top of his lungs. Sandy didn't like the looks of this at all. He had no business being there. Tee was married now. She walked over to the radio and turned it off.

"Get the frick out! I won't let you do to her what Armondo did to me. Get out!" she shouted.

Mac was unaware anyone else was in the kitchen except him. Sandy startled him and he almost spilled the orange juice he was making. He smiled weakly, "Oh, hey Sandy. I didn't know you were here. So nice to see you. What are you talking about? Who is Armondo? I am only being a friend. See, I brought breakfast. Are you hungry? Of course you are; pregnant women are always hungry. Have some hash brown casserole?"

He held up the container of food as if it were evidence of an innocent gesture.

Sandy looked at the food and smiled back at him. That casserole really did look good.

"You know what? You're right. I am overreacting," she said. "I think I'll take you up on that offer. However, I brought some things for Tee, and they're a little too heavy for me to carry with me being pregnant and all. Will you get them for me?"

"Sure. It would be my pleasure," Mac lied. The only thing he wanted to help her do was leave.

"You always were a sweetie. The car is unlocked. They're on the front seat," instructed Sandy.

Mac was glad Sandy didn't continue to yell at him about being there. He only wanted to be there for Tee in her time of need. Was that so wrong? He went to Sandy's car to get the things she spoke of, but the car door was locked. He could see clearly through the front window, and there was nothing there. He walked back toward the house and saw his jacket and keys sitting on the front step outside the door. He turned the doorknob, but the door was locked. He banged forcefully on the door. He'd been tricked!

"Go away, Mackenzie!" Sandy yelled from inside. "I know you are up to no good. Leave my sister alone. She's a happily married woman now. You had your chance, and you blew it. Scram loser!"

"No, you've got it all wrong," Mac yelled back. "I only want her friendship. Let me in so we can talk about this!"

"Bull crap. Tee and I appreciate the breakfast, but neither of us needs your company today. Adios amigo. Get to stepping!"

Mac knew there was no reasoning with her. He walked to his car and left. Operation Shoulder to Lean On didn't go at all like he planned.

Ten minutes later, Tee returned to her kitchen in a baggy University of Memphis sweat suit. She was surprised to see her sister sitting in her breakfast nook eating the food Mac brought. There was a second plate already set for her at the table with a glass of fresh squeezed orange juice.

"Good morning. Sit down and have some breakfast with me. The grits are good but not as good as the ones we make at Mae Lillie's," said Sandy.

Tee looked around for Mac but didn't see him anywhere. She sat down, said her grace and began eating. "Where's Mac?"

"I threw him out," said Sandy.

Tee let out a sigh of relief. She didn't know why Sandy put him out and at the moment, she didn't care. What mattered was he was gone. She regretted him being there the minute he hugged her. While upstairs changing clothes, she was trying to figure out how to politely ask him to leave. Now, she didn't have to.

"Thank you," she said.

"That's what sisters are for. After we eat, let's go see Lenora."

"Sounds like a plan to me."

"Oh ham!" said Sandy.

"What's wrong?"

"There's a dag gone seed in my juice."

"You really need to stop with the pseudo profanity. You sound ridiculous," said Tee.

"What the frappuccino are you talking about?"

"Never mind, Sandy. Eat your food."

Chapter 31

Confession Is Good for the Soul

Michael wanted to throw every TV in the house out into the street. He knew doing so would solve nothing, but it might make him feel a little better. It wasn't the TVs that were bothering him. It was those unfounded stories that were constantly airing. He asked his family not tell him what the media was saying unless it was something different from the initial reports. He stopped answering phone calls from everyone except his immediate family and his attorney. He understood that the NCAA technically couldn't do anything to him since whatever they believed might have occurred was over a decade ago, and he was retired. But they could launch an investigation into the matter and make their findings public. He had nothing to hide, but his reputation and integrity meant everything to him. What if they reported things that weren't true or what if what Peter said was true? He hadn't talked to his father about it yet. His awards and record-breaking performances on the field were a result of his hard work. Could they really make it look like they never happened? He didn't want his legacy tarnished this way.

Michael knew he needed to talk to his father but didn't know how to approach him. His father had always been his number one example for everything a man was supposed to be: smart, honest, God-fearing, strong, a great provider and an excellent husband and father. He knew taking money from boosters and agents could damage his career if anybody found out. He remembered the day his father showed up on campus with the slightly used black Corvette to surprise him. When he asked where he got the money, Michael, Sr. told him his father, Pop Warner, had a huge life insurance policy and had designated his only son as the beneficiary and that's where all the money came from. His father wouldn't lie to him. His grandfather died a month prior to him receiving the car so, it made logical sense to him.

Michael went downstairs to fix himself a snack and noticed that the door to the basement was open and the light at the bottom of the stairs was on. He thought everyone in the Stokes home was gone to school or work, except for him. He went down the steps and found his father sitting on the floor with his guitar and a beer. His only company was boxes packed with remnants of their lives--old clothes, toys, childhood awards, pictures and the like.

His father was never a good player, but every now and then, he'd pull out his guitar and play for his own enjoyment. He took a swig of his beer and then strummed a few more chords. Michael didn't recognize the song he was trying to play, but it was as sad as the expression on his father's face.

Michael, Sr. was a man in turmoil. Perhaps, he thought playing a few bad chords and drinking beer would give him some peace. Michael walked slowly toward his father. Michael, Sr. looked up at him with shame and sorrow.

"I'm sorry, son. This is all my fault. I never should have taken that money. If I hadn't, Peter wouldn't be doing this."

"You took money from Peter? Why? You knew what that could do to me if somebody found out. Why, Pop?" demanded Michael.

"We were broke, Junior. Vanessa was pregnant. I wasn't working, and I had a family to provide for. You were in college and even though you were on scholarship you still needed things. Maxwell needed braces and was going through a bad spell with his asthma. It seemed like he was going to the doctor every other week. My insurance from the military wasn't covering all the expenses. When Peter approached me and offered me some money to make sure he represented you when you graduated, I took it. Peter was still new to the business and needed some good clients. Everybody knew you were going pro, but he wanted to make sure you were larger than life. He told me his plans, and they sounded good. He said he had some investors that were willing to sponsor his endeavors. I agreed to steer you in his direction, but I made sure that we, as a family, got our fair share. I wasn't going to let them use me or my boy. If they were going to put you on the auction block, you were going to get something out of it. Looking back, it seems like I did the right thing. Peter kept his end of the deal. He kept you out of trouble and made you a sports icon. Look at you. You've got more money than you can spend, and the checks are still coming." He took another swig of his beer and strummed a couple more chords.

Michael's ears burned. He was in this mess because of his own father!

"How much did you take, Pop?"

"The amount doesn't matter."

"It matters to me. How much?"

"$500,000," Michael, Sr. confessed.

"You took half a million from them. Peter didn't have me on the auction block, you did! Why?"

Michael, Sr. put down his guitar and began to rise. He was a little tipsy from the five beers he drank but he managed to get to his feet without toppling over.

"You watch your tone with me. I am still your father. I told you why. I did it for our family and your future. Peter did an excellent job representing you."

"For me? You bought me a used Corvette. I didn't need a Corvette!"

"I saw the cars those rich kids at your school drove. You were the star of your team, and you didn't even have a car. It hurt my pride to see you do without."

"My friends had cars. I got around fine," said Michael. "I didn't need a car."

His father picked up his guitar and strummed a few more chords. He turned his body away from him as he did so. He couldn't even look at his eldest son.

He paused and said, "I didn't want you to get around fine. I wanted you to get around in style. I paid your momma's and Maxwell's medical bills, bought you and myself a car, paid the rest of the bills and saved the rest. Peter made sure that it looked like insurance money from my dad so no one could trace it back to whatever investors he got it from."

"You have got to be kidding. Who were these investors?"

"Son, I don't know all the details. Peter said it was better that I didn't. All I know is I got a lot of money to make sure you agreed to make Peter your agent. Don't be mad. Desperate times call for desperate measures. I only want the best for all of you." Michael felt his father's sense of reasoning was grossly wrong.

"Dad, all you had to do was hold out a little while longer. We could have taken out loans to pay the medical bills, and I could have paid them off easily once I got signed. You didn't have to do that. Neither of us knew it, but Peter is evil. He says he's going to ruin me if I don't start hosting parties at strip clubs to help him make the money he won't be getting since I don't play ball anymore."

"You don't understand. There was no time left. I took out a second mortgage on the house and was several months behind on the payments. We were getting cut off notices for the utilities. Our only car kept breaking down, and the dealership I got the raggedy thing from was threatening to repossess it if I didn't pay the notes. We were going under fast. I couldn't let my family end up on the street. You had at least another semester before you graduated."

Michael, Sr. strummed a few chords on his guitar and motioned for Michael, Jr. to come closer. He didn't move.

"That's what this is all about--parties with naked women? Money?" asked Michael, Sr. "If it's money that he wants maybe you can give Peter some and that will shut him up."

"No. I'm not paying him or anyone else hush money. But you are going to go before the NCAA and tell them what you did and that I had nothing to do with it!"

"I can't do that," said Michael, Sr. I'm a deacon and a community leader. I was thinking about running for the school board next year. Something like this could kill my chances for election. It would also embarrass your mother. She has no idea I took that money."

Michael couldn't believe what he heard. His father basically sold him to Peter and jeopardized his entire career. He was being massacred in the media, and his father was more worried about his reputation than doing what was right. What about his reputation? What about his position in the community. He had thousands of people, young and old, who considered him a role model. His father wasn't concerned about his reputation when he pulled a shotgun on three news reporters the day before. Why weren't they running that on the news?

Michael didn't feel well; he had to leave. He wanted to go somewhere where he didn't have to look at his father. He used to think home was the safest place on the planet. His parents' home was normally his refuge, but right now, it was the last place he wanted to be. He suddenly had the urge to feel the tender touch of the woman who loved him like no other. He needed Tee.

"I'm disappointed in you, Pop," said Michael before he ran up the basement steps and out the door.

Chapter 32

Daddy's Home

There was a brown box lying in the middle of Tiffany's porch. She wasn't expecting a package. She picked it up and examined the address. The only one on it was hers; there was no return address to help her identify where it may have come from. She tore it open and inside was a large manila envelope and a small box. She knew a jewelry box when she saw one. Tiffany popped open the top and squealed at the exquisite diamond ring with green emerald baguettes on each side. Green was her favorite color and diamonds were a girl's best friend! She put the ring on her left ring finger and held it up so she could admire it. It was beautiful. She returned her attention back to the package and opened the envelope. It contained a hand-written letter from Quincy and what appeared to be legal separation papers from him wife.

> Butterfly,
>
> I promised you I would leave my wife, and I'm doing it now. These last few weeks without you have been torture. Please accept this promise ring. It will eventually become an engagement ring but I've done things terribly wrong, and I want to start doing them right. I will get on one knee and propose properly once my divorce is final. I love you.
>
> Q

The man she loved was finally going to marry her! She, Quincy and Quincy 2 would be a real family. Tiffany believed this must be God's answer to her prayers. She was being faithful, and he was moving mountains on her behalf already. She asked him to fix her financial situation and now he had. As Quincy's wife, she wouldn't have to worry about money. He was rich. Tiffany was elated. She danced around the room, giggling and admiring her ring. She couldn't keep her eyes off of it. Her joy was momentarily interrupted by the sobering thought that she had no one to call and share her news with. None of her friends would be happy for her and her family wouldn't be either. There was one person she knew she could call. She picked up the phone and dialed Quincy's number.

"Do you like it, Butterfly?" he answered.

"Yes, Sugah. I love it!"

"I knew you would. I love you so much. Now, all I need you to do is drop this silly child support case. It's costing me a ton in attorney fees, and that's money you and I are going to need to start our life together."

"Sure," said Tiffany. "I'll call my lawyer today. When are you moving in?"

"What? Who said anything about moving in?" asked Quincy.

"If you and your wife are separated there's no need for you to stay there with her, right? I want to start living our life together right away. Get your things and move over here with me and your son. We miss you."

Quincy was silent.

"Quincy, when are you moving in?" Tiffany repeated.

"Butterfly, it's not that simple. My wife and I haven't told our daughters yet, and we agreed we would wait until after the youngest one's birthday so we wouldn't ruin it."

"And when is that?"

"January."

"That's two months from now! Do you really expect me to be fine with you living in the same house as your wife while I'm engaged to you?"

"Butterfly, did you read my note? We're not engaged, yet. Divorces generally take a minimum of three months. My wife agreed to the divorce, but she asked me not to ruin Sasha's birthday. I told her I wouldn't. Sasha is a Daddy's girl, and this will break her heart. I also have to do this delicately to make sure my wife doesn't take me to the cleaners during the divorce. You don't want a broke man do you?"

"I suppose I don't, but I want you here with me," pouted Tiffany.

"And I will be. Be patient. We're going to be together."

"I've been waiting for years, and I can hardly contain myself now that it's really about to happen."

"Give me a little more time. I tell you what. To show you I'm serious I'll move some of my things over soon. This is a delicate process. One step at a time."

"I'll try to be more patient. Will I see you soon, Quincy?"

"Of course. I can't wait. Bye, Butterfly."

Tiffany hung up the phone feeling less enthusiastic than she had a few minutes earlier. She was always being put on the back burner. When she became his wife there would be no more of that. She would demand that she and their son come first. She needed to get dressed. She had a spa appointment in an hour and didn't want to be late.

She decided to read some more scriptures first. She scanned the list Tee gave her and her eyes rested on Proverbs 4:23.

"Guard your heart for it is the well spring of life."

God if you're trying to tell me something I need you to make it plain. I'm new to this so you have to be straightforward with me, prayed Tiffany.

Her phone rang, and it was Quincy. "Butterfly, I'm on my way to your house?"

"Now? Why?"

"To show my future wife how much I missed her. If you have any plans, I suggest you postpone them for the next couple of hours," he instructed.

Tiffany smiled. She really did miss him, and they were going to be husband and wife soon. She saw no need to postpone the inevitable.

"Will do. Hurry up."

"I'm about 10 minutes away. You better get ready because Daddy's home."

Tiffany giggled and hung up the phone. She didn't have long to get ready for his arrival. She went to the mirror to apply some lip gloss and to make sure her hair was properly tousled. The pace of her heart quickened when she heard the front door open and close. She often treated their lovemaking like a production. Quincy never knew what surprises she had in store. She thought about putting on one of the many costumes she owned, maybe the nurse's uniform, the naughty schoolgirl outfit or her cat suit. None of those seemed appropriate. Instead, she took off all her clothes and laid across the bed in a sexy nude pose. She caught a glimpse of herself in the mirror and briefly admired the way her new ring sparkled in the sunlight streaming through her window. It was absolutely beautiful! She said aloud the new name she hoped to have in a few months, "Mrs. Tiffany Ann Tate-Matthews." The words rolled off her tongue easily and sounded like music to her ears. She could now hear Quincy's feet moving down the hall toward her. She was glad she didn't change the locks. This southern belle was beside herself with anticipation. She closed her eyes, sucked in her stomach to hide the pooch she couldn't seem to get rid of no matter how many crunches she did and stuck her chest out further to make her large breasts look even larger. She opened her eyes and Quincy was standing in front of her.

"Hello, Butterfly," he said. He then kissed her and proceeded to make her feel the depth, the magnitude, and the true meaning of the words, "Daddy's home."

Chapter 33

Get Well Soon

The next morning, Lenice received a call from the hospital informing her she could come see Lenora. She was warned if there were any more acts of violence she would be banned from further visits. Lenice assured them there wouldn't be. When she arrived, she sat on the side of the bed and French braided her sister's hair while they chatted about nothing in particular. An hour later, Tee and Sandy arrived. The trio sat and talked with Lenora, carefully avoiding any subject that might upset her. They knew how emotional she was.

The friendly stress-free interaction did Lenora some good. She was grateful no one asked her to explain her overdose. They all let her know how happy they were she survived and they loved her. She had no desire to talk about it or Herman. She also didn't want to hear another person telling her what she should and shouldn't be doing. Lenora already had Herman trying to tell her what to do; she didn't need them trying to do it, too.

Lenice wanted to tell Lenora what she should do to her ungrateful husband, but her sister's recovery was more important than giving her a piece of her mind, at least for now. She knew Lenora was unhappy with her for choking Herman, and if she brought up the overdose, Lenora was sure to start crying. There would be plenty of time to make her feelings known when she took her home with her. She was happy Lenora would be staying with her for a few days. They were awaiting her test results. Lenora hoped they were favorable so she could be discharged. Herman hadn't called since his visit last night, but she did receive a wake-up call from the children. She was appreciative that her in-laws thought enough of her to let her hear their voices before they took Hermie to school.

Lenora grew drowsy and settled down for a nap. Lenice left for work and promised to come back that evening. Tee and Sandy both went home.

Chapter 34

Bad News

Sandy was exhausted. She still wasn't sleeping well, but she couldn't take the nap she desperately wanted because it was time for the children to come home from school. They would be hungry and she needed to fix them an after school snack.

Upon her arrival, she was greeted by Donovin and Nicole. They kissed their mother and then kissed her stomach to say hello to their baby sister. They looked so much like Patrick. They both had his forehead and his smile. Nicole also had his bright brown eyes with long lashes, and Donovin had his thick lips and his walk. Their features left no doubt he was their father. She hoped her third child would share the same physical features. Her mother, Pearl, was there with the children, instead of Patrick. She was in the kitchen fixing them peanut butter and jelly sandwiches and Kool-Aid. That was odd because today was his regularly scheduled day off. Her mother said he received a call to do some emergency dental work and asked her to pick them up from school.

Patrick usually called or sent a text when he got an emergency call, but Sandy was too tired to dwell on his deviation from his normal behavior. She was grateful her mother was there so she could try to take a nap.

She went to her office to place some orders for the restaurant before bedtime. There was another note from

Armondo on her computer informing her that his request for leave was granted.

This was terrible! Sandy felt a sharp pain in her abdomen. She decided she needed to lie down now and hoisted herself up from the chair behind her desk to make her way to her bedroom but did not take more than two steps before another sharp pain crippled her. She screamed for help. Donovin heard her and came into the room. He saw his mother lying on the floor and ran to get his Momma Pearl.

For the second time in one day, Sandy was in a hospital. This time she was the one who needed medical attention. She was taken by ambulance to Collierville West, near her home. Sandy had gone into premature labor. The doctors were able to prevent her from delivering the baby but feared that it would happen again. Her mother, Tee, Patrick and her obstetrician, Dr. Dorsha Walker, were all gathered in her room.

"We were able to stop your labor, but I am afraid the worst may not be over," said Dr. Walker. "The baby appears to be in distress. Her heart rate is elevated. Your resting will help, but we need to get to the root of the problem. Often this type of condition is brought on by stress. Are you stressed, Mrs. Pierce? I know you are a restaurateur, wife and mother. Have you been trying to keep up your hectic schedule while pregnant?"

Patrick answered on her behalf, "No, Doc. That can't be it. My wife barely works four hours a day now, and she only goes in about three days a week. I made her cut back weeks ago when I noticed how tired she was, but she has been acting strange lately. She doesn't seem happy to be pregnant. I think she's depressed. Is that common during pregnancy?"

"Many women experience a heightened sense of emotion when they are pregnant. So, if they are sad it can be a deep sadness. Are you sad, Mrs. Pierce? What seems to bring about this sadness?" asked Dr. Walker.

"Yeah, what's going on, Sandy? Why are you so down all the time?" Patrick had a look of genuine concern and waited for Sandy to issue a reply.

Sandy looked around the room at all the concerned faces. She closed her eyes to shut them out. Maybe she and the baby would feel better if she confessed. Keeping her secret was becoming unbearable. She began to cry. "I'm friggin' sorry. I'm so friggin' sorry," Sandy said softly over and over again but offered no other words.

Momma Pearl moved closer to her oldest daughter. "I know that cry anywhere. It's the same cry I heard when you admitted to me you wore the freshwater pearls your daddy gave me to school for senior picture day and lost them. Whatever it is that's eating you inside, Sandy, you have to confess it because it's also eating away at my grandbaby. Calm down, take a deep breath and tell us what you did that you think is so unforgivable that you have to hide it. It might not be as bad as you think," said her mother. She kissed her daughter on the forehead and stroked her hair.

Tee reached for a nearby box of tissue, pulled out a few and handed them to her. She wanted to reveal her sister's secret badly, but she swore that she wouldn't.

"Tell him, Sandy," she said sternly. "Give yourself some peace."

Patrick leaned over to his wife, kissed her on the lips and whispered softly in her ear. "I know about you and Armondo. I love you, and I forgive you." He turned toward Dr. Walker and his in-laws, "Everyone, will you please give me and my wife some time alone. We need to talk."

Everyone quietly left the room. Sandy looked at her husband in bewilderment, "You know, Patrick? How? Did Tee tell you?"

"No. I didn't know she knew. I was in the office today and went to look for a pen on your desk. My arm brushed against the mouse, and your email came up. I guess you forgot to log out. I saw the email Armondo sent you questioning the paternity of our child. I followed your conversation stream. I saw you told him to leave you alone and how the only man you want is me. I haven't been at the office working on a patient. I've been in my car praying. I was so angry with you. I even thought about leaving you. God told me to put aside my anger and love my wife. We may not be perfect, but you and the children are my world. This is my fault. If I hadn't cheated on you with Sheniqua, you would have never felt that you needed Armondo."

"I'm so sorry, Patrick. I was so gosh darn…."

Patrick silenced her with another kiss. "I don't need details, nor do I want them. You said you're sorry, and I forgive you. I know how you feel. I felt better after I told you about my affair. Once it was out in the open, I could let the guilt, the shame and the sorrow go. Let it all go. I need you and the child you are carrying well. I'm hurt, but I'll be fine. Right now, I'm not planning on going anywhere."

Patrick kissed his wife again. This time slow, long and passionately. By the time he finished, Sandy felt lighter. Her heart was lighter. Her mind was lighter. Her spirit was lighter. She felt so heavy the past few months. The guilt was like 500 pound weights chained to her ankles. She was so relieved. She loved Patrick deeply, and it did her heart good to know that he wasn't angry with her.

She asked Patrick to tell her mother and sister everything was fine and to leave because she wanted to get some rest. She also asked him to ask Dr. Walker to come back later, and she would answer any questions she had. Sandy was tired. She hadn't slept well in months and she had a strong feeling she and the baby were going to sleep well tonight. Sandy felt so good she forgot Armondo said he was coming.

Although Patrick tried to whisper, Tee heard him say he knew about the affair and he forgave her sister. After witnessing that, she knew she had to go to her husband. She shared her plans to leave for Akron that night with her mother. Momma Pearl encouraged her to go. She would help look after Sandy.

"I think that's a wise decision. A wife's place is with her husband. Baby, can I ask you a question?"

"Yes, ma'am."

"I'm not familiar with that word Sandy used. What is friggin'?"

Tee smiled. "Momma, I have no idea. Sounds ridiculous, doesn't it?"

Chapter 35

Slap Attack

Tiffany was three hours late for her spa appointment at Urban Xscape. The receptionist told her they were completely booked for the day but if she was patient, she would try to work her in. They had a special private party and would be servicing several people at one time. Tiffany tried to patronize black businesses whenever she could, and she absolutely loved this place. Their prices were reasonable. Their customer service was excellent with great extras like free beverages and sweets for their patrons. She planned to get a facial, a manicure and a pedicure.

While she sat in the waiting room eating chocolate covered strawberries, a group of eight young ladies, who looked to be in their late teens and early 20's entered. She watched as the receptionist ushered them into the back. Tiffany let out an exasperated sigh. She had been sitting for an hour. Perhaps, she should reschedule for another day. She stood to tell the receptionist she was leaving when one of the young ladies from the party approached her.

"Miss, are you waiting to be serviced?"

"Why yes, I am. I was late, and I lost my appointment, but I'm tired of waiting for a new spot to open up. I think I'm going to reschedule," answered Tiffany.

"No need to do that," said the young lady. "One of my sorority sisters didn't show up, and we have an extra slot available if you would like to join us."

"Thank you, but I don't want to intrude. I'm sure you want to have girl talk with your sisters."

"It's no intrusion. Please join us. I insist. You look like you could really use a day at the spa," said the young lady very sweetly.

"You have no idea," Tiffany said. "Thank you so much."

She wasn't about to tell the child in front of her that she was tired from having sex repeatedly with her baby's daddy. Quincy behaved as if he were trying to make up for all the times they hadn't had sex in the past couple of months. She tried to persuade him to come back later that evening, but he told her he was leaving to go out of town on business for a few days and wanted it all right then and there.

Tiffany followed the young lady to Urban Xscape's private party room. An esthetician was in there applying mud masks to a few of the other young ladies' faces. The rest of them were in the corner of the room stretched out on tables waiting for a massage. After the mud masks were applied, they were instructed to sit in the large spa pedicure chairs in the middle of the room with their feet in warm swirling water. Tiffany took off her clothes and put on one of the spa-issued white terry cloth robes. She was instructed to sit in one of the chairs as well. She carefully slid her feet in the blue water. It was warm and relaxing.

She was grateful for the young lady's kindness. The two of them didn't even exchange names. She made a mental note to properly introduce herself before she left. The girls chatted about boys, classes and parties—typical college life. Tiffany tried to act as if she wasn't listening because they were not talking directly to her. The esthetician soon came over and applied mud to her face. It began to tighten in a matter of minutes. She hated that taut feeling, but loved how soft and smooth her skin was afterward. She looked at the two young ladies on each side of her. She admired their lean, toned bodies. She reminisced on her pre-cellulite, pre-stretch mark days. Back then, her breasts were perky without the help of custom-made bras. These days her girdle and Spanx helped her keep all those extra pounds hidden when she wanted to put on something tight and sexy.

She closed her eyes and enjoyed the moment. A hard slap across her face abruptly interrupted her enjoyment. She opened her eyes to find herself surrounded by six of the girls. Some of them looked like zombies in a horror movie. They had the cracked green mud on their faces, and they all looked menacing. She looked around frantically. Where had all the workers gone? Her face stung in the place where the slap landed.

"What was that for?" she yelled.

"It's for the hell you put me and my family through, you whore. I bet you have no idea who I am, do you? I'm Quincetta Matthews," said the young lady who invited her to join them.

She wondered why she didn't recognize her before. Tiffany had seen her picture in Quincy's wallet several times. She was Quincy's oldest daughter and the spitting image of her father. She had his wiry build and his long nose, eyes and eyebrows. Tiffany didn't know what to do or say. She had no idea she even knew who her father's mistress was. This girl probably hated her. She tried to get out of the pedicure spa chair, but was pushed back down and reprimanded with another slap to her face.

"You might as well get comfy cuz you ain't going nowhere until I say you can," said Quincetta.

She tried to scream for help, but one of the other girls slapped her again and told her to shut her face. Tiffany tried to get up again. Two girls on each side of her grabbed her arms and pinned her against the cushions of the chair. The chair's built in-massager was accidently activated and the rollers within the seat cushion began moving against her back and buttocks. Under normal conditions, Tiffany would have enjoyed the massage but with the girls pushing her down against the robotic rollers, it was extremely painful. She winced but didn't scream for fear of being slapped again.

"I knew this day would come," said Quincetta. "I used to imagine how I would tell you what a tramp I think you are. I've never seen a more pathetic excuse for a woman than you. Having sex with a married man for years, giving birth to his bastard child and then you had the nerve to give him my father's name like that makes him legitimate or something. The only reason me and my girls aren't dragging you by your hair around this room is because my daddy finally came to his senses and left your trifling behind. But you better trust that if you ever try to mess with him again, I won't be so nice. Leave my father alone!

"Life at our house has been so much better since you've been gone. My father is home more and spends more time with me and my sisters. My mother smiles more. She's nicer to everyone around her. They even renewed their wedding vows last weekend and are leaving for a second honeymoon tomorrow. I don't know what he saw in your fat butt. You look so fake with all that make up and those spider looking eyelashes. Don't you ever come near my father again! In case you are not completely comprehending how serious I am, we're gonna give you a spa visit you'll never forget. Bianca, go get her stuff."

A fat young lady with an afro puff went to the back of the room and retrieved Tiffany's belongings from the hook where she placed them when she entered the room and disrobed.

Tiffany watched in horror as Quincetta dipped her clothes in the blue pedicure water while another girl poured the mud mask in her Prada purse. She struggled to get up, but the girls held her tight in the chair. The massagers continued to press hard into her skin.

Tiffany screamed.

"I said shut up," said the girl who slapped her last and stuffed a wad of cotton balls in her mouth. Tiffany sat helplessly watching the girls as they poured mud mask over her head and rubbed it into her hair. She closed her eyes to keep it from getting in them as the concoction oozed down her face. They even put mud in her shoes.

They all laughed as Quincetta took her pants and shirt out of the water, stooped down and mopped the floor with them.

"Wait, I have a better idea," she said. "Let's do what you normally do with trash and put her out. I hope this makes you think twice before you screw another woman's husband, slut."

The girls dragged Tiffany kicking and attempting to scream to the back door of the private room. It was a fire exit and led outside to the alley located behind the spa. One girl opened the door wide and another one ripped the terrycloth robe from her body. Tiffany was hurled outside into the alley with nothing on but her hot pink Frederick's of Hollywood bra and thong. She landed on the ground and scraped her hands and left leg. The steel door slammed hard behind her. A few seconds later it opened again and someone tossed her mud-filled purse, shoes and her sopping wet clothes in her direction. Some of the contents of her purse spilled out as it careened through the air. It hit her on her ample bottom as she lay there in the chilly November air encircled in embarrassment. One shoe hit her in the back of the head and the other landed at her feet. The girls laughed and slammed the door closed, again.

Several people were passing by as she was being ejected from the building and stopped to see what was going on. Some looked at her in horror. One couple laughed, and a male passerby whistled at her, told her that he liked her "assets" and asked if she needed a ride. Tiffany pulled the cotton balls from her mouth. She was not going to lie there for their entertainment. She hauled herself off the ground, picked up her purse and searched for her keys and wallet within the muddy muck. Luckily, they were still inside along with her cell phone, but her makeup and various toiletry items littered the ground. She decided to let them stay there, as well as her clothes and shoes. They were ruined anyway. She ran to her car barefoot. She pressed the button to remotely unlock the driver's side door but in her haste to get her scantily clad body out of view, she dropped her keys. She stooped down to retrieve them and realized that both tires on the driver's side were slashed. She didn't dare stay a minute longer. She opened the car door, got in and started the engine. Her car's diagnostic system alerted her that all four of her tires were void of air. She didn't care. She was leaving. She pressed the gas pedal and endured the bumpy ride as she drove out of the parking lot on her expensive rims.

Tiffany knew she couldn't drive all the way home on her rims because she would ruin them. The Audi dealership where she purchased the car was nearby. She found some tissues within her car to wipe her Blackberry off as best she could and called William, the salesman who assisted her and Quincy when they selected the car. She quickly explained her tires were slashed and she needed to get them fixed as soon as possible. She told him that she had no intentions of coming in the dealership, and she needed to have a courtesy car waiting for her when she arrived. William said he understood and told Tiffany to meet him at the far end of the parking lot to save her further embarrassment.

William thought Tiffany didn't want to come in the dealership because she was the embarrassed victim of a tire slashing. He wasn't prepared for the mess he saw when the usually impeccably put together Tiffany Tate drove on her rims into the lot. Her hair and face were caked with hard green mud. Splotches of it were also on her body and undergarments. He tried not to stare, but it was hard to keep his eyes off her curvaceous figure. He liked his women thick. He offered her his jacket, which she readily accepted. William then helped her transfer her belongings to the courtesy car, and he assured her he would personally drive her vehicle out to her home when the repairs where completed. Tiffany thanked William for his kindness and asked him not discuss what he saw with anyone. He agreed. Tiffany was relieved he didn't ask any questions.

If what Quincetta said was true, Quincy had no intention of leaving his wife. You don't renew vows with someone you are planning to divorce. He told her he was leaving to go out of town on business, and he was actually going on a second honeymoon. That meant the separation papers he gave her must be false. Quincy tried to trick her into dropping her child support case against him but not only that, he also tricked her into letting him back into her bed. She didn't want to believe he would really stoop that low to protect his finances but she had to admit it was possible.

Tiffany was angry and humiliated, but she wasn't only angry with Quincy, Quincetta and those horrid little monsters who helped her, but she was angry with herself. How could she have been so stupid? Tiffany finally had to face the facts. Quincy had no intentions of ever leaving his wife for her. She was for his personal pleasure and that's all she would ever be.

If this was God's way of making it plain, she got the point. She cranked up the car and drove home to take a shower before she went to pick Quincy 2 up from her parent's house. On the way, she called her lawyer and alerted her to Quincy's underhanded attempt to get her to drop her case. Daddy was no longer welcome in her home, in her bed or in her life, but he was going to take care of his child whether he wanted to or not.

Chapter 36

I Got Your Back

Tee went home and packed herself a bag. She didn't know how long she would need to stay in Akron, but she packed clothes for five days to make sure she had enough. With so much activity, she wasn't able to watch television but she received news alerts on her phone all day. Her husband was still a hot topic on all the major news stations. She checked the answering machine at home and there were several interview requests from inquiring media. She had missed calls on her cell from numbers she didn't recognize. She wished they would leave them alone. They had no proof of any wrongdoing, only the testimony of a bitter man who refused to give any facts regarding the matter before he met with the NCAA.

Tee dropped Chesnutt off at a pet motel and by 7 p.m., she was on the highway, headed to her in-laws. Seeing Sandy and Patrick in a tender moment made her miss Michael even more. She repeated to herself the attributes of love found in the book of Proverbs. She needed to be reminded that this wasn't all about her any more. "Love is patient. Love is kind. Love is long-suffering. It keeps no record of wrongdoing. Love conquers all," she whispered softly to herself. "Here I come, Michael Stokes whether you like it or not."

Tee pulled in front of her in-laws' house at about 8 a.m. It was a long drive. She got sleepy along the way and parked at a truck stop to rest. She slept a little longer than she intended and probably would have slept longer if a bum hadn't knocked on her window asking for spare change.

As she was getting out her truck, Michael exited the house. He looked upset. She prayed all the way there that he wouldn't be mad that she came after he told her not to. He ran toward her, swept her off the ground and kissed her on the lips.

"I've never been happier to see you in all my life. I'm ready to go home if you are. We can leave right now."

The words escaped his mouth swiftly, and Tee wasn't sure she heard him right. "What? Ready to go? I just got here. Can I go in the house and speak to your parents first? Why are you in such a hurry to leave?"

"I just got back and no one is here. They are all out, and I am really ready to go. Let me go upstairs and grab my bag, and we can leave."

He was running from something, and Tee knew when Michael ran it was usually to avoid dealing with an emotional situation. She was not going to help him run without knowing all the details.

"Did you tell anyone you were leaving? I know you're not going to leave without telling Michelle goodbye. She'll be crushed. What's wrong with you, Michael? Did you go running this morning? Why are you sweating so much?" she asked.

Michael's bald head looked like it was raining outside instead of sunny with no clouds in sight. He wanted to leave now and forget the things he'd learned.

"Let's go inside," she suggested.

Michael took her bag in one hand and held her hand with the other as they walked inside the house. Tee followed him upstairs to his bedroom. There he told her everything that occurred since he left Miami. Except, he omitted the call he received from the woman who sounded like Becca. He refused to believe she was alive because there was too much evidence that she wasn't. Tee could see the pain in Michael's eyes as he recounted the details of his conversation with Peter and his father. He felt betrayed and used by all parties involved. Tee convinced him to stay a litter longer and try to reason with his father. It always puzzled her how her man could take a hit on the football field as well as any other NFL player, but when it came to a hit on his heart or his feelings, he had to run, hide and avoid whoever it was that was hurting him. It was time for him to stop running.

Michael agreed to stay in Akron but insisted they check into a hotel. He wanted some alone time with her. He finally knew what it was like to need someone who wasn't related to him or doing business with him. For most of his life, he had been pretty self-sufficient. When it came to women or relationships, other than his first girlfriend in college and Becca, he could take them or leave them. Tee made him better. Her mere presence made him feel stronger. When he looked out the window and saw her sitting in her Denali, it was one of the most beautiful sights he ever saw. He was glad she ignored his instructions to stay away. He wasn't by himself anymore. Mr. *and* Mrs. Stokes would face this thing with his father together.

He and his father needed to talk, but he wouldn't be home for hours. Michael still needed time to figure out the best way to approach this matter. In the meantime, he tried to cheer himself up by spending time with two of his favorite girls. He and Tee went to breakfast, and afterward, they picked Michelle up from school and took her to the aquarium. She made him feel better, too.

Chapter 37

Sister, Sister

Lenora enjoyed being able to spend time with her sister. Before she met Herman, they were together all the time. Their time together decreased after she got married. And once the babies started coming they had even less time together.

Lenora's doctor gave her a clean bill of health. He told her to avoid the diet pills and focus on losing weight through diet and exercise. Lenice decided to use a couple of vacation days and took it upon herself to become Lenora's personal trainer and nutritionist. Lenice was going to show her sister how to take the weight off the right way. She had never been over weight, but she had a passion for health and fitness. She worked out regularly and watched what she ate. Not because she didn't want to get fat but because she wanted to live a long, healthy life. The day after Lenora was discharged from the hospital, the two of them, along with Webster, got up at 7 a.m. and went for a brisk walk in a nearby park. Then, they returned to the house for some light weight lifting. It was followed by a low calorie breakfast of fruit and cottage cheese. Lenora yearned for some pancakes dripping in butter and sweet maple syrup with sausage and scrambled eggs with cheese. But, she realized that it was those eating habits that put her in this unhealthy state. She was surprised that she actually enjoyed the sliced pineapples, peaches and oranges. The cottage cheese wasn't all that bad either.

After their showers, the twins changed clothes and headed to see a movie at the Throwback Theatre. It specialized in second run and classic movies. The middle of the day was the perfect time to go because hardly anyone was in the theater. They went to see an oldie but goodie called *12 Angry Men* starring Peter Fonda. Lenice had motives behind selecting that movie. She often used it in her effective leadership communication training sessions at work. In the movie, Peter Fonda's character, Juror #8, was able to change the minds of 11 other jurors who were ready to sentence a young man to death for allegedly killing his father. Fonda's reasoning and persuasion techniques were brilliant. By the end of their jury deliberation, he got them all to agree the young man was not guilty and saved his life. Even the toughest guy in the room had to admit that he wasn't guilty. She hoped seeing Fonda stand up and defend his beliefs to 11 other men, with differing opinions, would give Lenora some inclination of how to stand up to one man.

Lenora was feeling better already. It's amazing what a different environment can do. She missed her children terribly but she needed a few days for herself. Herman called her cell phone several times, but she refused to answer. She wasn't ready to talk to him, again. She never knew she could become so wrapped up in someone else that she no longer cared for her own well-being. After they returned from the movie, Lenice told her she was going to the store to get some groceries so she could show Lenora how to fix a few easy low-calorie dishes a little later. Lenora decided to take a nap.

Lenice decided to take a less abrasive approach when it came to Lenora and her marriage. So far, she hadn't mentioned Herman's name once. She wanted to yell at her sister and shake some sense into her, but she knew that would only make matters worse. She would let her sister come to her own decision in her own time. Lenice's main goal was to help Lenora find herself again. She used to have her own opinions and way of doing things. Lenice didn't recognize or like the subservient, people pleaser her sister was now. She wondered what kind of hold Herman had on Lenora to turn her into such a spineless, wavering creature. She wanted the old Lenora back, and she was going to do everything she could to make it happen. She had more tricks up her sleeve.

Lenora woke up from her nap to find an easel, three new canvases and a paint kit with an assortment of colors placed at the foot of her bed. She felt like a little kid on Christmas morning. She ripped the packaging off each item and began working on a masterpiece right then and there. She hadn't painted in years, unless you counted finger painting with her children. The brush felt good in her hands. Lenora mixed colors together in order to create more shades to work with. She didn't stop to contemplate what she should paint. She let her hands guide her instinctively as her brush swept across the canvas with precise strokes. She thought about all the things she drew and painted in college that were hidden away in her garage. She hadn't looked at them in years. Her art supplies were there as well. When she got home, she was going to dig them out and find a place in her home that would be suitable for a studio. She was going to do something nice for herself for a change.

About an hour later, Lenice knocked on the door to see if she was ready to prepare dinner. Lenora's clothes and face contained flecks of paint that clearly indicated she wasn't. She was so involved in her painting that she completely forgot about their evening healthy cooking lesson.

"Can we play Betty Crocker tomorrow?" asked Lenora.

"Webster and I will cook dinner by ourselves tonight and put a plate in the microwave for you. Eat it whenever you are ready."

Lenora didn't wait for the answer before she returned to her painting.

"Okay. Sure. Whatever," she absently answered. She then thought about what her sister said and yelled, "Keep that dog away from my food! Pets have no business in the kitchen!"

Lenice smiled to herself. Her plan was working.

Chapter 38

Little Girl Lost

Michael finally received the call he was waiting on. He hoped Dr. Foster had some good news. He was full of questions. Even though she wasn't really a doctor, when they met she was undercover and pretending to be one. Out of habit, he continued to address her with that title.

"It took me a while to find out who she really is, but Becca's real name is Elizabeth Margaret Taylor. It seems her mother was a big fan of the actress. She grew up in a small town called Stage Coach, Texas," said Dr. Foster. "Turns out what she told you was true. Her father was a doctor, and her mother was a lawyer. They met when her mother was taken to the hospital after having a schizophrenic episode. At the time, her father was a medical school student doing residency there. He wasn't intimidated by her illness, and they started dating. I'm told Becca's mother was a brilliant woman and as long as she stayed on her meds she was fine. But when she wasn't she was prone to acts of violence. Seems she got her schizophrenia under control and went to law school. After she passed the bar, Becca's parents got married."

"Her mental illness was probably hereditary. How were you able to find that out?" asked Michael.

"I talked to her old neighbors. Becca lived in the same house from the time she was born until the time her parents died in that car accident. I went by the house and met this talkative elderly couple, Phillip and Allie Baker. They said they used to babysit Becca and her brother. The Baker's talked about how pretty and smart she was. They also talked about how her parents caused quite a stir in the neighborhood when they moved in. A lot of their white neighbors didn't take kindly to having an interracial couple in their neighborhood. They even had a few death threats. People still wonder if their car accident was really an accident. Anyway, they said after her cousin, Preston, got custody of them, Becca and her brother never came over to their house again Preston wouldn't allow it. I was even able to locate him. The town is so small everyone one knows everyone. Preston relocated to Austin."

"Great! What did he have to say?" asked Michael.

"He couldn't say anything. He's dead. He was brutally murdered about a month ago. According to what I saw in the police investigation files, he was a two-bit hustler, and the cops figured somebody got tired of his hustling ways and took him out. But I don't think so."

"Why not?"

"You told me her cousin made Becca become a child prostitute, right?"

"That's what she told me," said Michael.

"Well, her cousin was found dressed like a life-size doll. He had on panties, stockings, patent leather shoes, makeup—the whole nine. The dress had holes in it because he was stabbed multiple times and the words *kiddie pimp* were carved into his forehead. The coroner's report said he was dressed up and then stabbed over a period of hours, meaning he was tortured before he was killed."

"That's a horrible way to go. Sounds like Preston might have tried to do what he did to Becca to someone else and they decided to take revenge," said Michael.

"Do you think that maybe Becca got to him? With everyone thinking she's dead that would be the perfect time…"

"Becca is dead, Dr. Foster. D-E-A-D, dead. You're the one who killed her, remember?"

"I know, Michael, but this keeps getter weirder and weirder. I like to explore all options. Even the farfetched ones."

"I can agree that this is getting weird, but Becca is six feet under. Any leads on her brother, Cameron?" asked Michael.

"Not yet, but his real name isn't Cameron. It's Sean Connery Taylor. Their father was a huge James Bond fan."

"They sure did like movies. I appreciate your helping me, Dr. Foster"

"Don't mention it. You're like one of my grandsons now. I have to look out for you. Besides, you pay me really well," Dr. Foster chuckled.

Chapter 39

Daddy Dearest

Sandy stayed in the hospital another day. After her confession, her mood and health improved drastically. The baby's heartbeat was now normal, but the doctors wanted her to take it easy and released her to go home with strict orders to remain on bed rest. Momma Pearl came to stay with the Pierce family for as long as they needed. Patrick cut his hours back at work to half days and hired another dentist to take on his afternoon clients. He spent the extra time doting on his wife. It wounded him deeply that she gave herself to another man, but he had more important things to worry about than himself. His wife and their unborn child needed him. He was grateful for his mother-in-law's assistance. That gave him more time to focus on Sandy. Today, he crawled in bed with her for the majority of the afternoon. Patrick massaged her legs and feet, kissed her belly and talked to the little girl within. He even read to her. As far as he was concerned, this entire mess was his fault. His indiscretion with Sheniqua initiated a series of unfortunate events that landed them here. Neither of them brought up what if the baby wasn't his. It was the elephant in the room they both tried to ignore, for the time being. Patrick wanted his life back to normal and having a baby who possessed his DNA would allow that to happen.

But there were also moments that he didn't want to be around her. On those days, he spent more time with their children. Donovin reminded him so much of himself. He was handsome with a strong affinity for math and science. Nicole was his little princess. She liked frilly clothes and never went anywhere without her purse. It was generally filled with lip gloss and tissue, and her wallet contained whatever monies the seven year old collected from around the house. Patrick often left dollars and quarters where he knew she could find them just to see her face light up at her discovery. At night, when he went to check on them he found himself standing in the doorway admiring his gifts as they slept soundly in their beds.

Unbeknownst to Sandy, Patrick changed her password and was checking her email regularly. He did not want anything or anyone upsetting his wife. He saw the email Armondo sent stating he received permission from his superiors to come home but there hadn't been another one since then. In anticipation of his arrival, Patrick purchased a brand new 38 Smith and Wesson. There was no way Armondo was coming anywhere near his wife or their baby.

Chapter 40

Lights, Camera, Action

Tee and Michael couldn't believe their eyes. Peter was on TV doing an interview with Ultimate Sports. He talked about how tired he was of the dishonesty and the lack of integrity in sports, and that's why he came forth with the sordid details of how NFL great Michael Stokes rose to his iconic football status. He said he wasn't at liberty to give details right now, but he assured everyone they would be shocked. He claimed he had a private meeting with the NCAA soon and would give his statement then, complete with corroborating evidence.

Tee was fed up with Peter and was determined to find out why he was doing this. Last year, she coordinated a benefit dinner with NBC News anchorwoman Solay Peterson as the keynote speaker. The ladies talked occasionally, and Tee decided to reach out to her to see what she could find out. She called her cell phone, and Solay answered on the first ring.

"Girl you must have ESP. I was going to call you. My producer knows we're cool and asked me to see if I could get an interview with Michael. How are the two of you doing?"

"Under the circumstances, we're pretty good but Michael isn't doing any interviews until he knows exactly what Peter has up his sleeve."

"I can tell you that," said Solay. "He's trying to ruin Michael's career and make himself a celebrity in the process."

"What? How do you know that?"

"He's been calling every sports show on the planet to land an interview but initially, no one would bite because he wouldn't give any details to work with. It seems Ultimate Sports took him up on his offer in exchange for a promise to have the first interview when he could give more details. Peter claims he can't tell the media what he has before he tells the NCAA, but he wants an abundance of face time on TV anyway. I used to work at Ultimate Sports, and I still keep in touch with several of the people there. He told the host when the cameras were off he was tired of working with ungrateful athletes. He was tired of busting his butt to elevate them into the position of earthly gods and not being credited properly. Peter is trying to make himself a celebrity this time. He's pitching himself for sports commentator jobs and anything close to it. This will allow him to start commanding the big bucks for himself. And in this business everybody loves a scandal. It's the quickest way to get your name in the paper, that and reality TV. I'm sure he'll even do that if asked. I wouldn't be surprised if we saw Peter on an upcoming season of "The Apprentice."

"This is all starting to make sense now," said Tee. "Thanks for the info, Solay. When and if Michael decides to do an interview, you will be the first to know."

"Thanks, girl. I appreciate it. I'm praying for you two and you need to make a trip to New York so we can have a girl's night out."

"Sure thing. When this blows over I'm going to need one. Talk to you later."

Tee had to figure out how she could use this information to Michael's advantage because her gut was telling her things were going to get worse before they got better. Peter was determined to smear the Stokes name in order to make one for himself.

Chapter 41

Say It Ain't So

"Mom, come here quick!"

"Boy, you know I'm not supposed to get out of bed!" Sandy yelled to Donovin.

"Oh yeah, I forgot!" He ran into his mother's room with his laptop. Nicole was right behind him. To help keep his mother entertained, he often found funny videos online. Sandy wondered what he wanted her to see this time. She was feeling a little restless today and could use a good laugh.

"Ms. Tiffany's on YouTube getting her butt kicked," Donovin announced. He placed his laptop in the bed beside his mother.

"Let me see," said Sandy.

He clicked the play button and sure enough, there was Tiffany being held down in a chair and slapped by what appeared to be a bunch of young girls, but their faces were distorted to prevent them from being identified. She watched in horror, with her hand covering her mouth, as Tiffany was humiliated on camera for the world to see. After the girls shoved Tiffany out the back door in her underwear, the video faded to black and several words scrolled across the screen. *This is what happens to women who sleep with other people's husbands and threaten to break up their homes. If you need our help dial 1-800-Slap-A-Slut and we'll help you get your husband back.*

"Say it ain't so," said Sandy

"It is so," said Nicole.

"Yeah, Miss Tiffany got pimp slapped!" said Donovin and pretended to slap his little sister.

Nicole found it amusing, laughed and pretended to slap him back.

Sandy needed a reason for them to leave the laptop without putting up a fight, so she pretended to be angry.

"Both of you get out of my room and stay out of grown folk's business. Leave your laptop here and go read a book. Evidently, you can't find anything better to do with your time than watch violence and then imitate it. Donovin, don't you ever let me see you hit a girl. Don't even pretend."

"Aw, Mom. I was just playing. I don't hit girls," he said.

"Don't aw Mom me. Get out of here before you get pimp slapped."

After they walked out, she reached for the cordless phone on the nightstand and dialed Tiffany's number. It went straight to voicemail. She left a message asking her to call her because she wanted to check on her. The next call Sandy made was to Tee. She wasn't going to believe this. Michael wasn't the only person who had to worry about negative media attention.

Chapter 42

Tee to the Rescue

Tee was tired of seeing Peter's crooked grin on television. After his interview aired on Ultimate Sports, it seemed the other sports shows didn't want to be left out and one by one they were all interviewing him. Not only was he on television but also the radio, internet and in the papers. Michael found out that his meeting with the NCAA was almost a week away, giving Peter plenty of time to make his rounds with the media to tell them how he had some information on Michael Stokes that was going to shock the world but he couldn't tell what it was yet. It made no sense.

She and Michael devised a plan to try to convince Michael, Sr. to hold a press conference before Peter's NCAA meeting admitting what he did and that Michael had no knowledge of his wrongdoing. That should take some of the wind out of Peter's sails.

So far, Michael Sr. had been uncooperative. He was willing to admit his sins to the NCAA privately, but he had no desire to issue a public apology.

Michael was still avoiding the media, but he did allow his lawyer to issue a statement in his behalf. Edgar told them that Michael had no knowledge of inappropriate donations by University of Miami boosters, and he would respond further after he received all of the details concerning the allegations. But that didn't stop the media from calling relentlessly. He left the suite that morning to go exercise. Sweating it out in the gym would do him some good. There was a private facility that allowed him to come there whenever he was in town. Doing so, allowed him to work out without being disturbed by fans or the media. He seemed to be doing well, but he was very concerned about how this could affect his speaking engagements, book sales and other deals. So far, his endorsements with McDonald's, Nike and Gatorade were still solid. They were probably waiting to see what information Peter had, too.

Tee realized that spending time with her and Michelle was helping him stay calm. Michael seemed to really enjoy their visit to the aquarium the day before. He paid the facility handsomely to shut down for an hour so they could have some peace. Michelle had a way of making him smile whenever she was around, and she adored him. She didn't care about media reports, controversy or Corvettes. All she knew was Uncle Mike was on TV and to her that was cool.

Tee had work to do. While Michael was gone, she completed conference calls with her clients. Sheba continued to impress her. She was knowledgeable of the business and seemed to need very little direction to complete assigned tasks. Tee still wasn't sure if she could be trusted, but she did have confidence in her skills.

Sandy called as she was preparing for her next conference call. She gave her the rundown of the "Tiffany Tate Show" that recently surfaced online. Tee found the video on her iPad and watched in disbelief. It angered her to see her good friend being publicly humiliated. It didn't take her long to recognize where the assault took place. She rented the private room at Urban Xscape several times to host pamper parties for her most valued female clients.

She tried to call Tiffany herself, and it went straight to voice mail. Tee sent her a text to call her ASAP. If she were home, she would have driven to Tiffany's house but since she wasn't, she would have to do whatever she could from Akron. She decided to find out who recorded the video and see if she could get it taken down before it went viral. According to the YouTube view counter, it had already been viewed 100 times. Most of them were probably kids like Donovin. Perhaps, she could save Tiffany further embarrassment.

Tee called Trixy, the manager at Urban Xscape, and asked her the date of Tiffany's last visit. It was the day before. She then asked what group of girls used the private room the same time she was there. Normally, Trixy wouldn't give out such private information, but she was extremely grateful for the thousands of dollars worth of business Tee brought her establishment annually. She eagerly told her a group of sorority girls booked the room to celebrate their crossing. Tee asked which sorority and almost started cussing when Trixy told her it was her own sorority, Phi Beta Pi. She loved her sorority, and she wasn't keen on the fact they appeared to have inducted a group of bullies into their sisterhood. She asked who reserved the room and was given the name Diana Mason. Tiffany thanked Trixy for the information and called the undergraduate chapter advisor, Soror Graham, to inquire about the new inductees. Tee was very active in the Memphis alumni chapter of her sorority and spoke with several of the other members often. Soror Graham was all too happy to talk about the new members. She was quite proud of them and was pleased that Tee was taking an interest in them. She bragged about how they had wonderful GPAs, were extremely active on campus and would be an asset to the sorority. She gave Tee Diana's number and encouraged her to mentor as many of them as possible. Tee called her immediately.

"Hello, may I speak to Diana?" asked Tee.

"This is Princess Diana," she said playfully.

"This is Soror Tina Long. How are you?"

"You mean THE Tina Long? OMG you're like a legend in this chapter. I heard no body could step like you, and you won all kinds of awards when you were here. We really appreciate how you give back to the chapter now that you're all famous and stuff. We couldn't believe you got Rihanna to stop by the Pan Hellenic Step Show last year. People are still talking about how ill it was! I hear this year Icy Blak might perform during homecoming. I think he's the best rapper ever! He's cute, too. Do you think you could introduce me? I am honored to have you call my phone," spouted Diane with awe-struck excitement.

"Thank you, Diana. I am calling to congratulate you and your line sister's on becoming a member of Phi Beta Pi. I hope you realize what an honor it is to be selected to join us. We don't accept just anyone. Only ladies of excellence will do."

"Boy, don't I know it. I had three interviews before being selected to go through the intake process, but it was soooo worth it. I've met some wonderful women. It means so much to me that you would call me personally."

"It is my pleasure," Tee said sweetly. "I'm going to do something even better. I would like to get something special for you and the other young ladies on your line. How many of you are there?"

"There are nine of us in all. We call ourselves the Divine Nine," Diane said proudly.

"That's a cute name. Do you mind giving me all of your first and last names? I want to get the items monogrammed for you."

"Not at all." Diane provided Tee with each of their first and last names, complete with their line numbers and line names.

"Now, there is one more thing I need you to do for me," said Tee.

"Oh anything, Soror Long. You name it."

Tee's demeanor went from nice to nasty in an instance. "Whoever put that video up of you and your line sisters abusing my friend Tiffany Tate better get it down within the next 10 minutes! I now have each of your names, and I will turn them in to the police and campus judicial affairs. Soror or not, I will make sure you are prosecuted to the fullest extent of the law. I will get each of you ejected from your chapter and kicked off campus quicker than you can say Phi Beta Pi. The only stepping you'll be doing is in a jail cell, and the only degree you'll be able to get is online. Have I made myself clear, Soror Mason?"

Diane was so scared she almost wet her pants. Her parents would kill her if she got kicked out of school.

"But it wasn't my idea," she squealed. "Quincetta said she wanted to teach her father's jump off a lesson and…"

"I don't remember asking for an explanation, young lady. I am taking your assault on Ms. Tate personal. Get that video down now and destroy it! If it ever surfaces again you and your entire line will regret it. Don't play with me, little girl. I've got enough pull in this sorority and this city to make or break every one of you. Do as I told you and you'll be safe. Don't and suffer the consequences."

"Does that mean you're not getting us any gifts?" asked Diana.

"Are you slow? My gift to you is a stay out of jail card if you do as I told you."

She hung up the phone before Diana could respond and waited ten minutes before checking YouTube again. She smiled to herself when she tried to play the video and a "This Content Has Been Removed by the User" message popped up on the screen. Mission accomplished! She wished she could fix Michael's problem as easily.

Tee attempted to call Tiffany again, but she still didn't answer. She left another message asking her to call her back. She needed to give the twins a call as well. She knew Lenora was staying with Lenice for a few days to recuperate. She wondered how they were both doing.

Chapter 43

Love Hurts

Lenice was falling in love and she knew it. She was doing almost everything her therapist told her not to do. She told her not to focus on one man but to go out with several men to help get herself back into the dating game, but Lenice wasn't interested in any man other than James. She also told her not to get serious and not to have sex, either. Abstaining was the only part she seemed to be listening to. But she wanted to get very serious with James. She hadn't seen or heard much from him lately because she was attending to Lenora, and Lenice missed his company. They were scheduled to go to dinner tonight, but she was considering canceling to spend the evening with Lenora and the kids. Family first. She agreed to pick up Hermie, Heather and Heston after work and bring them home with her. Perhaps she should give them some time alone. She was sure the children missed their mother and probably wanted her all to themselves.

Lenora was doing much better. She happily spent her days exercising, eating less, job hunting and painting. She wouldn't show Lenice what she was working on but whatever it was, it was keeping her occupied. She was painting day and night.

Since Lenora didn't seem to need her, Lenice went to work that morning. She was now on her lunch break and waiting for the waitress at Tony's Pizza to bring her the thick slice of veggie delight she ordered. Her mouth was already watering for the spinach, tomatoes, olives, artichoke pieces, mozzarella and Feta cheese treat. She searched her purse for her hand sanitizer and couldn't find it. Lenice was a stickler for sanitation and headed to the restrooms in the back of the restaurant to wash her hands. She spotted James sitting in a booth with another woman. As the woman spoke, he looked at her tenderly and intently. They looked like they were having a very serious conversation. What was going on?

Lenice moved closer. That couldn't be her James. Her James told her he liked her. What was he doing with another woman? James looked up and saw Lenice staring at him. He smiled and called her name. Rather than answer, Lenice turned around and walked away. James tried to get up, but his chair was underneath the table and he struck both thighs as he rose.

"Ouch! Lenice wait!" he shouted.

Lenice put a hand behind her head and stuck up her middle finger as she fled from the restaurant. She muttered to herself, "All men should be caged or on a leash because they are all dogs." She needed to schedule another session with her therapist soon. Dating didn't seem like such a good idea anymore.

Chapter 44

A House Is Not a Home

Herman stood outside his sister in-law's townhouse fidgeting. He wanted to push the button to ring the doorbell but couldn't bring himself to do so. Instead, he played with his keys, transferring them from one hand to another and taking them in and out of his pants pockets. He needed to apologize to his wife. He needed to tell her how much he and the children missed her. The past few days without her seemed like eternity. He knew he mistreated her. He knew he took her for granted. He looked down at his wrinkled tan shirt and black dress slacks. Lenora would never let him go out in public like this. She always made sure everything was neatly ironed. He heard his stomach growl. Lenora wasn't there to cook him meals. That morning he made oatmeal but it was a soupy, inedible mess. All three children screamed for their mother when he tried to make them eat it.

Yesterday, Hermie needed help with his spelling words but, Herman lacked patience. He became frustrated and yelled at the kindergartener after he misspelled the word duck repeatedly. Hermie ran to his room, locked the door and didn't come out until morning. That same night the twins wouldn't go to sleep. He read them three bedtime stories, gave them warm milk and threatened to spank them but nothing worked. They were not interested in going to bed, and they wouldn't let Herman go to bed, either.

Heston and Heather finally fell asleep around 2 a.m. Herman had to get right back up at 5 a.m. to get them all ready for work, school and daycare. He was tired. Also, without Lenora there to watch the twins while he was at work, he had to put them in day care. He had no idea day care was so expensive. There was no way he could continue to send them there every week. How did Lenora deal with him and them all day and make it look easy? He definitely had a new appreciation for her.

He needed and wanted his wife back. He wanted his house to feel like a home, and he wanted to feel whole again. A very important part of him was missing. He wanted to see her and hear her voice, but he feared if she did talk to him it would be to tell him she wanted a divorce. Herman couldn't get up the nerve to push the button. He turned around and walked back to his car.

Lenora stood in the window and watched him the entire time. She wanted to open the door and invite him in but couldn't. She knew they needed to talk, but she was afraid she couldn't find the words to tell him how angry she was with him right now. He needed to know how much he hurt her with his name-calling and constant complaining about her weight. She didn't think she wanted a divorce, but she was sure this separation was the best thing for her, right now. Outside of being a wife and mother, she no longer knew who she was and fulfilling those two roles were no longer enough. She watched Herman as he drove away in the Ford F-150 truck he seemed to love more than her these days. She went back to her sister's spare bedroom to finish working on her paintings. She decided she would be the bigger person and open the door to communication. But she'd let him suffer a little while longer.

Chapter 45

A Message and a Prayer

Tiffany threw herself into her work to help her forget about being attacked at the spa. Her face still hurt a little from the slaps. Luckily, there was no bruising or swelling. She wore a dress, today. But she wore thick nylon stockings, instead of her usual sheer pantyhose, to cover the scratches on her legs. She wanted to avoid any possible "what happened?" questions. However, her hands were a different story. They hurt badly from being scraped on the ground, but she was determined to work through the pain as she administered her massages during class. She also had a client that afternoon, and she wasn't going to miss the opportunity to make some money. It was almost graduation day, and she was anxious to receive her certificate of completion so she could apply for her license.

Tee's idea of giving complimentary massages to pique people's interest was working in her favor. She showed up looking her best at each appointment. The men were always smitten with her beauty and then, impressed with her technique. Some of the women appreciated her flare for style, while it was obvious others were a little jealous or intimidated by her. But their initial hostility usually dissipated after she put her magic fingers to work. Her classmates, Sierra and Siendy, informed her that Peter was moving them to Miami after graduation. He still planned to launch a national mobile massage service without her. From the way they described their living quarters, it was the same house he offered to her. She wondered if Peter propositioned them for sex, too.

Tiffany checked her cell phone after class and saw the missed phone call from Sandy and Tee as well as her text message. She didn't feel like talking to her friends today. She looked down at her left hand. She was still wearing the ring Quincy gave her. She knew she should probably take it off because it was now meaningless, but she didn't want to. This might be the only time in her life she had the opportunity to wear a ring there, and she wanted to enjoy it as long as possible.

Her attorney advised her not to have any further contact with Quincy. So far, she was doing a good job avoiding him. She was outside her school loading her equipment when Tee called her, again.

"Hi, Sugah!" she said with as much enthusiasm as she could muster.

"Tiffany girl, where have you been? We've been worried sick about you," said Tee.

"Why on earth would you be worried about me? I'm fine. Busy as a bee. Thank you so much for the referrals. Everyone I've visited has scheduled a paid appointment with me or given me a referral for someone they know who might be interested in my services. Sometimes both. The tips are good, too. I'm believing that God will keep them coming."

"He will but be patient. Rome wasn't built in a day and neither will your business. Are you alright?" asked Tee.

"Of course I am. Why wouldn't I be? How's Michael?"

It was evident Tiffany had no idea her spa experience was now a webisode or that others outside the spa even knew. Tee didn't know how to break the news to her.

"He's fine. Peter is running around telling the world he's going to ruin him but won't give any details as to how. The suspense is killing us all. How do you put together a good plan of counter attack if you don't know what kind of weapon your enemy is using?"

"That's a tough one. Well, I'm here if you need me," said Tiffany.

"I know, girl. Thanks! Have you talked to anyone else?"

"No, I've been so busy with Quincy 2, school and massages. I haven't had time. How's Sandy? She called me today, too."

"She's fine. The doctor has her on bed rest. Would you do me a favor and go visit my sister and Lenora for me? I feel bad that I can't be there for them right now."

"Honey, you are exactly where you are supposed to be. You're a wife now."

Tiffany began to sing the words to "Stand By Your Man" by country singer Loretta Lynn She actually sounded pretty good. "Sandy and Lenora both have husbands and other family members to help look after them, but I'd be happy to go see them. I need to do that anyway. They're my friends, too," she said.

"Thanks." Tee couldn't hold her tongue any longer. "Tiffany, I know what happened at the spa. I found out who did that to you. I have their names and you can have them if you want to press charges." She promised Diana she wouldn't press charges, but she never said she would prevent someone else from doing it. Tiffany deserved the opportunity to confront her attackers, if she chose to.

"I noticed one of the names resembled Quincy's. Any relation?"

"Tee, that was the most embarrassing thing that has ever happened to me. It was Quincy's daughter and her friends. I was hoping no one would ever find out. How did you?" asked Tiffany.

Tee decided not to tell her about the video if she didn't have to. It would only upset her more. "I have my sources," she said.

"There were so many of them," Tiffany wailed. "I was afraid to fight back. I was scared of what they might do to me if I did. I don't think I fully understood the magnitude of my actions all these years until I looked into Quincy's daughter's eyes and saw the hatred in them. I've been so selfish. In my quest to get the man I loved all to myself, I was also taking a father away from his daughters. I don't want to press charges. I've caused her enough pain. How could God let his happen to me?"

"God? How is this God's fault?" Tee didn't understand her thinking.

"Now that I'm acting like a Christian, isn't He supposed to protect me from hurt, harm and danger?" asked Tiffany.

"Sweetheart, that slap attack you got is a direct result of your own actions. It had nothing to do with the Lord. The Bible is full of parables that illustrate how you will reap what you sow. For years, you have been sleeping with another woman's husband and living well because of it. You've got a house in an exclusive neighborhood. You have a nice car. You don't have to pay for either one, and you haven't held a job since you met the man. Quincy 2 attends the best private school in the city. You mean it never crossed your mind that at some point your actions would yield some consequences? You can't blame God. Who do you think has been protecting you all these years? Quincy's wife could have shown up at your house and put a bullet in your chest years ago. His daughters could have bashed your head in and put you in the hospital instead of slapping you three times and kicking you outside in your underwear. You need to check yourself, Tiffany Tate. God does not bless mess. This isn't His fault, it's yours!"

Tee was upset. The nerve of that woman! Before Michael, she had to work her behind off for everything she owned while Ms. Tiffany merely laid on her back and waited for someone to give her the finer things in life. She was glad she was on the phone because she may have slapped her friend again.

"Don't yell at me, Tee. I can take it when Lenice does it but not you. I get it. This is my fault, not God's!" squealed Tiffany.

"Then, stop talking foolish and I won't have to yell at you. I've been telling you to leave that man alone for years. I've been on my knees praying for you and your son's safety for the same amount of time. God has had a covering on you all along, and you were too blind to see it. You are spoiled and yes, you have been very selfish. It's time for you to grow up. Also, something tells me there's something you're not telling me. If you've started messing with Quincy again I suggest you stop before something really bad happens. Stop sleeping with married men. Period. I've always stood by your side, but I won't if you keep up such harlot behavior."

Every muscle in Tiffany's body tightened. She had been called names like that before from other women who didn't approve of her relationship with Quincy but never by her best friend.

"Is that what you think of me, Tee? You think I'm a whore."

Tee lowered and softened her voice. She knew she'd hurt Tiffany's feelings. "That's not what I said. I said you've been acting like one. You went from one married man's bed to another without batting an eyelash or thinking of anyone but yourself all because you like money. You're acting like you're for sale. Then, you keep choosing men who care so little about their wives and you, for that matter, that they are willing to take up a long-term mistress. Peter's wife was at the hospital watching her mother fight for her life when he was busy screwing you. She's still in a coma, and instead of being by Ce Ce's side, he's gallivanting across the country slandering my husband's name. What did Quincy's wife do to deserve his infidelity? If he's no longer happy he should be communicating that to her instead of making babies with you. If a man doesn't know how to love his wife how can he possibly give you what you need?"

"But I left Peter alone, Tee!" Tiffany shouted in her own defense.

Tee wondered what it would take to get through to this girl that her behavior was self-destructive.

"After you slept with him. My husband shouldn't have to knock on bedroom doors to try to prevent you from sleeping with his married friends. You have got to start making wise decisions on your own. You have to take responsibility for your actions and value yourself in the process. I want more for you. God wants more for you. He's given you warning after warning through myself, your family and others. Now, Quincetta has come along to slap some sense into you. What else do you need, Tif?"

"I need someone to love me. I need to feel special. I don't like being alone. I want to be taken care of. Is that so wrong? I'm not proud of my actions, and I want to do better. This is hard for me, Tee. I've always had someone to take care of me," explained Tiffany.

Tee was tired of preaching. Especially, to someone who didn't appear to be listening. "Will you listen to yourself?

My husband and I loaned you $12,000 to help you help yourself, and you're still complaining. It's time for Tiffany to learn how to stand on her own two feet and take care of herself. You'll get no sympathy from me in that area. I've been working since I was 16. My mother worked her butt off to take care of me and Sandy and as soon as we could help relieve some of her burdens by bringing some income into the house we did!" She was shouting again. Tee took a deep breath and softened her voice, again.

"I hope you mean it when you say you're going to do better. If not for yourself, do it for Quincy 2. I have to go now. Michael and I are going to his parent's house today. I need to get ready. I'm still praying for you. God loves you and so do I."

"Thanks, Tee. Tell Michael I said hello."

"Will do. You are precious, Tiffany. Keep that in mind every time a man comes into your life and asks you to open your legs for him. Value your vagina."

"I will," promised Tiffany. "Bye."

Tee hung up the phone to get ready for her in-laws. Had she been too hard on her?

Tiffany opened the door to her courtesy car and a faucet of tears flowed from her eyes. She felt weak. She fell to her knees and laid her head in the middle of the driver's side seat cushion and issued a prayer of repentance to God. She didn't care that she was outside where anyone could see her. She told God she would do better. She told Him she would work daily to live a life that was pleasing to Him. She was on the ground dirtying her pantyhose and pouring out her heart to her Heavenly Father for at least 20 minutes. When she finished her eyes were red, her face was streaked with tears and her nose was running, but she felt much better. She slid the ring she admired so much off her finger and put it in her purse. She didn't need that ring because God was going to bless her with one from a man who wasn't already married. It might not be today but someday. She was sure of it.

Chapter 46

News Flash

Tee and Michael arrived at his parent's house for a late lunch. His mother begged him to come over and try to work things out with his father again until he agreed. They rang the doorbell, and Vanessa answered in her usual cheery manner. She gave her son and daughter-in-law a kiss on the cheek. She wasn't happy with her husband's actions, either. She was also a victim of his lies. All those years, she believed the money he received from Peter was from her father-in law's life insurance policy. She was deeply disappointed in Michael, Sr. but he was her husband and no matter what he did, he would remain her husband. Michael was her oldest son and most beloved. A parent isn't supposed to have a favorite, but she did and he was hers. His entire life he went the extra mile to show how much he loved his family. He was a good son, and he showered his mother with gifts every chance he got.

Vanessa hated to see what this was doing to her family. She had to get them to work it out. They could not defeat the devil divided. The Stokes had to stand strong together. Vanessa asked Tee to accompany her into the kitchen to help finish preparing lunch. She sent Michael into the den where his father was watching TV.

Michael, Sr. was lounging in his La-Z-Boy recliner viewing Michael's college highlight reel and smoking a cigar. The chair was identical to the one Michael had in his Miami condo. His father came to visit him one weekend and liked his chair so much Michael bought one for him to enjoy at home. Michael really didn't have much to say to him. He was still upset with his father for taking that money and believing he would get away with it. He was even more upset that he refused to publicly confess and exonerate the name they shared.

Michael, Sr. heard him enter the room and began talking without turning around to acknowledge him.

"I've always been so proud of you, son. You never gave me and your mother any trouble. You got good grades, did what we told you to, excelled in sports and wasn't running around getting a bunch of women pregnant. You never let your success go to your head. You were almost perfect. Your major flaw is you believe the world is good. The world is evil, and we as Christians, fight every day to combat that evil. Sometimes we win. Sometimes we lose. Satan knows our weaknesses. He knows how to tempt us. Sometimes that evil gets inside of us, and we start committing sins: lying, stealing, killing and so on. I only wanted the best for my family and when a man is down to his last and his back is against the wall, he'll do what he has to do to provide for them. What he does might not be the most honorable thing, but you have no right to judge me. You've never been in that situation. You've been rich since you were 21 years old. I'm sorry for what I done, and I'm going to do what I can to make it right. I'll let Peter have his turn first. Then, I'll call a press conference and tell the world it was all me. I know I disappointed you. Ever since you were a little boy you've had me on this pedestal, but I'm just a man son. I'm just a man, and my greatest accomplishment is my children. You, Maxwell and Tomeka are the best thing I've ever done. I hope you can forgive me."

Michael walked over to where his father was sitting. Michael, Sr. was wearing an old pair of jeans, his brown leather house shoes and his University of Miami jersey. It was the same one he used to wear to Michael's college games whenever he came to see him play. It was faded now, but it was once identical to the one Michael wore on the field except for the name on the back. His read Stokes, Sr. Michael's read Stokes, Jr. His father loved that jersey and the attention it brought him. On more than one occasion Michael, Sr. was the recipient of generous discounts on food, lodging and other items simply because Michael Stokes was his boy. Sometimes it was even free. He was as proud as a Papa could be.

"Of course I forgive you, Pop," said Michael. I'd rather you have the press conference before Peter makes his announcement, but we can wait until after if that's the way you want it. Either way, I need the truth to be told."

Michael, Sr. shook his head up and down in agreement.

Michael patted his father on the back, lit himself a cigar and sat down to watch his reel. He hadn't seen it in years. He marveled at how thin he used to be. He was twice that big now. When it was over, they turned to CNN to see what Peter was up to now and running across the bottom of the screen was a breaking news alert. It read, *Michael Stokes' former agent Peter Parker found dead in his hotel room. Suicide suspected to be the cause.*

Michael, Sr. was in mid pull on his cigar when he read the alert. The smoke entered his nose, mouth and lungs and he began coughing. "Well, I'll be," he choked out.

Michael put his cigar down. "That can't be right," he said. He flipped through the channels to see if he could find more information on another station.

"Peter wouldn't kill himself. He loved himself too much. "I'm as sure of that as I am that my name is Michael Stokes, Jr."

Chapter 47

Email Fail

Sandy hated being confined to a bed. She felt so helpless. Her mother, children and husband were all wonderful, though. They waited on her hand and foot, attended to her every need and it was driving her crazy. She was use to taking care of everyone else and having it the other way around felt abnormal. Tee advised her to enjoy it because she didn't know when it would happen again, but she couldn't. The only time she left her king-size bed was to go to the bathroom. All meals, conversations and recreation took place in her bed. Last night, she helped Nicole with her homework from her bed. She was glad she could still be of some use, but she would rather be at Mae Lillie's greeting her customers and trying out new dishes. Yet, she was determined to give birth to a healthy child so she had no choice but to follow the doctor's orders.

She had been avoiding checking her emails. She was afraid there might be another message from Armondo announcing that he was in town. If he was, she needed to know but at the same time, she didn't want to know. Sandy decided to stop being a coward, reached for her Blackberry and attempted to access her personal email account. She didn't understand why her password didn't seem to be working. She typed it in again more slowly. It still didn't work. She clicked the "don't remember password" link and tried to recall the answer to her security question to retrieve her password. She could not remember which ice cream she said was her favorite. She had so many. It looked like she wouldn't be checking her emails today, either. Maybe no news was good news.

Chapter 48

Wisdom

After her prayer, Tiffany wanted to go home and take a hot shower. She would have loved to reschedule her client but she couldn't. It was with Mrs. Tolliver and while she was in class, Mrs. Tolliver's housekeeper left Tiffany two voicemails reminding her of the appointment. She seemed to be looking forward to it. Tiffany hadn't seen or talked to the older woman since their last appointment, and she was a little curious to know if the marital advice she gave her worked.

Tiffany approached the house and wondered if she would ever have enough money to live this lavish. There was a Bentley parked in the driveway and an old man in a chauffer's uniform outside waxing it. The house was massive with a pool, pool house, tennis and basketball courts. The lawn was immaculate, and the sun even seemed to shine a little bit brighter over her house. Maybe that was her imagination, but either way this woman was paid. She knocked on the door expecting the housekeeper to answer, but Mrs. Tolliver opened the door and greeted her with a wide smile.

"Come in, Tiffany. I am so happy to see you. My entire body is sore. I hope you brought your magic fingers. Would you like something to drink? How about some lemonade or raspberry tea?" she offered.

"Hello, Mrs. Tolliver. Some water would be nice. I'm sorry to hear you are not feeling well. I'll do what I can to make it better."

Mrs. Tolliver looked at her and smirked. "I said I was sore, but I have never felt better. Since our little chat, my husband has been coming straight home after work each day. Yesterday, he even came home for "lunch"—if you know what I mean. He cancelled his golf trip this weekend to take me to our cabin in the mountains instead. He also told me he ended it with his little girlfriend. Tiffany dear, from now on I want you to stop by the house and give me a massage at least once a week and provide me with more tips I can use to spice up my marriage and keep my husband away from that hussy."

Tiffany looked at Mrs. Tolliver a little closer. She was glowing. She was the exact opposite of the woman she first encountered. She stood straighter. Her tone was joyous. Her salt and pepper hair was down. It framed her delicate face in a bob, and she was wearing makeup. Her eyes sparkled, and she couldn't stop smiling. She looked like a woman in love.

"Thank you for helping me realize how neglectful I've been towards my Larry. He really is a good man. I'm still extremely hurt by the affair, but he is bending over backwards to make it up to me. I must say I am enjoying all the extra attention. We're behaving like we did before we had children," Mrs. Tolliver laughed. It was a full laugh that comes out of the pit of one's belly.

Tiffany smiled. She was happy she could do something right.

Mrs. Tolliver's laugh came to an end, and she took a good long look at Tiffany.

"Tiffany darling, what's wrong? Your eyes are red. Have you been crying? Why are your knees dirty? Did you fall?"

"I'm glad I could help you, Mrs. Tolliver. Unfortunately, I'm not the nice person you think I am. You know how I know so much about married men? I used to be the other woman. For years, I treated another woman's husband like he was my own. I didn't have to work. Quincy bought me everything I wanted and needed. I even had his child. I was thoroughly convinced that man loved me, and he would be better off with me and my son rather than his wife and their daughters. I know my friend Tee means well but telling me what to do and calling me a whore doesn't help. I still love him, and I loved having someone special who made me feel special. We broke up, and he won't even come see his son. I'm taking him to court for child support. And even though what he's doing is wrong, I miss him so much. I'm trying to do right and be a good Christian, but it's hard. I like sex. Is that so wrong?"

Mrs. Tolliver tried her best to keep up since Tiffany ran down the story of her pain in less than 30 seconds. She didn't know who Quincy or Tee was, but it didn't matter.

"You're human child, and there's something you have to understand about being human. Once you understand it, you can handle it better. Sit tight." She went to another room and returned a few minutes later with her Bible. She opened it and said, "I want you to read this passage I have highlighted here out loud."

Tiffany took the book from her and began reading Romans 7:14- 25.

"We know that the Law is spiritual, but I'm made of flesh and blood, and I'm sold as a slave to sin. I don't know what I'm doing because I don't do what I want to do. Instead, I do the thing that I hate. But, I'm doing the thing that I don't want to do; I'm agreeing that the Law is right. But now I'm not the one doing it anymore. Instead, it's sin that lives in me. So I find that, as a rule, when I want to do what is good, evil is right there with me. I gladly agree with the Law on the inside, but I see a different law at work in my body. It wages a war against the law of my mind and takes me prisoner with the law of sin that is in my body. I'm a miserable human being. Who will deliver me from this dead corpse? Thank God through Jesus Christ our Lord! So, then I'm a slave to God's law in my mind, but I'm a slave to sin's law in my body."

Tiffany found the passage to be a little confusing and depressing. "I think I got most of it, but will you explain it to me to be sure?" she asked Mrs. Tolliver.

" The Bible itself tells us the nature of man is sinful and it is the job of Christians to use the knowledge of God's word and the love God and His son Jesus Christ has for us to combat it. This flesh itself is prone to sin but when we sin we displease God. But when we call on God, he can give us strength to overcome it. It's not wrong that you like sex. What's wrong is that you let your fondness of sex impair your judgment. Sleeping with another woman's husband is wrong, but here you are mourning doing it because you like sex and love the man you did it with. Ask God to help you stop. He can do it.

"In addition to calling on Him, get in this word and study it. Memorize some of it and when the enemy comes against you recall what you know to be true in your mind and heart and beat him down. You can defeat this Quincy fellow, but the first thing you have to do is loose yourself from his grasp. Quincy thinks he owns you because he bought you material possessions. He's denying you and his child access to his money in hopes that you'll come back. Tell him where he and his money can go!"

Tiffany gasped. "He bought almost everything I own. You don't understand. I've never been poor a day in my life. As a child, I had the best of everything and when my parent's cut me off it was Quincy's money that allowed me to continue to live the lifestyle I was accustomed to. I don't want to be poor. I've had a small taste of it, and I don't think I like it. Look at my nails. I haven't had a mani or a pedi in weeks."

Mrs. Tolliver chuckled. "No one likes being poor, but poverty is nothing to be afraid of. Millions of people live in it every day, and they're still alive. Your life of luxury has been at the expense of another woman, yourself and your child. It's cost you your dignity, your self-esteem and your peace of mind. I've met women like you before. I bet Quincy walks in and out of your house and your life whenever he sees fit. He knows what buttons to push to make you melt like butter. He's been your puppet master for years, and you don't even realize it. The strings he uses are false love, hope and money. If he really loved you, you wouldn't be broke. A good man wants his woman to be financially secure even when he's not around. He left you, and your well ran dry. Why didn't he set you up a savings account? Why doesn't your son have a trust fund? Why didn't he give you a business to run or some rental property so you could have some assets and income? Because he wanted you to always be dependent on him, that's why.

"You say you're a Christian then believe in God to replace everything he gave you. Quincy gave you that nice Audi you drive. I serve a God who can get you a Bentley. He bought you a house. I serve a God who specializes in mansions.

"Did you know my great grandfather was supposed to be a farmer? That was the family business, farming. He wanted no parts of it. Instead, he put himself through college and became an engineer. After years of sacrifice, hard work and faith, he built one of the largest railroad companies in the United States. Because of his faith, my family never has to worry about money again. Get that man out of your life. Give away some things, sell some things and move to another location. God has kept you this far. You're in school. You're about to embark on a career you enjoy, and you're excellent at it. I know a winner when I see one, Tiffany, and you're a winner. Stand on your own two feet, work hard and build your son a legacy he can be proud of. You don't have to make any decisions tonight but think about it. I want you to read a couple more Bible verses. Turn to Matthew 6:24 – 34."

Tiffany did as she was instructed. "No one can serve two masters. Either you will hate the one and love the other, or you will be devoted to the one and despise the other. You cannot serve both God and money. Therefore I tell you, do not worry about your life, what you will eat or drink; or about your body, what you will wear. Is not life more than food, and the body more than clothes? Look at the birds of the air; they do not sow or reap or store away in barns, and yet your Heavenly Father feeds them. Are you not much more valuable than they? Can any one of you by worrying add a single hour to your life? And why do you worry about clothes? See how the flowers of the field grow. They do not labor or spin. Yet, I tell you that not even Solomon in all his splendor was dressed like one of these. If that is how God clothes the grass of the field, which is here today and tomorrow is thrown into the fire, will he not much more clothe you—you of little faith? So do not worry, saying, 'What shall we eat?' or 'What shall we drink?' or 'What shall we wear?' For the pagans run after all these things, and your Heavenly Father knows that you need them. But seek first his kingdom and His righteousness, and all these things will be given to you as well. Therefore, do not worry about tomorrow, for tomorrow will worry about itself. Each day has enough trouble of its own."

Mrs. Tolliver looked at Tiffany and smiled. "Where is your faith, Tiffany Tate? God will enable you to take care of yourself and those you love. Now, turn to Psalms 37:25."

Tiffany turned the thin pages to the appropriate place. "I was young and now I am old, yet I have never seen the righteous forsaken or their children begging bread," she read.

"I'm a living witness to that," said Mrs. Tolliver. "I know you think I've always had money, but I haven't. When I chose to marry my husband, my parents didn't approve. He was the son of our housekeeper, and they wanted me to marry someone of pedigree. They actually forbade it, but I didn't care. They didn't come to the wedding and afterward, they wouldn't give me a dime. They thought their money would make me come running home. I showed them. I was always good with numbers. I got a job as an assistant to an accountant and helped put my husband through college and then law school. There were some days when we didn't know how we were going to pay our rent, and we ate Vienna sausages and crackers for dinner because that's all we could afford. Yet, God provided month after month. Somehow, we managed to pay our bills and stay afloat. When my father saw Larry was going to make something out of himself, Daddy apologized and gave me my inheritance. He said it wasn't logical to make me wait until he was deceased when we needed it immediately. It helped out immensely because by that time, I had given birth to our firstborn, and I wanted to stay home and raise him. It appeared, I would have to go back to work out of necessity. Larry was in his second year of law school, and I was our only source of income. God made it where I didn't have to.

"Tiffany, the heart doesn't think. It's a muscle. It's one of the strongest muscles in the body, so it feels deeply and sometimes we have to use our mind to override it. You're an intelligent young lady. I have every confidence you will do the right thing. Let's not worry about a massage today. Maybe next week. Now, you get out of here and think about what I said. My husband will be home soon, and I promised him I would cook his favorite dinner tonight. I've been cooking a lot more lately, too. I cooked him breakfast this morning. I forgot how much I love watching him enjoy my meals and him telling me how delicious they are."

Mrs. Tolliver challenged Tiffany to start over. She didn't know if she was strong enough to do it. There was one thing she did know and that was she felt good about herself. Something good, other than Quincy 2 came out of her relationship. In her quest to break up a marriage, she learned how to save one.

Chapter 49

More Wisdom

Lenice didn't know where she was going. She didn't know why she felt like James was cheating on her when he wasn't her boyfriend. She continued to drive her car down street after street with no destination in mind. She turned left or right whenever she felt like it. She somehow found herself in Sandy's neighborhood. She and Sandy were more of acquaintances than friends. The only reason they had any interaction was because of their individual relationships with Tee. However, Lenice did hear Sandy was ordered to stay in bed for the remainder of her pregnancy and decided it would be wrong of her to be so close and not stop by to check on her. The last time she came to Sandy's house was to help cheer her up because she thought Patrick was cheating. That was the same night she decided to seek professional help to assist her with releasing her animosity towards men. She thought she'd done it, but after today, she wasn't so sure. Lenice hoped Sandy wouldn't be upset she stopped by unannounced.

Momma Pearl answered the door. She recognized Lenice right away and welcomed her in. She had met most of her daughter's friends, at one time or another. Lenice admired how young she looked for her age. She had to be in her 60's and looked to be in her 50's. Her skin was still smooth, and her white crown of hair complimented her beautifully. She hoped she would age as gracefully.

"Lenice, I think you get more beautiful every time I see you, but you look a little thin. I know skinny is in these days, but you might want to try eating a little more. Come on in the kitchen and let me fix you a plate. I just finished fixing dinner for tonight, but Patrick and the kids probably won't be here for a couple of hours and Sandy is asleep. Bless her heart. This pregnancy hasn't been easy on her. She has a hard time getting comfortable. The nurse stopped by today and told her that the baby is resting her head in her momma's rib cage, which is contributing to the discomfort. I know you probably came to see Sandy, but I don't want to disturb her now that she's been able to nod off. I hope this isn't a sign that my grandbaby is going to have a big head. Well, I'll love her all the same." Momma Pearl motioned for Lenice to follow her.

Lenice no longer had a reason for being there because Sandy was asleep, but she never did get her pizza. Some food might improve her mood. Since Lenora moved in, she always tried to walk into the house with a smile on her face to help keep her sister's spirits up. Tee's mother always was kind to her. Maybe a friendly chat would help improve her mood.

Once in the kitchen, Momma Pearl said, "Sit down Baby. Let me fix you a plate of these greens. I also made a pot roast with potatoes and carrots."

"Sorry ma'am, but I don't eat red meat or pork," said Lenice.

"Then greens, potatoes and carrots it is."

Lenice didn't have the heart to tell her she didn't want any vegetables either because she was sure the greens were seasoned with fatback or bacon, and the potatoes and carrots were cooked in the roast beef juices.

Instead she said, "I'm not very hungry, so please only fix me a small plate." Perhaps, that would save her stomach.

"Nonsense, baby. Whatever you don't eat you can take with you. There's plenty here. You know Sandy got her cooking skills from me. When we lived in North Memphis the whole neighborhood used to try and stop by for a plate of my greens."

Momma Pearl sat a huge plate of vegetables in front of Lenice and sure enough, nestled among the collard greens was a piece of swine with a large portion of fat attached to it. Lenice hadn't eaten pork or red meat in almost eight years. Her stomach made a gurgling sound she didn't like. She picked up the fork and forced herself to eat a couple of bites before she put it down and blurted out, "Ms. Pearl, why are men so stupid?"

Momma Pearl laughed. "I knew something was bothering you. I could see it as soon as I opened the door. The vein in the middle of your forehead is popping out like you want to beat somebody senseless. Man problems, huh? I don't believe all men are stupid, just individual ones. Why don't you tell me about the gentleman in particular you are referring to?"

Lenice told her about the day's events, her many conversations with her therapist and why she didn't think dating was for her. She was a one-man woman.

Momma Pearl listened attentively. Nodding her head where appropriate and when Lenice was done, she offered this advice.

"I think your problem is you give men too much power in your life. Here you are a beautiful, intelligent, successful woman and you let yourself get all worked up because you saw a man you care for sitting at a table with another woman. A man isn't supposed to be able to control your emotions like that, especially one that isn't yours.

"Your therapist told you to date multiple men so you can experience what it's like to be single without latching on to one man the way you did. You're learning how to love, again. That can be hard once you've been hurt. Before you give someone new the option of loving you, you have to get to know him to determine whether or not he is qualified for the position and worthy to love you. Two or three dates is hardly enough time to determine whether or not he's boyfriend material. Furthermore, it sounds like you gave him the position before he even put in an application for the job. Did he ask you to be his girlfriend?"

"No, ma'am," answered Lenice.

"Did he tell you he wanted to date you exclusively?"

"No, ma'am."

"Then, how in the world did you come to the conclusion that he was only supposed to take you out?" Momma Pearl looked at her like she had lost her mind.

Lenice felt foolish. "He said he liked me," she said softly.

"I'm sure he does, but he might like a few other people, too. His feelings and thoughts about them have nothing to do with the ones he has for you. He's probably trying to do what you should be doing, getting to know you to determine whether or not he wants to dedicate himself to you. It's a bad idea to hand a man your heart when he didn't ask for it. It's like entering someone's house without permission. You put them on the defensive, and you might get shot if they mistake you for an intruder.

"You have no reason to be upset with that man, Lenice. He didn't do anything wrong. He hasn't lied to you or misled you. I can tell you like him, but you better stop acting possessive before you scare him off.

"I know your last boyfriend cheated on you. I know it hurt, but you've gone from one extreme to the other. That's not healthy. You went from never wanting to date again to wanting to be in a relationship right away. Baby, find your way back to the middle. Take your time. Get out there and have some fun and when I say have some fun, I don't mean have sex with every man you go out with. That's what's wrong with the world now. Everybody seems to be hot in the pants. People think because they like someone they are supposed to have sex with them. That's bad judgment if I've ever heard it. Enjoy some laughs and good conversation over a good meal. Get to know these men and let them get to know you and like good cream the best one will rise to the top. Please excuse me for a minute while I go check on Sandy. You can never be too careful with these at-risk pregnancies."

Momma Pearl left the room and left Lenice with a lump in her throat. She owed James an apology. She hated apologizing, but she had to try to undo the damage she had done. She grabbed her purse and headed for the door. She hoped Momma Pearl wouldn't be too upset she didn't say goodbye or finish her plate of fatty greens and beef soaked potatoes and carrots.

Chapter 50

Oops Poop!

Tiffany arrived home to find William sitting in her driveway with her car. It had brand new tires on it and even a new set of rims. He hadn't called her with the cost of the tires before putting them on, and she didn't ask for new rims. Now that she was counting her pennies, she was almost certain she couldn't afford them.

"Good evening, Ms. Tate," he said.

"Well hello there, William. I see you brought my baby back to me with new shoes."

William thought her deep southern drawl was incredibly sexy. Actually, he thought everything about Tiffany Tate was sexy. He never told her how he felt because she was with Quincy. Quincy accompanied her to the dealership and bought the car. He assumed things must be over between them because a week ago Quincy came in asking if there was any way he could get out of his deal without ruining his credit. His assumption was confirmed when the pretty damsel in distress rolled up to his dealership in her lingerie. He was more than happy to be her hero. He wondered how he could make this situation work in his favor.

She looked beautiful today. She was wearing what appeared to be a doctor's lab coat over her outfit. It had her name embroidered on the right side.

"William, have you heard a word I said?" asked Tiffany.

William snapped back to reality. "Yes, ma'am. Yes, ma'am," he said. "What did you say?"

Tiffany laughed. She was used to mesmerizing men. She never really noticed William before, but he was a handsome young man, with a nice build. He looked to be about 26 or 27. It was evident he worked out regularly. The bulging muscles in his arms and legs could easily be identified beneath his clothes. His cocoa complexion looked nice in the setting sun. His thick lips encircled a nice wide smile with a small gap between his two front teeth, but she didn't view it as an imperfection at all. She thought it gave him character. He was wearing beige slacks with a striped beige shirt and a brown tie. His shoes were the same color as his tie, and she really liked whatever cologne he was wearing. The spicy scent reminded her a little of her father. It was a strong, masculine scent. She took a deep breath and let it further invade her nostrils. She did notice that whenever she was at the dealership William never tried to hit on her like the other men working there. She hated going in there for even an oil change because of the mass attention she received when she did. Tiffany enjoyed attention from the opposite sex as much as any other woman, but you can begin to feel like a piece of meat with multiple men ogling you and trying to come up with something witty to say to get your attention. Some days a woman doesn't want to deal with the unwanted invitations. She wants to handle her business without any one asking for her phone number or hearing some lame pick up line.

"I asked if you minded helping me unload my car. I need to take my supplies in the house," said Tiffany.

"No, Ms. Tate. I don't mind at all," William replied.

Tiffany took off her lab coat and put it in the car. She refused to wear scrubs. She found them unattractive.

Instead, she opted for a lab coat. It still allowed her to get dressed everyday in fabulous Tiffany Tate fashion. She was always careful to take off her heels and her accessories whenever she was in the classroom or with a client. She could always put them back on later.

She opened her trunk, and William took out her table and the bags containing her sheets, oils and any other supplies she needed. He followed her to the house and waited patiently while she unlocked the door. It was like she was leading a puppy. He stared openly at her shapely behind. *She truly is a masterpiece*, he thought to himself. Once it was open, she asked him to place her things on the floor.

William was very impressed with her home. It was nicely decorated and white seemed to be the dominate color, which he found odd for a woman with a child. The floor was marble, there were several pieces of Victorian-inspired furniture and a white baby grand piano.

"Thank you, William. I appreciate you bringing my car and my things in the house. I need to go pick up my son from my parents shortly. How much did the repairs cost me?"

He began to tell her, but they were both startled by a loud banging on the door.

"Tiffany! Tiffany you open this door right now! We need to talk. I've been calling you all day, girl. My daughter told me what you did to her at the spa. Now, you got a man in the house I bought. I see you've forgotten your place. Open this door!" yelled Quincy.

Tiffany's face showed sheer panic. Quincy had a terrible temper. What had Quincetta told him? That brat and her friends attacked her!

William knew an opportunity when he saw one. He was not a small man, and he wasn't afraid of a fight. In college, he received several awards while on the wrestling team. He worked out a minimum of five days a week and entered at least one bodybuilding competition a year. He usually placed in the top three. William made his way to the door and opened it with a *What do you want* look that made Quincy stop yelling. The two men stared at one another through the glass in her wrought-iron security door. Quincy wasn't tall in height, but he was tall in stature. He was one of the most respected architects in the city and served on the Memphis City Council. William wasn't surprised to see him, but he was surprised to see the tow truck that was being hitched to the car he delivered.

Quincy smiled. "Hello, William. Are you enjoying my leftovers? Excuse me for my intrusion, but I wasn't quite finished licking that plate. I would appreciate it if you would step aside, so I can finish some unfinished business with my woman.

"Open this door and step out of the way. This is my home. I bought this house, and I make the payments on that car. I bought that woman. That's right, I OWN her." Quincy looked over William's shoulder at Tiffany as the word, own, exited his mouth. "Right now, I would call what you're doing theft. Isn't that what it's called when you take another man's property without his permission?"

"Man, you're sick," said William. "Ms. Tate is a woman not a piece of machinery. You need to leave that car alone."

"Or?"

"I'm going to call the police."

"I play golf with the police chief. Would you like me to call him for you?" He took his cell phone out of his pocket.

Tiffany was standing behind William listening and whatever fear she had dissipated into thin air. She was now fuming. "Hold up, William! I got this!" she yelled. Quincy had finally pushed her too far. He made her sound as if she was his property to do with as he pleased. She made her way past William and forcefully pushed her wrought iron door open almost striking Quincy with it. He was able to jump out of the way before it did. She stepped outside and stuck her index finger in his face. William stepped out behind her to show his support.

"You own me! Is that what you said? You don't own me, Quincy. As a matter of fact, you can take your stupid car."

The keys were still in William's hand. She snatched them from him and forced them in Quincy's chest pushing him backwards. They fell to the ground. Quincy stooped to pick them up and then took a couple of steps back to put some distance between the two of them in case Tiffany felt the urge to push him again. Tiffany had been angry with him before, but she usually kept her sweet southern belle persona while she fussed, at least with him. Her philosophy was to always be a lady. That was one of the things he loved about her. She wasn't a drama queen like his wife, who seemed to have yelling and crying about something on her agenda at least every other week. He could usually calculate Tiffany's next move, but at that moment, he didn't know what she was about to do.

"You're despicable," snarled Tiffany. "You know I use that car to take your son to school, and that's how I get to my clients to make sure he eats every day. You haven't contributed a dime to his care in weeks. You did it to make me weak but guess what? It only made me stronger. I hate you! What kind of a man doesn't take care of his child? Me and my son will be moving out of YOUR HOUSE by the end of the month."

His money and status meant nothing to her now. She no longer wanted any part of him. "As a matter of fact, you can take all this crap back. She took off her Christian Dior pumps and threw them at him, missing his face by an inch. She then took off the diamond earrings and tennis bracelet he gave her one Mother's Day and threw those items at him, too. She realized she was wearing a dress Quincy bought her on a weekend trip to New York last year. She pulled the red KLS Collection dress over her head revealing a black silk full slip. It was sheer, and anyone could clearly see the black lace bra and matching panty beneath it. She then stretched her hand back and began beating him with her dress. It was fall and much to cool to be parading around in one's underwear, but Tiffany had rage to keep her warm. The heavy material was perfect for warding off chilly temperatures and perfect for beating her former lover unmercifully. With each blow, she released frustration derived from years of being lied to. She dreamed so many times of walking down a long aisle in a white dress with the man she loved waiting for her at the altar. It wasn't going to happen. She no longer wanted it to happen.

Quincy ran toward his car. "Woman, have you lost your mind? Put your clothes back on!" She made quite a spectacle as she ran behind him barefoot and nearly naked, hitting him repeatedly with her dress.

"No. I'm through taking orders from you! You think I'm a puppet! It's my turn to make you dance!" Tiffany yelled.

Quincy continued to run with her close behind him. He tried to cut through the yard to get to his car more quickly but slipped on some fresh poop left by the neighbor's dog. His feet flew from underneath him and straight into the air. He was airborne for at least two seconds before he landed hard on his back on top of the poop. The 50-year-old was paralyzed by the pain and lay there defenseless as Tiffany dropped to her knees and pummeled him with her fists. "Take that!" And give this to Quincetta!"

This was the second time William had seen Tiffany in her underwear within 24 hours. Although he was enjoying the view, he felt it would be best to intervene before she hurt him or Quincy tried to hit her back. He ran over to Tiffany, wrapped his arms around her waist and picked her up from behind. She kicked and screamed to be released because she wasn't finished beating Quincy's behind yet.

Quincy was grateful for the assistance. He regained motion in his body and stumbled to his car. He stopped momentarily to give the tow truck driver, who was doubled over with laughter, instructions to continue removing the car from her driveway. He would see how long Tiffany kept up this tough act with no transportation.

William ignored Tiffany's pleas. His might allowed him to easily transport her from her front yard back into the house. She was behaving like a child throwing a temper tantrum. "Let me go! He's getting away!" she screamed.

Once in the house, he swung her around facing him and grabbed her by both wrists. As they breathed heavily in one another's face, he looked in her eyes and was once again reminded of how beautiful she was. He could stare in her large brown eyes all day. In them, he saw her pain. He wanted to be there for her. It tugged at his heart to see someone so lovely so distressed. William pulled her to him and hugged her tight. Tiffany's fighting spirit waned. Her body grew limp and slid to the floor. She refused to cry. She had already shed enough tears today, but she was in agony.

William allowed his body to descend with hers, while still holding her close. He could feel the rapid beat of her heart.

"He said he owned me," said Tiffany. "He said he owned me. I thought he loved me."

William admired her strength. "Welcomes to yo' emancipation Miz Tif-ney. You's free. You's free. Thank God almighty you's free!" He said in a raspy Negro dialect and raised his arms above his head and shook both fits for emphasis.

Tiffany smiled at his horrible attempt to cheer her up.

"William, will you do me a favor? Will you drive me to my parent's house to pick up my son, and then take us to the dealership to pick out a new car? Quincy can keep that one."

"It would be my pleasure, Ms. Tiffany, but can I make a suggestion?"

"Sure."

"Why don't you hold on to the courtesy car a few more days. Let me look around and see if I can find you something a little more affordable. I heard you say Quincy isn't giving you any money. I'm sure I can find you a used car that looks almost as good as the one you were driving. Also, put on some clothes first. You don't want to go pick up your child in your underwear. I like it, but he and your parents might get the wrong idea."

Tiffany laughed. "Shut up, boy!" She playfully punched William in the arm before getting off the floor and running to her bedroom to find another dress.

Chapter 51

Reciprocity

The Stokes house was in a state of emotional confusion. Michael's best friend turned nemesis was dead. Michael, Sr. was saddened to hear Peter was dead but was relieved his problem had come to a swift end without embarrassment. Without Peter, there was no need for him to issue a statement. Without Peter, there was no meeting with the NCAA, no big announcement and no story. It was over.

Michael excused himself from the den and retreated to his childhood bedroom. He called Peter's wife to offer his condolences. Her sister answered. Audrey explained that Ce Ce was in no mood to talk. She received the news of Peter's death while sitting by their mother's side at the hospital. An hour later, their mother died. Michael offered his condolences to the entire family and told her that if they needed anything not to hesitate to call.

As soon as he hung up, the phone rang and out of reflex he answered.

"Hello, Binky. How are you?"

"Would you stop calling me!" he growled.

"I only called to get my thanks," said the voice.

"Thanks for what?"

"For taking care of your little problem. Nobody's going to take you down but me," said the voice.

Michael felt his heart plummet into his shoes. "You? You killed Peter? Why?"

"That's what you do to cockroaches. Pesky little critters that seek to make a home in places where they are not wanted. They carry disease and germs, you know. I saw a nasty little bug about to try and take my man down, and I exterminated it. I think it was rather clever of me to make it seem like a suicide. Don't you?" The voice laughed. "You should have heard him beg me for mercy like a little girl. He even offered to help me get to you."

"Becca, you killed my best friend. We were having our differences, but I'm sure we could have worked it out. You didn't have to kill him."

"Yes I did, Binky. He was never your friend. He was using you. You won't believe how much dirt he had on you and your daddy. You should be thanking me. I made him give me every shred of information he had. I threw it in the incinerator along with his laptop. He had several detailed documents about extortion, blackmail and payments made to football officials, referees, journalists and others. He was going to nail you to the wall. There were also pictures of you and a woman. Does the name Porsche sound familiar? She was secretly taping your sexcapades. I almost kept those. Imagine if that video got out and your precious Tee saw it. Miss Goody Two Shoes would be humiliated. I'm sure I could have found some way to torture you with Peter's evidence, but that wouldn't make me any better than that cockroach. You're safe for now."

Michael couldn't believe what he was hearing. Becca killed Peter for him?

"You're insane. If you wanted me miserable, why didn't you let him help you?" asked Michael.

"There is nothing wrong with me, Michael. It's called revenge, and it's perfectly normal to want it when someone ruins your life. When you lose everything you hold dear, I want to be the only one responsible. That's the only way I will reap any satisfaction from it. I gotta go now, Binky. Do yourself a favor. Don't mourn for that fool. He doesn't deserve your sympathy. He was rotten to the core. He was jealous of you, you know. He wanted everything you had for himself, including me. He could never be you, and he knew it. So, he decided to bring you down instead. You really should be thanking me."

"One question before you go. Did you kill your cousin who molested you?"

"I see you've been doing some investigating? The prick had it coming," said the voice and then hung up.

Michael dialed Dr. Foster's number. "We have to get some help with this. Becca killed her cousin and now Peter. We have to stop her before she kills again," he said.

"Now you believe it's Becca? I understand your concern, but we have no proof. Do you know how crazy I'd sound calling the authorities and telling them a dead woman is calling you from the grave and killing people? I have to have some kind of evidence she's alive before I do that. We can't even ask a judge to have the body exhumed to prove she's really dead or alive without some hard evidence. I'm glad you called because I was about to call you. I have something you need to see. I'm in Akron. I came here to pay a visit to the mental facility where Becca was being treated. Can you come down here now?"

"Sure. Give me 30 minutes," said Michael.

Chapter 52

Patience Is A Virtue

Lenora called Lenice to inform her she was going to dinner with Herman and the kids, and she didn't need to pick the children up. Lenice was relieved to be freed from the task. She wanted to leave her evening open to spend time with James. She called his phone to see if he was home. He answered on the first ring.

"Hi. I didn't expect to hear from you so soon."

"I'm sorry, but I need to talk to you. May I come over?" asked Lenice.

"No. I don't think that's a good idea. I'd like to go ahead and say what I have to say. Lenice, I think you're a nice woman, and I like you a lot, but I don't think this is working out. You're too emotionally unstable right now. I had my reservations after that incident with Herman at the hospital but after today, I'm sure. The woman you saw me with was my sister. Today is her birthday, and I met her for lunch to celebrate. She's having a lot of problems right now, and I was there being the listening ear and big brother she needed. I would have introduced you to her, but you flipped me the bird and ran out of the restaurant so fast I didn't have a chance. I don't like drama. You seem to have a lot of it. I don't think we should continue to see each other," said James.

Lenice felt more ashamed at that moment than she did when she was talking to Momma Pearl.

"James, I'm so sorry. Please give me another chance. This is all so new to me. I'm starting over, and I'm still learning what it takes to have a healthy relationship or even a courtship."

"I understand, but I don't know if I can deal with your erratic behavior," said James.

"James, don't do this. We can fix this. How about if we stop spending so much time together and take things slower? Will that help?" asked Lenice.

"Your therapist thinks you should see other people, and I do too. The only problem is I don't want to date around. I'd rather pick one woman and dedicate my energy to her. I'm sorry, Lenice, but I don't think we're right for each other."

"Please reconsider, James. We've had some good times together, and I would like to continue having them," Lenice pleaded.

James paused. It wasn't everyday that a woman who looked like a model asked him to stay in her life. He was a numbers cruncher not a jock. Maybe he should reconsider. This was good for his ego.

"Because you asked me to, I will take some more time to think about this. Give me a few days. I'll call you when I've made my final decision."

"I guess that's fair. So, I'll just wait until then?" Patience had never been one of Lenice's strengths.

"Yeah. The therapist, the anger management, the emotional damage, that's a lot for a guy to digest. I'm looking for a wife and right now, you're not even ready for a relationship," said James.

James' statement cut Lenice like a knife. She didn't need anger management! She needed people to stop making her angry! Yet, not even she could deny that she was emotionally damaged. She still had a lot of healing to do. She was glad Lenora and the kids were going out tonight. After this conversation, she needed to be alone.

Chapter 53

Let Me In

Tee was looking forward to returning home with her husband. She hoped that she and Michael could smooth things over with her father in-law that day and then drive back to Memphis that night. She wasn't sure that would happen now that Peter was dead. In a perfect world, everyone would forget that he ever opened his mouth or even existed. She wanted this scandal to die with him.

Michael walked into the kitchen and announced he was leaving. Tee silently rejoiced. She loved her husband, but she had a life outside of him she was ready to get back to. Her joy quickly subsided after he explained he was going for a drive to clear his head and would be back in an hour. She thought leaving meant going home.

"Where are you going?"

"I don't know. I'm just gonna drive and see where it leads me," he lied.

"Do you want some company?"

"No. I'd rather be alone."

Tee wrinkled her forehead. "Didn't we have a talk earlier about you shutting me out?"

"Woman, the man partially responsible for my career was found dead today and all you can think about is you? Give me a break."

"I want to be there for my husband. Why is that so hard for you to understand?"

"I want to be alone. Why is that so hard for you to understand?"

"Fine. Leave. See if I care," said Tee.

"Baby, I'll be back in an hour." Michael leaned in to kiss Tee on the lips. She turned her head. He kissed her on the cheek instead and said, "I love you."

Tee melted every time he said those three words. She smiled. "I love you, too. Did we just have our first married fight?"

Michael smacked her on the behind. "That wasn't a fight; it was merely a difference of opinion. I promise I won't be gone long." He took the keys to her truck and left.

Tee informed her mother-in-law she was going upstairs to lie down.

"Michael, Sr. is the same way," said Vanessa. "When he's upset, he doesn't want to talk and wants to be alone. Most times, he eventually tells me what's wrong. Some men need to try to work things out for themselves before they turn to others. Rest your mind, Tina. My son is head over heels in love with you." She gave her daughter-in-law a hug.

"Thank you, Vanessa. I'm trying to be okay with that, but I always feel like he's leaving me out of an important part of his life. Aren't husbands and wives supposed to share everything?"

Vanessa laughed. "You will always keep some secrets. Especially, if it's to preserve the well-being of those you love. Some things people don't need to know. But you have to give it time. The two of you haven't been together six months. It takes time to develop the type of marriage you want. As times progresses, your husband will trust you more and confide in you more."

"I hope so," said Tee.

Wearily, Tee headed to Michael's old room to take a nap. She was learning her idea of marriage wasn't what it was really like at all.

In Michael's haste, he left his cell phone on the bed. Normally, Tee wouldn't go through it, but his behavior warranted some investigation.

The last call was from Ida Foster. Then, there was a call from a restricted number. She continued to scroll through his call history and saw two more calls from a restricted number. One of them was on the last day of their honeymoon, shortly before Michael fainted. She wondered who could have called her husband and made him so upset that he fainted.

Chapter 54

I'm Coming Home

Lenora hadn't seen her children in three days and for her, that was three days too long. She felt good. She thought she looked good, too. Lenice refused to let her wear another mumu and bought her several colorful jogging suits to wear while she lost the weight. Today, she wore a bright pink one with white stripes going down the arms and the legs. She spent most of her day painting and calling local schools to see if anyone needed an art teacher. She received some favorable feedback and planned to drop her resume and art portfolio off at a few locations the next day.

She called Herman earlier and agreed to go to dinner with him and the kids. If things went well, afterward the two of them could talk about her coming home. Lenora saw their car parked in front of the house and ran out to join them. She climbed in the car and gave Herman a cordial hello. Then, she turned around to give her three babies in the back seat a warm smile. They were each strapped into their car seats and awaiting their arrival to their favorite restaurant, Big Boy's Hamburgers. Lenora gasped. She had never seen her children look so unkempt in all her life. Heather's hair was all over her head. Heston's face was smeared with what appeared to be chocolate, and his nose was running. Hermie's shirt was on inside out. None of their clothes matched, and they were wrinkled. She suddenly felt selfish for leaving. It was obvious her husband was not able to adequately care for them in her absence. She rubbed their little hands and blew kisses. The twins were excited to see their mother and struggled to get out of their car seats to embrace her.

"Hi, Mommy. I missed you," said Heston.

"I missed you, too," said Heather.

However, Hermie rolled his eyes.

"Mommy missed you more," said Lenora. "Now, settle down and when we get to Big Boy's I'll let you out of your seats." The twins were generally obedient children. They sat back in their car seats but didn't stop smiling at Lenora. She smiled back.

"Hermie, did you miss Mommy?" she asked and pinched his chubby cheek.

He didn't answer. Instead, he wiped his face in the spot she touched, turned his head and looked out of the window as if she didn't ask him a question. Lenora's feelings were hurt, but she wasn't about to show it. What was the matter with her baby?

As Herman drove to Big Boy's, she thought about how funny and fickle love was. She and Herman used to be so happy together. He clearly no longer felt the same love for her he once did because of what she looked like. She no longer loved him the same because of the way he treated her.

The drive was short, and the moment the twins were released from their car seats they latched onto their mother's legs. They held her tightly, making it impossible to walk. Hermie leaned against the car and pouted. He looked at her and rolled his little eyes again. He had a serious attitude. Lenora didn't like seeing her son with his lips poked out and rolling his eyes like a little girl.

"Daddy said you left us. Is that true, Mommy? You don't want us anymore?" he questioned in a high shaky voice.

"Hermie, no that's not true! Mommy was sick and took a few days to herself to get well, but I'm feeling much better now. I'm so happy to see you. I missed you all very much. She bent down and kissed each of her children. She reached for her first born, hugged him tightly and then tickled him until he could no longer fight the laughter building up inside of him. He nuzzled his face in her neck and proceeded to give a report on how unhappy he was without her.

"Mommy, come home. Daddy can't cook. Breakfast this morning was gross, and he made me put back on the underwear I had on yesterday."

"What? You're wearing dirty underwear?" asked Lenora.

"We all are. We need to wash baaaad. The house stinks, too. There are dirty dishes all over the kitchen. Daddy said washing dishes is women's work, but there's no woman around."

Lenora sucked her teeth and said, "Herman, I thought your parents were helping?"

"My mother and father left for their trip to see my Aunt Sylvia yesterday. I had to pick them up. It won't kill them to wear the same underwear two days in a row." He was displeased his son was commenting on his lack of parenting skills. He could be such a tattle tell.

"And you know what else," continued Hermie.

"No, baby what else?" asked Lenora.

"Daddy gave us all a bath with detergent because we ran out of soap. It's making me itch. It's your fault cuz you left, Mommy."

Lenora was shocked. Was that stuff safe to bathe with? She didn't want to imagine her daughter's delicate vaginal interior being washed with something that was guaranteed to get the toughest stains out and contained color safe bleach. She only used that for her and Herman's clothes. She still washed her children's clothes with Dreft baby detergent. Hermie had sensitive skin, and the twins were still babies.

The twins continued to cling to her legs like little bear traps. Their grip was so tight, Lenora could feel her toes going numb, and she was still bent over hugging Hermie. It was an uncomfortable position. She let go of Hermie, pried the twins from her body and stood the full length of her 5'6 frame. Herman was smiling. He seemed to find satisfaction in his son's last comment. She stepped in front of her husband, and put her hands on her wide hips. He tried to walk around her. She stepped to the side and blocked him.

"Herman, what is wrong with you? Why didn't you take your trifling behind to the store?"

Lenora was upset about the underwear and the lack of soap, but she was furious her children were fed lies about why she wasn't there.

"So, that's your plan to get me back? You tried to turn my children against me."

"I told them the truth," said Herman still smiling. He clearly thought he had the upper hand.

"Did you tell them how you're mean to their Mommy? Did you tell them you got Mommy so upset she made herself sick trying to please you? I'm sure you didn't. I didn't leave them. I left YOU, and I didn't officially leave. I took a break from the mental and emotional abuse you have been causing me for far too long. You are a jerk, Herman, but you're my jerk. When I took my vows I meant them. I said for better or worse, and I must say, right now we're at our worst. I'm coming home because my children need me. But get this straight, there will be some changes whether you like it or not. The old Lenora, you tried to get rid of, is back, and she is not going to take your disrespect any longer. I'll lose the weight, but I don't need any nasty comments or guilt trips from you. I'm going back to work, and I'm building an art studio in the house. I put my entire life on hold to be a good mother and a door mat wife. Well, no more! I've got to have some balance and self-gratification in my life. I deserve to be happy, and I will. Do you have a problem with that?"

The smile on Herman's face was gone, and it was replaced with a blank stare. "If I did would it matter?" he asked meekly. At that moment, his wife was behaving more like Lenice than Lenora. He had no intention of getting beat up in public.

"Nope. Not at all," responded Lenora matter-of- factly.

"I didn't think so," said Herman.

"It's settled. Let's eat. Afterward, we can go back to my sister's house and get my things. Then, we are going to go home and clean our house as a family. No longer will you be able to shirk your responsibilities around the house. You have got to start setting a better example for our sons. Men cook and clean. I am not raising male chauvinists or filthy pigs. Don't you ever try to use anyone I birthed against me again!"

She turned her attention to her children who were watching their parents have an adult conversation. They were usually banished from the room during moments like this, but since they were in the middle of a parking lot there was nowhere for them to go.

Lenora smiled at the trio to let them know everything was going to be alright.

"You hear that my little munchkins. Mommy is coming home!"

"Yay! Heather we get new un-nerwear!" yelled Heston while playfully bouncing up and down.

His twin sister was wearing a dress, and Heather began taking off her *Princess and the Frog* panties right then and there in hopes of receiving a fresh clean pair.

"No, no, baby. Mommy will get you some more panties when we get to the house. Okay." said Lenora.

Heather looked confused for a moment and then, pulled her panties back to their proper position. Lenora ordered all of them to hold hands, and the three of them playfully skipped to the entrance of the restaurant. Before being seated, she took them to the restroom to get cleaned up and combed Heather's hair.

Herman walked slowly behind them wondering what else the new and improved Lenora had in store for him. He didn't really care because he was glad she was coming home. He stopped momentarily to scratch his behind. It was itching. He was wearing dirty underwear, too.

Chapter 55

Dinner Time

Mac's plan to get back into Tee's life hadn't gone as he planned. He never should have listened to her. He couldn't believe he was run out of Tee's house by a pregnant woman.

Maybe he should give up. After leaving her house, he went back to his downtown law office and found a beautiful woman sitting in the lobby waiting for his paralegal to return from lunch. Her name was Ashley. She had long auburn hair, and big brown slanted eyes. She wore a tight blue pencil skirt and a blue ruffled blouse that made him think of the singer Prince. Beautiful women always made Mac feel better. He asked Ashley out to dinner to help get his mind off Tee. That was two days ago, and this was the third time he'd agreed to see her since the day they met. He usually didn't make himself so easily accessible to women in the beginning. This helped prevent them from believing he really like them or developing the notion they were in some type of relationship.

Ashley stopped by his office earlier and asked if he would trust her enough to give her the keys to his house. She wanted to cook him dinner and have it waiting for him when he arrived home. Mac didn't trust any woman with the keys to his home. He was afraid she might make duplicate keys and enter his home uninvited one day. Instead, he gave her his garage door opener. He never locked the kitchen door. It was located inside the garage. She could let herself in that way.

Ashley wasn't the type of woman he normally dated. She didn't have a career. She was currently a cashier at Qwikie Mart gas station and was hoping to enroll in Southwest Community College next semester to take some class. What Ashley did have was a large behind, a giving heart and the girl could cook. It was obvious she wanted to be his woman. When they were together, she spent the entire time catering to him. It never ceased to amaze him what women would do for a man with money. He was sure when Ashley saw him she saw dollar signs like the rest of them. If he was broke and driving a Pinto, she wouldn't be in his home cooking him dinner.

Mac was tired and hungry and looked forward to a hot home cooked meal. He couldn't cook. He usually stopped by some restaurant after work and grabbed a bite to eat. He entered his house and looked around in approval. It was the opposite of how he left it this morning. It was clean. He fired his housekeeper two weeks ago after she accidently bleached one of his favorite shirts. That shirt cost $300 and such idiocy was not allowed in his home. The house hadn't been cleaned since. He was pleased to see the furniture dusted and the carpet vacuumed. He walked into the kitchen and noticed the clothes he placed in the dryer before he left were neatly folded, and a new load was in the washing machine and the dryer. The kitchen was clean and something delicious was baking in the oven. He didn't see Ashley anywhere, but he assumed she couldn't be far.

He had to admit he enjoyed her company. She had a great sense of humor and made him laugh often. He was tired of the high maintenance women he encountered in his elite circle of society. They were used to the finer things in life, were expensive to impress and even more expensive to maintain. Ashley thought Red Lobster was fine dining. She jumped for joy when he came by her job and told her to fill her tank up on him. The $30 it took to fill up her late model Maxima was nothing compared to the $100 he had to pay to achieve the same result on his Navigator truck. The weird thing was Mac had no desire to bed her, yet. He was attracted to her, but it wasn't only her body that made him want to spend time with her. He wondered what was happening to him. Was getting older starting to make him view women as more than sex objects? He knew the reason. It was Tee. After they broke up, he engaged in a buffet of women in order to try and forget her. It didn't work, and he began to realize all the sex in the world wouldn't make him feel better. The celibate relationship he shared with Tee taught him the importance of having a woman who fed your soul. The only way to truly figure out if she could do that was to focus on what she could offer besides the physical. In the brief time the two of them were together, Tee taught him the true meaning of the words *I love you.*

The house smelled wonderful. He peeked in the oven and saw two Cornish hens with dressing and another pan of what appeared to be sweet potato casserole. A pot on the stove contained green beans. He was going to eat good tonight. Mac walked to his bedroom. The bed was neatly made and lying on top of the comforter were three different sets of lingerie. One was pink, one was purple and one was red. They were each a different style. There were bras, panties, bustiers, garters and thigh-high stockings to choose from. She had even laid a pair of stilettos that matched each ensemble on the floor beneath them. Mac couldn't help but lick his lips at the thought of seeing Ashley in any one of them. He began to touch each one to see what the material felt like. His cell phone rang. It was a restricted number. He hated that he had no way of contacting her. He had to wait for her to contact him, and he never knew when she would call. He didn't even know her name, so he began referring to her as Casper—like the friendly ghost.

"I don't want any more help from you," he answered.

"No one told you to go running over to Tee's house and try to sleep with her. The woman got married less than a month ago. You know she's a good Christian woman," the voice said sarcastically.

"Did you really think she was going to sleep with you? I gave you valuable information about her marriage having some trouble and her being home alone and you had no idea what to do with it. You should have invited her out to dinner to talk. Let some people see the two of you out together. I'm sure word would have gotten back to Michael. Better yet, we could have made sure that it got back to Michael."

"Why didn't you say that in the beginning? How do you know what happened at Tee's house," asked Mac.

"I make it my business to know everything. And I thought you were smart enough to devise a plan on your own. Clearly, I was wrong. I'll have some more information for you soon. Next time, I'll make sure you know exactly what to do with it."

"I don't feel right about this. Leave me out of your personal vendettas. Whatever Michael did to you has nothing to do to me. I can't believe I'm taking advice about how to get the woman I love back from someone I've never even laid eyes on. Don't call me again. I should move on anyway," said Mac.

"I am going to deliver Tee to you lock, stock and barrel like I said I would. Next time I call pick up the phone. I'm sure you'll like what I have to say," said the voice.

The thought of having Tee back in his life made Mac smile.

"We'll see."

"That's a good boy. Ciao."

He smiled at the thought of holding Tee in his arms again and kissing her sexy lips. In the meantime, Ashley would do. He heard her enter the house and sing out, "Baby, I'm home. I ran to get some ice cream for dessert."

It was time to eat!

Chapter 56

Tee Hee

Michael was greeted by Dr. Foster in the waiting area of Accent Behavioral Health Center. This was the facility where Becca was being treated when she escaped a few months ago. This was Michael's first time being there. He felt it was best if he didn't visit Becca during her treatment since her obsession with him was what prompted her psychotic behavior. Accent looked more like the show room of a furniture store than a facility that treated the mentally ill. The waiting area contained a brown leather couch and love seat with two oak table ends. There was a large beige and black lamp sitting on top of each one. The oak coffee table that sat in front of the couch was covered in art books with paintings by contemporary artists Michael wasn't familiar with. A large grandfather clock stood in the corner. The gold pendulum swung slowly from side to side softly keeping time. Its chime rang out twice indicating that it was 2 p.m.

Dr. Foster introduced him to an older gentleman named John who said hello and then laughed. Dr. Foster explained that because of his propensity for laughter at any moment everybody called him Tee Hee. Tee Hee laughed when nothing was funny, but he couldn't help it. It was some type of nervous tick he couldn't control, and it always came out sounding like TEE-HEE.

Tee Hee was a long-term patient at Accent. He had several phobias and was afraid of almost everything, but he'd resided at Accent so long he wasn't afraid of it. For him, it was home. The staff allowed Tee Hee to spend his days roaming the large hallways and assisting the staff. He often chatted with other patients and helped new residents transition to the Accent way of life. He could go wherever he wanted as long as he didn't leave the grounds. Although, there was no fear of him trying to escape. Tee Hee had some terrible experiences in the outside world because of his condition, and he was afraid of stepping past the Accent property. He knew he was safer at Accent and no one there treated him like he was crazy because everyone in there had some type of mental illness. Some were violent and needed to be confined 24 hours a day and others, like Tee Hee, wouldn't hurt a soul. Tee Hee befriended Becca while she was there and agreed to tell them what he knew.

"I want to show you something," said Tee Hee.

Michael and Dr. Foster followed him as he shuffled to the recreational area. They entered a large room that contained ping pong, foosball and table hockey tables. There were several metal folding chairs surrounding round plastic tables. On the wall, was a mural of a family. The mural was done in intricate detail with rich, bold colors and it was of Michael, Becca and Michelle. This dysfunctional, fictional family portrait was the only artwork in the room, and it stretched from the floor to the ceiling. It had to be at least 10 feet tall. Michael and Dr. Foster looked at one another with, *what in the world* expressions but neither of them said a word. Tee Hee broke the silence.

"Rebecca worked on this thing for two weeks straight. She told me you were her husband, but I didn't believe it 'cuz you never came to visit. Other folks here with a husband get a visit sometime. She talked about you all the time and your daughter, Michelle. *Tee hee.* She talked about the condo you had in Miami and the rich family vacations ya'll took together. She said she was president of the football wives, and Michelle was a cheerleader at her school. She said she was gonna be out of here and back with you soon. She was real cooperative and taking her pills at first. Then, somehow she got news that you moved to Memphis to be with some woman. *Tee hee.* She stopped eating, stopped taking her pills. She would go to the toilet and throw'em back up as soon as the nurses made her swallow it. She wasted away to skin and bones and everything outta her mouth was 'bout how she was gonna cause you and your lady friend some kinda of pain. *Tee hee.* One day, she was gonna burn you alive. The next, she was gonna poison your food. Miss Rebecca got downright scary.

"You know how she got out? She gave one of the janitors some money to let her out. She had some money hidden away somewheres. Anyway, ole Julio snuck her out the back and drove her outside the gate in his truck. *Tee hee.* When he wasn't looking, she hit him with something, knocked him out cold and stole his truck. They found him the next day about a mile down the road wandering around in his underwear with a huge knot on his head. She had took his clothes and his wallet. All he got for his troubles was fired. *Tee hee.* Next thing I knew, she was dead for trying to kill you. I reckon' she wasn't you're wife, huh and that ain't your daughter, is it?"

"No, sir," Michael said but offered no further explanation. He shook his head. He would have thought the portrait was beautiful if it hadn't been a twisted manifestation of Becca's delusions. Why did the facility allow her to paint that and more importantly why was it still up? The picture of Michelle looked exactly like her, right down to the dimple in her chin and the small scar on her right arm.

"Miss Rebecca didn't have not a visitor the entire time she was here, but in the past month, you two are the second and third person to come 'round here asking about her. *Tee hee.*"

"Who else was here?" asked Dr. Foster.

"Some man. Said he knew her in college. I gave him Becca's diary. I took it when the news came 'round she was dead. I knew the nurses here would put it in the trash. I didn't think it was right to throw the story of a person's life away. *Tee hee.* I took it and kept it safe. I knew someone would be 'round for her sooner or later. I been here 30 years. Someone always gets curious about what happened to dey loved one and comes 'round asking questions. *Tee hee.*"

"Did you read the diary before you gave it to him? What did it say?" asked Michael.

"Sorry, Mister, but I can't read or write too well. I can tell you she loved you. I could see right through all that killin' talk. Yep. That woman loved you a whole lot. *Tee hee.*"

"Can you remember anything else about the man who came here asking about Becca? Do you remember his name?" asked Dr. Foster.

"Nope. I sure don't. I only remember what I told you. That was over a month ago. I'm getting old, and my memory ain't what it used to be. *Tee hee.*"

"Thanks, Tee Hee. You've been a big help," said Dr. Foster. "I'm going to send you those chocolate chip cookies I promised. Can you make phone calls?"

"Not supposed to without special permission, but sometimes, I sneak and use the phone to call my sister. *Tee hee.*"

"Well, here's my number and if that man comes here again, get his name and call me. I want to know everything he says to you."

"Okey. Dokey."

Tee Hee placed Dr. Foster's card in the pocket of the grey flannel shirt he was wearing.

"It's time for me to help with snacks. We got cupcakes today. They got good cupcakes here. Nice to meet both of you. *Tee hee.*"

"Same here. Take care, Tee Hee. Thank you for talking to us," said Michael.

Tee Hee shuffled towards the door. Michael looked down and saw he was wearing a pair of worn tennis shoes with velcro straps. There was a lot Tee Hee could do, and there was quite a bit he couldn't do. Tie his shoes was one of them.

Michael shouted after him, "Tee Hee, what size shoes do you wear?"

"Thirteen!" Tee Hee shouted back.

Michael was going to send him a pair of his shoes. What good was a Nike endorsement deal if you couldn't give shoes to people who really needed them?

Michael and Dr. Foster exited the building and headed to their cars. Michael spoke first.

"I wonder who came here asking about Becca. It wasn't someone from college because Becca never officially enrolled. She only pretended to go to college so people would give her money. From what I remember, the only friends Becca had were the ones she did drugs with. If you can call someone who supplies your drug habit a friend. Have you been able to dig up anything on her brother? I bet it was him."

"Not yet. His last known address is in Cincinnati, but I decided to stop in Akron first to visit here and check on you. I'm going to go there and do some investigating tomorrow. We have to find someone who has a connection to Becca in order to flush her or whoever is calling you out. I'm pretty sure if we find that person we'll be able to find out who has been harassing you. I promise you, Michael, I'm going to do my best to put an end to this quickly. I don't want her to kill again any more than you do. In the meantime, what are you going to do? How are you feeling? I've seen the news. I don't even have to ask because I know you didn't do it. Don't let your haters get you down."

Dr. Foster always did remind him of his mother and expressed a genuine concern for his well-being like she was his mother. He appreciated her faith in his integrity.

"Thanks, Dr. Foster. I'm fine. I have to keep it together if I'm going to continue to keep this from Tee. She has enough on her plate, and I don't want to worry her until I have a good reason. Now that my situation with Peter seems to have come to an end, I'm going to take my wife home. She's got a bedridden pregnant sister and a career she loves to get back to. The only reason she's here is for me. I need to take her back where she belongs. I'm not ready to tell her about this, and the best way to avoid having her find out is to keep her preoccupied with her already busy life. Thanks for all of your help. Let me know what you find in Cincinnati. Send me the names and numbers of the people who run this place so I can get the mural taken down. Becca really is twisted."

Chapter 57

What's In A Name?

Sandy laid in her bed looking at the ceiling. She did this often when she was alone and no longer felt like watching TV, reading a book or surfing the internet. Her mother brought her some dinner earlier, but she wasn't hungry. The uneaten portions sat on the nightstand beside her bed. She was disappointed to learn she was asleep when Lenice came by. She welcomed the company. She could hear her family downstairs playing video games and having fun without her. She wished she could join them. Her only company at that moment was her cat, Ms. Tiara.

Today was one of those days Patrick didn't seem to want to be around her. He tried to hide his feelings, but every now and then she saw the look of disdain he gave her. It came and left quickly, but it pained her that it was there at all. Some nights he refused to sleep in the bed with her. He claimed it was so she could have plenty of room, but she knew better. On the nights she slept alone, Patrick slept on the fold out couch in the den. One night, she was almost certain she heard him crying, but she was too afraid to confirm it.

She prayed again that this baby was her husband's. She knew God was merciful, and she needed Him to rain down a double dose of it on her situation. She patted her stomach. She was six months now, and her stomach was nice and round.

She wondered how Tee was doing. Their last conversation was the day before when she told her about Donovin's online discovery. Tiffany never did return her phone call. She tried to play the video again that morning, and it was gone. She knew Tee was busy tending to her own family. Michael needed her whether he wanted to admit it or not. Men could be so stubborn at times.

Armondo seemed to have gotten the picture. At least she hoped he had. She still wasn't able to get into her email.

Later that night, Patrick came into their bedroom, pulled the covers back and slid himself next to her. He wrapped his arms around her and said, "I've made a decision. If this baby isn't mine, I'll raise her as my own but that man is to never set one foot near her. This baby will have my last name and call me Daddy. I'm the only father she will ever know. I don't care what that man says or wants. You are not to talk to him under any circumstances."

Sandy let out a deep breath and shook her head up and down. She was relieved to know her husband wasn't planning to leave her if the baby wasn't his. She slid her hand in Patrick's hand and guided it down to her swollen abdomen. Their baby kicked as if she were letting them know she agreed to his terms, too.

"Patrick, what are we going to name her? We haven't discussed names at all," said Sandy.

"I thought about that. Let's wait and see what she looks like and then give her a name." Sandy wasn't so sure she liked the sound of that. She was sure he meant who she looks like.

Chapter 58

Choose Wisely

"What are you gay?" screamed Ashley.

"Gay? Are you crazy? What would make you say that?" yelled Mac.

Ashley rolled her neck. "Look at me." She took her hands and pushed up her breasts. "You got all this loquacious woman standing in front of you ready to make good love to you, and you wanna sit here and talk You can't be serious. Man, nobody turns me down. You must be gay."

This was the first time a woman had ever accused him of being gay, and Mac didn't like it one bit. Loquacious? Didn't she mean luscious? Maybe she was on to something, because right now, she was talking way too much for her own good. And she was being ghetto. He tried to respect Ashley, and she accused him of being a homosexual. He had nothing against gays, but he wasn't one of them. She was less on his level than he previously thought.

He grabbed Ashley's oversized purse off the chair in the kitchen and began walking towards the door with it. It was obvious it was one of those cheap knock offs found at flea markets.

"Where you going with my Loui?"

"This isn't Loui, it's Doui. When you have money and can afford the real thing, you can spot a fake from a mile away, and I'm not going anywhere with it. You are. You are getting out of my house," said Mac.

"Fine. I bet you ain't all that anyway."

"Oh yes I am all that and then some. If you want details call your cousin, Dynasty. She knows all about it, but I bet you knew that, didn't you? You're so desperate to land a man with money, you're willing to sleep with the same man your cousin did. Let me give you a piece of advice. You've got to know how to do more that cook and throw your goodies around to land a man like me. A man like me needs a woman with class and intellect, you broke, low-caliber woman. You can't even appreciate a man who isn't trying to rip your clothes off."

"I don't need you," said Ashley. "And why you calling me low-calorie? That's stupid and you're stupid."

You're stupid, Mac thought to himself. Ashley took her purse from him and walked out the door. She wondered what she did wrong. She could usually get any man she wanted if she cooked, cleaned and gave him some of her cookies. Mac had to be on the down low. No man could resist her. She turned around to ask if she could at least get the lingerie she left on his bed. She spent a whole $25 on each ensemble at Walmart and planned to take back the two sets he didn't like. She also planned to take all the shoes back to the $9.99 shoe outlet. She never had a chance to utter a single word because Mac slammed the door in her face.

"Dumb broad," he muttered. Had he really turned down an offer for sex from a woman he found incredibly attractive because he wanted to get to know her better first? What did Tee do to him?

Chapter 59

Night Out

Lenice wasn't happy to see Lenora go. She understood that her sister's children needed her, but she felt a few more days with her would give Lenora more confidence and a better exercise and nutrition regimen. She also enjoyed having her around.

Herman entered her home to get his wife's things. She didn't speak to Herman, and he didn't speak to her. He was careful to stay out of her path the entire time he was there. He also carried a small can of mace in his pocket in case she got the urge to teach him another lesson. The bruises on his neck were gone, and the scratches were healing nicely, but the bruises to his ego were still there.

Lenice didn't shed one tear on the outside, but she shed a million on the inside. Her conversation with James was still fresh in her mind. Webster wasn't enough to comfort her tonight. She needed a diversion. She almost called James three times to try to make him understand how truly sorry she was for her behavior. She knew doing so would only push him further away. With no man in her life, Tee out of town, Teresa still on her cruise with her husband and Sandy on bed rest, she did something she'd never done before. She called Tiffany and asked her to meet her for appetizers. Why not? They'd put their differences aside, and they should act like it. It might be fun.

Tiffany was at her parents' house when she received the call. She readily accepted the opportunity to forget about her troubles for a few hours. She asked her parents to watch Quincy 2 and left.

They met at a restaurant downtown called Blush. The place consisted of bright lights, happy people and live entertainment provided by a R&B singer named Tim. No last name, simply Tim.

They were spotted by two guys sitting at the bar and asked to dance as Tim belted out Usher's "Love in This Club." The gentleman who asked Lenice to dance was named Paul. He was pudgy with red hair and freckles but moved pretty good across the floor. Lenice didn't find him attractive, but she didn't care. She was determined to have a good time. Tiffany's dance partner was named Alan. He was Asian and had no rhythm whatsoever. Tiffany tried her best to avoid getting bruised feet courtesy of Alan's two left feet. She also tried not to laugh in his face as he struggled to keep up with her fly girl pace. She knew how to shake her big ole booty with the best of them and bounced her groove thang all over the floor for the whole place to see.

Once Paul and Lenice grew tired of dancing, he escorted her to a table, pulled out her chair for her and had a seat himself. They made small talk until their friends were also tired of dancing and came to join them. The foursome listened to music, ate fried dill pickles and chicken wings, talked about life and cracked jokes until it was time for Blush to close. Paul insisted that he and Alan pay for the soft drinks and appetizers. Tiffany and Lenice expressed their gratitude and commented on their gentlemanly mannerisms. They also offered to walk them to their cars, but Lenice and Tiffany declined. They wanted to walk together undisturbed and chit-chat for a few minutes.

Before going their separate ways, they all hugged, exchanged numbers and promised to meet up again for another evening of fun.

"I had such a good time," squealed Lenice. "Girl, I didn't know you could dance like that. You looked like a member of Destiny's Child out there."

"Thanks, Sugah. Alan looked like he was stomping on roaches out there. Moving fast was the only way I was going to keep him from messing up my French pedicure. Do you like it? I did it myself. Tiffany held up her foot to show three manicured toes protruding out of her peep toe shoes.

"You did a good job. Thanks for coming out tonight," said Lenice.

"My pleasure. I needed this more than you know."

"That makes two of us. Maybe taking the time to date for a while without getting serious about anyone won't be as bad as I thought."

"Now that I got Quincy out of my hair, I should probably date for a while myself before looking for a permanent boo. The last thing I need to do is bring another man into my son's life so quickly," said Tiffany.

"Then, that's what we'll do. We'll date and on nights like this when we need a pick me up, you can be my date and I'll be yours," suggested Lenice.

"Sounds like a plan to me. I need to go pick up Quincy 2, now. Call me tomorrow. Good night, Sugah."

"I'll do that. Good night."

The two parted like there was never any bad blood between them.

Lenice thought to herself, *Momma Pearl was right. I need to find my way back to the middle.*

Chapter 60

Home Is Where the Heart Is

Michael returned to his parent's house and told Tee he was ready to go home. He ate his lunch and bid them farewell. Michelle gave her Uncle Mike and Auntie Tee a tight hug and a sloppy kiss. The couple then returned to their hotel room, packed up their belongings and left the city.

Michael was exhausted, and Tee knew it. She offered to drive and 30 minutes into their trip, she looked over and saw he was fast asleep. She was glad he was finally able to get some rest. She looked over at him and admired how handsome he was. He even looked sexy in his sleep. Their lives were so turbulent lately. She hoped his sleep would be a peaceful one. He had a nightmare last night and woke up in a cold sweat. When she asked what it was about, Michael told her he couldn't remember.

Tee ran down her mental to do list. She needed to call Sheba and see how things were going at the office. She needed to call and check on Sandy, Tiffany, Lenora and Lenice. She needed to check on the status of the I'm A Good Woman Empowerment Conference. She instructed her intern to complete several tasks before she left. All of those calls would have to wait until the next day. She was not going to get on the phone and wake Michael. Besides, her sister and her friends were all grown. Their issues were no longer her top priority, her marriage was. But Michael needed to learn to stop hiding things from her and putting a wall up when things went awry. He needed to learn to allow her to share in his concerns. They were now her concerns as well. She shouldn't have to go through his phone to look for clues to help her figure out what was bothering him.

Michael slept like a baby most of the way home. He woke up and took the wheel when they were three hours away from Memphis. Tee slept the remainder of the trip. Once they arrived, he helped his wife make her way to the bedroom. It felt good to be home. Tee began taking off her clothes to change into her nightgown and enjoy a good night's rest in her own bed. Michael loved to watch her undress. He was well rested and decided it wasn't time to go back to sleep. He had other things in mind.

"Thank you for coming to Akron, Tee. I'm glad you didn't listen to me and stay away. Your presence brings me comfort, and your wisdom helps me make difficult decisions. Having you with me after learning Peter was murdered makes his death a little easier to deal with. Since you took care of me, let me take care of you."

Michael led her to the bathroom, turned the water on in their dual head shower and allowed it to warm. He finished removing her clothes and then, removed his own before guiding his wife under the steady stream of liquid. The water felt wonderful after sitting in the car for hours. They stood there and let the pulsating fluid massage their naked bodies as they clung to one another kissing passionately. Tee was his favorite dish. Michael pulled his lips away from hers and began to gently slather a thick lather of soap all over her slick body. He took great care to caress and kiss her most sensitive areas as he did so.

Tee moaned in pleasure and said, "I love being married to you."

"Ditto," he said in between suckling bits of her soft flesh.

Tee wondered why Michael said Peter was murdered when all of the news outlets reported he committed suicide. Now wasn't the time to ask because it would surely ruin the mood, and that was the last thing she wanted to do.

Neither one of them said another word. What they were doing didn't require conversation. Together they made the sweetest of love songs. He was the beat, and she was the melody. Their bodies kept time with one another in a serenade of intense passion. It was like the steady boom emanating from loud speakers that invades your body and makes you feel as if you are one with the music. It's inside of you. It is you. Tee had never experienced anything like this with another man. What they shared was physical, emotional and spiritual. He was her king. She was his queen, and together they made such a powerful force that the walls came tumbling down around their kingdom leaving them breathless and exposed. Pleasure seemed to know no boundaries when they were together.

Daybreak came much too soon for both of them, especially Tee. She needed to go to the office. There were a few things she couldn't complete remotely. She quietly dressed and left Michael in bed snoring soundly. She also left him written directions to pick Chesnutt up from the pet motel. She even gave him the green light to start scouting out new homes for the three of them. As proud as she was of her current home, it was only a house. If Michael felt he needed more room to be comfortable, what harm would it do to move?

On her way to work, Tee called Sandy to check on her. Sandy assured her she was fine, and Tee promised to swing by the house during her lunch break. She was anxious to get to the office and get back to work, but she didn't look forward to seeing the people. Sheba warned her there was plenty of gossip floating around the office about her husband's alleged NCAA infractions and to be prepared for the stares and whispers.

She really wasn't in the mood for nonsense, but it comes with the territory when you are married to a celebrity. She was still adjusting to people staring at them whenever they were out in public together. She hated the constant interruptions from fans hoping to get a hug, an autograph or a picture. Then, there were those with some business or product he should invest in. Tee always felt like she was on display. If she wanted to pick her nose or pull her underwear out of her behind, she didn't for fear that it would be on "TMZ" the next day.

Tee drove into the parking garage and spoke to their friendly security guard, who was also named Herman. He had a crush on her and actually got a little huffy when he found out she was getting married, as if the snaggle-toothed man actually had a chance with her. He was old enough to be her father. Eventually, he accepted that she was no longer on the market and returned to his normal jovial self. Perhaps, he realized how silly he was being.

"Gooth Morning, Mth. Long. I mean Stokes," he spat.

"Hey, Herman. Anything exciting happen while I was gone?"

"Nope. You and your honey wuz de exthitment."

"I see," said Tee. "Well, don't tell me about it. I can't take it right now."

"I won't, but I'm thure those cackling hens in there will. Have a gooth day."

"You too," said Tee as she drove through the security checkpoint.

The office didn't officially open until 9 a.m., and it was only 8:30. She busied herself checking emails and voicemails. She returned the urgent emails and left the rest for later. At 9:00 a.m., Sheba entered her office with a fresh cup of coffee and her mail. She placed the most urgent ones on top, except for a thank you letter from one of her nonprofit clients. Tee helped this organization raise $50,000 to assist the homeless. Sheba thought giving her new boss a warm fuzzy would be a great way to begin the day. She hadn't had a drama free day since she started. The two ladies chatted briefly about an upcoming private political fundraiser Tee was coordinating for one of the mayoral hopefuls. As Sheba left her office, Tee instructed her to shut the door and put up her Do Not Disturb sign. Although, when it came to Edgar it might as well have said enter without knocking. Her door swung open five minutes later.

"Oh, no you don't! I have barely heard from you in almost two weeks, and if you think you can hide yourself in here without so much as a hello you have got another thing coming.

Tee laughed. "You know it's nothing personal love. I've got a lot of catching up to do. How are you?" From that point on their conversation developed an interesting back and forth banter that resembled verbal volleys during a tennis match. They quickly passed comments back and forth to one another without pausing.

"Oh, I understand that. What I don't understand is how the NCAA can try and investigate your husband for something he may or may not have done forever and a day ago. Don't they have some new recruit they can investigate? For Christ's sake, the man is retired and whatever money he may have made from some illegal deal, he has made 40 times over by now. I read somewhere when he retired he was worth at least $200 million. I'm wonderful by the way."

"Edgar, my husband didn't do anything wrong, and since the man who supposedly had all this proof is dead, they can't pursue or prove anything. As far as I'm concerned, it's water under the bridge. You know I don't discuss his finances. How's Marva?"

"She's fine. Still at home refusing to get a job and spending every dime I earn. Sometimes I wonder why I married that woman. Then, I come home and she smiles at me, and I remember I love her. We live a nice life with one income but with two, we could live a fabulous life. I don't understand why she won't get a job. It's not like we have any children. His finances are now your finances."

"Keep praying about it, Edgar. Maybe one day she'll wake up with some motivation and concern for someone other than herself. I can't believe she won't even cook for you. A hardworking man at least deserves a hot meal when he gets home. You look nice today. New suit?"

"Yes. Thanks. She's doing a little better. Last night, we had Hamburger Helper lasagna. No sides to go with it, just lasagna." He let out a loud sigh. "I was hungry again before nine. By the way, she wants me to get her a ticket to your conference. She suddenly has the urge to do something in the community but doesn't know what and feels listening to the motivational speakers at your conference will help her get a clue. Your office smells much better."

"Thank you. I rather like the smell of clean air myself. I'll put her name on the guest list. Is there anything else?"

"Just that---"

Edgar left the door to her office open when he entered, and Katty Kathy took that as an invitation to waltz in and interrupt their conversation.

"Has Queen Tina arrived at work today? If I married a man that rich there's no way I would keep trudging up in here every day. Although, you do seem to come to work when you feel like it now."

Tee was irritated with everyone's fascination with her husband's money.

"Not that it's any of your business but I have been away attending to a family matter. Also, I like earning my own money, Kathy. It gives me a sense of accomplishment. I had goals and dreams before I met my husband. I'm not going to abandon them because I no longer have to worry about a paycheck. Although, I'm sure you wouldn't know anything about that. You've been in your same position for about five years now, haven't you? You don't seem interested in advancing at all," said Tee.

"Don't take your husband's problems out on me. All I know is if my husband was as fine as yours, the only goals I would have would include our bedroom. The only dreams I would have would be fantasies that we act out while making porn." Katty Kathy then moved her body in a hunching motion, slapped herself on the behind and laughed.

Tee was not at all amused to hear her talk about her husband sexually. The two of them were not friends. They only tolerated each other because they worked for the same company. She never liked her. Katty Kathy was a jealous gossip, and Tee had better things to do with her words than spread other people's business. She also had no desire to see her bouncing those silicone air bags around in her office and slapping herself on her manufactured behind. Everyone in the office knew what she did with her Christmas bonus. She showed off her enhanced mammaries and butt implants whenever possible. Everything was skin tight with a plunging neckline. Edgar once joked that if you took off her clothes you would find a serial number and made by Mattel etched somewhere.

"Did you have a reason for coming into my office unannounced, Kathy?" asked Tee. She wanted her gone as soon as possible.

"Only to tell you the boss wants to see you in his office, now." The smirk on her face was a good indication that something wasn't right. That girl loved being the bearer of bad news.

Chapter 61

The Doctor Will See You Now

Tiffany thought she would enjoy a day with no classes or clients but she wasn't. It gave her too much time to think about her troubles. However, they didn't seem so bad since she no longer had to worry about paying her bills. At least she didn't for now. She was living frugally in an effort to make the money Tee and Michael loaned her last as long as possible. Her child support hearing was in a couple days. If things went well, she wouldn't have to worry at all once she combined it with her massage income.

She hadn't heard from Quincy since he towed her car, and William found her a used Audi that was only two years older than the new one she had. It was in great condition and came with a note she could easily manage. He called earlier in the day to check on her and asked if she wanted him to bring her lunch. She declined because she was going to Quincy 2's school to eat lunch with her son today. Since she and Quincy broke up, he hadn't seen much of his father. He used to see him at least two to three times a week. Those visits were the only time he felt like he had a family. The three of them often went to dinner, watched TV and occasionally took a trip together. His absence seemed to indicate the only reason he came was for Tiffany, not because he took a genuine interest in being a good father to his son.

Quincy 2 used to be a happy active child, but he was no longer behaving like himself. He seemed sad and somewhat withdrawn from the outside world. When he came home from school, he went straight to his room. When asked how his day went, his usual reply was, "It was cool". He didn't want to go outside and play with his friends or attend his Boy Scouts meetings. All he did was eat and play video games. Tiffany was concerned about her son and thought surprising him at school with food from McDonald's would be a way to brighten his day.

Quincy 2 was in the third grade at Brighton Christian Academy. It had a reputation for being the learning environment of choice for city and business leaders of Memphis. Tiffany attended the school herself. The curriculum was rigorous with a focus on high achievement and excellence. She was happy her son was being given the same opportunity she was.

Tiffany entered the attendance office and took off her oversized Versace shades. She squinted as her eyes adjusted to the light. The school secretary greeted her with a sweet hello and asked how she could assist her. Tiffany informed her that she wanted to have lunch with her child, and the secretary informed Tiffany that Quincy 2 was not there. He was checked out 30 minutes early by her mother. The secretary showed her the daily log with her mother, Mrs. Aurora Tate's signature.

"Ms. Tate, your mother has been checking Quincy out around this time once a week for a little over a month now," said the secretary.

The way Tiffany raised her eyebrows let the young woman know she had no idea her child was missing school regularly.

"Why didn't you inform me?" demanded Tiffany.

"We saw no need. You mother is on your approved check out list. We have it documented that she has permission to pick him up. Therefore, we assumed you knew. Each time, he returns the next day with a doctor's note. Therefore, we excuse the absence and allow him to make up any work he missed. We thought he was ill."

Tiffany was fuming. Her child was not ill. He had a physical last week, and the doctor said he was healthy. He had to have one to go on an obstacle course trip with his Boy Scout troop. Quincy 2 said he didn't want to go, but Tiffany insisted. She was tired of seeing him moping around the house.

"I assume you keep the doctor's notes on file?" she asked.

"Yes, we do."

"May I see them?"

"Of course, Ms. Tate."

The secretary walked to the back wall behind the counter to a long row of brown file cabinets. She opened one of them and retrieved a file. She walked as quickly as she could back to Tiffany and handed her the manila folder that housed her child's personal information.

Tiffany opened the folder and saw five doctor's excuses from a Dr. Stanley Fleming of Smile Pediatric Center. She took a pen out her purse and wrote down his name along with the address and phone number of his practice. She planned to go pay Dr. Fleming a visit and get to the bottom of things.

There was a wreck on the highway, and it took her almost 30 minutes to get to his office. She was a woman on a mission. She swiftly opened the car door and barely had one foot on the ground when her mother came rushing out of the building.

"Mother, where is my child?" she asked angrily.

"He is in there with the doctor." Mrs. Tate replied calmly.

"What right do you have to take my child on regular doctor's visit without my knowledge or permission? He already has a pediatrician."

"I'm his grandmother. The boy has issues that need to be addressed."

Aurora Tate was a caring woman who loved her grandson dearly. Her husband, Sullivan, forbade her to have any contact with him or Tiffany once he found out Tiffany was pregnant by a married city official. At the time, he was running for another term in Congress and didn't need a scandal preventing his victory. Family values were an integral part of his platform. Tiffany felt he was being a hypocrite because her father was infamous for his extramarital affairs. But the Tate family had been a part of the city's political arena for five generations and many Memphians voted for a Tate from name recognition alone. Her father demanded she end her affair with Quincy, and Tiffany refused. She was a woman in love and didn't care that he was married. However, since her break-up with Quincy things were much better between them and to the delight of his grandmother, Quincy 2 spent time with his grandparents regularly.

Mrs. Tate readily volunteered to pick him up from school, babysit and whatever else she could do to help make-up for not being a part of his life for the past eight years. She began to notice he was showing his adorable dimpled smile less and less and took it upon herself to intervene without consulting Tiffany first. She saw how hard her daughter was working and wanted to give her one less thing to worry about.

"Issues? What kind of issues?" asked Tiffany. "He never told me he had any issues?"

"According to him, you've been too busy to notice much of anything. Did you ever stop to think about how all of this is affecting him? Quincy feels abandoned."

"Abandoned? That's ridiculous. I see him every day!"

"Are you spending time with him? Think about it. His father, who he used to see regularly, no longer comes around. His mother, whom he used to have all to himself because she was a stay at home mistress, is now in school and working. Not to mention, you are dealing with your own emotional issues stemming from the break-up.

"Quincy knows he is the illegitimate child of one of the most prominent men in Memphis. How would you feel if you saw your father in the paper and on the news with his family that didn't include you? To know you have sisters that you've never met. You aren't allowed to go over their house to play, but you don't understand why. That boy will be nine soon. Do you think he doesn't know that he is his father's dirty little secret? I started taking him to a psychiatrist so he could talk to someone about his feelings," Mrs. Tate explained.

"Dr. Fleming is a psychiatrist! You've been talking my baby to a kiddie shrink without telling me. If my child should be talking to anyone it should be me! For all I know he could be some quack filling my son's head with nonsense and telling him I'm an unfit mother."

Tiffany wanted to know what they were talking about, and she wanted to know now.

"Move out of my way, Mother."

Tiffany swept past her mother and entered the building. The waiting area was brightly painted in the various shades of the color wheel. In one corner of the room was a small play area for little children. In another, there were electronic games to help keep older children occupied while they waited to have their head examined by a man she'd never heard of. No one was there. She rang the small bell on the counter, but no one came. She knocked on the door that separated the waiting area from the private offices and again, no one answered. She saw no need to wait for an invitation and turned the knob. She walked down hall calling Quincy 2's name and opening every door she saw along the way. No one seemed to be in any of the rooms. A tall bearded gentleman with a friendly face stepped out of the last room on the left. He wore a corduroy jacket, with suede patches on the elbows and jeans.

"Ms. Tate, You're here. It's a pleasure to finally meet you. I've been requesting a meeting with you, but your mother said you were in class at this time and were unable to make it," said Dr. Fleming and offered her his hand.

Tiffany shook it reluctantly.

"Well, I can't say the same considering today is the first time I've ever heard of you." Tiffany was flustered. What right did her mother have to try and parent her son? And why was Quincy 2 more comfortable talking to a stranger than her?

"I'm sorry to hear that, but it's important you're here. I've been meeting with Quincy one on one for a little while now, and I think we could get more out of his sessions if you joined us from time to time."

"How about I join you now? I'm curious to know what you've been telling my child and what my child has been telling you," said Tiffany.

"I think that's a mighty fine idea, Ms. Tate. Come right on in," said Dr. Fleming. He held the door to his office open so Tiffany could enter.

Chapter 62

Men Suck

Lenice sat nervously in the restaurant. She was waiting for him. She hadn't seen Scott in two years. She was making great strides with her therapy, but she knew the only person who could truly help her slay her demons was him. It was time for her to get some closure. She thought about simply calling him, but that wouldn't be enough. She needed to look into his eyes. She had to learn how he could keep that kind of secret from someone he was supposed to love, while knowing if it was ever exposed it could tear her heart apart. It had done exactly that and sent her into an abyss of distrust, anger and self-inflicted loneliness.

Lenice tried to seal the pain away in the recesses of her heart in order to function. But some of it seeped out and she became cold, unfeeling and afraid of love. She swore off all men and retreated to the comfort of her dog, her friends and her vibrator. She wanted to feel again. She wanted to love again. She believed she was now ready to trust a man, even if it was only just a little.

Her mind drifted back to the day she found out the man she adored was on the down low. She left work early and came home to her live-in boyfriend to sneak in some extra quality time. She wondered why their lawn man's truck was in their driveway since he cut the grass two days earlier. It was a dreadful sight to behold. She walked into their bedroom and saw Scott lying in the arms of another who didn't resemble her in appearance or gender. She ran from the house screaming like someone shot her. She drove to her sister's house and stayed the night. When she returned the next day, all Scott's belongings were gone. He left her check for $1,500 for his half of the rent, utilities, and other bills. Was that all she was to him, a roommate? He also left a simple note. What kind of man breaks up with his girlfriend in a seven-sentence note he wrote on a napkin? He should have faced her like a man. For the past two years, she wondered what another man had that she didn't. What did he offer to make Scott forsake her?

Lenice never tried to contact Scott after her discovery, and he didn't try to call her either. There was no closure. She severed all ties with their mutual friends and his family. She had been especially close to his mother, Samantha, and his sister, Madeline, but it hurt too much to keep in touch. She often yearned for the closeness they used to share. With both her parents being deceased, times spent with Samantha were welcomed maternal moments.

She sent Scott an email asking him to meet her. He said he would but he was 30 minutes late. Scott was always late. It was one of the things she didn't like about him. When they were together, he made her miss several planes and important engagements with his tardiness. Lenice asked the waiter to bring her another glass of water. She was hot and needed to cool off. She drank the first glass hurriedly and requested another. As her wait approached one hour, Lenice knew he wasn't coming. He was still a coward. She had to accept that her healing process wouldn't include him. Every relationship leaves an impression, but it was as if this one was solidified in cement. Lenice was determined to find a jackhammer to break up those painful memories and move on with her life.

She called the waiter over again and ordered herself a chicken salad with ranch dressing and a cocktail. After her drink arrived, she raised her glass in the direction of no one in particular and said aloud, "Here's to moving on and finding love again. Men suck!"

Chapter 63

Mommy Dearest

Tiffany felt like an unfit mother. How could she have not realized her child was in such turmoil? She, Dr. Fleming and Quincy 2 talked for two hours. Quincy 2 told her how much he missed his father and that he hated no longer being the most important part of her day. He understood she had to work, but when she got home, she was tired or needed to study and barely paid him any attention. He told her he called his father several times, and often, he didn't answer. When he did, he only talked to him a few moments and lied to him about coming to see him soon. He told her about one time he called, and a woman answered. She called him a bastard and told him not to call again.

Tiffany sat and listened as her only child poured his heart out with a little assistance from Dr. Fleming. When he was finished, she assured Quincy 2 he was still the most important part of her day and the reason she was working so hard was to take care of him. Things were different between she and his father now, and she had to go to school and work to provide for them. She wanted her son to continue to have the best in life, and she was working hard to give it to him. She never meant to make him feel like he was unloved or that she was too busy for him. The juggling act she was now required to do was new to her, and she was still learning how to do it right. She said she would speak to his father about his behavior and the woman who answered the phone. She let him know that no matter what he was loved by her and her parents. Tiffany promised Quincy 2 that the coming Saturday and Sunday would be mother and son weekend, and they could do some of his favorite activities together.

Dr. Fleming informed Tiffany the clinical diagnosis for Quincy 2's condition was depression. He didn't want to put a child so young on medication, but it would take some work to help him adjust to the changes in his life. Tiffany made an appointment with Dr. Fleming to discuss the best way to assist her son through this trying time in both their lives.

She wanted to take Quincy 2 home with her, but he begged to go home with his grandmother to see his grandfather, who he affectionately called Papa. He looked forward to spending time with his Papa. Tiffany was happy Quincy 2 and her father were forming a bond. This allowed her son to maintain a father figure in his life. On the way home, Tiffany decided she needed to do something to make herself feel better. She needed some therapy as well.

Chapter 64

WOW

Tee reviewed the day's events in her mind. How could that happen? One moment she was one of the most successful, highly sought after and well-paid event planners in the city. The next, she was unemployed. Mr. Anderson treated her like a criminal. He fired her and instructed security to escort her from the premises.

Security walked her to the elevators the long way so they could make a spectacle of her. The entire office--managers, co-managers and subordinates--were lined up along the hallway staring as her. They stood and looked at her with faces that showed no concern, disgust or anger. What had she done to be the recipient of such ugliness?

As far as they were concerned, she hit the jackpot. She married a man with money who could give her a life most of them would never experience. Instead of being happy that one of their own received the favor of God through a wealthy Christian man, they were jealous. There was no sympathy for an unemployed rich woman.

Before she was dismissed, Tee stood in Mr. Anderson's office and listened to his list of reasons for terminating her employment. He told her that she was no longer focused. Was he not paying attention? She was stabbed and almost killed. She endured a slow recovery process. She got married and went on her honeymoon. Upon her return, she was forced to watch her husband being slandered repeatedly. Of course she wasn't focused! Mr. Anderson said she was using company resources for personal gain. She paid everyone at the company who helped her with I'm A Good Woman out of her own pocket. He also said her contribution to the company's revenue was low. Her numbers were low because she took some time off from work to recover and to get married. But she also made sure all her clients were in good hands. Others in the company received the majority of the commission because they did the majority of the work. After everything she had done for Innovations, she couldn't believe he behaved that way. It was her hard work and ingenuity that built the events division of Innovations Marketing & Events. When she came to the company, events only contributed to 20% of the revenue generated and now it made up 40% and some months as much of 60%. When the recession hit and companies significantly reduced their marketing budgets, it was her department that kept the company afloat. She built him a winning team, recruiting and hiring some of the best talent the city had to offer. All she could say at the moment was WOW!

The last thing Mr. Anderson said to her was, "Don't take it too hard. You won't have to worry about where your next meal is coming from like so many of the unemployed today. And if you should decide to continue doing events, your contract states you cannot do business with any of the companies on my client list for at least five years. If you do, I'll see you in court."

Tee wasn't out of the building five minutes when her phone rang. She knew it was Edgar without having to look.

"Hey! How are you?" said Edgar.

"How do you think I am? I just got fired from the company I helped to build."

"Dumb question. I'm sorry that happened to you, but you will be fine. You always land on your feet, Tee."

"Yeah, but right now it hurts," said Tee. "Do you know how embarrassing that was, and it appeared everyone knew it was coming except me. The walk down the hallway to the elevator felt like it took forever with everyone staring at me."

Tee was devastated. Innovations was like home to her, and she thought her team was her family. She had been evicted. Did her family turn against her merely because she had millions now? She always made a good salary. Why was money a factor now? Besides, many of them enjoyed their lucrative salaries because of her. She made sure every member of her team received what they deserved and then some. She was a firm believer that happy employees were more productive and more productivity meant more revenue.

"Everyone didn't know because I didn't. Don't you worry about a thing. Me and that flat booty assistant of yours will clean out your office and bring you your things. I don't want any of those heartless, jealous niñas touching them. You probably wouldn't get it all back if they did."

Tee giggled. "Edgar, don't say such mean things about Sheba. She's a sweet girl."

"I know she is. We had some nice chats while you were gone. She seems to be a big fan of yours. She had nothing but rave reviews for her new boss. I was even ringside to a couple of conversations where she put Katty Kathy in her place when she came around trying to gossip about you and pump Sheba for info about Michael's situation. But don't act like you didn't notice she has virtually no figure. If you stood her backside next to a wall and compared the two, I bet the wall would have more curves."

Tee giggled again.

"Thanks for making me laugh, Edgar. I love you, and I'm going to miss seeing you almost every day."

"Same here. The boss is calling me so I better go. Keep your head up, girl. God has something greater for you. I can feel it in my bones. Bye."

Edgar was probably right, but Tee was still upset. Mr. Anderson treated her as if all the time and sweat she put into Innovations meant nothing. Several companies tried to lure her away from him, but she was loyal. She took pride in watching the company thrive and wanted to see how far the two of them could take it.

She heard the familiar chime of her phone indicating a text message arrived. It was from Michael. He wrote, go to the hospital. Sandy's in labor.

Tee's heart started to race. Labor? Her niece wasn't due for another three months.

Chapter 65

Momma's Baby, Daddy's Maybe

Sandy breathed in and out in short spurts and held Patrick's hand tightly. She couldn't feel a thing below her bosom, and the hospital staff was down there working. That morning she went to use the bathroom and noticed some spotting. Patrick took her to the doctor as a precaution and an ultrasound revealed that the baby's umbilical cord was wrapped around her neck, and her heart rate was low.

Everything after that was a blur with words like "emergency surgery," and "the baby could die," being said. People were rushing all around her without really talking to her or Patrick. Sandy heard one of the nurses say to someone they were lucky the OB's office was so close to the hospital.

Dr. Walker was prepped and ready to perform the emergency C-section. The baby had to come out now. Sandy noticed the worry in Dr. Walker's face when the baby's heart began beating slower and slower. She held Patrick's hand tightly and prayed her little one would be alright. Her two previous pregnancies went to term, and she was afraid the baby's organs weren't fully developed or she wouldn't live or perhaps the lack of oxygen damaged her little brain.

Earlier, while the doctors and nurses scrambled frantically to get Sandy into the operating room, Patrick called their parents and Tee. He got in touch with everyone but Tee and left a message on her voice mail. He also called

Michael and told him to make sure she got the message. Michael assured him he would get in touch with her.

Patrick was going to be a father again, and he was excited. There was a cloud of sadness hovering above him, but he was determined to make the best of this situation.

There were people everywhere, and they all seemed to be anxiously waiting for the baby to be born. He had no idea why they needed so many people, and he watched as Dr. Walker and her staff worked frantically to deliver the baby. He felt himself getting uncomfortably hot in the paper scrubs and mask he had to wear in the operating room. He turned his head as they made the horizontal incision across his wife's lower abdomen and her insides. He turned his head back but quickly turned it again as they separated Sandy's abdominal muscles, pulled the baby out of the womb and unraveled the umbilical cord from around their daughter's neck.

The nurse yelled out the time of delivery, and someone whisked the baby over to another group of medical personnel waiting on the side. Patrick held Sandy's hand more tightly. He was so afraid. The baby was pale, and she wasn't making any noise – no crying or whimpering like Nicole and Donovin did on the day of their birth. Dr. Walker assured them that the Neonatal Intensive Care Team was doing everything they could to help her.

Patrick walked over to where they were working and tried to see what they were doing. She wasn't breathing. *Please God this baby has a purpose, let her live*, he prayed. Suddenly, there was a loud gasp, followed by a weak cry. It was the most beautiful sound he had ever heard. His baby was alive! She was weak but alive. He ran over to Sandy, gave her a kiss and lovingly caressed her face. She smiled. She was tired but good.

The team cleaned the baby up and brought her over to Sandy and Patrick for a quick glimpse. She was beautiful! She was also very small and fragile, but everything seemed to be fully developed, from the outside. She had 10 fingers and 10 toes. Her eyes were closed. He tried to look for any indication that this was his child. Babies were so funny looking at birth, and this one was premature. She was light-skinned with curly black hair. The baby's eyes suddenly opened, and they were a piercing shade of grey. Patrick's proud papa moment came to an abrupt end. He dropped his head and backed away from Sandy. She looked at him and knew exactly what he was thinking. With grey eyes, the baby couldn't possibly be his. Someone explained the baby was not breathing well enough on her own and needed oxygen to stabilize her. The nurse whisked the newborn away to the Neonatal Intensive Care Unit.

It was hot, Patrick couldn't breathe and it felt like the room was closing in around him. He exited the room, leaving Sandy alone while her doctor attended to her open abdomen. He tore off his scrubs and hit the wall with his fist, but he was not alone. He turned around and saw Momma Pearl watching him.

"Well son, tell me something. How's my child and grandbaby?"

"Dr. Walker said Sandy would be fine. The baby is alive, but it's too early to tell how she's doing. The doctors are working on her now," said Patrick softly and slowly. Tears began to form in his eyes. This was too much for him.

Tee and Michael walked up behind her. They had all been in the waiting area praying. Patrick knew his mother-in law had no knowledge of his wife's indiscretion, but Tee knew. He blurted in her direction. "That baby has grey eyes. She's not mine. She's not mine, Tee!"

Momma Pearl was perplexed.

"What would make you say that?" she asked.

"Sandy had an affair. I knew there was a possibility the baby might not be mine, but I was hoping when she came out she would look like me, and we could finally put this behind us. I don't know if I can raise another man's baby. I can't even look at Sandy right now. Tee, you'll have to tell her I need some air. I need time to think. I'll come back and check on her later."

"You can't leave. She just had a baby by C-section. She needs you, and your parents are in the waiting room. I'm not going to be the one to explain to them why you left," said Tee.

Momma Pearl laughed. Everyone looked at her in bewilderment. What was so funny?

"None of you would know that Sandy's father had grey eyes since you never met him. You do know she's part Creole, right? That ain't nothing but part white. Patrick, pull yourself together. She had an affair. Well, so did you. She forgave you. Evidently, you forgave her since you're here. Babies are a blessing no matter how they got here. You two need to learn to stop turning away from each other for comfort and turn to each other. Now, get out of my way. I need to go check on my daughter. I'm sure you have her all upset with this not my baby nonsense. You two get a DNA test as soon as possible and put your minds as ease. Mark my words. That's your baby, and I don't have to see her to know it. I bet she looks like her granddaddy. He was a handsome devil. I hope you two have learned your lesson about cheating. All it brings is stress."

Chapter 66

Sexual Healing

William could tell something was wrong by the sound of Tiffany's voice. She wouldn't tell him what it was over the phone. She only said she needed to see him. He wondered if Quincy made another visit. He told her he would come over after the dealership closed. It was a good day. William sold three cars. Normally after work he headed to the gym or church, but today he altered his schedule to see what was bothering Tiffany, his vision of loveliness.

William didn't expect for Tiffany to answer the door in a form-fitting, short black dress. He didn't expect to enter the house and be greeted by the sound of Teddy Pendergrass singing "Turn Off the Lights." The room was dim and the sweet scent of vanilla filled the room. Tiffany pressed her body against him tightly in an embrace and pulled away slowly before planting a soft kiss on his cheek. She offered him a glass of champagne. William accepted the flute she extended to him but did not drink. He didn't drink alcohol.

She told him to have a seat on her living room couch. The vanilla scent was from candles burning on the mantle of her fireplace. They cast a warm glow on the bricks behind them. On a small table in front of him was a plate of strawberries and cheese. Tiffany picked up a strawberry and slowly sucked the end of if before she took a bite. She moaned softly, "Mmm, this is delicious, William. You should try one. I can feed it to you, if you like." He politely declined. He was allergic to strawberries.

Tiffany asked him about his day. She sat close to him with her shapely legs crossed in his direction. While sitting, her skirt rose higher exposing her entire leg. It barely covered the top of her thighs. She shifted to hide the scars from her attack at the spa. Tiffany hoped William found her enticing. She was tired of feeling alone and unwanted. As far as she was concerned, trying to be a good Christian was making her miserable. She prayed every day, and it appeared her situation wasn't improving. This was one of the most stressful times in her life, and sex was her favorite stress reliever. Trying to live a life of celibacy was denying her the pleasure of releasing that stress. She was used to having one specific man to assist her in her sexual healing, but Quincy was gone, and she needed a replacement. William was a handsome enterprising young man. He seemed like an excellent choice.

She listened as William talked about indecisive customers, unreasonable finance managers and families with cute kids. She reached over and loosened his tie. She really didn't care how his day went. She wanted him to kiss her, touch her, make her feel like a woman. What was taking him so long? She would have to make the first move.

"Come here, baby. I don't bite. Well, maybe a little," she said and kissed him softly on his cheek, again. It was followed by a nibble on his ear lobe.

"Tiffany, I need to tell you something," said William.

"I'm listening."

"I don't want or need a relationship right now. I-" Tiffany saw no need for him to finish his statement.

"I appreciate you telling me, but I don't want a relationship, either. Quincy and I are newly split, I'm in massage school, I'm seeing clients almost every day and all of this has been very hard on my child. He was diagnosed with depression today. He feels like his parents are neglecting him. The last thing I need is another person to worry about, but I could use a special friend for times like this when I don't want to be alone," said Tiffany. She slowly ran her hand down his muscular chest.

"We all get lonely sometimes. Occasionally, we could help each other out. You work on your feet all day. After work, you could come over here and let me massage your feet, along with the rest of you," she continued seductively. "Let's have some fun. Consider this my emancipation party, and you are the only invited guest."

William smiled. "You're a gorgeous woman, Tiffany, and I would like to be there for you. Do you mind if I touch you?"

"I don't mind at all. As a matter of fact, I welcome it," said Tiffany.

William sat his drink on the table and took off his suit coat. Tiffany was giddy with anticipation. She couldn't wait for him to put his hands on her. She knew she was in for a treat. He rolled up his sleeves and stood in front of her. Then, he knelt down before her, put a hand on her forehead and said these words.

Dear Father, this is your son, Rev. William Lewis, calling on you once again. I'm asking you to look down on Sister Tiffany and deliver her from the forces of evil that are now working against her. I ask you to deliver her from poverty, pain and sadness. I ask you to bless her finances. Make her client list so long she'll have to hire help. On the day she goes in that courtroom, I ask you to be the lawyer and the judge and allow her to get the money she needs to help her to take care of her son. I ask you to deliver her son from his depression and help him to see that his mother loves him. But dear Lord, I mostly ask you to make her feel your presence. Let her know she is never alone, you're always with her. Not a day goes by that you don't look at her and say that's my child and I love her.

You've known her since the day she was born. You see her pain and deepest desires. Reveal yourself to her. She is seeking you, but she is a new child in Christ. Help her to get in your word and understand that she doesn't need a man to fulfill her needs because you can give her everything she needs. The pleasure of the flesh is temporary but the pleasure of God is eternal. Help me to be the friend she needs. Help me to help Tiffany understand Christianity isn't about depriving yourself. It's about releasing yourself from the sin in this world and recognizing what it has to offer doesn't compare to what you have to offer. Move mountains on her behalf. She needs you. These and many other blessings we ask in your name, Father. Amen

Tiffany was dumbfounded. She had no idea William was a minister. She was trying to seduce one of God's chosen ones. Could she go to hell for that? She also made a complete and utter fool of herself. But the prayer was beautiful. She'd never had a man pray for her before.

William rose from the floor, looked Tiffany in her eyes and said, "You're stronger than you think you are, Tiffany. The last thing you need is another man in your bed who isn't ready to make you his wife. We barely know one another."

Tiffany looked him up and down as he kissed her on the forehead, retrieved his suit coat and left. Tiffany began to pray.

Okay God, I get it. Your way is the best way. I'm sorry. Please forgive me for making all those promises and then being willing to easily break them when things don't go my way. I'll do better, but I need your help. I'm weak. Please give me strength Father.

She hoped God heard her. She felt like a fool. Tiffany laid down on her couch and cried herself to sleep. What had she become? Was she that desperate?

Chapter 67

One Day At A Time

It didn't take Lenora long to find a job. A private Montessori school was looking for an art teacher and hired her during the interview. The principal was very impressed with her love of children and her artistic skills. As part of her portfolio, she presented the painting she completed while staying with Lenice. It was a portrait of the two of them, and they were the same size. Lenora considered this her vision board. She was going to lose the weight.

Things at her house improved greatly in a short amount of time. She and Herman sat down and had a heart to heart talk. He expressed as gently as he could that he was less physically attracted to her, but he still loved her. It hurt Lenora to hear it, but she appreciated his honesty. She promised to lose the weight, but he had to be patient. She didn't gain it over night, and she wasn't going to lose it over night. She was now eating healthier foods and exercising regularly. She already had a five-pound reduction to show for her efforts.

She asked him where he was the night of their anniversary. Herman admitted he went to a strip club with some of his buddies to celebrate someone's birthday. He had too much to drink and forgot about their anniversary. He assured her there was no other woman in his life. He also agreed to go to counseling. They decided to select a Christian marriage counselor. This would allow them to not only grow closer as a couple but in Christ as well. Lenora believed with the Lord's help they could repair their marriage.

The children were happy Lenora was back. The house and their underwear were clean. Meals were edible again, and they felt loved by both parents. Each evening after dinner, they cleaned the kitchen as a family. Herman was willing to shed his chauvinistic ways if it would bring more harmony to his home. They found small tasks for the children to do to make them feel useful and teach them responsibility. Lenora was taking control of her life, and she felt better than she had in years.

Chapter 68

Family Ties

"I found Becca's brother, or at least I found out where he is," said Dr. Foster. "He's in Nashville. According to his wife, Sean moved there a couple of months ago. Shortly before Becca was admitted to the mental facility, she reached out to him. They patched things up, and he was planning to visit her. That never happened because she was captured, and they lost touch. Sean didn't find out she was institutionalized until after I shot her. The wife said he took it pretty hard. She still lives in Cincinnati, though. They're going through a divorce."

"Do you think he and whoever is calling me are working together to ruin me? I'm still not sure it's Becca," asked Michael.

"Me neither. He could be working with someone, but if you think about it other than calling to scare you, she really hasn't caused you any harm. Maybe Sean is helping her gather information on you and Tee to use against you. Try not to worry, Michael. I plan to stay on this case and see if I can't figure out what she's planning to do to ruin you."

"I appreciate your help, but be careful, Dr. Foster. She's killed twice already. I'm sure she would do it again. If she has a vendetta against me, she probably has one against the woman who shot her as well."

"I'm not worried. I was a cop for over 25 years, and I helped bring down some tough criminals. She don't want none of this," said Dr. Foster.

Michael laughed. Dr. Foster had to be at least 55 years old. "Alright, Lone Star Ranger. I assume you'll be coming to Tennessee. Be sure to let me know when you arrive."

"I sure will. How are you sleeping?"

"Not well. The nightmares have started again. Only they're not like before. I couldn't see anybody's face because of a black shroud. This time, I see Becca's face clearly, and she's mad as heck. I keep wondering if I should tell Tee about the phone calls. My wife's not stupid. She knows something is wrong, but she's been through so much because of me. I don't want her to have anything else to worry about. I only want to bring her happiness," said Michael.

"I can understand, that but if keeping secrets from Tee is causing you more stress, I say tell her. You two are newlyweds, and it's not a good idea to start the marriage off giving Tee insecurities because she suspects you're hiding something from her," advised Dr. Foster.

"I'll think about it. I'll talk to you later. I'm at the hospital with Tee. Our new niece came into the world today."

"Congratulations. Give Tee my love."

"Will do."

Chapter 69

This Is Bliss

Sandy and Patrick were beaming. The doctors confirmed their daughter was healthy. She was breathing better with the help of a breathing tube. All of her organs were fully developed, and the doctors were confident there was no brain damage. However, at four pounds, her birth weight was low, and she would have to stay in the hospital a few weeks to allow them to fatten her up and monitor her improvement. She was still in the NICU, and Sandy hoped she would be taken there by wheel chair to see her soon. After the birth, Dr. Walker stitched her up and gave her a mild sedative so she could get some sleep. It didn't seem to be working, yet.

Tee felt better already. The fact she was humiliated and unemployed seemed miniscule to the joy this new little person ushered into their lives. She, Momma Pearl and Patrick were in Sandy's hospital room talking.

"I can't wait for you to see Little Tina. She's so cute," said Sandy.

"What did you call her?" asked Tee.

"Sandy decided to name her after one of the biggest influences in our lives. You've always been our cheerleader. You've been a great friend to me and an amazing aunt to our other children. We thought naming our baby after you would be fitting," explained Patrick.

Sandy chimed in, "Her full name is Tina Penelope Pierce. Doesn't that have a nice ring to it?"

Tee was overcome with emotion. She would have her very own namesake. How fantastic was that?

"It certainly does, but what made you select Penelope?"

"I read it in a book once, and I've always liked it. I can't go anywhere right now because of my stitches. Plus, I'm numb below the waist, but you can go see her. Why don't you and Momma go now? Patrick went earlier. Tell her Mommy's coming soon."

Patrick escorted Tee and her mother to the NICU. They both washed their hands thoroughly and put a sterile gown on over their clothes. Little Tee was sleeping soundly in an incubator. The room was quiet except for the soft beeping of monitors and the sounds other neonatal care machines used to sustain premature life. There were several babies in the NICU, but each was given a small amount of privacy by light green curtains separating the rooms from one another.

Little Tina only wore a pamper and a pink cap on her head. Tubes and cords ran from various parts of her exposed body, but she seemed to be resting peacefully. She was so tiny. Tee was afraid to touch her for fear of causing her niece injury. Tee placed her hand inside the plastic contraption and stuck her finger inside the baby's little hand. Little Tina latched on to it in her sleep. She then let out a soft sigh.

"She's beautiful," said Momma Pearl.

"Hey, Little Tina. Your Auntie and Momma Pearl came to see you," said Patrick. To their surprise, she smiled in her sleep. Tee looked up at Patrick.

"This is bliss. Thank you. This is the best gift either of you could have ever given me," she said.

She silently thanked God for putting everything in perspective for her. She didn't have a job but, she no longer cared. She was surrounded by love.

Chapter 70

Inside Out

Tee was overjoyed to see Tiffany and Lenice in Sandy's hospital room when she returned. Lenora was at her new job and wouldn't be there until later. The ladies were disappointed to learn only immediate family was allowed in the NICU, but they admired pictures of the baby Patrick took with his cell phone. Tee even threw in a few comments about how the baby looked like Patrick. She hoped this would help make him feel a little bit better about the pending results of the DNA test he took after Little Tina was stabilized. They were told the results would be ready in two or three days.

It was obvious Sandy was worn out, and her sedative was beginning to work. Tiffany and Lenice made their exit after 20 minutes. Tee and Michael decided to leave as well. Michael went to get the car from the garage, and Tee stood in the lobby and talked with her friends while she waited for him to return. The hospital was busy. Several men and women sat waiting for someone or for something to occur. A group of restless children decided to occupy their time running around the room. They playfully ran in between the three of them as they talked.

Tee noticed how close Tiffany and Lenora seemed to be. A few months ago they couldn't stand each other. They chatted and laughed about topics Tee had no knowledge of as if she wasn't there. She suggested she let Michael go home and the three of them go to get a bite to eat and catch up.

Tiffany declined because she needed to pick up Quincy 2 from school. She rearranged her schedule for the next few weeks to make sure she could pick him up from school and not her parents. This would give them more time together.

"Maybe some other time," said Tee. "I haven't forgotten about your custody hearing tomorrow. I plan to be there to support you. I'll call you later for an update on your life. We should schedule a Bible study session. Are you reading the scriptures I gave you?" asked Tee.

"Thanks. I appreciate your support, said Tiffany. "I'm nervous about the outcome, but God is in control. No matter what the outcome, I will survive. And yes, I've been reading the scriptures. They are really helpful, but there's no need to do the Bible study. I've been studying on my own, and a couple of other people have been explaining things to me. I think I can take it from here."

She gave Tee a hug. "It's good to see you. I'm happy you and Michael are doing so well."

She then gave Lenice a hug. The two of them snapped fingers and did the bump. Tiffany's wide curvaceous hip thrust was so powerful that she bumped petite Lenice over into Tee and almost knocked them both down.

"Girl, watch where you put that thing," laughed Lenice.

"My fault, Sugah. Sometimes, I don't know my own strength. I'll call you tonight."

"Yes, we must plan our next girl's night."

"You two have been hanging out?" asked Tee.

"Yep. We're two single women ready to mingle. We would have invited you, Tee, but you were out of town with the hubby," said Lenice.

"I understand, but I'm back now. Next time you go out try to include me in your plans. Lenice, I haven't talked to you in a few days either. What's going on with you and James?"

"Tee, I don't even want to talk about it. Of course we'll include you in our next get together. I'll definitely call you when we have things finalized."

"Yeah Tee, James is bad news," said Tiffany.

Tee's feelings were hurt. Lenice took the time to inform Tiffany about her man problems but didn't tell her. She used to tell her first.

Michael returned with the car. The ladies hugged again and left. Tee felt a wave of jealously pass over her. She used to be included in the plan making. She was happy they were able to put their differences aside, but it felt like Lenice and Tiffany were putting her aside, too.

Chapter 71

Guess Who?

Patrick didn't want to leave the hospital, but his receptionist called and said Mayor Wallace had an abscess and requested him for the procedure. Patrick thought this would be good publicity material. He could let everyone know the Mayor of Memphis was one of his patients. Sandy saw this as a golden opportunity as well and insisted he go. She told him to drop by Mae Lillie's afterward and check on the restaurant. She was confident in the abilities of her staff to run things without her, but they still needed to see the boss' face every now and then. A surprise visit would help keep them on their toes. Patrick had no reason to feel guilty about leaving her, now. Her mother was still there to keep her company. Although, she was currently in the NICU with the baby.

Patrick kissed Sandy on the lips and said goodbye. As he turned to leave someone with a big bouquet of flowers entered the room. The arrangement was so large they were unable to see the person's face, but the structure of the lower body clearly indicated that it was a man.

"Please put those over on that small table located in the corner," said Patrick. He reached in his back pocket for his wallet to give him a tip.

"Shouldn't the lady decide where she wants the flowers? After all, they are for her," said Armondo.

Sandy was frozen with shock. It was as if time was suspended, and she couldn't move a muscle.

Armondo lowered the flowers to reveal his handsome youthful face. He shifted the arrangement over to one hand, walked to Sandy's bedside and kissed her gently on the cheek.

"Hello, my fantasy. I've been dreaming about you. How's my child?" he asked.

Memories of their lustful night came flooding back to Sandy. That smile, those eyes and that hair were all as she remembered. He smelled like outdoors, but it wasn't repulsive. It was the inviting scent of a hard-working man. Armondo looked good.

Patrick stood on the other side glowering at the man he considered his enemy. This man invaded his home, invaded his marriage, invaded his wife and now he was invading the hospital where is infant daughter was being treated.

Armondo acted as if Patrick was invisible. He stared deeply into Sandy's eyes. He longed to feel his lips on hers, but he remembered what she said in her emails. It was over between them. He could respect that, but she would not keep him from his child. He extended his hand to push a strand of long black hair that fell in Sandy's face to the side. Sandy sat in her hospital bed in disbelief. Armondo in all of his fineness was standing in front of her, but so was her husband, the handsome man she loved and adored.

"Don't touch my wife!" commanded Patrick.

Armondo smiled and retracted his hand, but never took his eyes off Sandy. She was heavier because of the pregnancy, but her skin was glowing. In his eyes, she never looked more beautiful. The details of their afternoon together were seared into his memory. While in Iraq, he replayed it over and over like a video to help him get through lonely nights.

His most vivid memory was the feel of her silky smooth skin against his as they explored each other. Her softness rivaled that of babies. He desperately wanted to feel her body in his hands, again.

The heat from his gaze bothered Sandy. Her illicit lover still had an effect on her, and she knew it.

"I tried to go visit my daughter in the NICU, but they told me only family members were allowed. I couldn't convince them I was family," said Armondo.

"What makes you think she's yours?" growled Patrick.

"I went online and saw her pictures. She's got my lips and my chin. Her skin tone is even closer to mine than yours. Something as dark as you could never produce someone so perfect. I wonder where she got those gray eyes."

Sandy wanted to talk, but she couldn't. Her mouth was dry, and the words wouldn't form. She hoped they wouldn't argue in a hospital.

"What exactly are you trying to say?" Patrick asked angrily.

"I said it," Armondo responded with a smirk.

"I'm positive she's not yours. But to ease everyone's mind, we've already performed a DNA test. We should have the results in two days," Patrick informed him before he walked to the door and held it open. "Leave. Don't come back. If she's yours, we'll call you. Understand?"

Armondo laughed. Then, backed away slowly from Sandy and said, "Spero a presto, abbraccio." It meant, *I hope to see you soon, Love* in Italian. As he passed Patrick, he looked him up and down as if he were an ant.

Patrick was physically fit, but standing next to a solid as a rock soldier made him feel out of shape. Armondo wore a tight black shirt with the word army on the front in bold green letters. It was similar to the one he wore the day he had his way with Sandy, and it showed the outline of his chiseled pectorals perfectly. His identification tags hung from his neck and rested on his six pack abdomen. Patrick almost understood why his wife was attracted to him, but she was his wife. Armondo was in violation. The two men clenched their jaws and their fists as if they were about to come to blows but didn't. Armondo laughed again before strolling out the door. He could easily break Patrick in half. Patrick slammed the door rattling the contents of the room, including Sandy. She instantly became unfrozen and began to cry.

He pulled his cell phone from his pocket and dialed his office. The receptionist answered on the fifth ring.

"What took you so long? My phone shouldn't ring more than three times before someone answers," he shouted. "Call Dr. Price and see if he would like to come out of retirement temporarily. I need him to take care of the Mayor's abscess. I also need him to cover for me the rest of the week. If he says no, reschedule all of my appointments for next month and give the mayor a referral. Tell him I am truly sorry, but I cannot leave my wife at this time." His receptionist apologized and said she would handle it. She also inquired if there was something wrong.

"Yes and no, but Sandy and the baby are fine, if that's what you mean. I have some unfinished business to handle, and I have a feeling it's going to need all the time I have to dedicate to it. I'll call you later for a report."

Patrick hung up the phone and went to Sandy's side to console her. He was smart enough to know making her feel worse would only run her into the arms of the army stud, again.

Chapter 72

Business As Usual

"Tee, open the door! It's Sheba and Edgar!" yelled Sheba.

"Will you stop yelling and knock on the door like regular people," scolded Edgar.

Tee wasn't expecting visitors. She didn't want visitors. She came home and put on her pajamas. Her plans were to snuggle under the covers with a good book, take a nap and possibly go see Sandy and the baby again a little later. Michael was out running errands.

Tomorrow she would occupy herself with the I'm A Good Woman Empowerment Conference. It was four months away, and there were so many things left to do. Her former intern, Samantha, sent her a text message that Mr. Anderson called everyone in the events department into his office and told them if they assisted her with any project, they would be terminated. Now that she was a free agent, he viewed her as the competition.

"I need you to do better. The terry cloth robe, headscarf and flip flops are overkill. No one here is going to help you throw a pity party. We're here to help you throw a get over it party," said Edgar. "We brought cake and everything. It's your favorite."

Tee was already over being fired, but eating yellow cake with chocolate frosting would be a good way to celebrate. She assumed the small box Sheba carried contained the cake. Edgar held a much larger cardboard box that housed the contents of her former office.

"You are a newlywed. Michael doesn't want to see you like that. For at least the first five years, everything you wear needs to be sexy," he advised.

"Who told you that lie?" inquired Tee.

"You forget, I'm married. Why do you think Marva and I are still together? My wife doesn't work, and she doesn't cook but she sure looks sexy in a pair of jeans. I work hard. When I get home and see my hot Latina love, I forget about how tired I am and the fact that I'm hungry. Trust me, Sweet Tee. Go put on some clothes and comb your hair. Hurry up."

Tee smiled at her old friend and her new one. Edgar gave her the name Sweet Tee when they first met. He used to use it often, but these days he only called her that every now and then. She liked it and always had. She decided to take his advice and ran upstairs to change. Tee put on a pair of jeans, her I'm A Good Woman t-shirt and a pair of black ankle boots. She then pulled her hair into a ponytail, put on a little lipstick and went back downstairs. Edgar, Sheba, and Michael were seated at the dining room table, eating her cake. Obviously, her husband was back from his tasks.

"Aren't you supposed to wait for the guest of honor before you cut the cake?" she asked.

"You took too long. Lifting boxes is hard work. I needed something to help me regain my strength," said Edgar.

"Tee, I don't like what Mr. Anderson did to you one bit. He hired me to work specifically with you. Then, he got rid of you. That's not cool at all. But I don't expect to be at Innovations much longer after he finds out what I did," said Sheba. She licked some frosting off her finger.

"What did you do?" Michael asked with a mouthful of moist yellow cake. He broke off a small piece and fed it to Tee.

"Yum," said Tee. "This is good but yeah, Sheba what did you do?" She took Michael's plate and began eating the cake he prepared for himself. He let her have it without protest and cut himself another slice. Rather than get another plate, he ate it out of the palm of his hand and dropped crumbs on the floor. Tee looked at him and shook her head. Chesnutt scurried over and licked up the crumbs. She wagged her tail happily and waited for more to fall.

"I downloaded all the files on your computer onto an external hard drive and wiped the computer clean. I also copied every document in your office and shredded the originals. I've got a list of contacts for every client they ever had and every client you were targeting. I took them from your Outlook account and the company database. I'd like to see that fool try to manage your client list now without information to reference," said Sheba. She was very proud of her actions and sat there with a wide grin as she took a bite of her cake.

"Sheba, you didn't have to do that! That's destroying company property. He is going to fire you for sure when he finds out. He's so petty he might even try to press criminal charges."

"Let him. I ain't never scared. Besides, I already found another job."

"Oh, really. Where?"

"I was hoping I could persuade you to hire me as your new assistant. You can't launch a company by yourself. You're going to need administrative staff if you don't have anyone else to back you up," said Sheba.

Tee put down her fork. "What makes you think I'm planning to launch a company? Right now, the only plans I have are to work on my conference. I'll figure everything else out after that."

"You're too good to quit, Tee. The event-planning world needs you. Screw Innovations. You were Innovations. Launch your own business and hire me as your assistant. I didn't get a chance to show you how good I am. I can help you grow your business from the ground up and land clients outside of this city. Mr. Anderson's vision was narrow. He only wanted Memphis. Let's go national, no international!" Sheba was extremely animated, and her enthusiasm was contagious. Everyone in the room was catching it.

"She's right you know," said Michael with a mouth full of cake, again. "If you think about it you've already got clients. But I was thinking more marketing and management, rather than event planning. I guess you could do all three. I'm currently without representation. You should make me your first client. Tiffany could probably use you, too. Peter was actually on to something with that mobile massage team. The guys at my bachelor party loved her and the black Barbie twins. She really could become a massage therapist to the stars."

"Tee, I told you God had something better for you. Think about it. Everything you need is right in front of you," chimed Edgar. Yellow crumbs were scattered around his mouth. They looked out of place on his well-trimmed face.

Tee had to admit they were right. She could use I'm A Good Woman, her husband and Tiffany as a great starting point. She would need to acquire some more personal management knowledge, but she was sure it couldn't be much harder than event planning. Both required attention to detail and good people skills. She looked at Sheba and said, "Alright, young lady. As my assistant, your first official assignment is to find me a realtor, so we can start looking at office space."

"I'm one step ahead of you," said Michael. "I took your advice and started looking at condos today. I found one downtown I liked that sits on top of a storefront. It has two levels and needs some major renovations, but the owner is willing to sell them separately or together. I'm thinking together might be the way to go. Get your jacket and we can go see it as soon as I eat one more piece of cake. Do we have any milk? You can't have chocolate frosting without a tall glass of milk."

"See, that's what I'm talking about!" said Edgar. "This man knows how you eat cake."

Sheba told Tee to finish her cake, and she got up to get the milk. Tee smiled. She was even assisting when she wasn't being paid. Michael and Edgar were the two most important men in her life but listening to them talk about cake one would swear they were still little boys.

Chapter 73

How You Like Me Now?

Lenice decided to make tonight a movie night with Webster. She ordered Chinese food, put on her pajamas and got ready to watch *Training Day* with award-winning actor Denzel Washington. Webster also wore his pajamas. They were yellow with brown dog biscuits all over them. Lenice absolutely adored Denzel. She thought he was the modern day Billy Dee Williams. No matter how old he got, he still looked good to her and millions of other women. When he's in his 80's, you'll still hear 25-year-old women in the beauty shop talking about how he can "get it."

She was disappointed Scott didn't show up, but it was probably for the best. She didn't know how she would feel emotionally when she saw him. Would she be angry and fly into a rage or sad and begin to cry? He was the last man she was intimate with and the only man to break her heart.

She put Scott out of her mind and pressed the button to start the movie. Denzel was the only man she wanted to see, right now. Her phone rang.

It was James. Her heart skipped a beat. She let the phone ring a few more times before she answered so it wouldn't seem like she was waiting for his call, even though she was. She answered in a sleepy voice.

"Heeel-looo."

"Hey, Lenice. It's James. Did I wake you?"

"No, not really. I was resting. I had a hard day at work today."

"Oh, well I can call you back if you want," said James.

"No, that won't be necessary. It's good to hear your voice."

"It's good to hear yours, too. I've missed you. Do you feel like company? I was thinking I could come over tonight. We could order some take out and rent a movie or something."

Great minds think alike, thought Lenora.

"I appreciate the offer, but I don't think that would be a good idea," she said drily.

"Really? Why? I thought you enjoyed my company?"

"I do, but maybe some other time. I decided to take your advice and see other people. I was actually resting up before my date tonight," she lied.

"I don't know if I like the sound of that. I was warming up to the idea of having you all to myself."

"So, you haven't made a decision concerning us?"

"Not quite," said James. "But that doesn't negate the fact that I miss you, and I would love to spend some time with you while I continue to think about it."

"Don't bother. I've decided that I'm not ready for a committed relationship. I'm just getting over my heartache, and I'm not ready to give my love to another man. Don't worry, I'm not trying to get rid of you. I'm free Sunday. Let's go to brunch after church."

"Sunday's good. I'll let you go now. Enjoy your date, but I'm sure you won't enjoy yourself nearly as much as you will with me Sunday," teased James.

"We'll see, won't we?" said Lenice. "I'll talk to you later, James. Enjoy your evening."

Lenice hung up the phone, reached for her bowl of shrimp fried rice and turned her attention to the movie.

"If James thinks he can keep me dangling on a string while he decides whether or not he wants to be with me, he's got another thing coming. Isn't that right, Webster?"

Webster barked in agreement.

"Alright, Denzel. Let me see what you're working with."

Chapter 74

Results Don't Lie

Patrick planned to spend the night at the hospital with Sandy tonight. He went home to grab a few items and check on Momma Pearl and the kids. Sandy would probably be discharged in a couple of days. They dreaded having to go home without Little Tina.

After Armondo left, Patrick called Dr. Walker's office and demanded they put a rush on his DNA test. He couldn't wait. He had to know as soon as possible. He hoped Momma's Pearl's intuition was right. Little Tina had to be his because he never wanted to see that man again. The only way they were going to keep Armondo out of their lives was with official paperwork to make him back off. Patrick talked so harshly to the receptionist, she promised him she would call the DNA testing center and have the results the next day, even though she had no authority to do so. She was only supposed to schedule appointments and take messages.

Patrick told Sandy not to worry about Armondo. He would take care of everything. She had a large cut in her abdomen and a premature baby. Her only concern should be getting better and bringing their daughter home.

He packed an overnight bag and went to see what the children were doing. Donovin was in his room completing homework, and Nicole was already in bed fast asleep. He walked in Little Tina's nursery and ran his fingers down the side of her $3,000 crib. He couldn't believe his wife paid that much money for an infant's bedroom suit. Momma Pearl was in the guest room watching the "700 Club." He went to the office and checked his email. He also checked Sandy's.

> The army has summoned me back to Iraq immediately. It seems they went on a mission without me and we lost some of our team. I'll be back as soon as I can. You looked radiant today. I love you Sandy, but if I can't have your love then the love of our daughter will be the next best thing.
>
> Armondo

Patrick was happy that he didn't have to deal with him, for now.

Chapter 75

More Than You Bargained For

The next morning, Tee felt horrible. She was nauseous, and she could barely stand without the room spinning. She tried to go about her day as if nothing was wrong.

She loved the condo office combo Michael selected. It was big enough for Michael to feel as if he had plenty of room, and the office downstairs was what she would need to launch their business and more. There was room for more employees, if the two of them decided to expand. The owner of the property accepted their offer, and they hoped to close the following week. She hadn't thought of a name for their business, but she wanted it to be something that was indicative of the wonderful place she was at in her life.

She and Sheba were out scouting for home and office furniture when she lost her breakfast in a display umbrella stand. She offered to buy it, and the store manager readily accepted her offer. He agreed to have it cleaned and delivered along with a few other choice pieces. Tee planned to purchase items and place them in storage until their new home/office was ready. Michael planned to make extensive renovations, so it would be a while. He was use to having the best of everything. He was already talking about an elevator, Jacuzzi, voice activated security and secret compartments.

Sheba helped Tee walk to her car. She felt better after she threw up, and the fresh air helped as well. Tiffany's custody hearing was today, and she was going to be there to support her friend even if she had to take a barf bag into the courtroom.

"I hope I'm not coming down with a cold. I hate being sick," said Tee.

"Maybe, but when was the last time you had your period?" asked Sheba.

"It was before my honeymoon," said Tee.

"Boss Lady, I think you might be pregnant."

"Michael and I wanted to wait at least two years into our marriage before we had children," said Tee.

"That may be true. I suggest you get one of those home pregnancy tests and pee on a stick when you get home today."

"I'll think about it, but it's probably nothing. Sheba thanks for being there for me. I know we don't know each other well, but you've been a big help. I feel like I can trust you," said Tee.

"You can, Boss Lady. Me and you, we're going to do big things. You wait and see. Now, you do what I tell you and stop by the drug store and pick up that test. I'll call you later tonight to get the results."

Tee looked at her watch. She was late. Tiffany's hearing was already underway. Good thing she wasn't far from the courthouse. She hoped she could find a parking space quickly and get into the room before the judge gave his ruling.

Chapter 76

More Than a Conqueror

Tiffany was nervous. She prayed that morning and read a few more scriptures. She was still working her way down the list Tee gave her. She read Romans 8:31-38.

"What then, shall we say in response to these things? If God is for us, who can be against us? He who did not spare his own Son, but gave him up for us all—how will he not also, along with him, graciously give us all things? Who will bring any charge against those whom God has chosen? It is God who justifies. Who then is the one who condemns? No one. Christ Jesus who died—more than that, who was raised to life—is at the right hand of God and is also interceding for us. Who shall separate us from the love of Christ? Shall trouble or hardship or persecution or famine or nakedness or danger or sword? As it is written: For your sake we face death all day long; we are considered as sheep to be slaughtered. No, in all these things we are more than conquerors through Him who loved us. For I am convinced that neither death nor life, neither angels nor demons, neither the present nor the future, nor any powers, neither height nor depth, nor anything else in all creation, will be able to separate us from the love of God that is in Christ Jesus our Lord."

Those words gave Tiffany confidence for the day. She repeated over and over to herself, "I am more than a conqueror. I am more than a conqueror."

She hadn't heard from William since she tried to seduce him. She hoped he wasn't mad at her, but she had more important things to worry about at the moment.

The courtroom was packed. It was a busy day at juvenile court. The tension in the room was thick. Several parents and spectators where there to see who would be responsible for the well-being of a child. You could hear conversations all around the room about low down, gold digging baby mommas and trifling, broke baby daddies. There was so much angst between people, who at one point, cared enough about each other to share their reproductive organs with one another. Tiffany's case was the first one after lunch. She hoped the judge enjoyed his meal and was in a good mood. The bailiff entered and asked everyone to rise for the Honorable Judge Larry Malone. He was known around the judicial system as Iron Man. Judge Malone ruled his court with an iron fist and did not tolerate any outbursts, disrespect or foolishness. He was known for being hard but also fair. He wasn't one of those judges who automatically ruled in favor of the mother. He believed the father deserved a say so in the matter too, unless he was trying to shirk his parental responsibilities. He had no tolerance for that. His philosophy was children did not ask to be here. They were a result of the actions of two other people, whether intentional or unintentional. Therefore, a child was the responsibility of the mother and the father and should be adequately cared for by both.

Judge Malone came in and stood behind the bench. He had a distinguished look about him. His salt and pepper hair and mustache looked good against his black robe. He scanned the courtroom before he sat down. His expression wasn't friendly, but it wasn't mean either. The bailiff announced court was now in session. Judge Malone looked down and flipped through the files pertaining to the case that were sitting in front of him.

The DNA test confirmed that Quincy Albert Matthews was indeed the father of Quincy Albert Tate. The Matthews' and Tiffany were ordered to submit their financial information to help the court determine what amount of child support should be awarded. Tiffany's lawyer, Wilmetta Willis, stood and asked the judge to grant child support in the amount of $2,000 a month and make Quincy responsible for private school tuition and his medical insurance. Judge Malone continued to flip through his documents without saying a word. After a few minutes, he asked Attorney Willis to have a seat. Tiffany didn't understand what was going on. Why didn't the judge want to address her lawyer? She feared for the worst.

Quincy and his wife, Marilyn, were also in the courtroom with their lawyer. Judge Malone narrowed his eyes at all three of them. He then addressed the couple as if no one else was in the room.

"Mr. and Mrs. Matthews, I looked over the financial statements you supplied to the courts, and I found it hard to believe your annual income is what you two said it was. I know Mrs. Matthews is a homemaker and Mr. Matthews, you are the sole breadwinner in your household, but something kept telling me you were hiding something. Therefore, I asked one of our investigators to dig a little deeper. It seems you two have several assets that were acquired during your marriage using Mrs. Matthews' maiden name of Galveston. My investigator found over 20 rental properties, most of which are paid for and several shares of stock in major companies like Google, Nike and Pfizer. So in addition to Mr. Matthew's architectural business, which pays over $100,000 annually, and your City Council salary you make an additional $170,000 annually that you neglected to report to the court. I take such matters very seriously, Mr. & Mrs. Matthews. But what concerns me more is you have agreed to care for young Quincy financially but have not requested any type of visitation. It is my understanding, Mr. Matthews spent quite a bit of time with his son while he was having an affair with Ms. Tate. But now that she no longer wishes to continue and is seeking child support, you don't even want to spend a weekend with him. This is not only wrong, but it is reprehensible. I have decided to award Ms. Tate the sum of $3,500 a month in child support. Mr. and Mrs. Matthews, you are also responsible for his health care insurance and private school tuition. You must also set up a trust fund of no less than $30,000 that he can access at the age of 21 along with two of your rental properties. I am making it mandatory the three of you, along with your lawyers, come together and work out an amicable visitation arrangement. This boy needs a father, Mr. Matthews. Since you donated the sperm for his being, I'm afraid it is going to have to be you. You have one month to handle this matter. Don't make me have to tell you to be a father, again. You have three other children who seem to be doing well. So, I suspect you are qualified for the job."

Judge Malone smiled in Tiffany's direction. "Ms. Tate, it has been a pleasure having you in my courtroom." His smile suddenly disappeared, and he turned his head in the directions of Quincy and his wife. "Mr. and Mrs. Matthews, you should be ashamed of yourselves!

"We'll take a 10-minute recess, and then we'll begin the next case. I have a lovely weekend in the mountains planned with my wife, Loretta Tolliver, and I'm not trying to be in here all day with you people." He banged his gavel and left the bench.

The Matthews' and their lawyer were speechless. Mrs. Matthews turned and cut her eyes at Tiffany, but Quincy smiled. He still looked dashingly handsome to her, but she didn't have the urge to find an empty office and take his clothes off like she used to. He rose from his seat and approached her side of the courtroom.

"Tiffany, I'm sorry for the way I've behaved lately. If you say it's over, then it's over. You and Quincy are welcome to stay in the house. I'll even put it in your name. I gave the car to my teenage daughter, but I can get you a new one. I hope you can forgive me," he said. "Also, Quincetta told me she attacked you. I promise you, it will never happen again. I took her credit cards as punishment. I'm sure she's learned her lesson. I look forward to working out visitation so I can continue to be a part of our son's life. I'd like to be friends, Tiffany. Once upon a time, we were friends. I would like to get back to that."

Tiffany was moved by his sincerity. "I'd like that too, Quincy. You can set up a meeting with my attorney, Ms. Willis, to arrange visitation. Your son really wants to see you. And let me know what day you would like to meet to give me the house. I already purchased a new car; your daughter can keep that one. Now, please excuse me, I have something I need to say to your wife."

Tiffany smoothed out her suit and carefully approached a seething Marilyn Matthews. She was nervous, but she knew she had to do this

"What do you want? Are you happy now?" Marilyn spat at her.

Tiffany did her best to muster a smile and nervously said, "As a matter of fact I am, but I came over her to say I'm sorry. I sincerely apologize for all the pain I've caused you and your family. Quincy was and is your husband. I was young and silly when I met him, but I always knew he was married. We had no right to do what we did. I know you and I could never be friends, but please don't punish my son. He is a nice boy, and I'm sure he could bring some joy to your lives, if you let him. He wants to meet his sisters.

"Please, forgive me. I promise you, it's over between Quincy and me. And I will not contact him for any reason other than to discuss his son. He loves you, you know. That's the reason he would never leave you for me no matter how many times he told me he would."

Marilyn's voice lost some of its venom, but the scowl on her face remained. "You have no idea how many times I wished you were dead. I even thought about paying someone to kill you. I don't know if I can accept your son as part of our family. Quincy always wanted a son to carry on his name. I hated you even more when you gave him what I couldn't. We'll have to take it one day at a time and see what happens," she said.

"I understand, and that sounds more than fair to me. But, if you ever call my son a bastard again, I'll slap the taste out of your mouth. Be blessed, Mrs. Matthews."

Tiffany then sashayed over to those who came to support her before Mrs. Matthews could respond. Tee, Lenice, Lenora and her parents were there. They all shouted for joy and did a little victory dance right in the courtroom. This was a cause for a celebration!

Tiffany could hardly believe God put her in the courtroom of the husband of one of her best clients. She never realized Loretta Tolliver was using her maiden name instead of her married one. God is sho' nuff, sho' nuff good. Hallelujah!

Chapter 77

Whose Is It?

Patrick sat in Dr. Walker's office nervously awaiting the results. He didn't tell Sandy he was coming. If she knew, she would have made him put her on speakerphone while Dr. Walker gave them the paternity news. He needed to hear it by himself. If it was bad, he could prepare himself to face Sandy without upsetting her more. He planned to love and raise Little Tina no matter what, but he was going to be extremely disappointed if science proved she didn't belong to him biologically.

He looked around the room at the various degrees framed and mounted on the walls. Like Dr. Walker, Patrick had his high school diploma, undergraduate degree and medical degree on the walls of the office, located inside his dental practice. Pictures of her husband and child were placed on the desk. They were a handsome family. He wished she would hurry up because the suspense was killing him.

One of the nurses walked in and greeted him. "Hello, Dr. Pierce. Dr. Walker is tied up at the hospital with a delivery. However, she asked me to give this."

She handed him a white envelope. He opened it hurriedly and pulled out the documents. He scanned them quickly and when he found what he was looking for he could hardly contain himself.

"Yes!" Patrick shouted. "That there grey-eyed baby is mine!" He stood and danced around the office wiggling his butt and shaking his hands in the air.

The nurse giggled. "I'm glad the results are to your liking. Congratulations, Dr. Pierce."

"Thank you. May I ask you to do me a small favor? Will you scan these documents and email them to me?"

"I can do that," she said. The nurse wrote down his email address and exited the room.

Patrick wasn't going to wait another minute to email the results to Armondo and tell him to never contact his wife again. That should get rid of him. He called Sandy to share the good news with her.

Chapter 78

Plus or Minus

That night all of the girls, with the exception of Sandy, gathered at the Stokes' residence to celebrate Tiffany's victory in court and Tee's new entrepreneurial endeavor. Tee even invited Sheba. It seemed she was going to be around, and Tee wanted her friends to meet her. Teresa was back from her cruise and was happy to be reunited with everyone. The girls tried to quickly catch her up on everything she missed.

There was also an unexpected guest. Ida Foster decided to come to Memphis to see Michael after she wrapped up her investigation in Nashville. She wanted to tell him her findings but realized she should have called rather than dropping by the house unannounced.

Tee hadn't seen the woman who saved her and Michael's life since their wedding. She was forever indebted to her, and Dr. Foster was welcome in her home anytime.

"I'm sorry for the intrusion. I see this is a bad time," said Dr. Foster.

"No, this is perfect timing, but Michael isn't here. He went out with my brother-in-law, but we're having a girl's night, and since you're a girl, you should join us. We'll arrange for the two of you to meet tomorrow. I insist you go in the kitchen and fix yourself a plate." Tee hoped she could get a few minutes alone with her to find out what she and Michael had been talking about.

Dr. Foster did as she was told. The food and drink flowed freely and everyone seemed to be enjoying themselves. Sheba walked up behind Tee and whispered in her ear. "Did you do it?"

"No, I didn't, and this is hardly the time to discuss it," said Tee.

"Of course it is," Sheba said loudly enough for everyone to hear. "You said yourself your friends are like family. I knew you wouldn't do it, and that's why I brought this." She pulled a home pregnancy test out of her purse. All conversation in the room came to a halt. You could hear a pin drop it was so silent. All eyes were on Tee and Sheba.

"Tee, Sugah, you didn't tell us you thought that you might be pregnant," said Tiffany.

"That's why you're not drinking anything tonight," said Lenora.

Tee didn't like being put on the spot one bit. "I started having symptoms earlier today, and I don't see why I have to rush to take the test. It's probably stress or something. You all know Michael and I have been going through a lot lately. Would anyone like some more punch? Hand me your glass."

Tiffany took the box out of Sheba's hand and handed it to Tee. "No, thank you, Missy Miss. You are not about to charm you way out of this one. You take this test, and you go take it right now." She gave Tee a gentle push toward the bathroom.

***

Tee stared at the home pregnancy test in disbelief. There in the small results box was a plus sign. She was pregnant! She knew she couldn't tell her friends before she told her husband. She used her cell phone to call him from the bathroom. She hoped he would answer, and he did.

"Baby, are you busy?" she asked.

"Patrick and I are at a cigar bar having a couple of stogies and some drinks to celebrate the birth of Little Tina. What's up?"

"I have to tell you something."

"Sounds serious, is everything okay? Do I need to come home?"

"I would love it if you came home, but I can't wait until then. I'm pregnant!" she shouted.

"You're what? That's great!" He turned around toward the other men in the cigar bar and shouted, "Hey everybody! I'm gonna be a daddy! Free cigars for everybody! I'm gonna be a daddy!

The girls were standing outside her bathroom door listening and heard her announcement as well. They cheered and clapped loudly. Some shouted congratulations.

Michael smiled widely. Not too long ago, he thought he was a father but later found out he was really an uncle. This time there was no doubt, this baby was his. He almost forgot Tee was on the phone until he heard the girls in the background.

"Where are you? What's that noise?"

"I'm at home. The girls are still here and apparently they are eavesdropping. Oh, Dr. Foster is here, too," she said loudly to make sure they heard her.

"We're sorry," said Lenora.

"No, we're not," said Lenice.

"You are going to be an amazing mother. How much longer do you think the girls will be there?" asked Michael.

"I don't know. Maybe an hour."

"You ladies wrap up. Then, I'm coming home, and we're going to have our own celebration."

"You got it, Mr. Stokes. I can't wait to have your baby."

Michael smiled from ear to ear. I love you, Tina Desiree Long-Stokes! See you soon. Tell Dr. Foster I'll call her tomorrow."

He hung up the phone and looked around at all the well wishers. The cigar bar was full of patrons. The other smokers issued their congratulations and gave him pats on the back. Suddenly, Michael felt a small pang in his heart for Peter. He really hadn't had a chance to mourn his death, and he had been thinking about him on and off all day. Peter was his best friend and confidant but greed made him turn on him. He was still in disbelief that for years Peter was collecting dirt on him to use at a later time. God was a keeper and didn't let it come to pass, but he hated that Peter had to die. Part of him wished he was there to share his joy with him. If they were still on good terms, he would have made Peter his child's Godfather.

Michael snapped out of his sad moment and handed out $70 cigars to several men. He noticed Mac was also there enjoying a few drinks with friends. He wasn't one of Michael's favorite people. He did propose to Tee while they were dating, but he gave Mac a cigar anyway. He was in an excellent mood.

Mac accepted the cigar, issued his congratulations and stepped outside to make a phone call. Casper finally gave him a number where he could reach her. She was asking for more money. This time it was $10,000, and Mac didn't have it to give. Especially, when he didn't know what he was getting for his money. He wanted Tee back but not at any cost. Maybe Casper would be willing to cut him a little slack once he delivered this tidbit of information.

Patrick was on cloud nine. Now, he and his brother-in-law each had a reason to celebrate. He spent most of the day at the hospital with Sandy and the baby. She was now able to be transported by wheelchair to the NICU. He watched both of them with pride as the tiny infant suckled from her mother's breast. Little Tina was so beautiful. Her smile caused him to grin every time he saw it, and her grey eyes sparkled like precious jewels. She was a reminder that God was real, and He answers prayers. He planned to go back to the hospital and spend the night with them after he finished celebrating. The father of three smiled and slowly puffed away on his cigar.

Chapter 79

One + One = Three

Michael left the cigar bar and came home to the arms of his beautiful wife. Everyone was gone, and Tee completely forgot that she needed to talk to Dr. Foster before she left. They knelt and said a prayer of thanks to God for the wonderful new life growing inside Tee. They asked Him to make him or her healthy, strong and smart with a servant's heart for God. They asked for wisdom to help them be good parents. They thanked Him for bringing them through Michael's situation with Peter and the NCAA and giving Tee the opportunity to now conduct business on her terms. They asked Him to continue to bless their friends and family. They prayed for Sandy and Little Tina's health. Michael and Tee both loved God and had no doubt He would continue to bless their union.

Afterward, Michael turned on some relaxing music and, the two of them slow danced holding each other as close as they could for as long as they could. When they were tired of standing, the duo made their way to the bedroom. Michael ran a relaxing bubble bath in their garden style tub, and they lovingly bathed one another. Tee rested her back and head against his chest as they talked and sipped sparkling white grape juice until the skin on both their bodies resembled raisins. Michael dried his wife off and carried her to the bed.

Mr. and Mrs. Stokes made love repeatedly until neither of them could continue. They both fell asleep happily exhausted. Michael didn't believe life could get any better than this. He had a beautiful Christian woman by his side, and they were in the beginning phases of parenthood. He was blessed beyond measure. His rest was peaceful. There was no nightmare to interrupt his joy.

The next morning, Michael received a phone call, but he didn't answer. His phone was on silent because had no desire to talk to anyone but his wife. He was actually in the kitchen making Tee breakfast when the call came. The caller left a message.

"Hello, Binky. I hear you're expecting. Congratulations! Enjoy it while you can! I'll be watching. Tell Tee I said hello."

Her plan was unfolding beautifully, and it was almost time to kick it into high gear. She was going to make Michael's life mirror the one he took. He would know what it felt like to fall in love, have the one you love leave you and watch someone else raise your child. She laughed at how she would watch him fall into a pit of despair and beg for mercy. The only mercy Michael would receive was when she put a bullet through his head. She would have the ultimate revenge. Of that she was sure. God was now a joke to her. As far as she was concerned, she was the master of her own fate and those whose lives she wished to mangle. Before it was over, Michael and Tee would both bow before her.

THE END

Sneak Peek

Forever and A Day

The final installment in the *Someday* Trilogy

Forever and A Day
Chapter One

MiTee Management At Your Service

"Thank you for calling MiTee Management, how may I help you?" asked Sheba.

"Yeah, can I speak to my momma?" said a young male.

Sheba hated prank phone calls. She had better things to do with her time than play with somebody she couldn't even see.

"Sir, I think you have the wrong number. Everyone in this office is childless," she said rudely.

"No. Tina Stokes is my momma. Tell her that her son is on the phone. She'll know exactly who you're talking about," the young man insisted.

Sheba was sure he was mistaken. Tee didn't have any children, yet. If she did, whoever was on the other end was way too old to be her child, but she decided to humor him. "One moment please," she said and pressed the button to put him on hold. She then pressed the extension for Tee's office. "Boss Lady. There's a young man on the phone who says you're his mother. Do I need to get rid of him?"

Tee giggled. "No Sheba, that's my baby. I'll explain later. Put him through," said Tee.

Her phone rang two seconds later. "MiTee Management, where we are lifting our clients to new heights. Tee Stokes here. How may I help you?"

Tee loved to say the name of her and Michael's new management company. They selected MiTee because it was a combination of their names, and it sounded like the word mighty. That's exactly what they planned to be—stronger, bigger, and badder than any other management company in the nation. Together they were a force to be reckoned with. The company was two months old, and MiTee Management was responsible for maintaining the I'm A Good Woman brand and executing the I'm A Good Woman Empowerment Conference. They also managed Michael's career as a motivational speaker and book author, Tiffany's Magic Touch Mobile Massage and now gospel hip hop artist Isaac Blak. It was an eclectic bunch but nothing she and Michael couldn't handle. So far their assistant, Sheba, was the only employee, but they were looking for an additional manager. Tee planned to reduce her work hours after she had the baby.

Things took off much faster than either of them expected. After they publicized the launch of their company, many of the celebrities Tee and Michael knew called to see if they were interested in managing them. They turned most of them down because they didn't want to take on too much too soon. However, when Blak called there was no way Tee could deny him. He was special to her, and she was honored that he wanted her to help manage his career. They worked out the details, and Blak was coming in town the next day to sign the contract. She was quite proud of the businessman he was becoming.

"Hey, Momma! I liked your name better when it was Tina Long," teased Blak.

"Boy, I told you I am nobody's mother. At least not yet, and I think my new name is beautiful! Tee looked down at her small, almost 3-month, baby bump. She actually enjoyed being pregnant. She got to eat as much as she wanted, and everyone pampered her. The breast swelling was annoying, but she was secretly excited about the notion of added cleavage. They seemed to be getting bigger every week. She hoped the added inches would stay once the baby was born. Although, she didn't enjoy the morning sickness she initially experienced. It seemed to have subsided and odd eating habits were the newest phase in her pregnancy. She dipped a Cool Ranch Dorito in apple sauce and crunched it loudly in Blak's ear.

Blak was one of several young people God placed in Tee's life to mentor. When she met Isaac Blackston aka Icy Blak he was a hip hop superstar tormented by the fast life he no longer enjoyed or wanted to be a part of. Tee convinced him to follow his heart and submit to God's will. He did, and last year, he announced he was switching from secular hip hop to gospel hip hop and was now getting ready to release his debut CD, "Walking in the Light." Blak prayed his new CD would be well-received. He even changed his stage name from Icy Blak to Isaac Blak to help demonstrate the change in his life. Even though he stood to lose thousands of his secular fans, he felt good about the positive messages in his songs that anyone of any age could enjoy. Parental advisory stickers would no longer be needed on any of his CDs. He was determined to gain new fans and win souls for Christ through his music. He couldn't wait for his first single, *Living the Godly Life*, to drop.

"I hope it's a girl, so I can continue to be your only son," said Blak.

"That's so sweet. What can I do for you? Is everything alright? You usually call my cell phone," said Tee.

"Yeah. I thought I'd catch you off guard. Nothing's wrong. I had the urge to talk to you for a few minutes. I can't wait to see you," said Blak.

"Same here. Don't forget, I want you to do a private meet and greet with the group I told you about, Families of the Incarcerated. These little boys and girls have a mother or father who is locked up, and in some cases, both parents are in jail. I know seeing you would brighten their day. We're also going to swing by Mercy Children's Hospital and have you spend some time with the patients there, too."

"That's cool. I like doing stuff like that. You're picking me up from the airport, right?" asked Blak.

"Actually, I was going to send a car to get you."

"No deals. I haven't seen you since you convinced me to change my life. The only person I want picking me up is you."

Tee had a million things she needed to do, but she couldn't turn down her newest client. "Alright, Blak. You got it. Tee's escort service will be there waiting for you."

"That's the business! I have to go to rehearsal now. See you tomorrow."

"I'm so proud of you."

"Thanks, Momma. I owe it all to you. I'm glad you're going to help guide my career. Holla."

He hung up before Tee could say goodbye. So much had changed in only a few months, but the changes were for the better.

The holidays were especially good to her. Christmas brought a special present that couldn't be placed under a tree. Tee's premature niece, Little Tina, was allowed to come home on Christmas Eve. After weeks in the NICU of the hospital, she was now able to sleep in her own nursery. It was hard to believe the plump grey-eyed baby was only four pounds when she was born. On Christmas day she cooed, gurgled, and smiled to the delight of everyone in the family. Especially, her older brother and sister. They wore Sandy's nerves thin asking repeatedly when Little Tina was coming home. Now that she was home, they couldn't get enough of her. The children even stood over her crib and admired her while she slept.

Michael and Tee flew to Paris to ring in the New Year. They made some wonderful memories sharing kisses atop the Eiffel Tower and dining on French cuisine. They also took a train through the countryside and admired its beauty. Many romantic nights were spent under the starry skies of a foreign land living, laughing and loving as happily married couples do. Their trip was short, but they promised themselves they would see much more of Europe in the future. It was now February, and the dynamic duo was hard at work running their business. They were certain this was going to be a good year for MiTee Management.

Tee lovingly rubbed her stomach again. She could hardly wait for the baby to arrive. She and Michael were going to be wonderful parents. He was definitely a wonderful husband.

Forever and A Day
Chapter Two

It's Getting Hot In Here

Michael exited the mineral bath water and wrapped himself in a large, thick, white towel. The room was hot and steamy, but the warmth felt good to him. He welcomed this opportunity to release some of the tension resulting from a busy week. Running a management business was hectic. All of the things he used to have other people do for him he was now doing for himself, as well as others. As he tied the towel around his waist, Tiffany entered the room. She loved looking at Michael shirtless. They worked closely together and had developed quite a bond over the past few months. Michael, being a celebrity himself, took Tiffany under his wing and escorted her personally into the lives of the rich and famous. He, Tee and Tiffany often went to industry functions, award shows and movie premiers to promote their businesses and help Tiffany get the connections she needed to make her mobile massage service a success. Business was going so well Tiffany had to hire additional help. What began with her and her twin massage therapy school classmates, Sierra and Siendy, now included a total staff of five extremely attractive masseuses--four women and one man. They traveled anywhere in the continental United States to see their clients. She and Michael were even considering making her idea of opening a bathhouse a reality. Doing so would allow Tiffany to maintain a stationary location to work in. As the mother of a 9-year-old boy, she welcomed the opportunity to stay home as much as possible.

"Are you ready for me now, Michael?" she said while running her hand down his shirtless back. Even though he was retired, Michael still worked out regularly to maintain his solid NFL physique.

"I really need to go, Tiffany. I told Tee I would be back at the office at 1 p.m. and it's now 3," said Michael.

"Well, you *are* working just not at the office. I need you to stay and get the entire experience so you can tell me what would entice a man to patronize a bathhouse. Most men take showers, not baths," said Tiffany.

"So, I'm you're guinea pig?" laughed Michael. "I could have kept my clothes on and told you that. Quality service and beautiful women. The same two things that have been driving them to Tiffany's Magic Touch from the very beginning."

Michael's cell phone rang. He walked over to the area where he laid his clothes and located it. The name Dr. Ida Foster was on the screen. He had barely spoken to her since she came to Memphis to tell him that she was unable to locate Becca's long lost brother. She thought he was living in Nashville, but when she arrived, no one she talked to knew him or had ever heard of him. Michael told her to keep looking, but the trail went cold.

He looked at Tiffany and smiled. "Can you excuse me for a moment? I need to take this call in private."

"Sure, Sugah. Just call me when you need me." She exited the room and shut the door behind her.

"Hey, Dr. Foster," he said.

"Hello, Michael. How are you? Have you heard from Becca lately?"

"I'm happy to report that for the last two months I haven't heard a peep from whoever was making those crazy calls," said Michael.

"I'm happy to hear that, but I thought you would like to know that I received a call from Tee Hee today," said Dr. Foster.

"You did? How's he doing and what did he say?"

"He seems to be doing fine, but he told me Accent Behavioral Health Center is planning a big celebration in honor of a new donor. He also told me to tell you thank you for the tennis shoes," said Dr. Foster.

"Oh, that's good. I hope he liked the shoes. Did he invite you to the celebration?"

"Not exactly, but it seems that someone is giving them $20,000 to name the recreation room in honor of Rebecca Defoy."

"You can't be serious!"

"I'm afraid so. I called the facility and talked to the director. She said Becca's little brother is behind it. It seems he is trying to create a positive legacy for his big sister because one of the requirements of the donation is that the mural of you, Michelle and Becca be preserved as long as the facility exists."

"No way!!" shouted Michael. "I can't have a picture of me and another woman up for all eternity. I'm married now with my own child on the way. I've been meaning to call Accent and tell them to paint over it, but my life has been so busy I never got around to it. What if the media gets a hold of this? As soon as we get off the phone, I'm calling my lawyer to stop it," Michael slammed his fist on the bench he was sitting on.

"I understand how you feel, but I've been looking for Becca's brother for months with no success. This room dedication ceremony could be the only chance we have to pinpoint him. If you get the ceremony canceled, we may never find him. I suggest that you don't do that."

"I understand what you're saying, Dr. Foster, but I can't possibly allow them to keep up that mural. It's an untrue depiction of what happened between me and Becca. It makes it seem like we were a family. That never happened. She tried to kill me and my wife, and Michelle is not my child. She created that mural as a part of her delusional fantasy that we would one day be together. I don't have a problem with them naming the room after her, but that mural has got to come down. When is this dedication supposed to take place?"

"Friday."

"As in the day after tomorrow?"

"Yes. If we both go, we can meet Becca's brother and find out if he knows anything about the strange phone calls you received."

Michael was curious to meet Becca's brother. He was Becca's only known relative, which made him Michelle's only relative on her mother's side. Michelle would be five soon, and she seemed content with the family she had now. He knew at some point, she would want to know more about the rest of her family. It would probably be a good idea to find out what type of man her uncle is before she does.

"I'll meet you there," said Michael. "I'll call you back in a little while to get more details about this dedication ceremony."

Michael wondered how he was going to explain all of this to his wife. How could he reveal that he needed to go home to Akron to the mental facility where Becca was previously treated to stop them from keeping up a mural Tee didn't even know existed? Tee was also completely in the dark about several other things. Michael didn't tell her about the Becca-like phone calls he received or his hiring of Private Detective Ida Foster to find out who was making the phone calls. He also hadn't told her that he and Dr. Foster paid a visit to the mental treatment facility and met Tee Hee, a patient there who befriended Becca while she was there. Michael didn't see how he could tell Tee where he was going without telling her everything. Maybe it was time to come clean, but she was in the first trimester of her pregnancy. He didn't want to do anything to upset her. He heard that the first trimester was the most critical stage of pregnancy and that many women miscarried during this stage. He also witnessed how stress and worry caused his sister-in-law to deliver Little Tina prematurely. He definitely didn't want that. Maybe it was best to continue to keep her in the dark.

Tiffany knocked on the door. "Are you ready for some more one on one time with me?"

"Sorry Tiffany, change of plans. I'm no longer in the mood for a massage. Maybe some other time."

Tiffany's smile quickly morphed into a scowl. "What? I had something special planned for us--I mean you."

"And I appreciate it, but something came up and I need to leave. I have some business to attend to."

"I am your business. I'm your number one client," pouted Tiffany.

"Tee and I have an entire roster of clients to attend to. You know that," said Michael.

The last thing Tiffany wanted to do was get on Michael's bad side. Because of him, her business was thriving and she was on her way to one day making more money than the rich married man she used to sleep with.

"I guess I'll see you next week," she said softly.

"I'll call you. I like our weekly sessions, but things at the office have been hectic lately, and I may not be able to come as often. I really do appreciate you. Nobody does me like you," said Michael.

"And nobody ever will. I appreciate you too, Michael," said Tiffany. She gave him a hug of thanks. It was tight and warm. She enjoyed the feel of Michael's mahogany skin against hers. As she pulled back from him, she inadvertently brushed against Michael's towel and it tumbled to the floor. Unashamedly, she looked down and smiled. Michael wasn't shy when it came to his body, but at that moment, he wanted to run and hide. One of Tee's best friend's was ogling a part of his anatomy that should only be viewed by his wife. Rather than stoop and pick up the towel, he turned around and said, "Tiffany, I think you should leave now."

Tiffany had clearly knocked his towel off by accident, but she was not the least bit apologetic about it. She wished he hadn't turned around, but his backside was a sight to behold as well. She stood there admiring the hard defined muscles that rippled through Michael's entire body. He was a dark-skinned dream. She took careful survey of the hard lines in his thighs, gluts and back. Still somewhat damp from the bath and sweating from the heat, beads of moisture slowly slid down his body adding to her enjoyment. She licked her lips. It was her pleasure to touch him while giving him massages. He was quite a treat. She was usually able to easily maintain her professionalism but today was proving to be a challenge.

Tiffany rededicated her life to Christ back in November and was trying desperately to practice celibacy. This visual feast in front of her wasn't helping her quest to keep her mind off sex. She realized Michael was embarrassed but she on the other hand, was aroused.

"I'm so sorry, Michael," she lied. "But you have nothing to be embarrassed about. I've seen you nearly naked several times during your massages," she said.

"Nearly naked and naked are two different things, Tiffany. This is inappropriate. What if someone were to walk in? We are in a spa. Workers are in and out of here all the time. I asked you to leave. I need you to go, now. As I said, I have some business to attend to," said Michael sternly.

Michael was upset. Tiffany wasn't quite sure if he was upset with himself or her, but either way it wasn't good.

"As you wish, sir. It was an accident. No harm done. I'm leaving," She gave his backside another long glance before she turned around and exited the steamy room. She was trying very hard not to like her friend's husband, but how could she not? He was everything she ever wanted in a man: attractive, intelligent, sexy, charming, funny and rich. She was seeing someone, but he wasn't like the magnificent Michael Stokes.

Michael dressed hurriedly and left the spa. As he drove back to the office, he wondered if what happened was yet another thing he needed to hide from his wife, or if he needed to tell her before Tiffany did. He hated keeping so many secrets from Tee, but they were all things he felt she was better off not knowing until he had them under control.

Stay Connected

Websites

www.jaehendersonauthor.com
www.imagoodwoman.com

Facebook Fan Page
www.facebook.com/imagoodwoman

Twitter
www.twitter.com/imagoodwoman

Email
Imagoodwoman2@yahoo.com

Book Clubs

Book club discussion questions can be found at www.jaehendersonauthor.com.

CPSIA information can be obtained at www.ICGtesting.com
Printed in the USA
LVOW132300230412

278838LV00001B/1/P

9 780983 981930